Sundown Town Duty Station

Also by J. J. Zerr

The Ensign Locker

Sundown Town Duty Station

J. J. Zerr

iUniverse, Inc.
Bloomington

Sundown Town Duty Station

Copyright © 2012 by J. J. Zerr

All rights reserved. No part of this book may be used or reproduced by any means, graphic, electronic, or mechanical, including photocopying, recording, taping, or by any information storage retrieval system without the written permission of the publisher except in the case of brief quotations embodied in critical articles and reviews.

Certain characters in this work are historical figures, and certain events portrayed did take place. However, this is a work of fiction. All of the other characters, names, and events as well as all places, incidents, organizations, and dialogue in this novel are either the products of the author's imagination or are used fictitiously.

iUniverse books may be ordered through booksellers or by contacting:

iUniverse
1663 Liberty Drive
Bloomington, IN 47403
www.iuniverse.com
1-800-Authors (1-800-288-4677)

Because of the dynamic nature of the Internet, any web addresses or links contained in this book may have changed since publication and may no longer be valid. The views expressed in this work are solely those of the author and do not necessarily reflect the views of the publisher, and the publisher hereby disclaims any responsibility for them.

Any people depicted in stock imagery provided by Thinkstock are models, and such images are being used for illustrative purposes only.

Certain stock imagery © Thinkstock.

ISBN: 978-1-4759-6928-3 (sc)
ISBN: 978-1-4759-6929-0 (hc)
ISBN: 978-1-4759-6930-6 (e)

Library of Congress Control Number: 2012924188

Printed in the United States of America

iUniverse rev. date: 01/25/2013

Thanks

For all the help along the way, Steve Keibler, Jerry Arbiter, John Leder, Jessica Chowning, Mary Horner, and Peter Mersky.
Karen.
Donna, Lou, and all the C&C bubbas and bubettes.
Carol Gaskin.
Dianna, at 2 Rivers Communications and Design.
Remaining errors are all mine, not theirs.

For Karen Theresa.
For those who took the giant steps for mankind.
For those who contributed a baby step.
God bless them, each and every one.

Part I

No welcome in the wagon.

1

NOT MANY THINGS, ASIDE FROM the baby crying, rousted Teresa Zachery out of bed before 0700. That morning, List Almighty would determine their future, and her husband, Jon, could get a permanent bridge to replace his two upper-front false teeth.

She slid her feet into her bunny slippers and padded across the living room carpet to the kitchen. Jon stood at the sink, water running, and Teresa stopped to watch from the doorway. It wasn't spying; it was more like when she discovered two-year-old Jennifer deeply engrossed in her coloring book, one of those precious, and rare, motherhood moments. She frowned. Really, watching her husband felt like spying.

Jon turned off the faucet, shook water from what he was fond of calling his falsies, put them in, and looked down at the front of his Navy uniform shirt. She smiled as he ran through his get-ready-for-work routine: Teeth in. Edge of shirt, edge of belt buckle, and edge of fly in a line—gig line straight. Zipper up. Hat tucked under the belt on the left.

"Everything shipshape," Teresa said.

He spun around, an annoyed look on his face, but it didn't last.

"Sleeping Beauty up at …" he checked his watch, "0554? The handsome prince was about to awaken you with a chaste, fairy-tale, industrial-strength lip-lock."

She shook her head but couldn't keep from smiling. He loved to do that, to package "fairy-tale," "chaste," and "industrial-strength lip-lock" in one sentence. She crossed the kitchen and kissed him, dislodging his teeth.

"Rats, now I have to start the checklist all over again."

"You look squared away to me, sailor."

"I was about to come in and tell you I was leaving," he said.

She hugged him. "Call me after you leave the clinic. I'd like to know if they can do permanent Bucky Beavers for you."

He looked away. "I decided to skip the dentist."

"Jon Zachery, it took months to get that appointment. Heaven only knows how long to get another. I'm not ready to spend the rest of my life sleeping with a man who puts his teeth in a glass of water every night."

"It's only the two uppers."

"There's no *only* about it. You keep that appointment."

Teresa felt it happen, like it always did. Jon's blue eyes softened the hard edges of her scolding.

"Jon, I know you're worried about List Almighty, but even if it is posted today, you aren't going to change what's written on it by going in early."

"I wasn't looking for help with the logic of the situation."

"You were looking for sympathy?"

"I know. Dictionary. End of the S section."

"I love you, Jon Joseph Zachery."

"And you are a hard woman, Teresa Ann née Velmer, but I couldn't love you more."

She returned his good-bye kiss carefully. At the door to the carport, he stopped with his hand on the knob.

When he turned to face her, it surprised her, the way it always did, that she was married to this handsome man. He stood so straight and appeared to be taller than his actual five-seven frame. Broad shoulders and without a shirt, he looked almost as muscled as those men on the covers of romance novels. In profile, his nose did stick out a bit.

He gave her his mischievous little-boy grin that only used half his face. "Thanks, Teresa."

"For what?"

"For getting up."

The door closed before Teresa came up with an appropriate reply. He'd been irritated with her because she awoke early and didn't let him skip the dentist. Then he thanked her.

She poured a glass of orange juice, turned out the kitchen light, and sat in gloom at the table, at her table. She caressed the tabletop. After four years of living in furnished apartments, she appreciated owning a few pieces of furniture.

She sipped and thought men were complicated creatures. They never outgrew some parts of their boyhood. Aviators seemed a lot more juvenile than the officers Jon associated with on his destroyer. In flight training, most of the student pilots were just out of college. Despite, or maybe because of, the danger in flying, pilots had to act fearless.

Boys. Schoolboys.

She recalled asking Jon why flight training took so long.

"Navy flight training is like going through school," Jon told her. "Primary at Saufley Field is kindergarten. Next is basic. That's grade school. Advanced, high school. After advanced we pin on our wings. We're naval aviators then."

"That's a year and a half, right?" Teresa asked.

"About that, but there's still another six months of training in the specific jet I'll fly in the fleet. That's college."

Teresa finished her juice and thought about the night of the dog poop. Night of the dog poop. Encounter some life-altering experience, and Navy men had to trivialize it with a juvenile and profane name.

It was November 1966. Jon had just returned from a deployment to Vietnam on a Navy destroyer. At that point, they had planned for him to leave the service as soon as he completed his three remaining years of obligation. Then he would get a job as an electrical engineer and they "would live happily ever after."

The plan changed a week after his ship returned to San Diego. They had driven to Los Angeles to visit the Prescotts, Teresa's uncle Edgar and aunt Penelope. The Prescotts did not expect their daughter Christine to come home from Berkeley that weekend, but she caught an opportune ride. She entered the house while her parents and the Zacherys were still at the dinner table.

On previous visits, Christine liked Jon. She told Teresa, "He talks to my friends and me like we're adults, not kids." But in the three months she'd been away at college, she'd been caught up in the antiwar movement. "Baby killer!" she shouted at Jon and stormed back out.

Early the next morning, three of Christine's male friends trashed the Zachery car with dog poop and a garden hose. Jon heard the noise and fought with them, losing his top two front teeth. Two of the three boys were hospitalized though.

After the police and ambulances left, Uncle Edgar sat Christine down. Teresa had always thought her uncle spoiled and indulged his only child, but that morning he was furious.

"Explain yourself, young lady."

The boys she'd ridden home with were local friends, a year ahead of Christine at Berkeley. Shortly after the fall semester began, they had taken her with them to meet a group of four men and three women, none of them Berkeley students. The group had no name, only strong views. They considered the Vietnam War immoral. Soldiers, sailors, and airmen indiscriminately killed women and children. American servicemen were war criminals.

"You believe this crap?" Uncle Edgar leaned toward Christine, his hands on his knees.

Christine looked up. She looked defiant, determined, but her lips quivered, and she was close to tears.

Teresa felt uncomfortable being in the Prescott living room with the father-daughter confrontation, and she started to stand.

"Stay," Uncle Edgar commanded without taking his eyes away from his daughter. "Please."

"You called Jon a baby killer. Baby killers are cowards. What he did last night—charged into the middle of three guys, all bigger than him—whatever he is, is sure as hell not a coward."

Christine looked back at her hands.

"What the hell were you kids thinking?" Uncle Edgar asked.

Christine didn't want to answer, but he pushed.

The group, she said, met once or twice a week. They went over news accounts of the war. They talked about doing something, picketing the Naval Air Station at Alameda, maybe. But that's all they did: talk. During the ride down to LA Friday, they discussed the "all talk, no action" bunch. It was time they did something. If the group wasn't going to act, then the three of them would. They came up with wording for signs each of them would carry outside the Alameda main gate. Next week they would act. They agreed on that, and then Christine got out of the car and entered her home.

"Look at Jon, Christine. Look at what you did to him."

Jon's upper lip was swollen and purple. Blood spots dappled the front of his T-shirt.

Christine sobbed.

A week after the fight, Jon sat next to Teresa on the sofa. "I've been thinking," he said.

Cold fingers squeezed Teresa's heart.

"Before the encounter with Christine's friends, I didn't pay that much attention to all the protest going on in the country. It's in the papers and on TV all the time, but it didn't have anything to do with us. Now it does.

"Some of it I understand. Dr. King, for instance. The Emancipation Proclamation was 103 years ago. It's time it becomes real. I understand that protest. I think Dr. King is right about many things, but he would have us fight the domestic problem and forget about the foreign one. Our country has enemies foreign and domestic. The foreign enemies aren't going to let us say, 'Hey, Foreign Enemies, we've got some domestic problems to solve. Don't attack us for a while, okay?' I don't think he's right about us getting out of Vietnam and concentrating only on fixing race issues."

Teresa realized she'd been holding her breath.

"In the newspaper accounts and on TV, I don't think the protestors know what they are protesting," Jon said. "It's more anti-establishment than anything. These people scare me. They seem to want to tear the country apart, not fix it. And nobody seems to stand up to them and tell them they're wrong. It's like the country doesn't know what to do about these protestors."

Jon took both her hands. "I can't climb on a soapbox and try to shout these protestors down. What I think I need to do is to stay in the Navy, but I can't do that unless you support the decision."

Teresa couldn't think of what to say for a moment.

"I'm not just knee-jerk reacting to what happened at the Prescotts, if that's what you're thinking."

She'd been thinking just that. Finally, she said, "Jon, have you really thought this through? You've never liked being in the Navy. And you did enough, already, on the *Manfred*. You say it's not a knee-jerk reaction to the fight with Christine's friends, but it seems like it to me."

"I think I'm being objective, Teresa. I have thought about it. And you're right. I never wanted to be in the Navy in the first place. Pop pushed me in. Being a junior enlisted man was not fun, and I agonized over staying to get the Navy college scholarship. Being an ensign on the *Manfred* wasn't pleasant either, and I looked forward to getting out. I was going to be an electrical engineer, and we'd have four babies. But these protestors scare me. Christine went from a friend to an enemy in the seven months I was gone. The protest business seems to involve most of our generation. What's going to happen to our country when these yahoos take over? I just feel like I need to do something. Staying in is what I can do. It's not much maybe, but it's something."

Teresa sighed. "You have to do what you think is right."

Then he told her he wanted to apply for aviation, and she got angry, feeling as though he'd suckered her in with the "stay in" part. When she bought that, he hit her with aviation. Aviation was dangerous, even in peacetime. He wanted to drop bombs on North Vietnam, and the newspaper articles about the strikes into the north all reported US aircraft losses.

"You have to do what you think is right," she said again. Then she went into the bedroom and cried.

For weeks she prayed that he'd be found physically unfit for flying, but those prayers were not answered. Eventually, she found the bedrock on which Teresa Ann Velmer Zachery stood. God would not give them anything they couldn't handle. In the end, many times, you just had to trust in God and go forward.

Fourteen months and a second baby later, they were in Pensacola. Jon had completed kindergarten, and now they awaited List Almighty.

The list would tell them where they'd go for the next phase of Jon's training. Jon wanted jets. Helicopters or propeller planes would not do. It had to be jets. And jet training was in Meridian, Mississippi.

Wherever they were ordered, the move would happen fast. The Navy organized the flight-training program, as if all the students were bachelors with little or no household goods to move. If one was married, had two small children, and lived in a rented, partially furnished, three-bedroom house, as she and Jon did, the Navy expected that person to be just as mobile as a guy who lived in Bachelor Officer Quarters with all his belongings in one seabag. The next couple of weeks were going to be interesting.

Jets were more dangerous to fly than helos or props. Flying onto and off the carriers at night posed the greatest risk—or challenge, as the pilots called it.

Part of her wanted to say a prayer that Jon got jets and Meridian. Part of her wanted to pray for anything but jets. Another part wanted to pray that he'd wash out of flight training.

A tear ran down her right cheek and hung on her chin.

In you, oh Lord, I place my trust. Please bless Jon with Meridian, but Thy will be done.

When he'd first told her about wanting to apply for aviation, he'd made her angry. Now that jets were close, the fear of losing him left no room in her head or heart for anger.

And teeth, Lord. Permanent ones, please.

She didn't know whether to laugh or cry, and she did some of both. Then seven-week-old Edgar Jon sounded off, and there was no time for laughing or crying.

She looked at the framed eight-by-ten needlepoint hanging on the wall behind the table. Her best friend, Rose, had made it for her.

Toughest Job in the Navy:

Navy Wife.

The period after "wife" was oversized. Only Rose would say, "Go ahead, knock the chip off my shoulder," in needlepoint.

Teresa went to do her duty.

2

Harry Peeper gripped the steering wheel of his DeSoto. It was a quarter till two on Thursday morning. Fifteen minutes to the target. Cruising at the speed limit. No Meridian cops in sight. No other cars either. Driving north through town, he didn't even know what street he was on. The navigator knew. The navigator told him when to turn. Harry hated not knowing the lay of the land, and he especially hated having to depend on the backwoods peckerwoods the Klan saddled him with for the mission. The mission had all the signs of a monumental goat rope. He'd learned how to recognize an impending major screwup in the Army.

Harry glanced at Ford, riding shotgun. He was barrel-chested, slope-shouldered, rancid with a never-takes-a-bath smell coming off him, wearing bib overalls, but he was alert. His head swiveled, checking the sides, rear, and front, and he was quiet. Chevy sat in the back with the real shotgun, and he wouldn't shut up. His mouth ran constantly. He wasn't even talking to anyone, just babbling. *Jesus.*

"Goddamn nigger, dentist, civil rights, son of a bitch."

Jesus.

In the Army, Harry worked motor pool jobs, including his first year in Vietnam, when he repaired trucks at Tan Son Nhut Air Base. As the end of his tour approached, he began to worry about what he'd tell the guys at Boxley's Saloon back home about what he did in the war, so he extended a year for infantry. He was a good mechanic and a good soldier too, but he never got to prove it. The Army kept his infantry unit around Saigon, and the area had been cleared of VC by two large combined-force operations the year he worked as a grease monkey. As an infantryman, he went on plenty of patrols and night ambushes, but he never fired his M-16 at a Communist. When he returned to the States, Harry refused to talk about his experiences in Vietnam.

   His ability as a mechanic landed him a job with Germaine Cadillac in Jackson. Two weeks after starting work, he was invited to a Klan meeting in the garage attached to Sam Germaine's home. Sam liked military things as much as Harry hated the memory of the Army. At work, everyone called him Mr. Germaine. In Klan meetings he was Captain Sam. Harry thought that first meeting sounded like a bunch of old-fart blowhards, all talk and no action. But he attended a second meeting, because he didn't want to risk the good job he had. During the second meeting Captain Sam talked about civil rights agitators in Meridian who needed to be taught a lesson. He asked if anyone was interested in the job. One never volunteered in the Army, but Harry stuck his hand up.

   "What you got in mind, Cap'n Sam?" Harry asked.

   "I got a plan. It's simple. All you have to do is follow it. Take the job, and I'll brief you."

   It did sound simple. A colored Meridian dentist was way too vocal about his support of the civil rights movement. A shotgun blast through his living room window at 2:00 a.m. would teach him to keep his mouth shut. Captain Sam had the route to the target house marked on a map, along with the escape route.

   "I never been to Meridian," Harry said.

   "You're an honorary sergeant," Captain Sam said. "You get two soldiers, Chevy and Ford Henley. They know Meridian. Here's another map showing you where to pick them up. Mission is next Thursday. Also, I got a line on a moonshine-runner car. I'll loan you the money to get it.

If you're gonna be doin' missions for us, you oughta have the right kinda wheels."

"Next right turn," Ford said, snapping Harry back to Thursday, "need to take it. Two blocks, then a left."

Harry began to think better of Ford. When he spoke, he had something worthwhile to say.

"Uppity coon-assed," Chevy babbled on," don't know to mind your place."

Jesus.

He turned right.

At least the car worked out, he thought. Jolene, from Biloxi, sold it to him. She needed money after her moonshiner husband, Earl, got nailed by the feds. It was one hell of a car. The engine exhaust grumble came up from below like a lion lived down there, a lion powerful enough to rip an elephant apart to get a bite of its heart before it stopped beating. The grumble stirred him. Thinking about Jolene stirred him. *One fine-looking woman but hard-muscled too. Jolene!*

He made the left, and both Harry and Ford checked for cops while Chevy motormouthed.

Harry'd been happy with the DeSoto. He'd expected good soldiers too. Even though he had a low opinion of the Army, finding Captain Sam's soldiers felt like a personal insult. Even finding them hadn't gone easy. Nothing marked the dirt road off the Jackson-Meridian highway but two ruts leading back into the pine trees. After driving back and forth three times, he finally figured out the one to take.

Captain Sam said they were twins, but they sure didn't look like twins when his headlights found them sitting on the bed of their beat-up white pickup. One was black haired and beefy. The other was his own height and build, six feet and lean, but Harry wasn't blond. The blond was talking and swinging his legs. Beefy Black Hair just sat and stared.

Harry left his car idling and got out, and they made introductions.

"You got a shotgun, right?" Harry asked.

"Right here." Chevy reached around behind him and picked up a double-barrel and a stick.

"What's the stick for?" Harry asked.

"It's a ten-gauge, see? But I only got twelve-gauge shells. When I fire it, the brass gets stuck and I have to use the stick to punch the shell out," Chevy said.

"Jesus," Harry said.

"He hits what he shoots at," Ford said.

Harry didn't like it.

"We goin', or what?" Chevy asked.

Ford got in the front passenger seat of the DeSoto.

Harry slid behind the wheel. "What kind of shells you have?"

"Birdshot," Chevy said and slammed the back door.

"Birdshot?" Harry asked.

"Target's a window," Ford said. "Prob'ly five, six paces from the street. Birdshot'll do."

Jesus.

But he had to take them. There was no way he'd go back to Captain Sam and say he chickened out.

They moved from an area with streetlights on the corners and occasional garage lights to a dark street ahead of them.

"Take the next right turn," Ford said.

Harry muttered a curse and fought to keep his mind on the mission, not on Chevy's diatribe, which included every damn name for a colored man Harry had ever heard. It annoyed the hell out of him.

"Third house from the corner," Ford said. "You 'member when we scouted it, Chevy?"

Chevy's voice kicked up a notch, and he sounded like a girl. He stuck the gun out the window, cocked both hammers, leaned his upper body out, and strung together an impressive string of shouted profane promises of death and destruction for the "civil rights son of a bitch."

Chevy shouldn't have stuck the gun out the window so soon. He shouldn't have shouted. He'd wake somebody up before the gun went off. Harry's inclination was to step on the gas and get the hell out of there, but he was afraid the stupid bastard would drop the gun. Ready to explode with constrained anxiety, Harry forced himself to take the corner slow.

"There," Ford said and pointed the flashlight at the target window.

Chevy stopped talking, and Harry was surprised to hear the growl of his car engine.

The shotgun roared and roared again, and then Chevy brandished the shotgun and shouted, "Take that, you civil rights cocksucker," at the window he'd blown out.

"Stop," Ford said. "Stop."

It was the last thing he wanted to do, but Harry listened to Ford.

Ford bolted out the door, took the shotgun from Chevy, pushed him back inside the DeSoto, shoved the gun in after him, and got back in.

"Go," Ford said. "Not this one. Next left, take it. Then it's a straight shot out into the county."

*   *   *

Harry watched Sam Germaine fork up a mouthful of coffee cake, take a sip of coffee, and set his mug on the Formica tabletop of the diner booth. Crumbs floated on the surface of the white coffee.

"So how'd it go, Harry?"

He looked up and saw the sweat beads dotting Sam's forehead above his round white face. Harry wondered if it was hot in the diner, but he was too tired to try to figure it out. His head hurt, and his eyes felt like sand coated the inside of the lids. He'd been awake a long time.

"Sumpin' go wrong, Harry?"

"It was a goat rope. Those Henley guys showed up with a ten-gauge shotgun and twelve-gauge shells. They had a stick to poke stuck shells out of the thing."

The diner was crowded, but nobody looked at him. He lowered his voice anyway. "Chevy talked the whole damn time. Never shut up once. Jesus."

"Did you get the mission done?"

"The mission, well, sort of."

"You blow out that dentist's window or not?"

"Yeah. Chevy hit it with the first barrel, but he was so excited he missed the whole damn house with the second barrel."

"You blew out the window though?"

"Yeah. It took out the glass and the curtains. But the dumb bastards only had birdshot. Hell, I was thinking deer slugs."

"Whatever the hell they used was okay, as long as there was the roar of a shotgun and you blew out the window. Fine job, Harry."

"Felt like a major screwup."

"Loosen up, Harry. Your first mission and you pulled it off. You'll get better with each one you do."

"I don't want to work with those Henley boys again."

"You gotta. We just established good connections in Meridian, and they're part of it. This was the first time we used them too. They'll get better."

"You said they were twins."

Sam laughed. "There's a story about them boys. Just a little farther down that road where you met them last night, there's a moonshine bar. The twins' momma was fond of shine, and she hung out there a lot. Story is them boys was conceived right outside that bar in the backseats of the cars they was named after. Mind you don't say anything about it though. Ford, especially, is touchy about it. He looks kind of fat and soft, but he's strong as an ox. Word is he's one a those don't feel pain. Just as happy tasting his own blood as seein' another's. Ford'll make a fine soldier, with the right sergeant lookin' after 'im."

"Chevy though. Jesus."

"He'll take a little more work."

"They stink."

Sam laughed. "Roll down a window." He used his finger to wipe up the last of the icing and berry filling from the plate and licked his finger. "Okay, Harry. Business. Your next mission is at 0200. Same objective. Blow out the window of another Meridian civil rights agitator. Bollinger's his name."

"Christ, I'm on my ass!"

"Stop arguin', 'n you can git coupla hours a sleep."

"But two nights in a row, the same kind of mission, in the same town! That's crazy."

"No, it's not crazy. Last night, the mission was north, in the colored section. Cops'll be there. The next one is southeast and white. Got a great escape route into the county. It's all worked out."

"Jesus," Harry said.

3

When the load of student naval aviator teeth problems demanded, the dental clinic started seeing patients at 0700. Jon had lucked into a seven o'clock. First appointments of the day were golden too. With his second patient, a Navy dentist began falling behind schedule. Jon hadn't brought a book, which was a mistake since he arrived at 0625, five minutes before a sailor unlocked the door. His dentist came into the waiting room twelve minutes before Jon's appointment. He expected a "Let's go, Zachery," but Lieutenant Fleming nodded to him and then discussed tennis with the petty officer behind the reception desk until exactly 0700. The appointment didn't even take ten minutes.

At 0712, Jon climbed into his car, started it up, and pulled out of the lot. Finally, nothing stood between him and List Almighty but the drive out to Saufley Field, northwest of Pensacola. That's what he thought. Two blocks away from the clinic, a white Navy pickup truck with a large, round red flasher on top stopped Jon. The third-class petty officer on the master-at-arms force got out of the truck, walked up to Jon, and asked for his military ID and driver's license. He felt sure the petty officer deliberately prolonged writing the speeding ticket.

When he finished, he handed Jon the ticket. "Eleven miles over the limit, sir. Please be careful when you pull back onto the road." The tall, thin sailor walked back to his truck.

Jon knew how sailors enjoyed situations like that, being able to jerk an officer's chain. Understanding didn't make it rankle less.

When he got on the road again, he remembered the call he'd promised to make to Teresa. Permanent teeth would arrive in six weeks.

The two-lane blacktop road to Saufley Field was wet from an early-morning rain. Floridians used oyster shell in the makeup of their roads, they were told, and the shells made the roads extra slippery when they got wet. The Navy urged caution weekly. Still, students frequently plowed into the skinny pines lining the road or into a ditch. A number of others received tickets from omnipresent sheriff's deputies. He did not want a civilian ticket to go with his military police citation, and he had to keep lifting his foot off the pedal.

Gray clouds covered the sky. Hopefully it wouldn't rain anymore. Group 68-1 was scheduled for a group photo on the flight line that morning.

Jon was part of 68-1, the first group of student naval aviators to start through Navy primary flight training in 1968. All of them had anticipated List Almighty every day that week. Second Lieutenant Amos, the only Marine in the group, named the list. "The rest of our lives, what we do, what we are, everything we can become—all of that will be determined by the list. It's List Almighty."

Amos was arrogant. When he said something, Jon automatically disagreed. A lot rode on the list though. Amos called that right.

List Almighty would determine where the members of 68-1 went for basic flight training. More important, it determined the type of aircraft a pilot would fly during his Navy career.

"If you get jets, we have to move more often," Teresa said.

"Yes, but it's a small price to pay to avoid being a puke forever."

Jon had explained the hierarchy among naval aviators to Teresa. By self-proclamation, jet pilots sat at the top. Everybody else was a puke. There were prop pukes and helo pukes. Even air force jet pilots were pukes. They didn't land on aircraft carriers, and therefore they lived in pukedom.

The Navy loved ceremony. If List Almighty determined the future of people of consequence, sailors in dress uniforms would assemble in ranks, a band would play, and there'd be a gun salute. Since the list pertained to ensigns and second lieutenants, it would be posted on the bulletin board with the notices for the bake sale, free puppies, and "I've got stuff to sell cheap because I'm moving."

When the Navy compiled List Almighty, the overriding factor would be the needs of the service. Students filled out a preference card for the type of airplane they wanted to fly, called a dream sheet for very good reasons. If the Navy needed fourteen students in the helicopter-training pipeline, all fourteen from the group would be helicopter pilots, even though eleven wanted to fly jets.

Group 68-1 began primary in January. By March they'd lost seven of the twenty starters. Three were set back because of medical issues. Two had gotten downs for failing to pass the safe-for-solo check flight. They would get one more chance. The other two quit and were dropped on request, or DORed. One student joined 68-1 from 67-12. He passed his safe-for-solo check ride on his second attempt.

After Jon parked a long way from the hangar, he forced himself to transit through the cars at a controlled pace. Naval aviators projected cool. Student naval aviators practiced cool.

Jon headed for the bulletin board on the bulkhead outside the student pilot locker room.

There. List Almighty!

"Basic Flight Training Asignments for Group 68-1." He didn't notice the typo the first time he looked.

Second Lieutenant Amos   Helicopters

His eyes wanted to move to the bottom of the list, to his name.

Ensign Barnes   Props

Barnes wanted props. He and two others had a plan. They wanted to fly props, accumulate hours, acquire multiengine ratings, serve minimum time in the Navy, and get airline jobs.

Amos wanted jets. He graduated from the Naval Academy and was tall, trim, and used to getting what he wanted. Zachery couldn't help himself. He smiled about Amos.

Ensign Desmond   Helicopters

Desmond wanted jets.

If I can't fly jets, I don't want to be here went through Zachery's mind. He considered rapping on his head. It was the best wood available to ward off the jinx he'd called down on himself by giving voice to his desire.

Ensign Emerson   Props

Emerson got what he wanted.

Ensign Foster   Props

Foster wanted jets.

Ensign Kohl   Props

All three with the airline-pilot plan got what they wanted.

Ensign Samson   Props
Ensign Siling   Helicopters
Ensign Silver   Props
Ensign Smith   Helicopters
Ensign Tanber   Helicopters

They all wanted jets. Two names left. Not one was going to jets.

After the night of the dog poop, he had sold his soul to the Navy for another five years, not just to fly, but to go back to Vietnam. And not just go back, but to contribute to the fight in a more meaningful way than as one of three hundred on a destroyer. As a pilot, he would drive his own plane to the war. If he got props or helicopters, the whole reason for selling his soul to the Navy would be lost. He had to get jets.

Fifteen guys in 67-12 completed primary in December. Eleven wanted jets. All eleven got jets. The Navy looked at each man's dream sheet, his academic grades, and his flight grades; then the Navy looked at where it needed people to go.

Ensign Young   Helicopters

He wanted jets too. Jon looked away from the list and looked up and then down the passageway. No one else was there.

Lieutenant (jg) Zachery

In his peripheral vision, it looked like a short word to the right of his name. It didn't look long enough to be Helicopters.

Jets

Jets!

His breath exploded from his mouth, as if he'd swum underwater as long as he could stand it. His knees weakened, and he put both hands on the bulkhead beneath the bulletin board. Euphoria started building as a tiny bubble in the bottom of his belly and grew rapidly to the size of a hot-air balloon, expanding up into his chest and threatening to blast out of his throat as a scream. A scream would be uncool though.

Zachery looked up and down the passageway; still no one else was there.

Jets. Not a big deal really.

He went over the list again.

Lieutenant (jg) Zachery   Jets

Still there, and the only one going to Meridian.

In his mind, *hot damns* and *thank you, Gods* elbowed for position. Zachery hesitated in front of the door to the student-pilot locker room. List Almighty had disappointed the whole group, except for the future airline pilots and, of course, himself. He muscled the smile off his face and pushed open the door.

Lieutenant Amos stood with one foot on the bolted-to-the-deck bench between the rows of lockers. Even his flight suit—a green garbage bag with arms and legs when worn by anyone else—looked good on him. The other dozen in the group huddled behind him between the rows of six-foot-tall lockers. Thirteen sets of eyes hit him like a sucker punch.

"Mississippians hate Negroes, Jews, Catholics, and Communists," Lieutenant Amos said.

Zachery's mind had been occupied with calling Teresa about jets, the teeth, being cool, not being a puke, and not being an ass about getting Meridian.

Amos's saying froze Catholic Jon Zachery as he stood in the doorway, holding the spring-loaded door open.

He watched Amos lower his flight-booted foot to the deck. He had that *Amos* look on his face that said, "I know you want to be me." He started toward the door, and his adulators got in line to follow him out of the locker room.

Jon realized Amos expected him to hold the door for him. *Not going to happen, Amos.* Jon let go of the spring-loaded door, and Amos halted and glared down at his intended doorman.

"C'mon, Amos," one of the future airline pilots said and pulled the door open.

Out in the passageway, the voices cranked out: "See the look on his face?" "Man, you got him good." Then the door closed behind the last one, and Zachery was alone in the large room. He went over to his locker.

Mississippians hate Negroes, Jews, Catholics, and Communists. Everybody knew about the Negro part, he thought. Jews and Catholics though, he hadn't heard that. Could it be true? He wondered if it had been in the news and he missed it.

Zachery figured ten of the group had to be disappointed and jealous. And Amos, obviously, had no practice dealing with disappointment or with concepts like the needs of anything or anyone but Amos.

Amos's saying held a ring of truth though, like List Almighty. If Mississippians hated Catholics, he had Teresa and two babies to think about.

As Zachery pulled on the socks he wore with his flight boots, he realized he hadn't used foot powder. Athlete's foot was something real to worry about.

The rest are just jealous, and Amos is Amos.

He finished suiting up and went out to the flight line to get a group picture taken in front of one of the T-34 trainer aircraft, but it got complicated. The thirteen took turns communicating, not very subtly, with their middle fingers. The second-class petty officer photographer had seen student pilots try that stunt before though.

"Gentlemen, let's just get this over with. Okay, sirs?" the petty officer asked.

The photographer got ready to shoot again, but whispers and suppressed sniggers arose from the second row.

Jon, the senior officer in 68-1, knelt in the middle of the short-guy row in front. Being senior officer didn't mean much, but it made him responsible for things like getting the group picture taken. He said over his shoulder, "I'm sure the PO2 has something worthwhile to do. Let's do what he says. Let's get this over with."

Whispers and sniggers persisted.

Jon blew out an exasperated breath, stood, took three paces forward, and did an about-face.

"Sixty-eight dash one," Zachery commanded, "ten-hut!"

Nobody moved. Everyone watched Amos. He stood with his weight on one foot, looking off to his right. Jon noted the photographer's name stenciled above his dungaree shirt pocket.

"Petty Officer Evans," Jon ordered in a normal tone of voice, "take a picture of Lieutenant Amos. Do it now. The one I'm pointing at. Take the picture."

The camera clicked.

"Amos," Zachery bellowed, "you will stand at attention. You will act like a Marine officer, or I will place you on report for insubordination, conduct unbecoming an officer, and inciting mutiny. Second Lieutenant Amos, ten-hut! Sixty-eight dash one, ten-hut!"

For a moment, Jon thought Amos was going to try a stare-down, but he assumed the position. The others came to attention one by one.

They stood, rigid and hatless, on the flight line. Amos's jaw worked, as if he were chewing the tongue of his flight boot. The T-34 aircraft behind the tall-guy row posed passively. The others in the photo group seethed, especially Foster, Kohl, and Tanber in the tall row, who flushed red.

Jon heard engine and propeller noises. He smelled fuel, oil, and scorched rubber from the landing end of the runway. The wind messed with his hair. It was as if he could see, hear, smell, and feel, but they couldn't. They stood at attention in ranks, like statues.

"You ready to shoot the group photo, Petty Officer Evans?" Zachery asked.

He nodded.

"We're doing it with both ranks at attention. As soon as I get into position, shoot the picture. Understand?"

"Yes, sir."

"The rest of you—gentlemen," Zachery said, "we are taking one shot. If any one of you is not at attention, I will place the whole bunch of you on report. If any one of you sneezes, belches, hiccups, farts, or behaves inappropriately in any way, you will all be placed on report."

The Group 68-1 photo drew the eye to one figure. In the middle of the short-guy row, Zachery smiled amidst thirteen grim faces. He hadn't put his false teeth in after the dental visit.

4

It was a quarter till two on Friday morning. Driving the speed limit, Harry Peeper gripped the steering wheel of his DeSoto. Just like Thursday, quiet Ford watched for cops. Unlike Thursday, Chevy sat quietly too in the backseat with Harry's pump twelve gauge.

"Use number four shot," Captain Sam had said. "Better'n slugs for windows. We're not trying to kill anybody. We're communicating with them."

When Captain Sam mumbled that stupid McNamara quote through a mouthful of his second piece of coffee cake, it sliced through Harry's fatigue and he coughed coffee out his nose.

Harry's opinion of Sam slipped a notch. Just before he left his motor pool job, Harry and two other monkeys were working on a truck under a roofed-over pad of concrete at Tan Son Nhut. Shirtless in the stifling, moisture-laden air, streaming rivulets of beer sweat, the three weren't talking. They plugged away sullenly at the job, more focused on looking busy than actually working.

The mechanic they called Nine Toes ambled under the shade of the shelter and said, "Listen to this."

Harry, standing atop a stand and leaning over the carburetor he was installing, looked up. Nine Toes, a skinny kid, wore a white T-shirt with a package of cigarettes rolled in the sleeve. He opened a *Stars and Stripes* newspaper, got his finger under a line, and read. "McNamara says we're not bombing North Vietnam; we're communicating with them."

Nine Toes folded up his paper and held up a sack. "I think you guys can stop fixing the truck. Let's take a Coke break."

"Sarge'll be on our ass if we don't finish this job," Harry said.

"I'll communicate with him," Nine Toes said.

The truck didn't get itself fixed that day.

Then Sam used that same stupid line, and Harry wondered if he hadn't just gotten himself into something just as stupid as the Army. He did agree with Sam about one thing though. Civil rights agitators—especially Northerner civil rights agitators—needed to have the shit stomped out of 'em. They upset the natural order of things. *Northerners*—just the word made his teeth grind together. *Coming down from where they live and telling Southerners what's right and what's wrong. Had plenty of that ugly business in the early sixties,* he thought. Now that civil rights stuff was getting fired up again. He decided he'd do the second mission, but if it was as big a goat rope as Thursday, *Cap'n Sam could have his damn missions and he could take his damn job and shove it.*

After he picked up the twins, Harry stuck his new forty-five through the belt in the back of his pants. He wore a T-shirt with a button-up shirt over that, open in front. It didn't take long before the gun in his back became uncomfortable as hell. He took both hands off the wheel and got the piece located on his right side, butt forward. He'd practiced drawing the weapon from the rear of his pants. Stuck in the right, it had the same butt orientation and no discomfort.

"Next left," Ford said. "Need to take it."

He turned. No cars moved on the new street. Streetlights lit the corners. A light bloomed above a garage door down the block.

"Second left," Ford said. "Target house's middle of the block. Gotta take it slow to find it."

Harry worried about Chevy. "You awake back there?" Harry asked.

Ford answered, "He's fine."

Harry flicked the switches that turned off the headlights and the brake and taillights but kept his hand on the headlight switch in case he needed them.

"Left turn."

Harry slowed and turned the corner.

"Gun out, Chevy," Ford said.

Harry moved the car into the left lane. They passed out of the light from the streetlight on the corner. Houses were dark on both sides of the street except for a garage light above a driveway to the right three or four houses ahead.

"See it, Chevy? The flowerpot on the porch? That's Bollinger's house," Ford said.

The house across the street from Bollinger's had the garage light on, and it threw enough light for Harry to make out the flowerpot Ford mentioned.

"Now 'member, when you pump it, pull it back inside enough so's the shell lands in the car," Ford said.

Harry smiled. That was just the way he had briefed them.

"Safety off and fire," Ford said.

The gun roared, and the pump action ratcheted. Harry saw venetian blinds hanging from one side in the target window. The shotgun roared again. The blinds were still hanging.

Harry's ears were ringing, but he heard Chevy rack a shell into the chamber. The gun roared a third time and the blinds were gone. A girl screamed from inside the house.

"Safety on. Get the gun in," Ford said. He was turned around and watching his brother. "Go."

Harry stepped on the gas. The car shot forward. Euphoria shot through Harry.

That Bollinger civil rights son of a bitch, he thought. *People like him put nigger sergeants in charge of white people in the Army.*

They passed the last streetlamp at the edge of town, and Harry flicked on the headlights-only switch.

"Right turn coming. Need to take it," Ford said.

Harry took the turn fast, and the rear end skidded. He tromped on it and got them straight with the road.

"Damn, Ford," Harry said. "Just goddamn."

There was a long, straight stretch. The powerful motor growled. The car ate up the road. Gravel pinged under the fenders. He felt immortal, invincible, and he rode a rocket through the black-assed night. Not once during that extra wasted year in Nam had he had a mission like the one just behind them.

"Damn, Ford." Harry grinned. He didn't take his eyes off the road, but he felt Ford's eyes on him.

5

Jon passed the Meridian city limits sign at 0750 with time to drive around before his 0900 appointment at Binford's Real Estate. Base housing would be convenient and eliminate a forty-five–minute drive, but the Navy only provided on-base quarters for bachelor student pilots. According to the real estate agent he'd talked to, Binford's had houses to rent in the southeast section of town. That area contained the Catholic church. Church would be close, but currently no houses were available in the northeast section, the area closest to the Navy base.

Jon drove through the downtown section of Meridian. The one- and two-story brick buildings—not new but not run-down either, built to last—reminded him of a respectably sized Midwest farm town. They reminded him of home rather than a Navy town.

In some sections of the city, streets were laid out in a strict rectangular grid, but there were many places on the map where streets seemed to have been arbitrarily and obstinately plopped down with the intended purpose to disrupt orderliness. The Catholic church sat on such a street, but he found it after two pull-overs to check the map. The church building itself, red-brick construction, appeared to be well maintained. Large stained-glass windows promised a bright, cheery nave. The grounds were in good shape. A Catholic grade school abutted the church and rectory. All the parish buildings appeared to be well built and well maintained.

It was 0805. He had time to drive to the north side of town to get an idea of how long his drive to the base was going to be if they found a house close to the church. In eleven minutes he was lost, and he pulled into a graveled parking lot to check the map. The lot was adjacent to a newly constructed church—no, a synagogue, according to the sign. It would open for services in mid-May. Smaller than the Catholic church, it was an attractive light-colored brick structure.

Amos, you're full of crap, he thought. *If Mississippians really hated Jews and Catholics, how could they have such a nice synagogue and church? Amos. Amos, the helo puke. Okay, that's a confessable offense.*

Jon figured out where he was and drove to the road leading to the naval air station. If he rented a house back by the Catholic church, he was going to have to figure out the best route to drive to the base. Even with a good route, it would probably be an hour's drive.

Heading back toward downtown and the real estate office, he came to a barricaded street. The street was being repaved. To the left, the area looked run-down. Jon turned right. He couldn't turn left again for what seemed like a long time, and then he was in the colored section. He had never been in a colored section of a town before, but he recognized it, immediately. To his left three colored boys sat on a front porch step. They all stared at Jon as he drove by. Kids, eight or nine, maybe, but their eyes delivered an adult message: You do not belong on this street, in this part of town. Those three kids scared the hell out of him.

In broad daylight, with white-people territory only a couple of blocks away, why am I afraid? he wondered. The logic of it didn't diminish his desire to be back where he belonged, with white people. *Another confessable offense* flitted through his mind.

Jon could not recall being in a situation where he was in the racial minority. He grew up in the small Missouri farm town of St. Ambrose. No colored people lived there, and none visited that he remembered. No colored kids attended his Catholic high school. In the Navy, there were colored sailors, but not many. In his Officer Candidate School regiment, out of some four hundred men, only one was colored. At Saufley Field, there had been no colored student pilots.

Makes a difference if you're the surrounder or the surroundee, huh, Zachery? he told himself.

Talking himself out of his fear didn't work. Leaving the colored section did.

*   *   *

Jon dragged himself to the door of his motel in Meridian just after midnight. He fumbled with the key, dropped it once, got the door open, and carried his small bag inside. Despite his exhaustion, the drab, dingy room still imposed its depressing spirit. He considered just flopping on the bed with his clothes on, but he reeked of bleach and Pine-Sol. He knew the strong smell would keep him awake.

Before he found a house to rent, the Binford Real Estate agent had showed Jon seven houses, none of which came with the features Teresa wanted: a fenced backyard for Jennifer to play in and a kitchen sink with a window behind it, overlooking the yard. Back at the agency at 1400, Mr. Brown, the agent with whom he'd dealt, told him a house closer to the base had just become available.

Located on Fortieth Street, it would cut ten or fifteen minutes from the drive to work.

From the driveway, the red-brick ranch appeared attractive. Yard and bushes in front were in good shape. A carport adjoined the house with a storage shed walling the end. In the backyard, two huge oaks shaded the house. A large stump sawed off about five or six inches above the ground showed where a third large tree had stood. The shade would be welcome in the summer.

They entered the kitchen from the carport, and Jon wrinkled his nose at the smell of rancid cooking oil. The stove needed cleaning, as did the walls, especially behind the stove, but behind the kitchen sink a window looked out onto the unfenced backyard.

Jon knew how to clean stoves. Chicken wire and steel posts would make a fence.

Four bachelor student pilots had rented the house and left it a sty. Flocks of dust bunnies occupied the corners of the bedrooms and the living/dining room. Dust covered the blinds in all the rooms. Windows were blurry with dirt. Walls needed to be scrubbed. White paint would brighten the dingy, drab place.

When he had been a junior enlisted man, the Navy provided him with plenty of experience cleaning up huge messes. He would have to clean and paint the bedrooms, the kitchen, and the hallway leading from the bedrooms to the bath.

Then he opened the door to the bathroom. He grimaced at the smell of mold and mildew. A torn, soap scum–crusted shower curtain hung from a single hook into the tub that looked like it was coated with dried pond algae. The flushing handle on the toilet was broken off, the tank lid leaned against a wall, and a bead chain connecting to the flapper valve in the bottom of the tank dangled over the side of the tank. The tank was full of water. Jon pulled the chain, and a vigorous flush sound echoed through the silent house. He tried the faucets and waited until hot water came out of them.

Jon went back into the kitchen and stood at the sink, looking out into the yard, weighing pluses and minuses. The bathroom was close to a deal breaker, but the plumbing worked.

"Window air conditioner in the dining room works fine," Mr. Brown said.

Jon had forgotten about the agent. He stood in the doorway to the living/dining room. He was about Jon's height at five seven, with narrow shoulders, a widow's peak, and thin brown hair. His brown tie hugged his chest and rode the contour of his potbelly.

"Come July and August, you'll appreciate it." He flashed a smile. "You move in, give me a day's notice, I'll have the Welcome Wagon lady call on you."

Welcome Wagon lady closed the deal. In retrospect, he was sure he'd been stupid to get reeled in by the Welcome Wagon lady. But at the time, it had seemed like such an attractive thing. It seemed like something normal people had when they moved into a new house. The Beaver's mom, Mrs. Cleaver, probably had a Welcome Wagon lady call on her when she moved into her house. Teresa should have Welcome Wagon lady call on her.

That's what he'd thought hours, a bottle of Pine-Sol, and a quart of Clorox ago. Now he was tired. It had been a long day. He drove from Pensacola on a two-lane road with lots of small towns to slow down for. The hours spent looking at unsatisfactory houses sapped his energy as much as cleaning the sty.

When he'd bought cleaning supplies, he picked up a local Meridian newspaper. He planned to read it that night, but he was too tired. He needed a shower and sleep. He would read the paper over breakfast and tossed it on the bed. It flopped open.

A headline grabbed his attention: MONTHLY NEGRO CHURCH BURNINGS ENTER THIRD YEAR.

Monthly? Third year, twenty-five Negro churches burned? How could that be? he wondered. One Negro church burned, or even two or three, was imaginable. Twenty-five seemed enormous. He thought about Lieutenant Amos and his saying in the locker room at Saufley Field. He thought about the Catholic church and the Jewish synagogue he'd seen. It didn't make sense.

The article occupied the lower right quadrant of the page. He read it quickly, looking for indications of a synagogue or Catholic church burning, but only Negro churches were mentioned. He read it a second time. No leads, no suspects, no outrage, no *We've got to put a stop to this!* Just a catalog of times and locations. The church burnings occurred in the counties around Meridian, not inside the city itself. Inside the city, the article recounted, were two incidents of drive-by shotgun blasts into the windows of homes of both Negroes and whites with ties to the civil rights movement.

In the shower, Jon thought about news stories he'd watched covering the freedom riders, the marches, and integration efforts at a Southern college. Despite how ugly those things looked, it just never felt real before. It was the news, something that happened to other people.

He and Teresa had watched TV reports, read newspaper and magazine articles on racial violence, and hated the idea that something like that could go on in the United States. But Jon had no inclination to put his future on the line and join the freedom marchers. He sympathized, he prayed for them, and he admired them mostly. Admiration ran out during destructive riots.

As he crawled into bed, he remembered the unexpected visit to the colored section of town. That attack of Negro-phobia and the article roiled in his aching head in a stomach-upsetting jumble. *I probably won't sleep at all,* he thought, but he was wrong.

The next morning the article in the paper still bothered him, but there was a bathroom to reclean, bedrooms to paint, and a fence to build.

Every city and town had a wrong side of the tracks. That's where bad things happened to people. The Binford Real Estate agent, Mr. Brown, said he would have the Welcome Wagon lady call after they moved in. On the right side of the tracks, the Welcome Wagon lady called. Nothing would happen to them. The move to Meridian was what he wanted. It was a positive thing.

*   *   *

On the last Friday in March, Mayflower moved the Zacherys' belongings into the house on Fortieth Street. The window behind the sink and the fence he'd set up pleased Teresa. Mayflower departed, his family had a new house with a very clean bathroom to live in, and that afternoon Welcome Wagon lady would call. The following Tuesday, Jon would begin the basic jet-training syllabus.

After lunch and when the babies went down, Jon insisted Teresa take a nap. As he cleaned the stove, he hummed "The Best is Yet to Come," wishing he could remember more of the lyrics.

Forty minutes later, Teresa got up from her nap and entered the kitchen.

"We have a white stove!" Teresa's smile shone as brightly as the de-gunked appliance.

Jon was scrubbing the oven.

"For that smile I'd scrub another 999 stoves."

He stood and hugged her without touching her with his soiled sissy rubber gloves.

"Teresa," they separated, "What do I wear for the Welcome Wagon lady? Should I put on a tie?"

Teresa rolled her eyes. "Jon, I know you think Meridian's Welcome Wagon lady is going to turn out to be the Beaver's mother, but she knows the movers were here this morning. You're fine."

"Mr. Cleaver always wore a tie."

"Jon Zachery, you are so, so—"

"Suave, debonair, handsome?" he suggested. He liked to be helpful.

It got a head shake, but a little smile too. Jon tried to be as funny to Teresa as he was to himself; that happened rarely, which was why he tried so hard.

Jon was in the kitchen when the door buzzer's nails-on-a-chalkboard, teeth-grating *bzzzt!* wounded his ears. Teresa hurried to the door. Another *bzzzt* would probably set Edgar Jon off. On his back in the playpen in the living room, the baby peacefully but spasmodically reached for the plastic toys strung above him until the buzzer startled him. He didn't crank up his air-raid siren though, which was only restrained by a hair trigger. Edgar Jon's wail at the threshold of pain would not be a proper way to welcome the Welcome Wagon lady. Jon felt sure of that.

Teresa opened the door.

Watching from the kitchen doorway, Jon thought the woman looked like Dinah Shore with a little bit of something strange in her dark-brown eyes—Gracie Allen or Lizzie Borden maybe. Blonde, tall, and slender, she wore a short-sleeved dress, white with a black swirl pattern. She blinked a smile onto her face.

Teresa introduced herself and invited the thirty-five-or-so woman in.

Still standing on the porch, the Welcome Wagon lady said, "Mid wehyust." It was a declarative statement. "Ah pride mahself on ahkcents."

The smile blinked on and then off again, and she charged through the door, past Edgar Jon's playpen, and through the living room like a combination of Scarlett O'Hara entering a ballroom and an affectionate poodle looking for an ankle. Jon had to get out of her way. Teresa followed the woman, and when she passed Jon, she pushed up on his chin.

Jon closed his mouth and watched Teresa manage the older woman as an equal, a guest.

Teresa wore slacks and a short-sleeved white blouse, and she'd been cleaning kitchen cabinets. Jon thought she carried herself rather well next to the older, or more mature, Welcome Wagon lady. Teresa's shoulder-length brown hair never appeared to need attention—except for that one time when she'd been in labor for twelve hours with Jennifer before they decided to do the emergency C-section. But she was poised and a perfect hostess.

Teresa poured iced tea for herself and her guest. Seated across the table from each other, they exchanged introductory information. Mrs. Ellison had a practiced spiel, and she delivered it quickly and efficiently, touting a number of services and merchants. She acknowledged that Teresa would probably do most of her shopping at the naval air station but that the prices at the local merchants were very reasonable.

"Ma'am," Jon said in a pause while both ladies sipped tea, "I heard that we might be able to find some domestic help here. Someone to help Teresa with household chores: cleaning, ironing, that sort of thing. Is there such help available, and what's the going rate?"

"Oh, certainly. Some of our local colored women do that. As to rates, it varies with the individuals. You do have to be careful. Some of them are just shiftless wastrels. I can recommend someone."

"I'd appreciate that, ma'am. And another question, if I might?"

"Of course." She smiled and sat forward.

"I'm wondering, ma'am, I read in the local paper here that there are monthly Negro church burnings, and that this has been going on for three years now. So is my family safe here?"

"Oh, certainly, Mr. Zachery. There's nothing to worry about. Our colored people know their place."

"It's not the colored people I'm worried about, ma'am. I mean, they aren't burning their own churches down. It's the people burning the churches I'm asking about."

The smile appeared again. "You have nothing to worry about. Meridian is a friendly li'l ole town."

She dug in her purse, pulled out a notepad, scribbled furiously on it, tore off the top sheet, and thrust it at Jon.

"Sissy Smith" and her phone number were scrawled on the paper. Jon looked up to see her muscle another smile onto her face.

"Don't get up," she said and blew out of the Zacherys' house.

Jon stood next to Teresa by the living room window and watched last year's Ford station wagon back out of the drive.

"There was no welcome in that wagon," Teresa said.

"I guess I shouldn't have asked Welcome Wagon lady that last question."

"And she was no lady," Teresa said.

"She had white gloves in her purse."

"Jon, you are so, so—"

"Midwestern?" he suggested, just trying to be helpful. It earned him a swat on the arm.

6

Mississippians hate Negroes, Jews, Catholics ... They'd find out in a couple of hours about the Catholic part.

Jon got the coffeepot going. He woke twenty-six-month-old Jennifer (who didn't protest), two-month-old Edgar Jon (who did), and Teresa (who groaned and pulled the pillow over her head because she knew what came next). Jon had adapted the theme song from the TV show *Rawhide* to the Zachery family Sunday-morning get-ready-for-Mass ritual: *Get 'em up, clean 'em up, feed 'em up, dress 'em up ... for church.*

He pulled the pillow off and kissed her.

"I love you on Sunday, Teresa Ann Velmer Zachery, but if you don't get up, I will be forced to sing the song again."

Works better every Sunday.

* * *

Jon waited outside the fourth-grade classroom, where he'd left Jennifer with a nice young lady. Teresa had taken Edgar Jon to the nursery at the other end of the school building. He watched her come out of the far door, negotiate the two steps carefully in her heels, and set off on the sidewalk toward him.

Every once in a while, he thought, *the world stops racing by and you get a chance to really see something.* Such a fine-looking woman, slender, endowed with curves in the right places, in just the right proportions. Her green wool suit set off her pale complexion perfectly. No movie star, no model could make that suit look as good as Teresa did. She worried she hadn't lost her pregnancy fat. He'd tried to convince her, but husbands' soothing words didn't count. As if "Well, yes, you are kind of fat" would float. That probably constituted justifiable homicide. The skirt had been a little tight around the waist, but it looked spectacular on her. She had very nice legs, perfectly sized feet, slender ankles, and luscious calves. The knees were attractive too, but under the hem of the skirt. He felt so blessed, so fortunate, so lucky to have her.

"I recognize that look on your face, Jon Zachery," Teresa said. "It's not sacred thoughts churning between your ears."

"You're wrong. Sacramental matrimony thoughts actually."

She swatted him on the arm. "You and your one-track mind."

"Deftly switching the subject." Jon took Teresa's hand. "I told you it was a nice parish. The school, the church building." Jon gestured, lifting an upraised palm to point out the red-brick walls rising to the steeple that pointed to the blue sky and heaven. The hand came to earth. "The shrubs, the grounds—the parish takes good care of it all."

"Babysitting during Mass is nice," Teresa said.

"Given the Church's position on birth control, it's the least they can do."

Teresa stopped and swatted him on the arm again. "Jon Zachery, since you started flying, you seem to get more sacrilegious every day."

She shook her head but let him take her hand again.

They rounded the corner to the front of the church and climbed the front steps. Looking through the propped-open doors, Jon saw that the pews were packed. *That's a lot of Catholics,* he thought. Were all of them hated by non-Catholic Mississippians? Any number of times, he'd convinced himself not to worry, but his mind kept dredging up concerns about that Amos pronouncement.

Stepping into the nave, Jon smelled incense from the previous service. Teresa wrinkled her nose. Incense bothered her. Strong smells sometimes triggered migraines. Behind the last pew, to the left of the center aisle of the church, an usher flashed a major smile at Teresa. He was a normal-sized man at five feet seven inches. He was slender and wore a dark suit and red tie. His oiled dark hair reflected light in spots. He bowed to Teresa. Jon thought he'd make a great Welcome Wagon lady, but then an image of Sister Mary Maurice from grade school frowned at him. "You are in church!" the image said. Sister knew that if a boy wasn't misbehaving, he was thinking of misbehaving.

The usher started purposefully down the aisle. Teresa followed. Jon caboosed the tiny train.

The large windows let plenty of bright, cheerful light into the nave. But he thought the stained glass seemed off, too modern maybe. The colors, he decided, were too bright, vivid, stark.

They stopped. The usher attempted to get people in a crowded pew to scrunch together more.

Teresa put her hand on the usher's forearm. "Move back," she whispered. He just stood in place and gaped at her. Teresa grabbed his arm, and he closed his mouth and allowed himself to be moved out of the way.

Then Jon saw the young colored woman on the second kneeler in from the aisle, alone in the eight-person pew. She knelt but rested against the seat behind her. The people in front of her were sitting. Behind her, a man and a woman were kneeling, their arms on the back of the pew. The young colored girl—Jon thought she was about eighteen, nineteen maybe—stared straight ahead.

The Welcome Wagon lady popped into Jon's mind: *Our colored people, they know their place.*

But not in church, not in a Catholic church, they don't have to know their place here.

At his Navy duty stations, at Purdue University, colored people attended Mass. Not many, but some did. He had always assumed Negroes preferred other religions, but if they wanted to attend Mass, well, certainly they'd be welcome. No big deal.

He followed Teresa into the pew and put the kneeler down.

He felt eyes pressing on him, like the pressure on the bottom of a deep swimming pool, and he began perspiring.

The people in the pew in front of them were seated. He and Teresa postured themselves, as the colored girl had. Jon noticed the silence. The generalized rustling of hundreds of closely packed people had stopped. Above his suit coat collar, it felt as if bugs were trudging through the jungle of his hair. He was scared one instant, embarrassed the next, and then scared again.

In the pews to the front, heads started turning and looking back at the Zacherys. Those eyes held nothing friendly.

Outside, it had been cool. Inside, the air held that extra dose of chill from proximate cold-soaked stone, and as his sweat dried, Jon shivered. Even though there was a lot of room in the pew, he edged closer to Teresa so that their shoulders touched. She slipped her hand under his arm. With peripheral vision, he saw Teresa jut out her chin.

There, in that segregated Catholic church in Meridian, Mississippi, with animosity, and probably some hate, focused on the two of them more than on the girl, Jon felt overwhelmed with a sense of love and admiration for Teresa. She had known the right thing to do and did it, leading them into the pew.

If he had been paying attention, instead of gawking around at the windows, he wondered if he'd have had Teresa's presence of mind and courage to act. *I doubt it,* he confessed to himself. *I'd probably have allowed the usher to shoehorn us into an already-crowded pew.*

Next to him, Teresa's head was bowed. A little smile tweaked up the corners of her lips.

At the sudden jangle of the sacristy bell, Jon saw Teresa flinch. Despite the smile, anxiety gripped her too.

The altar boys and the priest processed out from the sacristy, and the organ cranked up. By magic, or maybe a miracle, nineteen hundred years of church history and ritual shouted down, for the moment, a century of local social pattern. The service ran according to form. The colored girl stood, knelt, and sat at all the appropriate times. Jon wondered if she was

Catholic or just sitting in on the service and following the cues of those around her. She seemed at home with the ritual.

Jon didn't pay attention to the early prayers. He anticipated the sermon. There would be pulpit direction to welcome his pew mate. There had to be, except the young priest acted as if the colored girl wasn't there.

When the usher came by with the basket, he didn't offer it to Jon. Apparently his money didn't belong there either. Maybe he and Teresa had disappeared through an act of collective will power. That seemed to be how they handled the colored girl. The congregation's initial hostility had burned like the last Fourth of July sparkler in the box. When it went out, the event was over. The universal animosity flared, went out, and with the extinguishing, the parts of the Mass marched forward. The colored girl and the two interlopers had been erased. Not even their ghosts remained.

When Jon and Teresa left the pew and joined the line to receive Holy Communion, he glanced back at the colored girl. She stayed in the pew. Nobody tried to stop them from receiving the host.

After the service, Jon waited until the people filed out. He started to stand, and Teresa grabbed his arm. She leaned over and whispered to the girl, "I'm Teresa Zachery. Are you going to be outside? Would love to talk to you."

She shook her head. "No, ma'am. I'm afraid if I leave the pew, I might not get another. I'm staying until after the noon Mass."

Jon hadn't looked at the girl closely before. There hadn't been time to take in anything but the color of her skin. She was about Teresa's height but had an athletic heft to her shoulders. Her skin was very dark, her face was pleasant, and her black hair was bobbed short. She wore a sedate, light-blue, flowered, short-sleeved dress with a royal-blue sweater over it, and she sat in the pew with her hands clasped in her lap, a picture of calm, grace, and composure.

"Would you like to come to dinner?" Teresa asked.

"Thank you, ma'am. Thanks, but no, I can't. Just after the next Mass I'll be picked up. We want to be out of Mississippi before the sun goes down."

"Oh, I didn't think." Teresa put her hand on the girl's forearm. "I hope I didn't make things more difficult for you."

"Oh, no, ma'am. Don't you be worrying about that. Thank you for sitting with me."

Teresa asked Jon for a three-by-five card from his shirt pocket. She wrote their names, address, and phone number on the card, and she handed it to the girl.

"We'll be in Meridian for six months. If you come back, or if you need anything, give us a call, please. And will you tell me your name? I'm going to pray for you."

"It's Clarissa, ma'am. Clarissa Johnson."

Teresa took her hand and squeezed it. "Please call when you get home, just so I know you got there okay." The girl nodded.

"Clarissa," Jon said as Teresa wrote, "would you be willing to give us your address and phone number too?"

She hesitated but nodded again. Jon thought she had a beautiful smile.

Jon and Teresa walked down the aisle of the mostly empty church. A half dozen older women knelt in some of the rear pews. An usher, Mr. Welcome Wagon Lady, stood just behind the last pew, handing out weekly bulletins. Six pews before Jon got there, he placed the bulletins on a small, dark wooden table next to the door, and he turned, presenting his back.

Jon took a bulletin, and they continued through the vestibule. Outside, three islands of male conversation were distributed about the sidewalk in front of the church. The young priest who had presided at Mass stood with the center group. He looked up, saw the Zacherys on the top step, and bolted back inside the church through a side door.

When Jon got to the grade-school classroom to retrieve two-year-old Jennifer, she was the only child there and was seated at one of about thirty small desks. The young babysitter, in her late twenties or early thirties, stood with her hand on a doorknob at the far side of the room. Jennifer got up and ran to Jon. He knelt and hugged her. When he rose, the woman was gone.

"Thank you," he said to the door she had been standing by. *Word gets around fast,* he thought.

Jennifer grabbed Jon's finger with her left hand, and they crossed the classroom to the far door. Jon opened it into a wide hallway with classrooms on either side. The hallway was empty of humanity. Jennifer raised her arms. Jon picked her up, and she hugged him around the neck.

"I'm glad to see you too, princess."

As soon as Jon opened the door to the parking lot, he could hear Edgar Jon. The kid had lungs, and he let you know if the world wasn't running the way it should. Teresa was almost to the car with the baby on her shoulder. He arched his back and raised his little arms over his head. Teresa had to work at supporting him. The little guy had a temper, but Jon had never seen him so upset.

He put Jennifer into the backseat of the two-door Impala; then he and Teresa worked together to get the screaming squirmer into his infant seat. She tried to get his pacifier in his mouth, but he kept turning his head and batting it away. After a couple of tries, Teresa managed to hold it in there long enough for him to figure out what it was and that it wasn't just another of the endless irritants he'd been enduring since the creation of the universe.

Edgar Jon had his way of winding down. With a few hard sucks on the pacifier, and snuffling intakes of breath through his nose, his tension went down a notch. With another suck, suck, snuffle, snuffle, it went down another notch.

"The baby"—Jon had never seen Teresa so furious either—"had a terrible dirty diaper. His poor little bottom is fire-engine red." She put her hand on Edgar Jon's head. "Mommy's sorry. Mommy should have come to rescue you sooner."

The baby was winding down fast. Eyelids drooped.

"He was in a crib, crying his little heart out. There was a woman in there, but she was in the back of the room. As soon as I came in, she left." Teresa shook her head.

"I found Jennifer just the same way. I was surprised the babysitters found out so quickly, but I guess someone told them. They don't want us to come back. That's clear. We're ostracized."

"No, Jon," Teresa said. "As far as those people are concerned, you, me, and Clarissa Johnson have never existed. We have been unborn off the earth." Her lips compressed to a line, and she shook her head from side to side. "Whatever they do to you and me, that's one thing, but taking it out on the little ones—"

"You remember what the girl, what Clarissa said, about being out of Mississippi before the sun went down? Do you know what a sundown town is, Teresa?"

She shook her head.

"There have been towns, not just in the South, with signs posted indicating Negroes had better be outside the city limits before the sun goes down. That's a sundown town. What Clarissa said is that Mississippi is a sundown state."

"Let's go home, Jon."

"Next Sunday, Mass on the base?" he asked

She didn't answer right away, busy as she was glowering at the windshield. Jon thought about Lieutenant Amos. He must not have known that Mississippi Catholics hated non-Mississippi Catholics. That sure would have messed up the symmetry of his catchy little saying. Then Teresa nodded, forced a smile on her face, and rubbed her hand over Edgar Jon's fine baby hair. He still worked the pacifier, doing his sharp, short inhales through his nose, but he about had his little world back in order.

7

Cyril Henley slammed the door of his new black Ford pickup, stood arms akimbo, and glowered at it for a moment. He'd been sitting in the church parking lot, listening to the Sunday morning news, when the radio died. The sound quit, and the light in the dial went out.

"Brand-damn-new truck," he said out loud, and then he quickly looked around to see if anyone heard him talking to himself.

There were a lot of people funneling themselves through the door of the church, but they were in a hurry to make it inside before the Mass started and were not paying attention to anybody around them.

Cyril liked to wait in the parking lot until five minutes after the service started. Most Sundays—not Christmas or Easter, of course—he could still wedge himself into the row of young-men-against-the-back-wall standers. If he had his druthers, he wouldn't be there at all, but he lived at home. There'd be no peace with his momma if he didn't go to church on Sunday to avoid losing his immortal soul to the fires of hell. Living at home enabled him to put money aside for the truck. So he stood in back and went to communion so his momma would see him. Then he filed back after, along with the entire rank of back-wall standers, and continued right on out the door without slowing down even a little bit.

Cyril paused below the steps to silently curse the bad luck that settled the Henley family next to Mrs. Albemarle, who got his momma fired up about letting the pope run their lives. His round head twitched. After climbing the steps, he stopped again to hitch up his pants. Climbing steps made his belt sag under his belly. He brushed the toes of his go-to-church cowboy boots on the back of his legs. When he looked up, about halfway to the front of church, he saw Ollie trying to usher a man and a woman into a pew. The woman pushed Ollie out of the way and got into a pew behind the one the usher intended.

Sweet Jesus. A nigra.

Cyril stood in the middle of the aisle and waited for Ollie. If Ollie's leather heels weren't clicking on the tile, he wouldn't have noticed how quiet it was. Generally, whispers buzzed, clothes rustled, kneelers dropped. Not that day though.

Ollie looked worried. *And he damn well ought to,* Cyril thought.

Cyril grabbed the usher by the upper arm and dragged him out through the vestibule, down the steps, onto the sidewalk, and spun him around to face him.

"Why the hell you let a nigra in?" Cyril asked.

"I didn't see her come in. Once she was seated, what was I s'posed to do?"

"Drag her black ass out."

"It's church, Cyril."

"Colored Catholics got their own church."

"This colored girl, she's probably a Northerner."

"I know that." Cyril shook his head. "Momma's daddy, John Calhoun, not gonna like this. Who's those two got in the pew? Know who they are?"

"He's a Navy guy. Just moved here. He filled out a registration card at the rectory."

"Know who's in the office?"

"Essie."

Cyril nodded once and stomped off around the side of church.

* * *

John Calhoun sure as hell did not like it.

"I knew blowing out windows wadn't gonna do no good. No need to get the police riled up, they said. Hurt somebody, police git riled, they said. Nobody makes a fuss over Negro church burnings in the county, they said. In town we got to be careful, they said. In town we got to be smart, they said."

Cyril knew to stay out of Uncle John Calhoun's way when he went into one of his rages, stomping back and forth in front of a long, open-on-one-side tin shed, where he kept his trucks, tractors, dozer, and front loaders.

Cyril knew some mistook Uncle John Calhoun for skinny. He just liked his bib overalls a little loose. Not a lick of fat on him, but what there was of him was all hard muscle.

"And strong," Cyril's pop, Darnell, said once. "Your momma's daddy, John Calhoun, can lift as much by hisself as takes three men to do. Once I seen him get that mean look on his face 'n 'e scared an anvil off'n the ground."

Cyril thought Uncle John Calhoun really got scary when he stopped pacing. Then he seemed to go from volcano to iceberg as he got to figurin' what he was gonna do about what fired him up in the first place. Until he wound down, Cyril stayed between the dozer and a stake bed truck under the shed. Sometimes it took a while.

John Calhoun said, "Bring your sorry ass outa there."

Cyril stopped at the edge of the shed overhang.

"I ain't gonna bite."

John Calhoun put his hand around Cyril's bicep.

"Okay, Cyril. These Navy people come to our town, they oughta know we got our own ways of actin'. Can't have 'em encouraging the niggers. We gonna have to teach 'em manners."

"Shotgun?"

"Don't try to think, Cyril. Listen."

He listened and waited for John Calhoun to finish the things he wanted Cyril to take to his twin cousins.

Cyril did not like going out to the twins' shack. His pop and momma had taken him away from the place sixteen years before, and nothing made going back attractive. A person just didn't argue with John Calhoun though.

He passed the city limits, heading west, and thought about the night that convinced his momma the family had to move to town and get civilized.

They had their own shack out there back then. His pop, momma, and he lived next to pop's sister, Mary Magdelene, and her boys, Chevy and Ford. Mary Magdelene wasn't around much, and Cyril's momma raised the twins more than their own momma did. Mary Magdelene was often gone for days at a time, so exactly when she finally disappeared was kind of hard to nail down. When Cyril turned six and the twins were seven, Cyril's pop started taking the boys with him to the still. The boys grew up chopping wood for the still and house, planting and tending the corn and the garden, carrying buckets of water from the creek during dry spells, and hunting with a single-shot twenty-two. Ford grew faster than his brother and his cousin. By the time he was fourteen, Ford was six feet tall and weighed 255 pounds. Toting supplies to the still, he could carry more than Cyril's pop. At night Cyril's momma taught the three boys their lessons with light from a coal oil lamp.

All three boys wanted to go with Cyril's pop when he made his moonshine deliveries, but he'd always refused. Then, when Cyril turned fourteen, his pop said it was time.

"Arlene, I'm taking the boys with me on a delivery run."

"That'd be a mistake, Darnell."

"Don't be such a worrywart. I'll watch 'em."

"You bring them boys back with shine on their breath, you'll get something to worry about."

Cyril's momma had a way of sending his pop off with a mighty sheepish look on his face.

They had to go out onto the Meridian-Jackson highway and drop off jugs at a dozen stops. The last delivery was to a shack bar just a hoot and a holler from where they lived.

Cyril's pop delivered the jugs and came back out. "Boys, come on inside. They got ribs."

The inside of the place scared Cyril. Two coal oil lamps didn't throw out much light through sooty chimneys. So much cigarette smoke hung in the air it stung his eyes and left an acid taste in his throat. The mumbled voices carried menace and threat, and when every eye swung around and stared at the boys, Cyril was ready to bolt.

His pop led them to one of the two round tables with four men around it.

"Mind lettin' my boys sit 'n eat?" his pop asked.

The four didn't move. Three of them watched the fourth to see what he would do. The fourth man stared up at one twin and then the other. He smirked and nodded toward the plywood bar, and the four scooted their chairs noisily back across the rough plank floor.

Cyril's pop set a plate of ribs in the middle of the table, and he sat too. They all grabbed ribs and started gnawing.

Every once in a while, one of the men who had vacated their table would turn and look at the twins and then turn back and mumble something, and they would all laugh.

"What they laughing at?" Ford asked Chevy.

"Nothing. Pay them no mind," Chevy said.

"Chevy knows. Cyril knows. Prob'ly time you know the story too," Cyril's pop said. "After your grandpa and grammaw Henley died, your momma started running with bad people. Story is she got double knocked up in the backseats of cars right outside this bar. That's how you come to be. Two weeks after you was born, Mary Magdelene came back to the bar here. She was asked what she named you. 'Hadn't yet,' she said. Well, that was a pure shame, the men decided, so they named you Chevy and Ford. Prob'ly right at this table."

"Boys." Cyril looked up as a man, the one the others had watched, placed four jelly jars with an inch of clear liquid in each on the table. "On me."

"Thanks, Harvey. But we can't. The boys are drinking Co'-Cola," Cyril's pop said.

"The boys 're old enough to say for themselves. What do you say, boys? Have a drink."

"Thanks, Harvey, but we're leaving," Cyril's pop said and started to get up.

Harvey pushed him back into his chair. "Okay, Darnell, you can speak for your boy, but the twins'll say their own piece." Harvey looked at Ford. "Now which one is you? The two of you look so much alike."

The three at the bar roared, bent over, slapped knees, and stood up again.

"Hell, Darnell," the blond, tall drink of water named Davey, standing at the end of the bar, said, "even your rotgut shine tastes good when it's chased with a belly laugh."

Cyril dropped a rib he hadn't taken a bite from, and it fell onto his lap and then onto the floor. He didn't understand what was going on. Harvey abruptly stopped laughing and glowered at Ford.

"You gonna drink what I brung ya?"

"I'll drink it," Chevy said as he reached for a jar.

"Now you take one, Ford." Harvey leaned on the table. "Like your polite brother here."

The expression on Ford's face never changed much. Cyril couldn't tell what he was thinking. Ford wiped his hands on his pants and looked up at Harvey.

"Hey, Ford, jist let it alone," Chevy said. "He don't mean nothing. He's jist joshing."

Harvey backhanded Chevy, and Cyril wet his pants as Ford seemed to explode from his chair and punch Harvey in the face. Harvey straightened up and started going backward, his feet trying hard to stay under him. He crashed into Davey, and both fell to the floor.

Cyril's mouth hung open, just the way Harvey's other two companions open-mouth stared at Ford as he approached them. Ford punched the one on his right in the gut. The man doubled over and moaned. Davey scrambled to his feet, grabbed the sawed-off baseball bat from the shelf behind the bar, and swung it at Ford's head. Ford turned just enough so the bat landed on his shoulder, eliciting no more than an "uh." He grabbed Davey's shirt, took the bat away from him, and clobbered him on the side of the head with it. Davey crumpled onto Harvey, who was on his hands and knees.

Darnell got the boys out of the bar right behind the fourth man, who was in more of a hurry than he was.

Cyril heard his pop tell his momma what happened. Two days after the fight, Davey died in Harvey's shack. Harvey told the deputy sheriff they had been drinking and there'd been a fight. Harvey couldn't remember who hit Davey. The victim had no kin, and nobody knew where he came from.

Cyril's momma told his pop, "That's it. You take my daddy's offer."

His pop didn't want to go hat in hand to beg a sawmill job from Arlene's daddy, John Calhoun, so the family could move to Meridian. "You go," his momma told him. He went.

Chevy and Ford refused to move to town. Cyril's momma said, "Suit yourselfs then." The twins stayed in their mother's shack and took over the still.

Cyril couldn't remember how many years it had been since he'd been to the twins' shack. Seeing Ford in town wasn't nothin' to fret on, but out there in his own territory, that was something else.

He parked his shiny black pickup next to his cousin's dented, rusted, and dirty white one and stood beside the driver's door. The pine scent in the still air under the trees was strong enough to taste. There wasn't a sound except the engine cooling. He rubbed his hand over his head, more a remembered than a functional thing, took a deep breath, hiked up his pants, and started for the rotted wooden step leading into the shack.

Cyril stepped back from the opened door, giving the escaping smells more room to move by him. Inside, both his cousins lay on twin mattresses on the floor. He stood looking at them, hesitating. It didn't do to startle his cousin Ford.

"The hell you want, Cyril?" Ford asked, and it was Cyril who was startled.

Cyril passed along John Calhoun's message and even remembered the part about "Don't say nothin' to the Jackson folks." When he left, Chevy gave him a jug.

Chevy was the sociable one.

8

Clarissa Johnson sat on the pew, her eyes on the altar. She had to work hard to contain the fear and turmoil that threatened to overwhelm her. The congregation had paraded out and left empty pews in front of her. Behind her it sounded as if the main entrance doors to the church were propped open. She heard children's voices from the parking lot across the street, a sound of springtime. The musty, confined indoor odor she smelled connoted winter. A car drove past the entrance to the church but didn't stop. No matter. It was still too early for the pickup. No part of the morning had been easy. Waiting for the car, which would rescue her, wasn't either. She wanted to look around behind her, but she thought that if she did, it would turn loose the violent disaster that hovered over her ever since she got out of the car and walked on rubbery legs into the church and into the pew. *Dear God in heaven, why did I let Billy talk me into this?*

Billy. He wasn't handsome. He was beautiful. He stood straight and tall, not proud or haughty, but with the grace of an angel so perfectly at home with his purity. He sang like an angel. The choir director liked to arrange a duet for them to perform each Sunday. Clarissa loved to sing with him. And Poppa and Momma would approve of Billy. That's what she thought. If only she'd found out about him before her stupid puppy love–besotted brain agreed to come with him on this "it's time for people like us to do our part" journey of his.

She wished she had stayed in Chicago and gone to her place of worship. She and Billy could have sung "Amazing Grace," but Billy told the choir director they were going to be absent today. In her mind she went through the song, just the way she would have with Billy. Then she checked her watch. *Thank you, God, almost time.* When the second hand reached the top, 11:23, she left the pew, genuflected, and turned around, not sure what she'd find behind her. Relief flooded through her. No one else was in the main part of the church.

She started walking toward the entrance. They promised to be there at exactly 11:25 a.m. Billy made her set her watch to his, to the second. What if they were held up? So many things could have gone wrong. The two of them could have run into trouble. The thought of having to wait for the car outside the church was more terrifying than anything else she'd gone through that morning. Inside the church, there was a promise of sanctuary, but outside on the street, in the white section of town, demons from hell waited to tear her body and soul apart.

Through the propped-open door she saw Albert Wexall's Plymouth Valiant pull up and stop at the curb. Her spirit soared, and her heart skipped a beat. She picked up the pace, wondering if someone would come from a hidden corner and stop her, but no one did.

As she descended the steps, she saw a group of six men huddled in a circle to her right and ten feet or so from the front of the Valiant. The six all turned. Their eyes made her feel like cornered prey.

Keep moving. Holy Mary, Mother of God, pray for us sinners.

She didn't complete the prayer. Mentioning death seemed like tempting or daring fate to unleash overwhelming hate and retribution. Keeping her eyes on the car, she fought the urge to run. It was as if she were watching some other Clarissa. She got in the car, as if she had all the time in the world, and closed the door with just the right amount of pull to latch it securely.

As Billy pulled the car away from the curb, she stared straight ahead but felt six sets of predator eyes follow her until the car rounded the corner.

"I never should have let you talk me into this, Billy. This was crazy. It was just awful," Clarissa said.

Billy was driving Albert's car, and Albert was under a blanket on the floor in back. It was not a good idea for white and colored people to ride in a car together in Mississippi.

Billy smiled at her. "How'd it go, Clarissa?" That smile could still melt her heart, even in the midst of fear and horror.

How'd it go! She wanted to scream at him, but she just shook her head, took a handkerchief from her clutch purse, blew her nose, and looked out the windshield.

Billy said over his shoulder, "How're you doing, Albert?"

"No problem. I'm gonna take a nap. But, you know, next time, I think we should get a motel in Memphis. This driving all day and all night's for the birds."

"Yeah, you sleeping all the time the sun's up gotta be tough on a man," Billy said.

"This whole damn thing was your idea, so what've you got to whine about?" Albert asked.

"So, how'd it go with you," Clarissa asked Billy, "bringing a white boy in a colored church?"

Albert answered. "Ha. We sure stepped in it. Turns out Billy's house got a shotgun blast through the window a couple of weeks back. His daddy was not happy to see Billy bring me to the service. 'You trying to get us killed?' his daddy asked him."

"Well, actually, Daddy isn't happy to see me at all these days," Billy said.

"Yeah." Albert laughed. "Daddy doesn't like Billy's choice of roommate. That's how he put it, right, Billy boy?"

Billy shrugged.

Clarissa didn't like his choice of roommate either, even without the homosexual issue and his roommate's flippancy. Billy was serious about everything: studies, music, Dr. King. Albert took only marijuana seriously. Coming with Billy, for him, was just a lark.

"You want a sandwich, Clarissa?" Albert asked.

"A sandwich! I'd throw up."

Clarissa heard wax paper crinkle from the backseat. Suddenly, she felt exhausted. It had been a long night in the car. She'd been jerked awake in panic by bumps in the road, sudden high beams from oncoming cars, a horn honk, and the car slowing. *Thank God,* she thought, *for Billy's high school friend Gail and her bathroom to wash up and change.* At least she had felt clean and properly dressed to face her ordeal. Access to the bathroom had revived and fortified her. Now, after what seemed like hours of tension, with the immediate threat removed, she was so very tired, and she leaned against the door and lay her head back.

"Clarissa, before you go to sleep, tell us how it went, will you?" Billy asked.

She didn't soften recounting the horror she felt, and to her, it was the main reason to tell the story.

"An usher tried to put two white people in the pew in front of you, and the woman pushed the usher out of the way and sat with you. That what you said?" Billy asked.

She nodded.

"Clarissa, that's wonderful. That's the whole point. Until we see these small victories from just ordinary people, not the freedom-rider sort of heroes, we can't realize Dr. King's dream."

"You know what I did, Billy?" Clarissa dabbed her eyes. "I lied to the woman who sat with me. She is such a nice person. I lied to her."

"How? How did you lie to her?" Billy asked.

"She asked if I was going to be outside church to talk to me. I told her I was staying for the noon Mass. That was a lie."

"We talked about that, Clarissa," Billy said. "If someone asked, you were to let them believe you would be there until 1:00 p.m. You did just what we agreed. That was the plan."

"After she was so nice, and it took courage to do what she did. It makes me feel dirty and ugly to have lied to her. I can't even remember her name."

"We outside the city limit yet?" Albert asked. "I want to crawl up on the backseat and sleep—if you two can hold the noise down, that is."

9

Jon reached across the kitchen table and took Teresa's hand.

"Sorry, Teresa. I wasn't expecting to drag you and the babies into all this hostility. Meridian was going to be a normal town, not a Navy town. The Welcome Wagon lady came to call. I looked at the church building and thought it was a nice parish. Stupid, stupid, stupid."

"Jon, it's going to be okay. We have a house to live in. From now on, we'll leave Mississippi alone, and they'll leave us alone. You'll be out at the base for six months, and then we'll shake the dust of this place from our sandals. We'll be fine. God won't give us anything we can't handle."

"Sometimes God seems to think we're awfully tough."

"We are when we let Him be on our side."

Some part in the refrigerator vibrated for a moment, and then it was quiet.

"The almighty dollar says, in god we trust," Teresa began.

"And the mortal Zacherys do too," Jon finished her saying. He kissed her hand. "Okay, Teresa, the babies are in bed. You need to take advantage and grab a nap."

"I want to help you clean."

"The move has worn you out. Nap."

"Yes, dear," Teresa said, got up, and headed for the bedroom.

Huh.

He thought of that Sunday two years ago, when Jennifer was a new baby. Teresa's friend Rose Herbert came over to see how mother and baby were doing. Rose took one look at Teresa, and she turned on Jon. "I swear to almighty God. Men are so oblivious! If one of Teresa's boobs fell off, you wouldn't even notice, as long as you had the other one to look at."

Jon didn't have a clue as to what set her off.

"Oh, for Christ's sake. Look at Teresa, Jon. She looks like a raccoon with those circles under her eyes. She's exhausted."

As Teresa slept, Rose gave Jon some instruction.

"Even an idiot can take care of a baby. Pay attention. You may be able to work your way up to that level." Rose aimed a disgusted look at him. "Or not."

Rose was five feet tall, weighed one hundred pounds, had red hair and green eyes, and was the toughest person Jon had ever met.

Twenty-six months later, Rose would, no doubt, still find fault with his observational powers, but he'd learned a few things. When he was home, he made sure he lifted two-year-old Jennifer and that Teresa took naps.

Jon got up from the table to follow Teresa and tuck her in.

"What are you smirking about?" she asked as he pulled the sheet up over her.

"You obeyed me," he said. "I think that is the first time you observed that part of our wedding vows."

She swatted him on the arm.

"And we've only been married for five years."

Which earned him another swat—a smile too though.

After he closed the bedroom door, Jon got a bucket and scrubbed out the rest of the kitchen cabinets. When Teresa got up, they could finish unpacking the kitchen things. As he worked in the kitchen, he thought about giving the bathroom another scrubbing. It really didn't need it. But his mind kept seeing that petrified pickle, lying on the bottom of the filthy bathtub the first time he went in the place. At first he thought it was a turd and almost walked out, but it was the last house the real estate agent had to show.

Perhaps after my mind is in Meridian a while, it can make the imitation-number-two memento get unborn from my head.

10

Harry Peeper crept the car along the highway from Jackson to Meridian so he wouldn't miss the dirt road slashed out of the pine forest. It was easy to miss the road in broad daylight, much less on a black-assed overcast night. But he found it, two red ruts leading off between thick stands of skinny pine trees.

"Damn road," Harry grumbled as his DeSoto bounced, and he had to fight the steering wheel. He glanced at Amanda Sue.

She stared straight ahead and hunched forward, her left hand on the dash, bracing herself against the jouncing.

Be a shame if she doesn't work out, he thought. He'd met her in Coleman's Tavern two weeks before with another girl. The girls took stools at the bar, near where Harry stood in a circle of guys from Germaine's service department. She was giving Harry the eye. He watched her too. She was blonde and had nice boobs. She looked fresh, soft, and clean. He compared her to Jolene, a brunette, built just as well, but with a hard and used look to her.

"Blondie's been giving you the eye, Harry," Baxter, the guy from the parts department, said. "Buy her a beer."

"Those college girls out slumming, you think?" Harry asked.

"The hell difference that make?" Baxter asked.

Harry bought her a beer. Amanda Sue Wellman had graduated from college the year before. Her daddy was a big-shot lawyer who blamed her for not being a boy. She hated the social events her second stepmother pushed her to attend. Harry learned a lot for the price of a beer. That night, he took her to his apartment, and the next day she moved in with him. That was all well and good, but what he needed to know was if he could use her as a driver.

Trees crowded right up to the edge of the wheel ruts. Pine branches scraped the top and sides of his car. Even inching along, the car bottomed hard in holes he couldn't see with the headlights dancing up and down. Harry swore. The big moonshiner motor grumbled, as if it too were impatient with the pace, eager to cut loose.

About a quarter of a mile from the highway, they came to a chain stretched across the road. Dangling from the chain was a wooden sign with faded black lettering on the remnants of some long-ago applied white paint: GO AHED TRESPAS.

"'Manda Sue, get the chain."

She sat frozen, staring at the sign. Her blouse was sleeveless, and Harry used his left hand to slap her bare upper arm.

"Get the goddamn chain!"

She looked at him as she rubbed her shoulder. Harry drew his hand back, but she got out before he could hit her again. Amanda Sue went to the tree to the right of the road. The chain was secured with a padlock.

"Other side," Harry said.

Amanda Sue unhooked the chain and pulled it across the road.

"Want me to hook it back up after you drive through?" He heard her voice quaver.

"Nah." Harry couldn't see her face as she stood by the tree, but he imagined big scared eyes. "Wait here. Be back in ten minutes."

"No!" she screamed. Harry laughed and drove away.

A half mile beyond the chain, Harry found the twins, sitting in the bed of their pickup, legs dangling. He parked with the car angled so the headlights weren't in their faces and stepped out.

"Got the coal oil?" Harry asked.

Chevy got out of the pickup, walked along the passenger side of the DeSoto, and got in the backseat.

"What's eatin' Chevy?" Harry asked.

Ford looked at his hands for a moment. "We shot Bollinger's window, 'n Chevy didn't say nothin'. You didn't neither."

"Chevy got his feelin's hurt, that what you're saying?"

"Coal oil's here. Three jerricans."

Ford grabbed two of the cans and headed for the rear of the DeSoto. Harry watched the shadow hulk of Ford move through the darkness. *Tending crybabies. Guess that's why I never wanted to be a sergeant in the Army,* he thought and grabbed the other can from the twins' pickup.

Harry got back in the car and turned around.

"Okay, Ford, Chevy—"

"Ever body says Chevy, Ford," Ford cut in.

Harry wasn't moving fast, and he put on the brakes and looked over at Ford, staring out the windshield.

He shook his head and moved the car forward. "Chevy, Ford then. This nigger church we're doing tonight, the target got handed us by the Jackson guys. Next month we scout our own target. That a problem?"

Nobody said anything. "That a problem, Chevy, Ford?"

"Need to ask him," Ford said.

Jesus.

Harry asked. Chevy said it wasn't a problem.

Harry listened to the grumble of the big engine in his car as they coasted along the rutted road. A few bugs danced in the headlights' beam, not as many as would be there in the summer. *Bugs, they're about as big an aggravation as Chevy,* Harry thought.

"Got someone else along tonight," Harry said. "Might work out to be our driver."

"Who?" Chevy asked.

"Right up ahead, holding the chain," Harry said, and he felt Chevy grab the seat and pull himself forward.

"A cunt? You want a cunt to be our driver?" Chevy asked.

Harry jammed on the brakes and spun around. "You want me to tell you who'd be more use to us?"

Chevy slunk back to his corner of the backseat.

Harry glanced at Ford. He stared straight ahead.

After Harry drove past the tree, Amanda Sue hooked the chain back up, without having to be told to do so.

Harry turned on the overhead light, got out of the car, and held the driver's-side rear door open for her. The uppity society girl had mastered her fear of the dark. He could see it in her face. There might be some backbone to the girl that he could count on. It didn't really matter too much if she measured up or not. There were others who could drive and do the things to support him.

Of course 'Manda Sue being a nympho and all, that'd be hard to replace, Harry thought. Soldiers, and especially sergeants, had to make sacrifices though.

But Harry liked what he saw in her face: no fear, just a wild excitement like before the sex games she was fond of playing.

Harry glanced at Chevy. His mouth hung open, his gaze locked onto Amanda's chest.

The tails of Amanda Sue's blouse were tied together under her breasts.

"Jee-eee-sus," Chevy said. "Look a' them jugs."

In a blur of motion, Harry lunged across Amanda Sue and held the tip of his switchblade under Chevy's left eye. "We're on a goddamn mission. Keep your mind on the business. You either tell me you can do that, or get out of the car without this eye."

"Jesus, Harry."

Harry's voice was quiet and calm. "Can you count to three, Chevy? One, two—"

"Wait, wait! Yeah, I got it, goddamn, Harry. I was jist lookin'."

Harry glanced at Ford. Ford didn't move; he just stared straight ahead. Harry pulled back out of the car and sat on his haunches. He looked at Amanda Sue for a couple of ticks and tocks, and then he rose and retrieved his new hardware from the trunk.

"Hold this," he told Amanda Sue and placed the stock of a Thompson submachine gun on the floor between her feet.

Harry stood and smiled. He'd given some thought to where to keep his forty-five. That was on his left under his belt. He carried his switchblade in the watch pocket on his right. After practice every day for a week, he could draw both really fast.

He got back in the driver's seat and turned around. There was a small red tear about an inch below Chevy's left eye. Chevy wouldn't look at Harry.

"So's ever'body knows the plan," Harry said. "Target's just twenty minutes' drive. When we get there, Chevy—Chevy, look at me." Chevy's eyes glanced at Harry's face but didn't stay there. Harry waited a moment. "Chevy." Harry wore his quiet voice again. "Take a five-gallon can of coal oil, break a side window, and dump your can inside. Bring the can back. Don't leave it."

Chevy nodded.

"Say it," Harry said.

"Side window. Bring the can. I got it, Harry."

"Ford, grab the ladder that's against the shed in back, and bring it to the front of the church. I'll carry the other two cans to the front and meet you there. You take a can up and spread it on the roof." He turned back to Amanda Sue. "You stay right next to me with the Tommie." He turned back to Ford. "When you're back on the ladder, holler ready, and we'll all toss our matches and hustle back to the car."

11

It was 2200. Time for the news.

Jon left the *Student Naval Aviator Handbook* on the sofa, got up, and turned on the portable TV.

As soon as it warmed up, the president appeared and announced he would not seek reelection. He would spend his remaining time in office, getting the country out of Vietnam.

Jon felt it like a kick in the stomach.

Following the night of the dog poop, he had decided to stay in the Navy, but that was the smallest part of what he felt called to do.

He had thought about it and boiled it down to a handful of key points upon which to base his decision: If Communism defeated America, it would be a tragedy for the human race. When draftees said, "Hell no, we won't go," and ran away to Canada, it made America vulnerable. Protestors shouting and waving signs against everything, implying no government was better than the existing one, made American vulnerable. And when Dr. King proclaimed we should forget about Vietnam and fix our racial problems, that made America vulnerable to foreign enemies.

Before he made his decision to stay in, he had weighed other factors.

The Revolutionary War had been fought over things like taxation without representation and religious freedom. Sometimes people had to stand up for what they believed. Sometimes they even had to fight for those beliefs. Before making his decision, he asked himself, *What's different between 1776 and 1968?* The question had no answer he could find, except that, to the colonists, the issues facing them were things to fight for. Jon felt sympathy for the "no nukes" protestors when ex-President Eisenhower advocated dropping the bomb on North Vietnam. But America had not nuked the north, and Jon was sure the protestors had nothing to do with that decision. Cool heads had prevailed. Jon felt no call to join the no-nukers. The antiwar protestors made less sense to him. *Could you envision the United States without any police in any of its cities?* he asked himself. An individual's capacity to commit evil, ugly violence magnified from twenty-two caliber to a megaton when it became a nation's policy. The next Hitler, the next Stalin was out there in kindergarten maybe. He was not supporting the antiwar protestors.

Weighing it all at the end of 1966, he was left with his perception that there were plenty of foreign enemies of the United States in the world. The personification of *foreign enemy*, for Jon Zachery, was North Vietnam. During his destroyer deployment to the South China Sea in 1966, there had been three, maybe four, times out of five months when he felt like he was contributing meaningfully to the war. Every day though, aviators flew off carriers and bombed the north. And that was what his decision to stay in really amounted to. He had committed himself, sold his soul, to the Navy for another five years to bomb North Vietnam.

But now, with the president's announcement, it appeared he had just thrown away five years of his life for no real purpose.

After the president's spot, the anchorman appeared, smiled, and put on a serious face. "In Memphis, tensions remain high. Spokesmen for Dr. Martin Luther King Jr. told reporters today that they have not given up on a second march supporting the garbage workers."

Jon clicked off the TV and listened to it hiss and snap as it died. *God bless you, Dr. King,* he thought, *I just hope you don't realize your dream only to have us wind up one more country of Communists.*

The flight-training program took eighteen months, if everything went well. Students got sidetracked or delayed for all kinds of reasons. After the training program, it took another six months of training in a combat aircraft to become a fleet pilot. *Two years. A long time. The war could end in two years. Heck, it could end in two months, if the prez did what he said he would.*

LBJ said he wanted to get out of the war, like it didn't matter who won, as if the United States would just quit fighting. A balloon of uneasiness started expanding in Jon's belly as he started for the bathroom to brush his teeth.

Why did I ever decide to stay in the Navy and apply for aviation? he asked himself. *I could be getting out next year. Zachery, you are a fool.*

He turned on the light in the bathroom and saw the fool looking at him from the medicine cabinet mirror over the sink. Only it wasn't Jon Zachery, the Sunday-evening fool. It was the Saturday-morning fool. He'd forgotten about him.

On Friday, the Welcome Wagon lady had written "Sissy Smith" and a phone number on a piece of paper before she left. Jon called, and Sissy Smith agreed to arrive at the Zachery home at 8:00 a.m. on Saturday. She agreed to do whatever kind of household chores the Zacherys wanted her to do.

Saturday morning at 0800 came. Sissy Smith did not. At 0830, Jon called Sissy's number. No answer.

He hung up and wondered if the Welcome Wagon lady would intentionally recommend a shiftless wastrel.

Help or no help, there was work to be done that Saturday morning, and Jon started in the hallway between the kitchen and the bedrooms. He was scrubbing grime off the walls and ceilings prior to painting them. At 0945, the door buzzer sounded.

A colored woman, about five foot two, about thirty or forty years old maybe, stood on the top step. She belched an invisible cloud of onion and alcohol smell.

Jon tried to not let his nose wrinkle. "Are you Miss Smith?"

He thought she might have been trying to smile, but her face wasn't pulling it off.

The woman looked solid, like a tall fireplug. The fireplug swayed around in a little circle. She wore a faded ankle-length dress. She had straight hair, as black as her face, but the ends were bleached—some kind of treatment, hair straightening maybe. Then she belched again, and he wondered what might be happening to his hair.

"You gotta pay the taximan. I ain't got no money," the fireplug said.

There was a yellow cab parked on the street by the driveway. The driver leaned on the passenger-side front fender. He watched Jon, sucked on a cigarette, held on to the smoke, and then exhaled through his nose.

Jon looked back at the woman. He was not letting her in the house. Jon got two dollars from his wallet and gave them to Sissy. Two dollars. That was what she'd asked for an hourly wage.

Jon walked out to where the taxi waited. The driver wanted six dollars for bringing her and seven for taking her away. Jon gave him twenty, in case she puked.

The tall, thin, gray-haired man took the folded twenty and gestured "Come on" to Sissy. The driver walked around the car. "Oh, Sissy never pukes," he said and got in. He held up the folded twenty and flashed a smile that looked right at home on his weathered face. "Thankee kindly," he said, nodded good-bye, and tucked the bill in his shirt pocket.

Jon stood in the driveway and watched the cab pull away. He wondered if he should have done something to help Sissy. Maybe call AA or something. Then the driver turned his head a bit, and he seemed to say something to Sissy in the backseat. Her cackle hit Jon just about the way her belch had.

"Twenty dad-burned bucks! No welcome in the wagon," Teresa said on Friday. *She deliberately set us up with a shiftless wastrel, because I asked about the church burnings?* Thoughts tumbled through his head like a drunk down a flight of stairs. The string concluded with *There's no fool like an old fool, but I know a young one who's plenty stupid.*

After a day of cleaning and a three-mile run on Saturday, and with church on Sunday, he'd forgotten about how the Welcome Wagon lady had made a fool of him with Sissy Smith.

The LBJ announcement on the news resurrected Saturday's fool and brought a new Sunday fool. The fools knocked loose memories of other times he'd been a fool, incidents he hadn't thought of for a long time, and they fell around him like walnuts after his uncle Ralph bumped Grandpa Zachery's tree with his pickup so the kids could pick them up.

The memory that always seemed to surface first was that he never wanted to be in the Navy. His dad shanghaied him into it. "Fed long enough at the family trough," his dad said. "Time the two young ones got to move up a notch," he said. Then he drove Jon to the recruiter's office.

After he'd been in a year, Jon found out about the NESEP program. The Naval Enlisted Scientific Education Program was begun in the late fifties to address a shortage of science and engineering degrees in the naval officer ranks. He almost didn't apply for the program. Being a junior enlisted man was not fun, and he got seasick. In the end, the chance to go to college was too good a deal to pass up. He won a spot but had to reenlist. It felt like selling his soul to the Navy for eight years, even if four were college years.

After commissioning, he reported for duty on a destroyer, which deployed to Vietnam. During the deployment, three North Vietnamese PT boats attacked his ship. The ship didn't even fire its guns. Aircraft from a carrier on Yankee Station sunk the PTs. Aviators fought the war. Surface Navy guys steamed circles in the Tonkin Gulf.

After college, Jon planned to serve the four years he owed them and then get out. But after his first year of obligation, the night of the dog poop changed his mind. If the antiwar protestor movement could inspire Christine to call him a baby killer, the movement was something to worry about.

Through that chain of circumstances, he had decided to sell his soul to the Navy a second time.

President Johnson's announcement made a house of cards out of that set of circumstances. The announcement could very well mean an end to the war and a reduction in the size of the Navy. He was being selfish. It was like thinking about Teresa dying in childbirth and then worrying about what an inconvenience it would be for him, having to raise a daughter alone. He couldn't help how he felt.

He had sold his soul to the Navy for flight training, and the reason for having done so had just gone up in smoke, like a pile of draft cards and bras in a burn barrel.

Sissy Smith and LBJ—they both did a job on me.

Jon flicked off the bathroom light and put the twin-image fools to sleep. After he got into bed, he wished he could put the real fool to sleep that easily.

12

Twenty-six-year-old Amanda Sue Wellman shivered. She was afraid but more excited than she'd ever been in her life. If they were caught burning a Negro church, her dad would—she couldn't imagine. Thinking about what her stepmother would do though—that would be worth being caught, almost. For a moment she forgot about the smelly twins. *Twins, right,* she thought. They couldn't be more different. One handsome, one ugly. One dark, the other light. One beefy, one nicely muscled. *Lord, they both stank though.*

Burning a Negro church didn't mean anything one way or the other to her. The excitement of the thing mattered.

In her senior year at college, she had talked with her roommate, Charlene, about wanting some of that excitement in her life.

Charlene had a funny look on her face.

"What?" Amanda Sue asked.

"I'm not sure you're up for it," Charlene said.

"If you can handle it, I can," Amanda Sue said.

Her sorority sister took her to an apartment near campus and introduced her to the "rape game." Football players removed the girls' panty girdles with scissors they used to cut the tape from their ankles after a game. The rape game spiced up her last semester.

After they graduated, Charlene taught third graders, and Amanda Sue worked in the accounting department at her father's law firm. Six months after starting their jobs, the girls got together and decided to search for something like the game they had grown fond of in college.

"We need to be careful," Charlene said. "We need to make sure it stays a game."

They visited six bars and left before accepting any of the many offers they received.

"Booze is the thing," Charlene said. "A man drinks too much, he isn't interested in playing games."

"Well, why are we looking in bars then?" Amanda Sue asked.

"Let's give Coleman's Tavern a look. If that doesn't pan out, we'll figure something else out."

After Harry bought her a beer and she took a sip, Amanda asked him if he was drinking. He held up his left hand. A beer bottle was stuck on the end of his index finger.

"Why you carry it like that?" Amanda asked.

"Reminds me it ain't water," Harry said.

Charlene went home alone, Amanda Sue with Harry.

That was two weeks ago, and now she was on the way to burn a colored church.

You should see me now, step-bitch! Amanda Sue's stepmother number two got on her case about the company she kept, when she remembered she had a stepdaughter.

Amanda Sue didn't remember her mother. Her mother never recovered from giving birth to Amanda Sue and had to go live where "they" could take care of her. That was the family story. Amanda Sue was five when her mother died and her first stepmother moved in. It was hate at first sight between the two Wellman females. It took Amanda Sue's father three years to hate and dump number one. Stepmother number two didn't arrive until Amanda Sue started high school. There was no animosity between Amanda Sue and Two. There was nothing between them. Her stepmother loved her charity balls, auctions, and causes. Amanda Sue avoided them.

The car hit a hole, and Amanda Sue bit her tongue.

They'd been driving down a dirt road for a long time and had passed three or four shacks with coal-oil lamp glow in the windows. Another shack was up ahead to the right with a window outlined with a dim yellowish glow. As she watched, the light went out.

"Ha," Chevy said. "Coons in there pissin' their pants. Shoulda brought the shotgun. They'd shit themselves too."

In the dim glow of the instrument panel, Amanda Sue saw Harry's head twitch.

They passed two additional widely spaced, dark houses, and then Harry swung the car left and stopped.

The headlights illuminated a one-room clapboard structure, freshly painted yellow. A small, white, wooden cross was tacked to the top of the inverted V of the roof. The side of the church sported two large windows.

Harry left the motor running, set the emergency brake, and got out. Ford got out at the same time and hurried around to the back of the church.

"Move, Chevy. 'Manda Sue, the Thompson, come on," Harry said.

Amanda Sue stuck on Harry's heels as he and Chevy got the jerricans and headed for the church. Ford came from the back, carrying a wooden ladder, propped it against the side near the front, and started climbing. Harry two-handed him a five-gallon can, and Ford carried it up, as if it were empty.

Harry pulled his forty-five from his belt, broke the glass from a window, and dumped the contents of a jerrican inside.

"Give me the Thompson," Harry said to Amanda Sue. "Put the empty can in the trunk. Wait by the car," Harry said.

Amanda was reluctant to leave him. "Move," he said and pushed her.

"Ready," Ford said from the roof.

Harry struck a match and touched it to the trail of coal oil he had poured on the windowsill. Chevy had his fire going. Ford was coming down the ladder, carrying his empty jerrican.

Amanda Sue leaned on the front fender, watching the flames rise and dance and throw freaky shadows inside the church. Up on the roof, flames were climbing up the shingles. The men hustled across the yard, Harry with his machine gun.

Amanda Sue untied the tails of her blouse.

"Hustle it up," Harry said as they ran across the grass to the dirt parking lot.

"Come here, Harry," Amanda Sue said.

The light from the flames on the roof of the church moved up and down her, like hands exploring, tasting her skin. "I want you to do me, Harry, right here. I want to feel that engine rumble under my ass and watch the flames—"

Harry slapped her hard. "Get in the goddamn car."

Ford and Chevy threw their jerricans in the trunk, got in the car, and slammed their doors, making one sound.

Harry opened the back door, threw Amanda Sue in, and got behind the wheel. "Button your goddamn blouse, you dipshit slut."

"Naw, leave it open," Chevy said.

The switchblade opened with a *snik*. Chevy shrank back into his corner. Harry spun around and put the blade point right above Amanda Sue's left breast.

"I've a mind to stick this in your heart and throw you out."

Amanda Sue didn't move. Harry was struggling with control. She saw his face change. Her mouth opened. A kind of moan came out. Harry pushed on the knife, and Amanda gasped. But he had pushed the little button that enabled the blade to fold. Harry held her gaze. She was unable to look away. When he finally turned around, she found Ford and Chevy both looking at her, and she hurriedly tied the tails of the blouse together.

"Take a look, quick, or you'll miss what you came for." At first, she didn't realize Harry was talking to her.

She turned. A red-yellow glow flickered inside the church, an almost cozy picture, except the flames and shadows did a spooky, macabre, spastic dance together. A sheet of coal-oil fire covered the roof over the entry door.

Flames climbed up the white cross tacked onto the top of the inverted V-shaped roof.

Amanda Sue blinked as tears puddled in her lower eyelids. When Harry popped the clutch and she wound up against Chevy, she pushed away from him. He smelled like he hadn't had a bath in years.

Nobody said a word while they were on the dirt road, having their brains scrambled. It seemed like a matter of seconds and they were on the Jackson-Meridian highway. Harry headed for Meridian at the speed limit, and he turned on the overhead light and adjusted the rearview so he could see Chevy in his corner in the back. Amanda glanced at Chevy, and he seemed to sink back farther into his corner.

"Nice job, Chevy," Harry said.

Amanda Sue thought Harry's smile was strange, and she began to worry what he'd do to her when they got back to his apartment.

13

W*HUNK!* The house shook.

Jon's heart beat hard. Teresa gripped his arm. He felt nailed to the bed.

Outside, a deep-throated engine grumbled. A rectangular halo glowed around the blinds.

He threw the covers off, tore through the bedroom, grabbed onto the doorjamb, and spun himself toward the living room.

"The babies!" he heard from behind.

He ripped open the front door. To his left, a pickup sat in the middle of the street and idled through a bad muffler. A big, beefy man wearing bib overalls sauntered around the back of the truck. He threw something into the bed that landed with a heavy clunk.

"Git your nigger-lovin' ass outta our town," the driver shouted.

A white elbow hung out the driver's window.

The big man stood by the open passenger door. The streetlamp illuminated an ugly sneer on the lower half of his face under a baseball cap. He gestured with his middle finger extended.

Jon clenched his fists. They thought they had all the time in the world.

They could just drive up to his house and threaten them. Teresa and the kids were in the house.

Arrogant, goddamn, shit-for-brains, inbred cretins.

The words started as thoughts and mutated into a whine, snarl, and part howl. It came from Jon, but he heard it as if from the neighbor's dog.

He started down the steps toward the pickup.

"Shit, he's coming." The driver dropped something out the window.

Jon vaguely registered the sound of glass breaking.

"Git the hell in," the driver demanded.

As the pickup accelerated up the rise of the street, the bad muffler made a prodigious racket.

Jon hit the pavement going full out and, like a dog, could almost taste the bumper. Then he stepped on glass with his left foot and transitioned from running to hopping on his right.

Damn, damn, damn, damn. Jon wasn't sure what he damned, the pickup getting away or cutting his foot.

The truck disappeared over the rise.

Standing on one foot, in his skivvies, in the middle of Fortieth Street, he listened until the bad muffler faded in the distance.

Across the street from his house was nothing but woods. On his side, there were houses as far as he could see downhill and one before the top of the hill. Not one of them had a porch light on or a light in any window. Somebody had to have heard the pickup. He started hobbling back toward the house, being careful to circumnavigate the broken glass.

"Jon!" Teresa's voice contained a mother's reprimand for a misbehaving boy.

Teresa stood in the open door to the living room. Jennifer was by her side, holding on to a fold of her nightgown. Edgar Jon squirmed and fussed in her arms.

The lawn rose from street level to house level, and just as he reached the top of the rise, he stepped on a rock with his good foot.

"God—"

Teresa didn't like it when he swore. "Jon Zachery, you make me so mad. This was just like the night of the dog poop."

Jon stopped on the sidewalk just below the three steps leading up to the front door. Teresa frowned down at him. She was angrier at him for charging into a fight than she was at the creeps who attacked them.

The night of the dog poop. He tallied up the changes that night had brought into their lives: *Lost my teeth. Sold my soul to the Navy. Brought Teresa and the babies to Meridian.*

"I'll get the babies settled. Then I'll take care of you." Disgust lay on the surface of her words like an oil slick.

She stooped and picked up Jennifer. Jon almost said something about her hurting herself, but it was too late.

He knew Teresa would tear into him. She didn't have to bother. He could already hear her scolding him.

He checked the bottom of his foot with light from the streetlamp and saw that the cut was just behind the ball of the foot. Dirt and grass stuck to the area of the cut, and a drop of blood fell to the sidewalk. At least it wasn't squirting.

He started up the front steps, keeping the weight on the outside edge of his left foot. Then he saw the piece of paper nailed to the front door.

He took off his T-shirt, tied it around his cut foot, and flipped on the light switch. A rusty railroad spike impaled some kind of drawing to the door. He almost ripped the paper off the spike but stopped.

The drawing showed two stick figures dangling from nooses. The figure on the left wore a hat—sailors called it a Dixie cup—on the circle head. The sailor face had Xs for eyes and a tongue hanging out of the side of the line mouth. On the right of the paper, the stick person wore a skirt, and the circle head was black and had long hair.

In the bedroom, Jon pulled on a pair of blue jeans and another tee. In the small mudroom connecting the kitchen to the carport, he put his running shoes on. It didn't matter if they got bloody.

After getting a baggie and one of his sissy rubber gloves from under the kitchen sink, he took a flashlight and went out into the street. Only two glass shards looked big enough to hold a print. He bent to bag them and smelled some kind of alcohol.

When he got back to the house, he used the rubber glove to close the front door. Two inches of shiny metal tip of the rusty railroad spike stuck through the back side of the door.

Jon checked on Teresa. She was nursing Edgar Jon, and Jennifer was back in bed. He went to the kitchen and called the police. The policeman didn't seem interested.

"Are you going to send someone, Officer?" Jon asked.

From the phone, he heard a muted mumble of voices and then "Fifteen minutes." *Click.*

The call left Jon feeling uneasy and foolish. He went into the living room, opened the blinds over the window so he could watch for the police, and started writing a timeline for what had happened.

It was 0227. He started putting minutes against what he remembered, working backward. About 0207 the drawing was nailed to the door.

Jon was still writing when he heard a car coming. Headlights topped the ridge. Glass crunched, and a police car—the bubble lights on top were not going—slowed and stopped just past the driveway. It backed up. A spotlight hit the front of the house, looking for the number next to the front door. The car pulled forward and into the driveway.

Two policemen bolted out the doors on either side of the car. All of sudden they were in a hurry. Jon jumped up and opened the front door, not wanting gestapo truncheons to start the babies going again.

Jon was standing just inside the front door as the first policeman started up the front steps. "I called. I'm Jon Zachery."

The first officer barged into the house with his right hand on the butt of his gun and pushed Jon back into the room with his left. He looked nineteen.

"Who else's in the house?" the first officer asked.

"Uh, my wife, Teresa, two small kids."

"Where?" the second policeman asked as he stepped in through the door. He appeared to be thirty-five or forty.

Jon pointed to the hallway to the bedrooms. "There, trying to get the babies to sleep again."

The second officer started for the bedrooms.

"Wait. She's not dressed."

The boy officer pushed on Jon's chest again, and he kept his right hand on the gun.

Jon heard the door to the children's bedroom open. A light flicked on, and Edgar Jon cut loose with a yowl.

Jon moved, but Boy Policeman pushed again, smirked, and said, "Stay." Then he turned and looked toward the bedroom.

A commotion in the hallway further distracted Boy Policeman. Teresa had the older officer by the arm and pulled him into the living room while Edgar Jon imitated an air-raid siren from the bedroom.

"There, pay some attention to that." Teresa pointed to the spike in the door. "Are you policemen or just another set of Neanderthals who come around in the middle of the night to scare babies? Jon ran off the first two, so they sent you bozos with guns. That it?"

Edgar Jon wailed, but Jon heard the patter of feet on the wood floor. Jennifer stopped beside Teresa and clutched a fold of her nightgown. She looked up at the older policeman with a stern scowl wrinkling her little face.

"You *scah oh* Jon-Jon." Edgar Jon was a mouthful for Jennifer.

A smile of admiration for Teresa and Jennifer tried to sneak out of Jon's mouth, but he clamped his lips together.

"Come along, Jen-Jen," Teresa said. "Maybe we can get some sleep now."

She started leading Jennifer back to the bedroom but stopped in the hallway. "Or can we expect those first two to come back again?"

"Not likely," Boy Policeman said. "They's prob'ly jist coupla peckerwoods on the way home after their bar closed."

"Shut up," the older policeman said to his partner. "Git your hand off your gun." He turned and looked at the spike.

Boy Policeman removed his left hand from Jon's chest, dropped his right from the grip of his pistol, and sheepishly glanced at the older policeman.

Both policemen were six-footers and solidly built. Boy Policeman was blond and *closer to pretty than handsome*, Jon thought. Man Policeman had dark hair.

Edgar Jon's wail changed timbre. Teresa must have picked him up.

"Officer," Jon said to Man Policeman, "can I make you gentlemen a pot of coffee, and can we talk about what happened in the kitchen?"

Man Policeman hesitated and then nodded. "Coffee'd be good."

He was in charge again, and that seemed to be good too.

Jon pointed to the kitchen table, and they both pulled out chairs. Jon handed Man Policeman the pad of paper with the timeline, and then he started the coffee.

Man Policeman looked up from the pad of paper. "You ran after them? Barefooted, wearing what, PJs?"

"Just skivvies."

"You gotta be shittin' me." Boy Policeman was loud. "What was you gonna do if you caught 'em? Ask 'em to not do that anymore?" He brayed a laugh. "Hell, you prob'ly never hit anybody in your life. All those peckerwoods carry guns. You're lucky you didn't get your ass shot off. You ever been shot at? What the hell was you thinking?"

"Smile, Jon." They hadn't heard Teresa come to the door from the living room. She held Edgar Jon as he worked his pacifier hard. She spoke quietly. "Smile."

Jon showed them his gap.

She fixed Boy, and then Man Policeman, with an angry stare. "A year and a half ago, Jon got in a fight with three guys who were trying to damage our car. Biggest one was bigger than you." She nodded to Boy Policeman. "Jon lost those two teeth, but two of them got carted away in an ambulance, including the biggest guy. The third one got away. Jon's been shot at. More than you have, I'm very sure. Now are we going to have to compare notches on guns, or can you put some attention to what happened here tonight? Are you going to help us, or are you going to keep acting like this was all our fault? And even if it was our fault, you should have some consideration for the babies. Keep your voices down, please."

Teresa glared at Man Policeman. After a couple of seconds, he looked down at the pad of paper. Then he stood up.

"Stand up, Rafe," he said. "Stand up."

Rafe—Boy Policeman had a name—scooted his chair back and stood.

"Sorry about the noise, ma'am. We'll hold it down. I'm Officer Billy Dobbs. This is Officer Rafe Calhoun."

Teresa swayed from side to side with Edgar Jon. "Thank you, Officer. Thank you. Please, sit down."

Officer Dobbs sent Rafe out to see if there were any more pieces of glass in the road to collect, and Jon poured coffee into two mugs. Dobbs wanted milk and sugar. Jon wrapped his fingers around his USS *Manfred* mug, and he felt the sting of the heat. *Too hot.* Scalded taste buds would ruin it.

Officer Dobbs asked a couple of questions. Jon answered. Both of them whispered. Jon asked him about dusting the front door for fingerprints, but the cop thought it would be a waste of time.

Jon fingered the mug, and it felt just right. He took a sip. "Ah, nectar of the gods."

Dobbs grimaced and put more milk in his mug. "You could use this tar to patch potholes."

After Teresa gave her version of events, the officers took the note but left the spike in the door. They'd get the spike later that day, when the noise of extracting it wouldn't wake the babies.

Before they left, Teresa asked them if they thought they might be able to find the white pickup. Rafe laughed and said there were probably hundreds of pickups in the counties around Meridian matching the description they'd given him.

When the officers' car pulled out of the drive and drove back up the rise, a heavy silence filled the kitchen. Teresa got a glass of orange juice from the refrigerator and sat back down at her place on the short side of the table. Next to her, Jon sipped his coffee and smiled. "Aaah."

When he looked up, Teresa pounced. "I was so mad at you, Jon Zachery." Her face went from hard to wrestling with tears. She took a breath. "You did it again, ran right out there after two men, and this time, they did have guns. That policeman said so. It wasn't like those boys in California."

Her hands were on the table on either side of her glass. He reached out and put his right on top of her left, and she jerked hers back.

"I had a good mad worked up against you. Then those, those—"

"Cretins?" Jon suggested, trying to be helpful again.

"Policemen," Teresa said. "They came busting in, and you know what they were going to do. They were going to tell us it was our fault for sitting with," she had to think a minute, "Clarissa. They made me so mad at them, it just ruined the mad I had at you. But I'm not done being mad at you. Not by a long shot."

Jon thought of Teresa as soft, without a hard edge anywhere. It was one of the things that had attracted him to her in high school. She had things she was set against, like drinking, but he had never considered her position to be hard. Hard just didn't fit with Teresa.

He had thought of her as soft and precious, something to be protected, while they courted, through the first two years they were married and she was unable to get pregnant, and through the start of the deployment on *Manfred*. But a month into that 1966 deployment, he began to discover facets of Teresa that were hard as steel. Her steel didn't bend or expand and contract from thermal effects. It had sharp edges though.

He took her hand again, and he wouldn't let her pull it away.

"Have I told you, Teresa Zachery, what a fine, fine hunka woman you are?"

Mad stayed stuck on her face for a moment. Then she got up, sat on his lap, and kissed him gently on the lips. Then Jon's eyes popped wider. She'd slipped the tip of her tongue through his lips.

She sat up. "Now, I need to look at your foot."

"Just what I was thinking about, my foot."

Teresa smiled and shook her head.

Nothing made Jon feel better at the end of a day, or the beginning of a new one, than to make Teresa smile. In his mind, it made up for some of that "for worse" stuff they'd carted into Teresa's life when they married her—he and the Navy.

* * *

Jon's hand rested on his wife's hip as she slept with her hand over his. He tried to get Meridian into some kind of perspective. It wasn't easy. He'd expected to face danger in the military. It had happened to him on his destroyer in 1966.

The first time occurred shortly after Jon had antagonized his CO. His CO sent him ashore as a gunfire liaison officer with a company of Marines operating south of Da Nang. Most of the time, the Marines performed their own calls for gunfire from supporting ships. Jon was certain the assignment was meant to get him out of the way for a couple of days. On his second night ashore, North Vietnamese attacked Jon and three Marines in their observation post. Jon and Sergeant Evans were asleep when the attack started, and they both lived, though the sergeant was wounded. The other two Marines were killed, but Sergeant Evans and Jon killed the six North Vietnamese sappers. Once the observation post was secure, Jon called for fire from his ship, USS *Manfred*. The ship was credited with breaking up a major attack on the Marine company and with twenty-one KIA.

The second time occurred in the northern Tonkin Gulf. Just before dawn, PT boats attacked *Manfred* and another destroyer. Aircraft from a carrier on Yankee Station scrambled and sank all three PT boats. There were three survivors from one PT. *Manfred* put a boat in the water to attempt to rescue the North Vietnamese sailors. The CO needed a boat officer. All his other officers had important jobs during battle stations. He assigned the mission to Ensign Zachery. As a sailor in Jon's boat was attempting to pull one of the North Vietnamese survivors into the boat, the man lunged up from the water and slashed the *Manfred* sailor with a knife. The North Vietnamese fell back and went underwater, and Jon frantically clawed his forty-five from its canvas holster and worked the slide to seat a round in the chamber. The North Vietnamese surfaced, his face and eyes blazed hatred, and he drew back the knife to hurl it at Jon. Jon one-hand gripped the forty-five and fired, hitting the man in the shoulder. Jon got two hands on the gun and fired again, striking the man near the collarbone. Jon brought the weapon down from the recoil and fired a third round into the top of the man's head as he sank under the water.

The third time, in the middle of the night, the ship was anchored in the Saigon River and supported operations in an area called the Rung Sat.

Jon was sent out in a boat again, this time to investigate some floating debris coming down with an ebbing tide toward the ship. VC were known to hide in driftwood to attach satchels of explosives to anchored ships. Jon found and killed the sapper.

He had a direct hand in killing twenty-nine people, and he wasn't bothered by any of those deaths. He felt compelled to confess the third round he fired into the North Vietnamese sailor in the Tonkin Gulf. The man was probably already dead, already sinking. Still, it felt like a sin to fire that third round.

That North Vietnamese sailor's face was the only one he saw alive from close range. He saw the six dead VC along the slopes leading to the Marine observation post. Those dead men's faces held no hate. He couldn't make out the facial features of the VC he shot in the middle of the night in Saigon River. The North Vietnamese sailor's face, in the light of the just-risen sun, radiated lethal animosity from a hate-filled soul. The memory of that man's face came to Jon's mind frequently.

When he returned from the Vietnam deployment, he worried that Teresa would see something in his face. The men he had killed—would she see the marks of their deaths on his soul when she saw his face, looked into his eyes? He'd worried mightily about that and what he could do if she saw him and turned away in horror. It hadn't played out that way though. She had been overjoyed to see him, to have him home again.

But that morning, even though it had been too dark to see, he knew the big man's face by the pickup wore the same hate he'd seen before. *Why did that man by the pickup hate me?* he wondered. *For sitting with the colored girl in church? Because I'm Catholic?* Jon didn't hate the North Vietnamese. The Marines respected them as tough fighters. The man by the white pickup came in the middle of the night and threatened his wife and children. Jon didn't know whether he hated the man or not. One thing he did know though was that he could understand how the Marines respected the North Vietnamese fighters. Jon did not respect anything about that white-pickup-truck cretin.

Throughout the deployment to Vietnam, Teresa had been safe in their apartment in Chula Vista, California. He hadn't worried about not being there to protect her. Now he was with his family, but could he protect them from the white pickup? *I wish Meridian had quarters on base for married student pilots,* he thought. *I wish I had my shotgun in the house, and I wish I had shells for it.*

Al Schwartz popped into his mind.

Al hated to hear "I wish" about as much he hated "If only."

14

Jon hadn't expected to meet Al Schwartz or anyone else before noon that first morning after school let out on his seventh grade. He was sleeping soundly in the unfinished upstairs until his father yanked the covers off him.

"Come. Get breakfast."

"But it's Saturday." He rubbed sleep from his eyes as his father walked away.

After Jon ate, his pop tied the trunk lid of the black Plymouth on his bike and drove him three miles past the church atop the hill above town to Heiny Schwartz's place. Jon had never met Mr. Schwartz, nor thought about who owned the farm next to the parish picnic grounds.

Jon's pop stood five foot eleven, Mr. Schwartz an inch or two shorter and not as thick through the chest and shoulders.

"You're working for Heiny." Emil Zachery removed the bike from the trunk and said, "Here," to his son and drove away.

"Come," the farmer said. Even dazed, Jon recognized the milk barn as the only new structure on the place. He followed the man into a room housing a large tank for the milk and then through a door into the milking chamber. Obviously proud of his new facility, Mr. Schwartz explained the setup. Jon didn't absorb many of the details, as his mind focused on the humid, fetid air, laden with the heavy, almost chewable, smell of cow poop.

"I run the operation from the pit," his new boss said and talked about ropes controlling doors, cows coming in and going out, pneumatic systems, and cows eating breakfast while they got milked.

Jon saw the pile of semiliquid cow poop at the end of one stall. A twin pile decorated the end of the other stall too. He grimaced and wondered if he'd be able to eat cereal with milk ever again.

"I'm finished milking by seven generally," Heiny Schwartz said. "Be here by then, and clean these stalls. I'll be out by seven thirty, quarter till maybe. Then we go to work."

Jon couldn't tear his eyes away from the black four-inch pile of cow poop at the end of the stall to the left.

"Scoop's outside," the farmer said, pointing to the door between the stalls one got to by climbing three steps from the pit. "Scoop as much as you can get. Then use the hose. Mind you get the stalls clean. An inspector comes through each month, and we don't know when. The walls, doors, floor—hell, the ceiling too, if it gets shit splattered. Ever'thing's got to be clean, hear?"

Heiny Schwartz left to get breakfast. Jon didn't know where to start. He didn't want to start. Then he remembered. "Wanting a job to be done makes it bigger," Pop said once. "Workin' makes it littler."

At seven thirty, Heiny entered the milking chamber, inspected the stalls and the pit, nodded, and gestured "Follow me." Another man, about Jon's height, stood outside the milk barn.

"My brother, Al," Heiny said. "You and him going to be clearing some woods to expand a pasture. You know how to use an ax?"

It seemed like one of those questions where the answer should surely be yes.

Al smiled, reached out, and messed up Jon's hair. "Nothin' to it."

Every morning, Jon completed the same muck-out-the-milk-barn job. Every day he learned something new, and after three weeks he could even back a wagon with a tractor. Heiny hadn't said anything about when he'd get paid. Jon asked.

"Your pop said I didn't need to pay you."

That evening, Jon asked about working for nothing.

"Boy needs to learn how to work." His father folded the newspaper and began to read a new article. "Doesn't need to learn how to get paid."

"Whyn't you tell me I was working for free?"

"Didn't see the need."

His mom had lost three premature babies before Jon came along. She doted on him. His pop treated him just the opposite.

"You mad at me?" he once asked.

"Nope," Pop replied. He acted mad though.

His father worked from early to late six days a week, and when he came home, Jon slunk away to his bedroom and read.

He rarely spoke to his pop, and messages from him came through his mom. Apparently, though, giving a son over as slave labor did require speaking a couple of words.

Two months after Jon started working for Heiny, he rode his bike home after a day of stacking hay bales in the barn. At about 8:00 p.m., he coasted on Church Street on the stretch that skirted the south side of the Catholic school. Ahead, just before the road turned right to head down the hill to the town, he saw the two Fant boys in the road.

Dick Fant, the biggest and oldest, had been held back twice in first grade and once in second. After that, the nuns moved him along each year. In September, Dick would be in seventh, a year behind Jon. Hank Fant, one year older than Jon, the same height but skinnier, always wore a belt too long for him with an extra hole punched in it and enough extra leather dangling from the buckle to go halfway around him a second time. Dick had big shoulders and long arms. If someone laughed or smiled around Dick, he assumed that person was making fun of him. Fortunately for the boys at Holy Martyrs Catholic School, Dick couldn't run very fast and didn't remember perceived insults from one day to the next. His brother, Hank the Weasel, however, never forgot a slight, nor did he seem to need one. The hair on the nape of Jon's neck tingled when the Weasel stood or sat at a school desk behind him.

As Jon approached the Fants, he slowed and moved to the left lane to go around them.

"Stop him," the Weasel said.

Dick reached out a big paw, grabbed the handlebars, and jerked. Jon fell onto the blacktop, skinned his palms, and hurt his left knee. He stood up and looked at the hole torn in the knee of his jeans. Suddenly his head filled with stars. He wound up sitting on the pavement with his mouth hurting. He couldn't bite down. His upper front teeth were bent back so that his lowers hit on the front side of his upper teeth. Jon put a hand up to his mouth. His swollen lips dripped blood.

The Weasel snarled, "Get up and fight."

Jon shook his head. He didn't want to fight. He wanted to be able to close his mouth normally.

The Weasel stomped on the spokes of the bike's front wheel. Jon continued to work his jaw, trying to find a comfortable way to hold his teeth.

The Weasel picked Jon's bike up and threw it into the ditch. "Chicken," he said and walked away. Dick followed.

Jon had been in third grade the first time he ran afoul of the Fant brothers. That time Dick threw him into a muddy ditch with a couple of inches of snowmelt runoff. He'd entered the kitchen of his home, bawling, and his mom took him into her arms.

That night after Jon got into bed, his pop came into the room and turned the light back on. "You come home bawling, it vexes your momma. Do not vex your momma." He turned out the light and left.

Jon pulled his bike out of the ditch and carried it home. "I tried to do a wheelie, Momma. I pulled back on the handlebars and the front wheel fell off. My fault."

His mom called their dentist. After he got Jon in the chair, Dr. Parnell said, "You bite me and I'll pull those front teeth." Then he stuck his thumb behind Jon's uppers and pulled them back into alignment while Jon's body went rigid and his butt lifted off the chair. But he didn't bite.

The next morning, Heiny asked Jon what happened. He told him the wheelie story. Al took Jon's chin in his hand and turned his head from side to side.

"Come with me," Al said. "I think you need to learn how to take care of yourself."

Al had been in the Marine Corps for twenty years and taught hand-to-hand combat. That first day, he gave Jon a two-hour lesson about fighting before they headed out to the fields.

"Somebody brings you a fight," Al said, "it's their fight. First thing you do is take the fight away from them and make it yours."

Suddenly, Al slapped Jon on the side of his head. Jon raised his hand to the hurt and took a slap on the other side.

"Hey."

"You don't want to be hit, stop me."

Jon raised his hands like he'd seen boxers do, and Al punched him in the belly. Anger blotted everything out of his brain, and he charged at Al, arms flailing like a demented windmill. Al wound up sitting on the dusty floor of the machine shed, laughing his head off.

"Help me up." Al reached up a hand.

"Don't trust you."

Al started laughing again and stood up, but he kept his eyes on Jon. "Fingers, fists, forearms, elbows, knees, and feet are weapons, but they're useless if you get hot mad. Now a cold mad," he said, "that's different."

Five minutes into the second day's lesson, Al said, "Stop ducking. You have good reflexes and fast hands. Use them and keep your head up so you can see where to hit."

Two weeks after the fighting lessons started, Jon and Al sparred using open-hand slaps. Jon connected with a left hand, after setting Al up to expect nothing but rights. Al stepped back and Jon grinned.

Al shook his head. "Nothing funny about fighting. Avoid it if you can. If you can't, don't back up and don't lose. Now, Mr. Wiseass, we got another hour."

Jon's smile fled.

After work the last Friday in August, Jon found the Fant boys standing side by side on Church Street again. The Weasel's vicious, ugly grin dumped cold fear into his belly. He stopped about twenty yards from them, laid his bike in the ditch, took a breath, and stuck out his chin. Hank the Weasel was to his left. Jon started walking toward Dick, and the Weasel stepped in front of his brother and clenched his fists.

Ten yards from the boys, Jon started moving faster. Hank took a step toward Jon, cocked a right fist, and swung. Jon's left hand slapped the blow aside. His right fist smashed into the Weasel's nose. The Weasel fell back against Dick. Dick caught his brother under his arms. Jon jabbed his index finger into Dick's right eye. Dick dropped Hank, howled, and raised his hands over his face.

The Weasel sat on the street and looked at the blood in his hands. "I'll kill you," he shouted and jumped up. Jon snapped his head back with a left jab and nailed him with another right. The Weasel sprawled on his back, blinking up at the sky.

With his right hand over his right eye, Dick bellowed and reached his left for Jon. Jon grabbed Dick's index finger, thrust back, and it snapped. Dick dropped onto a knee and cradled his left hand with his right. His right eye blinked repeatedly.

"Enough?" Jon asked.

Dick, kneeling and looking down at his left hand, nodded.

15

When she'd cleaned and bandaged his foot, Teresa had insisted he go out to the base for a tetanus shot. But when he got up to do what she wanted, she did not want him to leave the house.

"The white pickup truck guys'll be just like the VC. They only come out at night. Nothing to worry about until the sun goes down. I'll be back long before then."

She hadn't been so sure. And when she was asleep and Jon had put his hand on her shoulder to awaken her, she started awake with her heart beating so hard it hurt. Then he'd tried to be funny.

"I should have pinched Edgar Jon. Maybe that would have triggered your maternal instincts awake instead of the survival one."

It hadn't sounded funny at all when he said it. Now, just a little maybe.

As Jon backed the car out of the driveway, she wanted to stop him, make him stay home with her and the babies. On Sunday, sitting with Clarissa in church had seemed like such a right thing to do. But the only thing that had come of it was a terrible fright for her family.

That big man by the pickup was the scariest-looking man she had ever seen. While she feared for herself, she knew she would not be able to protect her babies if those creatures came back. They wouldn't run away from Jon again. He'd just surprised them. *Oh, God,* she thought, remembering her surprise when he started that animal growl and charged out across the lawn.

Edgar Jon yowled from the bedroom and brought her back to the present.

"Jen-Jen, you stay right here." She pointed at the high-chair tray. "Here."

"Hea o," Jennifer said, and she put the index finger of her right hand on the tray.

Teresa smiled. Jennifer was a wonderful baby. No trouble, really. Bright, inquisitive, mature in some ways, but she did such cute baby things. She never fussed. Well, sometimes, a little, when it was time for a nap. Jon-Jon was a demanding little—well, he was a male, after all.

Beside the door to the mudroom and carport, two other doors led out of the kitchen toward the rear of the house. One opened to the dark hallway that ran behind the living room, and the other into the living room/dining room—which was all living room because there was no furniture for a dining room. The dining room route added a few steps, but after last night, she didn't want to walk into that dark hall.

Edgar Jon had distinctive levels of crying. As Teresa passed near the front door, he cranked the intensity of his cry up a notch. Teresa told Jon the second level meant "I've been crying for ninety seconds. You have ninety more to get in here or the windows will shatter."

"Mommy's coming."

"Eeeeeeeeee!"

Jennifer's scream from the kitchen cut through the house, cut through the morning, cut through time. The scream stopped. Teresa stopped. Her heart stopped between beats, and then it thumped and pumped not warm red blood, but ice slivers that cut cold.

The universe started expanding again. For a lightning flash of time, Teresa considered going to Edgar Jon, but her feet took her to Jennifer.

Jennifer was in her high chair, just as she'd left her. Calm. Not a thing out of place. Nothing to be frightened of.

"What is it, sweetheart?"

Then Teresa heard the scraping, like beast claws on the side of the house. Fear fingers clamped around her chest. It was hard to breathe. *She wanted to scream, wanted to grab Jennifer and run.*

Jennifer had the same idea and reached up to be taken out of her high chair.

Once she had her daughter in her arms, the moment of insane panic ebbed away. She heard the scratching noise again from the back wall of the house.

"It's just tree branches, Jennifer, nothing to be afraid of. I'll show you." Teresa carried the toddler to the window behind the sink. "See? The tree hangs over the house, and the wind moves the branches. You see?"

Jennifer nodded.

"But it's still a little scary, right?"

Jennifer nodded again.

"When Daddy comes home, we'll ask him to take care of those branches. Now let's go take care of Jon-Jon. Hmm. He's quiet. I wonder if he stopped wailing when you screamed. Do you think so?"

Jennifer shrugged her shoulders.

As she was taking care of the baby, Teresa asked herself, *How could I have been brave last night and now be such a fraidy-cat during the day?*

Since Jon had returned from the cruise in 1966, he'd been home almost every night. There were duty nights and two weeks at sea a couple of times in 1967, but for the most part he was home.

In San Diego, she'd had Rose Herbert for company, a great friend and a very down-to-earth woman. By talking with Rose, Teresa always found a way through the most difficult of problems. Six months ago, Rose's husband Fred's ship had been moved from San Diego to Yokosuka, Japan. With Rose on the other side of the world, there was a hole in Teresa's life that neither Jon nor babies could fill.

Last night, when Jon had started running after those two men, Teresa saw him running to his death. He had just charged off stupidly, blindly, with no thought to what would happen to her if he was killed. What made him run after those two men? She couldn't understand it.

When he'd returned from Vietnam, she hadn't seen it at first, as wrapped up as she got with reuniting with him after seven months, but after he'd been home a week, he told her about the medals he would be getting. He didn't tell her much. Most of what she knew came from the wives of other officers on the ship. Jon didn't want to talk about it, and she could understand that. Her father had been in World War II, and he never talked about those experiences. But she had seen a change, a deep quiet to him that had not been there before he left. When she thought about it, she could see that experiences such as he had would have to affect a person. The key thing, though, was that he seemed to love his daughter, and his wife, even more than he had before.

Jon's Vietnam experience might be the explanation for why he charged after those men by the white pickup. Understanding where it came from did not prevent her from being angry about it.

Phooey, sometimes I wish I could cuss like Rose.

Talking to Rose would be such a relief. She couldn't talk to Jon. The Navy had rules about wives worrying their pilot husbands. She'd absorbed the message, or lecture, in the base chapel at Saufley Field just after Jon began flight training.

"Don't bother your husbands with trivial matters," the lecturer told the wives. "They need to have their minds on flying."

"What's your definition of trivial?" one young wife had asked.

"Do not worry your husbands. You could kill them."

Teresa shook her head. *I'm a Catholic woman. My psyche is already as sensitive to guilt as a princess to a pea.*

Thinking about Jon warmed her heart, but it reminded her of something Rose said. "Men don't have the sense to come in out of the rain unless a woman tells them to." Rose would know why Jon ran toward danger, instead of what normal, rational people did.

Holy Mary, mother of God, please can I find someone to talk to? Her mind prayed as her fingers snapped the bottom of Edgar Jon's outfit together.

She hoisted the baby onto her shoulder and began toting up her *trivial* matters. *I shouldn't tell Jon that Jennifer is afraid of our haunted house, and I'm afraid too. I shouldn't tell him that I feel like I'm alone in an alien land, don't know anyone, my only friend is on the other side of the world, I'm tired all the time, the second C-section is taking longer to recover from than the first, and the second baby is more than twice as hard as the first one.*

"When the going gets tough, blow your nose in toilet paper. Then get going." Rose had told her that a time or two.

Teresa put Edgar Jon in his infant seat on the floor of the bathroom and settled Jennifer next to him with a coloring book and crayons. In the shower she was careful with the shampoo so that she never had to close her eyes.

After her shower, she bathed Jennifer in the tub and Edgar Jon in the kitchen sink. At 1045, the door buzzer made its ugly rasping noise. She wrapped the baby in a towel, and Jennifer followed her as she answered the front door.

"Oh," she said, raising her hand to her mouth. She took a step back and grabbed Jennifer's hand.

A giant stood on the porch. He had thick black hair, a small brow, black bushy eyebrows, and intense black eyes. A large potato nose jutted from the middle of a scowl.

The threatening, dark face bloomed a smile.

"Teresa?" The smile widened. "God, Two Buckets is one lucky dude! He had your picture up by his bunk in the ensign locker, but man, the picture didn't do you justice. And, sorry, I'm Greg Haywood. He and I were on the *Manfred* together."

"Oh my gosh, Tutu!"

"Well, I'd just as soon no one ever say that nickname again. I did just call Jon Two Buckets though."

Greg pointed to the spike in the door.

"We heard about this on the base this morning. I didn't even know Jon was in the aviation-training pipeline. I wasn't scheduled to fly today, but we're supposed to hang around the ready room, just in case a hop comes up. I got permission to come see Jon. Is he here?"

"No. He went out to the base first thing this morning, but he should be back soon." Teresa waved him inside. "Come in, Tu—Greg."

Greg studied the spike sticking through the back side of the door.

"Wish I could have been here last night." He turned toward Teresa. "But listen to the story going around the base. These guys show up, wake you all up nailing the sign on your door, and Jon tears out after them barefooted and in his skivvies. Word passed via the rumor mill is the police don't believe little Jon could chase off two Kluxers until they find out he crippled five antiwar creeps in a fight in California and killed seventy-eight VC in Vietnam."

Teresa laughed. "A wee bit of exaggeration."

"What? You think the rumor mill would inflate Jon's body count?"

She liked Greg. Her initial fear had evaporated quickly and completely, but talk of "Jon's body count" sat uncomfortably in a corner of her mind.

"Come along, I need to get Edgar Jon dressed." She pulled Jennifer around to the front of her leg. "And this is Jennifer."

Greg knelt on the floor. "I saw pictures of you when you were a little bitty baby. You are such a big girl now. I'm Greg. Can I be your friend?"

Navy men, Teresa thought, *they talk of body count one moment and in the next they play with a two-year-old.*

In the children's room, Teresa dressed the baby on the changing table as Jennifer clung to her leg. Greg sat on the floor. He didn't push it with Jennifer.

"Jon said you left the *Manfred* in the Philippines, just before the ship came back to the States. What happened after you left? He said you were going to be assigned to Swift Boats," Teresa said.

As she snapped Edgar Jon's one-piece together, she looked back over her shoulder. Greg looked at her for a moment before answering.

"Well, you know, the ship didn't need all its officers for the trip home, just sailing across the pond, no combat watches to stand," Greg said. "The XO knew an admiral's staff was looking for a guy to work liaison with the Swift Boats, and since I requested duty in them, he thought it would be a great place to stash me until I got orders. Also," Greg flashed a smile, "maybe he just jumped at the opportunity to get rid of me."

"There was something—planting dead cockroaches in the CO's skivvies—that was you, right?" Teresa asked.

"The vicious rumor mill sometimes cranks out unsubstantiated baloney like that."

"Unsubstantiated baloney, right. But what about aviation?"

"After I got to the admiral's staff, I really got to see what the aviators were doing in the war, and I thought it was more than the Swift Boats were doing. I applied for flight training, and it turned out the Navy needed flyboys more than boat drivers."

"Jon was bummed that it took him a year after he applied before he could leave the ship. How long did it take you to start training? How far along are you here?"

"It took ten months to get off the admiral's staff. I'm a couple of months into the program here."

Edgar Jon went down for a nap, and the two grown-ups were about to head for the kitchen when the phone rang.

Teresa answered it in the bedroom. It was Jon. He had reported to his training squadron CO to tell him about the incident. His squadron CO sent him to talk to the base CO. That was what had taken so long. He was about to go to the commissary and exchange.

Teresa told Jon about Greg Haywood showing up on their front porch.

"What? Tutu, here? I thought he was going Swift Boats, not aviation."

"He's here, alright. I'll put him on."

After Greg talked for a couple of minutes and hung up, he said, "Jon'll be home in thirty-six minutes."

"Are you like that too? Thirty-six minutes, not about thirty-five or forty?"

"Actually, I think I caught that same disease on the *Manfred*. Maybe I got it from Jon."

Teresa pointed at the bed. "Sorry about the mess. I generally don't get it made until noon these days."

"What's a made bed?"

"That has to mean you're not married."

"True, but I have a girlfriend from here in town. Maybe it'll work out."

Greg knelt down and said to Jennifer, "Maybe we can have our own little girl. If I have a little girl, would it be okay to call her Jennifer? It's such a pretty name."

"I can see I'm already late in starting to teach Jennifer about smooth-talking bachelor sailors."

Bzzzzzzt.

Teresa started for the door, and the buzzer rasped its impolite, impatient, grimace-inducing buzz again. She was inclined to jerk the door open, but she had to be careful of the spike sticking through.

The slender man on the porch was about five foot ten. He was wearing a tan suit and a light-tan hat. He didn't remove his hat.

"I'm Wallace Binford. One of my agents rented this place to you. You are Mrs. Zachery?"

Teresa frowned at the man's abrasive manner. "I am."

"You're going to have to pay for that." Wallace pointed at the spike in the door.

"We will do no such thing. The police will catch the criminals who did this. Make them pay."

"The police're not gonna catch anybody. You Yankees come in here, don't even bother to find out how people act around here." Wallace stopped talking, his mouth opened, and a look of fear cascaded from under his hat and seeped down his face. "You're the one." He turned, and as he ran back to his new blue Buick, his hat blew off. He didn't stop to retrieve it though.

"What a jerk." Greg retrieved the hat from the sidewalk, poked a hole in it with the pointy end of the spike, and hung it on the spike on the outside of the door.

16

Jon walked into the kitchen from the carport and grinned. "Holy crap! I'd forgotten how big you are."

Greg stood, and they shook hands, pumping up and down, both grinning.

"Two Buckets in Meridian. Amazing!"

"No more amazing than finding Lieutenant Junior Grade Tutu here. How far along are you in flight training?"

"I'm in the third phase, basic instruments. A couple of months ahead of you."

"You were going Swift Boats. What happened?"

Tutu sat back down at the table. "Long story. Never thought you'd go aviation."

"Long story."

After ten minutes of the verbal serve-and-volley, Teresa cut in. "If you two can stop talking long enough to eat, I'll fix you sandwiches."

"Thanks, Teresa, but I tend to eat people out of house and home. I'm meeting my girlfriend for lunch."

Greg knelt on a knee and spoke to Jennifer. "I'm going to borrow some tools. This afternoon I'll take care of the *scawy twee bwanches,* okay?"

Jennifer hugged him around the neck. He picked her up and handed her to Jon.

"If Melody—she's my girlfriend—can take off this afternoon, I'll bring her back with me. She'll help you clean, Teresa. Then, after the evil tree gets tamed, I'll go shopping for dinner."

After the children were down for a nap, Jon poured a cup of coffee and asked Teresa to leave the dishes for a moment. "I need to tell you about my session with the base CO."

Teresa dried her hands with the dish towel as she approached the table. She had a way of levitating her left eyebrow to silently ask, *Now what?*

"My meeting with the squadron CO wasn't too bad," Jon said. "But he sent me to the base CO. He's a captain, a four-striper, and he was not happy with—me." Jon had almost said "us."

"What?" Teresa frowned. "The base CO is mad at you?"

"Captain Morgan."

"Captain Morgan then, he's mad at you?"

"Captain Morgan said that getting into the pew with that colored girl was either a stupid stunt or a blatant thumbing of our noses at the citizens of Meridian."

Jon paused, and the scene in the base CO's office replayed in his head. The beefy, bald, six-footer grabbed a cigar from a desk drawer, bit the end off, and spit it into a trash can. He flicked a lighter, anger in the glower on his face and in his motions. After sucking on the cigar, he blew a cloud of smoke at Jon. "So which was it?" he asked.

Jon struggled for a moment, trying to figure out how to answer the captain's question. But it was one of those chewings-out where lots of interrogatives were fired but, for the most part, answers were not required— nor a good idea. The CO and his officers had worked hard building a good relationship with the people of Meridian. Jon moved in and immediately obliterated months of effort. And he was a lieutenant (junior grade), not a wet-behind-the-ears, rosy-cheeked, just-out-of-diapers ensign.

"There's a lot of political bullshit stirring in the country right now, and you need to stay clear of the civil rights agitators and all the rest of that stuff."

"It wasn't like that, Captain," Jon said, which had been a major mistake. Afterward he realized the base CO had actually been winding down. The comment fired it all back up again.

"Until you got here, the only reason I saw a student pilot was to give him a student-of-the-month award. Hell, I don't even know how to give a proper ass-chewing anymore. Go see my legal officer." He pointed an accusing cigar butt at Jon. "Tell him what you and your wife have done."

His bushy black eyebrows danced up and down above his piercing blue eyes. "Get the hell out of here."

Before the chewing-out, Jon had admired Teresa for moving into that pew. Neither he nor Teresa had had many associations with colored people. Neither of them had ever supported civil rights activities beyond feeling sympathy for the cause. But, in that moment standing in the aisle in church, Teresa had first seen getting in the pew with Clarissa as the right thing to do, and then she had the courage to act and to actually do the right thing. He wondered if he'd have been quick enough to make the decision and to take the moral action Teresa did. *No,* he thought, *I'd have let the usher, Mr. Welcome Wagon Lady, shove us into the crowded pew.* The chewing-out only reinforced his conviction that Teresa had been right to get into Clarissa's pew.

The legal officer had spent most of his time laughing as Jon recounted the session with Captain Morgan. He did leave Jon with one admonition.

"You want to have your mind totally on the flight-training program here. You do not—do *not*—want to call yourself to Captain Morgan's attention again. Even if you get a student-of-the-month award, decline it."

He thought about not telling Teresa about the session with the base CO, but she needed to know how they stood. He did intend to tell her that getting in that pew was absolutely the right thing to do, and that he was proud of her for doing what he didn't have the sense, or courage, to do. But before he could deliver the last part, *bzzt, bzzt, bzzzzzzzzzzt* assaulted his tympanic membranes.

A sympathetic explosion of noise erupted from Edgar Jon in the children's room. Teresa and Jon hurried through the living room, she to the baby and he to open the door and stop the buzzer.

A man stood on the top step of the four-by-four-foot concrete porch. He was wearing light gray slacks, a blue double-breasted blazer, and a hat, very much like the one hanging on the spike in the door. A police officer stood on the next step down, behind the man.

"Where's Jon Zachery?" The man's manner was offensive.

Before Jon responded, the full volume of Edgar Jon's wail hit them at the front door.

Jon was angry, but he felt the policeman watching him intently.

"Officer, I'm Jon Zachery."

"He's not. Where's the big gorilla who threatened me?" Blazer Man piped in.

"Officer, I am Jon Zachery. The door buzzer scared my baby son awake. I also have a two-year-old at home. Both of them have been frightened enough for one day. If we can have a civil conversation, I will invite you into my house."

"It's not your house. It's mine."

The blazer man talked to Jon, but Jon worried about the police officer.

"Officer, I have a lease. I paid a cleaning deposit and two months rent in advance. Since this gentleman is not able to control himself, I'm closing the door."

"Now, see heah—"

"Mr. Binford, back away from the door," the officer said. "Let Mr. Zachery come out."

"Now, you listen here. I am evicting you from these premises. I hereby serve you notice. You have six hours."

"Mr. Binford, I have a lease. My wife and I have done nothing wrong. We're not leaving."

"Officer, arrest him. He's trespassing."

"No, Mr. Binford. I can't do that. Your complaint was that Mr. Zachery threatened you, and obviously, you've made some mistake about that. And until you get a court order for eviction, I can't do anything."

"Jon," Teresa said from the doorway as she patted Edgar Jon, who was upright on her left shoulder, "I think Mr. Binford bears a family resemblance to that man who stuck the spike in our door last night. Do you see it?"

A smile flickered on the policeman's face.

"You always see those kinds of things better than I do, Teresa," Jon said. "Maybe if he was wearing a ball cap."

Mr. Binford looked as if he'd been slapped. "Court order. I'll have one in less than an ow-ah." He started toward the police car. "Come on, Junior."

The policeman looked up at Teresa and took off his hat. "Ah'm Junior McCauley, ma'am. A right pleasure to make your acquaintance."

Then he took Jon's arm and pulled him toward the driveway.

"Quite a woman, Mrs. Zachery."

Jon nodded, waiting to see what would come next.

"Personally, Mr. Zachery, I'm sorry about what happened last night and with him." Junior hooked his thumb in the direction of the car. "But don't underestimate Mr. Binford. There's a judge in the county northeast of here with a last name the same as his."

"Junior, let's go!"

Junior ignored Mr. Binford in the passenger seat of his police car and stuck out his hand. "Hope this works out for you, Mr. Zachery."

"Thanks." He shook the policeman's hand. "I'm Jon." He noted the officer's athletic build. "Football?"

"Was." Junior grimaced. "Outside linebacker in high school. Had a full ride to Ole Miss. Then my knee got messed up in summer workouts before freshman year."

"Sorry." Jon looked him in the eye. "But I can't tell you how nice it was to get a civil word from someone in this town. Thank you."

"The knee. Just feathers. Some days the fox gets chicken, some days just feathers. And sometimes the farmer gets the fox. But, you, Mr.—Jon, probably have thirty minutes. If you have some strings to pull, you might want to give 'em a yank. And that wasn't intended to be a pun."

As the police car drove away, Jon looked at Mr. Binford's morning hat hanging on the spike, briefly considered removing it, but left it. He went inside and called Commander Harrington, the base legal officer. The commander said he couldn't promise that he could keep Mr. Binford from evicting them, but he would try. Then Jon called the CO of VT-7, the squadron he was assigned to. It didn't do to step around the chain of command.

With the phone calls done, Jon considered waiting to see if Commander Harrington's efforts paid off. The Navy expected him at work the next day, eviction or no eviction. He had work to do. He hopped to it.

* * *

At 1340, Jon was on the sidewalk in front as Greg Haywood pulled his green Corvette convertible into the driveway. A six-foot extension ladder and a pruning saw on the end of a six-foot pole stuck out of the passenger side. Greg's girlfriend, Melody Jansen, pulled in behind him.

Jon painted the hallway ceiling as Greg went to work on the tree branches in the back of the house. After an hour, Jon checked on Tutu. A considerable pile of pruned branches from the tall oak behind the house lay around the base of the ladder.

"If you just had a blue ox, Tutu."

"You should know better than anyone, Two Buckets, that I, Greg Haywood, am a man of many talents, including lumberjack."

Jon had met Greg four months into a seven-month deployment to Vietnam on the USS *Manfred*. Ensign Haywood had reported aboard as the replacement for another ensign who had been killed in an auto accident while on leave in Manila. Jon and Greg hit it off immediately. Their commanding officer, however, considered Greg to be an attitude problem. Jon tried to help Greg learn the ropes and fit in with the other fifteen officers in the wardroom but had only limited success.

"Man of many talents, alright." Jon laughed and went back inside.

As he picked up his paint roller, he thought about how flight training had unexpectedly reunited him with his friend. Teresa wanted and prayed for a friend like Rose. That was the way of things though. Instead of her prayer, one that he never even prayed got answered.

How about one for Teresa, God? Maybe Melody? Just trying to be helpful with the suggestion, you know, Lord?

As he painted the ceiling, he could hear Teresa and Melody in the kitchen. They were like two conversational Old Faithfuls, each with a period of a few seconds. When one fountain was spouting, the other was building up steam.

"Where'd you go to school, Teresa?"

"St. John's Mercy. A three-year nursing school in St. Louis. You?"

"LSU. Daddy said I had to go out of state. Where'd you meet Jon?"

"High school." Teresa shook her head. "Oh my. Ten years ago already since we started going steady."

"How did you meet Greg?"

"Christmas dance at the country club. My mother fell in love with him. He is a very good dancer."

Jon smiled as he worked the roller. It was good to hear Teresa's voice bubble happily in conversation with an adult female.

"Good dancer? I guess his nickname from the *Manfred* was appropriate."

"Greg never mentioned a nickname," Melody said.

"They called him Tutu."

"Tutu?" Melody asked. "They called him Tutu?"

"They are officers and gentlemen. They have a piece of paper that says so, but they can be such juveniles. Jon, explain to Melody how Greg got his name."

"Sure." Jon climbed down from the ladder, put the roller in the tray, and walked into the kitchen.

He looked up at Melody on her ladder, where she had been scrubbing the wall between the kitchen and the bath. She had a red bandanna on her head and knotted under her blonde ponytail. She was a tall, beautiful woman, her pale cheeks flushed and her blue eyes twinkling. She and Teresa seemed to hit it off about as well as he and Tutu had on the *Manfred*.

"On our destroyer, the ensigns had to take turns sampling the crew's dinner," Jon said. "It was Greg's turn one day when we were near a typhoon. The ship was pitching and rolling. Greg had just gotten a tray of food from the serving line in the crew's dining room and was looking for a place to sit when the ship took a big roll. The deck was very slippery from spilled food. Greg started sliding toward the rear of the room, made a couple of turns as he held his tray in front of him. He passed five tables sliding and turning, and then he smacked into the back of a seated sailor who was eating his dessert. Greg dumped his tray of chili con carne and rice in the poor sailor's lap. One of the other ensigns from the ensign locker said Greg looked like he was doing pirouettes across the mess decks. So he was Tutu."

Melody shook her head. "Greg in a King Kong suit—that I can picture."

Teresa laughed. "Mr. Binford, he owns the house we're renting, was here this morning. He was going to evict us until Greg stood behind me and scared him. Maybe if he'd been in a tutu, Mr. Binford wouldn't have been frightened. But I'm sure glad Greg was here."

Melody's turn to talk came, but she just turned back to the wall and started scrubbing again. Jon wondered what had upset Melody, or maybe he imagined something that wasn't really there.

Edgar Jon cut loose with one of his signature wails. Teresa dropped her sponge into her bucket.

"May I come with you?" Melody asked.

Jon went back to painting. The women started talking again as they walked through the living room to take care of the baby. *Maybe,* Jon thought, *I just imagined something strange in the kitchen.*

17

Jon ran the roller a final time across a spot near the door into the kitchen. *Ceiling job done,* he thought as the door buzzer made a polite *bzzt.* Teresa answered the door.

"Mr. Binford," she said.

Jon stepped into the living room with the roller in his hand. The base legal officer, Commander Chad Harrington, stood next to Mr. Binford on the top step. A policeman and two workmen, one colored, in white bib overalls, waited on the sidewalk.

Jon looked at the policeman. "Commander Harrington, are we—"

"No, no, it's okay," Commander Harrington said. "The officer will take the spike."

"Would you like to come in?" Teresa asked.

"Right kind of you, ma'am," Mr. Binford said. "The commander and I, if we could just take a minute of your time. And these men," he indicated the two workmen, "are here to replace the door. Okay for them to start?"

"Yes, Mr. Binford. My two-month-old is asleep, and if you gentlemen," Teresa looked at the two men, "could try not to make too much noise, I'd be grateful."

"Yes'm," the white man said with a smile and a head bob. The smile evaporated as he turned. "Abel, fetch the WD-40 from the truck."

Abel bobbed his head just the way the white man had and left to do as he was told.

Mr. Binford snatched his morning hat from the spike and followed Teresa into the living room.

The commander said, "Why Lieutenant Zachery, were you painting something, or was something painting you?"

"Just finished the overhead, Commander. I'll get more of the paint on the bulkheads—walls, I guess civilians call them." Jon introduced Teresa.

"Pleased." Commander Harrington extended his hand. "Mr. Binford has something to tell you," he said, his eyes moving from Teresa to Jon.

"Yes, uh, Mr. and Mrs. Zachery," he seemed discomfited having to manage a hat in each hand, "it has come to my attention that my agent rented you this property in a less-than-satisfactory condition. You have given my agency a cleaning deposit and two months rent. I want you to consider yourselves paid up for four months."

"That's very generous, Mr. Binford," Teresa said.

Jon cast a quick glance at the commander. "Too generous, actually, Mr. Binford. I made a deal with your agent, and I knew the condition of the house before I signed the lease. I do think Teresa and I have earned the amount of the cleaning deposit. That would make us paid up for three months. So you'll have my next rent check in July, not August, and I assure you, your property will be clean when we leave. Fair?"

Jon looked at the commander, but the lawyer's face betrayed nothing.

"I can see you are an honorable gentleman, Mr. Zachery. Deal."

Mr. Binford put both his hats in his left hand, and he shook Jon's hand with his right. After he checked his hand for paint, he smiled and left.

Commander Harrington watched Mr. Binford walk past the front window. When the car door slammed, he turned to Jon.

"Lieutenant, I'm this close to being real torqued at you. Do you know how hard the captain and I both worked to pull this deal together in a very short time? And it's not just you, it's everybody who comes after you we were working for too."

"Commander, I appreciate what you and Captain Morgan did for us today. I really do. I just felt that Mr. Binford had to win something. I thought it would be better if we allowed Mr. Binford to walk out of here with his head up a bit. That's what I tried to do, sir."

"Mistah Binfohd mo betto now," Jennifer said while hanging on to her mother's leg.

Commander Harrington knelt on a knee. "And who are you, young lady?"

"Jennifo."

"Well, Miss Jennifo, you may be right. I am pleased to meet you. You seem like a very smart young lady. Maybe you and your daddy are both smart and both right. Let's hope so."

The commander stood.

"Jon, Teresa, we have assurances that you are safe here. Though I would advise very strongly against any other demonstrations of affection for the civil rights movement. Jon, Captain Morgan and your training squadron commander are both concerned that you not be burdened with any distractions as you start flying jets. They are very concerned. Understand?"

Jon was about to answer when Teresa squeezed his hand. "We both understand, Commander Harrington. Thank you too for what you've done for us. Until you showed up here, this was just the most awful place. It's going to take our babies, and me, some time to get over what happened here this morning. But I know Jon has to have his mind on flying, not this other stuff. We got the message."

"Good. Jon, you need to be in Captain Morgan's office at seven. He will give you the message as only a senior aviator can. Then at eight you need to meet with your squadron CO and the training officer. Like I said, people are concerned. Usually, student naval aviators here don't get in trouble until after they check in. I think you hold the record." Commander Harrington locked eyes with Jon. "0700. Cap'n Morgan's office."

18

Jon placed his 7Up can on the ground as Greg sipped from a bottle of Heinekens. Both watched Jon's long-handled fork flip porterhouse steaks.

"You really think we needed six steaks?" Jon asked as he picked up his 7Up.

"We need eight." Greg reached out a big paw and messed up Jon's hair. "But your grill is small."

Greg looked around behind him at the open window over the kitchen sink and whispered, "Did you tell Teresa what we did to Captain Peacock?"

Jon shook his head. "Haven't told anyone."

He poured some water from a baby bottle to beat back a grease fire, and the flames subsided with a hissing protest and a cloud of steam.

"You?"

"Nope. After the XO wangled those orders to get me off the ship to end the bug wars, there was no one I could talk to."

"The bug wars," Jon said. "I'd forgotten those."

They both stared at the meat again.

Jon had been aboard the destroyer *Manfred* for eight months when two significant events occurred. In a regularly scheduled change of command, Commander Peacock relieved Commander Carstens as the commanding officer of the destroyer, and Cowboy, one of *Manfred's* five ensigns, was killed in an automobile accident while on leave in Manila.

The officers on *Manfred* all considered Commander Carstens to be a combat-oriented natural leader. Captain Brass, Commander Carstens's boss, however, thought differently. Brass worried about appearances a lot more than preparedness for combat.

After Commander Peacock assumed command, he immediately tried to win the favor of Captain Brass. His approach antagonized the wardroom. The executive officer, XO, worked hard to support the new CO but also tried to shield the officers from Commander Peacock's hair-trigger fault-finding sense. Just as the XO began to feel he had imposed a sort of balance on all the factors at play, Greg Haywood reported aboard as Cowboy's replacement.

Commander Peacock quickly identified Greg as an attitude problem and set out to squash the rebellious young officer. Greg responded to the pressure. The CO had a cleanliness fixation, and Greg broke into his cabin twice to plant bug body parts in the his skivvies. After the second incident, it was obvious to everyone aboard who had befouled the CO's underwear. It was obvious to Commander Peacock too. To the XO, Greg was dumping gasoline on the smoldering animosity between the new captain and the wardroom. Through classified personal messages, the XO got Greg orders to the same admiral's staff that Commander Carstens was assigned to.

Jon and Greg were both quiet for a moment, remembering the bug wars. "How was duty on the admiral's staff?" Jon asked.

"Not bad actually. I got to do a lot of running around meeting with Swift Boat sailors. And I met Commander Carstens as soon as I checked aboard the staff. Liked him right away. He asked me about life on the *Manfred*, and I almost told him what we did. But I decided to play the dumb ensign." Greg took a swig. "You know how well I play that role. I don't think he believed me, that I didn't know anything. He didn't push it though."

"Did Commander Carstens know about Commander Peacock screwing up?" Jon asked.

"Yep. He knew about the XO having to assume command when the North Vietnamese shore gun fired at us. He knew about the approach to the oiler that he screwed up, and he knew that we didn't find that downed helo off the coast because Peacock wouldn't take the ship close enough to shore. He knew Commander Peacock walked in front of a supposedly unloaded fifty-caliber machine gun, and that he almost got hit by a round cooking off."

Jon nodded.

"You have any second thoughts about what we did, Two Buckets?"

"I've thought about it, sure. Do I wish we hadn't done it? No. Would I do it again in the same circumstances? I don't know the answer to that one. Yeah. I've thought about it. What about you?"

"Oh, I'd kind of pushed it out of my mind. Every once in a while I think about it, and it seems like somebody else did it. When it was happening, I don't remember feeling any hesitation. Now it's kind of hard to believe we pulled it off. How about on the ship? There was an investigation. You must have been questioned."

"I was questioned," Jon said. "I didn't have to lie. There were the vodka bottles in his desk safe and more sleeping pills than he should have had. I didn't see what was in the board's report, but the XO told us the board concluded that the stress of combat drove Commander Peacock to drink and abuse sleeping pills. Then when he was almost struck by the fifty-cal round, it unhinged him. Most of the people on the ship thought he would have succeeded in killing himself if he hadn't been so drunk, but he only managed to shoot his pillow."

"Kind of amazing we got away with it," Greg said.

"Yeah. But we had to try to stop him. He was going to hurt a lot of people."

Through a strange set of circumstances, the CO trusted Jon. After the accidental discharge of the fifty-cal, Commander Peacock apparently thought his officers were out to get him because he had been hard on them. He decided to fire his entire wardroom, except for Jon, when the ship entered port in the Philippines in two days. Jon thought of two reasons the man trusted him.

First, every commanding officer needed a communications officer he could rely on. Jon had just taken over that job. The driving need for a trustworthy comm officer magnified a minor incident, the repair of the ship's IFF, the electronic system that identified radar contacts as friendly or hostile. Now the CO trusted Jon.

When Commander Peacock embarked on his program to square his ship away, Jon argued with him and attracted severe criticism. After thinking it over, Jon decided the junior ensign had no business arguing with the commanding officer, and that a new CO would naturally want to stamp a ship with his brand of leadership. He thought of one of Teresa's favorite musicals, *The King and I*, and the king wrestling with the notion of having to be right even when he was wrong. When the IFF failed, Jon's crew diagnosed the problem and determined that the required repair part was not carried aboard and had to be ordered. In front of the wardroom, Commander Peacock said Jon's diagnosis of the problem was wrong. Jon brought a circuit diagram and explained why the diagnosis had to be correct. The CO refused to believe him and insisted they place a bet as to whether the ordered part would fix the problem or not. When the part arrived, it did indeed solve the problem, but Jon paid off the debt publicly so that the CO could be right. Peacock understood what Jon had done—Jon could see that—but he was stunned to find the man trusting him as a collaborator in sacking all the officers.

"You gonna flip that meat, or you want me to?" Greg asked.

Jon flipped.

"You were right about only needing to force two sleeping pills down his throat along with the vodka," Greg said.

"Alcohol and pills are dangerous. We had no idea how much he had before we broke into his room. I didn't want to kill him."

"Wouldn't have bothered me, not against what he was trying to do."

"He was sick, Greg."

"Rabid dogs are sick."

Jon shook his head, thinking about that morning. The CO didn't answer his phone again. When the bridge watch investigated, they found the CO passed out in his urine- and feces-fouled bed, a bullet hole in the pillow next to his head, and a fired forty-five on the deck next to his bed.

"We shouldn't talk about this again," Jon said. "Even with each other."

Greg took a step closer and put his right elbow on top of Jon's head. "Just like me, what, you worry?"

"Oh good, Alfred E. Neuman as my comutineer!"

19

Greg leaned toward Jennifer, sitting atop two phone books on the chair next to him. "Your momma's a great cook, huh?"

Jennifer nodded an enthusiastic affirmation and smiled up at Unka Tutu.

"The steaks were delicious, Greg," Teresa said. "Thanks so much for treating us to such a wonderful dinner. We should have treated you, after all the work you and Melody did for us today."

"Greg likes to do the shopping for a dinner like this." Melody patted Greg's hand. "If he doesn't, either he goes away hungry, or the rest of us do."

"Isn't he cute when he blushes?" Melody asked Teresa.

"Help me, Jennifer. The women are ganging up on me," Greg said.

Jennifer assumed a lips-pressed-together stern look and waved her finger in a no-no signal at Melody.

"Ah am appropriately chastised, Miss Jennifer," Melody said, adding a little extra accent.

Greg whispered, "Thanks," to Jennifer as Teresa turned toward Melody. "It was so nice of your mother to make a peach pie for us."

"Momma always freezes some Georgia peach slices during the season for special occasions, and she wanted to welcome you to Meridian. If you are friends of Greg, she knows you are good people. She thinks Greg is just the sweetest," she made quotation marks with two fingers of both hands, "'l'il ole thing.'"

"Little! Compared to a moving van, he is little," Teresa said. "Vanilla ice cream with your pie, little man?"

"Yes, please. Jennifer and I would both like it that way."

Greg watched Teresa and Jon clear the table and dish up dessert. Melody helped them. Melody's mother liked him, and Melody seemed to as well. Still, there was something about Melody, like maybe there were secret parts to her.

Greg had envied Jon's attachment to Teresa from when he'd first met Jon in the ensign locker on USS *Manfred* in 1966. Jon wrote to Teresa every night. He even wrote her poems, and it was obvious Teresa meant the world to him. Until he met Jon and watched him write all those letters, he'd been content to be alone. He dated, and he knew he could be funny when he tried. Some girls too seemed interested in his size, and they just had to find out what he was like in bed. Greg blushed and looked to see if anyone was watching him, but they were all engaged in their tasks.

In the ensign locker, Greg had envied Jon Zachery for other things as well. Greg was impetuous. Because of his size, he had gotten away with it most of his life. Jon thought about things. He was careful and deliberate and decisive, all at the same time. And he was fearless.

There had been the night the *Manfred* anchored in the Saigon River after the day's merchant ship traffic ceased and fired guns in support of an operation south and east of Saigon. The Viet Cong tried to float explosives and a sapper down onto the ship in some driftwood. Jon had been sent out in a boat with three sailors to check out the floating debris. Jon spotted the sapper and shot the VC with an M-14.

Jon showed no emotion after the sapper turned out to be a teenage girl, and he went from the boat to the bridge and stood his midwatch. Just a minor incident in a Navy ensign's daily routine.

Out at the base that morning, word had gone around about the Klan attack on a student naval aviator in town named Jon Zachery. The Naval Air Station Meridian rumor mill said that Zachery had a Bronze Star.

The Bronze Star event had occurred before Greg reported aboard, but it was a hot topic on the *Manfred*. The ship had been credited with twenty-six KIA. The sailors talked about it, but Jon, when asked, evaded the issue. He said he just talked on the radio, that the Marines and the ship's guns had done the real fighting. Greg hadn't known about the Bronze Star. That would have been awarded after the ship got back to the States. A Bronze Star!

"You still take stuff in your coffee, Greg?"

"No, black."

Teresa placed a wedge of almost one-fourth of the pie, with two scoops of ice cream on it, in front of Greg.

"Will there be seconds?" Greg winked at Teresa. "Just kidding."

Melody sat at her place with her half-inch sliver of pie with no ice cream. "Momma thought she should send two pies, but this is the last of her peaches."

"You're not having pie, Teresa?" Greg asked.

"Jon will give me a bite of his."

"You'll get a fork in the back of yoah hand if you try to take a bite of Greg's," Melody said.

"I'd never hurt you, Melody."

"Oh, I know, Greg, honey. You're just the sweetest li'l ole thing."

* * *

Driving Melody home, Greg had both hands on the wheel. His belly was full. He'd found Jon Zachery again. Melody's subtle perfume reminded him of plumeria leis in Hawaii.

"We've been dating since the Christmas dance," she said, "and I think I learned more about you tonight than all the other times put together. I sure never expected to hear you ask Jon to let you change Edgar Jon's diaper."

Greg grinned. "I'm a man of many talents, Melody."

"One you should develop is driving the speed limit. The police like to catch Navy speeders, especially Navy people in Corvettes."

Greg backed off the gas. "Four miles over the limit. That do it?"

"You really like Jon, don't you?"

It was ten thirty, and about half of the houses still had lights on in at least one room. Greg stopped at a stop sign in a puddle of light from a corner streetlight; then he pulled forward.

"I looked up to my dad when I was little," Greg said. "He and Mom started having problems when I was in high school. Then we moved to Wisconsin, I started college, and he left. 'Too many stewardesses too available'—that's what my mom told her brother once. I never looked up to another person until I met Jon. Kinda funny, I guess, to have to look down to look up to a person."

"I really like Teresa," Melody said.

"Me too. Jon told me she was the one who moved into the pew with the Negro girl in church yesterday."

Suddenly the social atmosphere in the car changed. There were subjects you just didn't talk about with Melody. Greg wasn't quite sure how to handle the situation, and he wasn't used to watching what he said. He glanced at her. She was sitting up straight and staring out the windshield.

She turned toward Greg. "You were really called Tutu on that ship?"

Greg considered parking the car. The abrupt change of subject and Melody's pleasant voice surprised him. It was pretty clear though that Melody didn't want to talk about the previous subject. If there was ever to be something serious between them, they were going to have to talk about Negroes in the South, but it didn't seem like the right time.

"Melody," he said, "I hope you won't tell anyone that. That was almost two years ago, and I really don't want that nickname to come back to haunt me."

At Melody's parents' house, Greg pulled under the pillar-supported roof over the curved drive that led from the street to the front door of the white, two-story house. He helped Melody out of the car, and she kissed him lightly and briefly. Then she went up the two steps and into the house. Greg regarded the closed white door with the brass knocker for a moment. Every time the subject of Negroes came up, the good-night kiss went like that. And she refused to talk about what Jon and Teresa had done, getting into the pew with the girl. To Greg, all the names people had for dark-skinned people seemed ugly. Negro, colored, darkie, and all the others—not one of them seemed any better than n*****. It was hard to even think that word.

Greg got in the car and started driving toward his apartment. *On the* Manfred *we had one source of poison,* he thought. *We took care of Commander Peacock, and the poison in the ship was eliminated. Sure isn't that way here. You could eliminate half the town and the poison would still be there.* Melody puzzled him. In some ways, it was easier to talk to her mother than it was to her.

One evening as Greg sat with Mrs. Jansen, waiting for Melody to finish getting dressed, Mrs. Jansen had told him, "In our country, at times of major social change, you'll find half the country saying, 'Too much change, too fast,' while the other half says, 'Not enough' and 'Too slow.' My mother told me prohibition and women's suffrage taught her that."

Mrs. Jansen was tall and slender and always elegantly dressed. Her black hair was streaked with gray. Melody's blonde locks came from her father.

"Melody loved my mother. They were very close. I wish my mother was still alive."

Greg wished he could talk to Melody as freely and easily as he could talk to her mother.

20

Sam Germaine didn't know how Ike Larson was selected, or elected maybe, as the Grand Kleagle of the Mississippi Klan. Sam didn't know who picked him to be the planner either. If he continued to do that job well, one day he would know how that upper circle of secrecy operated maybe.

Sam didn't know Ike, didn't know where he was from. Not Jackson though. Sam knew all the local Klansmen. At least, he thought he did.

He was meeting Ike at "Desires," an all-nighter greasy spoon made from two railroad dining cars placed end-to-end with the entrance in the middle. Sam parked his new Cadillac three parking spots from the entrance. The dining car to the left had a counter with stools running the length of the car. Through the windows, he saw that about half the stools were occupied. The diner to the right had booths against the front windows.

Sam headed right. All the booths were empty except the first, the one with painted-over windows. He slid into it.

"Mr. Larson?" Sam asked.

The man sitting across from him was about his own height, five foot ten. He had broad shoulders, a gray crew cut, a couple of days of gray stubble on his cheeks and chin, and hard brown eyes. Sam squirmed, waiting for him to answer.

The man's head bobbed slightly.

"Sam." He offered his hand across the cigarette-scarred Formica.

Ike stubbed out his short butt. "I know."

A waitress entered the diner from swinging doors into the kitchen across the rear of the intersection of the two cars.

"What can I get you?"

"Black coffee." Ike said.

She looked at Sam.

"Peach pie, à la mode. Iced tea."

She scribbled on her order pad and left.

"In two streetcars named Desire we get varicose veins, saggy tits, and straggly gray hair," Sam said.

Ike lit up and blew smoke at the ceiling, but his eyes held on to and never left Sam's. Leaving entered Sam's mind.

The order came, and the waitress left.

Ike pushed the pie toward the window side of the table.

"Business," Ike said.

Sam's Adam's apple bobbed. His mouth felt dry, and he gulped a swallow of tea.

"So far, you haven't done half bad as our planner. But we're doing some things different now. One, we're stepping up our actions. I'll be telling you about that as we go. Two, you got to pay attention to security. You need to build some separation between you and your teams, especially the Meridian one."

Ike sucked hard on the cigarette. Finally, Sam realized he should ask a question.

"Uh, do things different, you said?"

"We're not trying to kill anyone. We're communicating with them. 'Member saying that?"

Sam tried to speak but couldn't. He nodded.

"We're done with that pansy-assed idea. We decide we need to do something, and people will die. Got it?"

"Sure, um, Ike."

Ike stubbed out his cigarette and lit another. "Okay, you're meeting your Meridian team leader."

"Mr. Peepers." Sam smirked.

"Stop with the trying to be funny. It's not working. Now pay attention. You got to start worrying about security. First, drop the military lingo. It calls attention. Next, your Meridian guy's girlfriend, Amanda Sue Wellman, her daddy buys a new car from you each year. This has got to be the last time you're seen with her. Last time. They'll be here in twenty minutes. This is what I want you to tell them."

* * *

Harry Peeper stopped just inside the doorway. Sam was three booths away. Nobody else was in the place, except the guy in the first booth. Gray Flattop hunched over a cup of coffee. He dressed rough. A drunk? The crew cut was too neat.

Harry pushed Amanda Sue in front of him, and she walked toward Sam's booth. Harry watched Gray Flattop. The man never looked at Amanda Sue. Most men would have. *Queer?* He didn't look like it. Harry began to worry about the guy.

Amanda Sue slid onto the seat opposite Sam. Harry stood next to Sam and motioned with his hand for Sam to slide in. Sam pointed to next to Amanda Sue. Harry shook his head.

"Sit," Sam said, pointing to the seat next to Amanda Sue.

Harry glanced back at Gray Flattop, shrugged, and sat, but he didn't like it with that man behind him.

Sam stared at Harry for a moment. "You can't work in my repair shop anymore." He held his hand up to forestall Harry's protest. "We got a series of banks we plan for you to do. After a job, you turn over half the take to me. You keep the rest to live on. You'll have more money than you do now. Other thing is we got more stuff for you to do. You goin' to be a busy boy this summer."

21

Jon lay propped by a doubled-up pillow, reading his flight manual for the T-2 trainer he'd fly on the base. Teresa came in and started closing the accordion doors to their closet. She liked drawers and closet doors closed.

"Teresa, can we leave that door open, please? I've got my shotgun in there, and I want to be able to get to it quickly if I need it."

Teresa looked at the closet shelf, the box of shotgun shells, and the stock of the double-barrel, and she turned, put her hands on her hips, and shook her head.

"You know I don't want guns and ammunition in the house. Jennifer is starting to get into things."

"I know. I agree with you, really. The cabinet in the shed in front of the carport has a hasp for a padlock. I got a lock today too. Before I go to work in the morning, I'll lock up the gun and shells."

"You should have talked to me about bringing that gun in here."

"I'm sorry."

"The base CO said we didn't have to worry. That's what you told me, that the police would be patrolling the street in front to make sure we're not bothered again."

"I hope he's right," Jon said, but he was thinking of something Al Schwartz said: "When the going gets tough, everybody's likely to get going."

Jon placed his book on the floor beside the bed. "I don't want to frighten you, but I'd like to be prepared. If those guys do come back, I'm not going out after them barefooted, in my skivvies, and with nothing in my hands."

Teresa *humphed* and climbed into bed.

"Teresa, I should have talked to you first. But if those guys do come back, I don't think it will be right away. I think the base CO put some heat on, so they'll lay low for a while. Maybe they won't come back at all. Whichever way it turns out, I just want to be better prepared than I was last night. And I'm not going to do something stupid."

"Right, like last night."

"I know you won't understand this. But the danger was in just standing there and not doing anything, letting them control the situation." She shook her head, didn't see it that way at all. "They didn't expect me to come running after them," Jon said.

"Not just them. I got to the door right when you started for the street, and just like that time in California, it's like I freeze. I just know that in an instant I am going to see you die. And I can't even say anything. At Aunt Penelope's, when the big guy came after you, I wanted to warn you, but I couldn't make my voice work. The same thing happened yesterday, only this time it seemed so much worse than in California."

"Once I opened the front door, and I saw those guys and they saw me, I knew there was only one thing for me to do. If I had closed the door again, it would only have encouraged them. That could have put us all in more danger."

"How do you know that, Jon?"

"I don't like to fight. I try to avoid fighting, but sometimes you can't help it, like yesterday morning. I do know a little bit about fighting."

What he knew about fighting told him that the big man in bib overalls would not have run from him. He'd been lucky that he'd spooked the driver. Teresa didn't need to know that though, he was sure.

Teresa got into bed and stared up at the ceiling. Jon waited to see if the discussion about fighting was finished.

He thought about when he came home from Vietnam. He had worried that the war changed him, that fighting and killing had smeared ugliness on him. He worried she'd look at his face or into his eyes and see the hard, vicious bastard who could do the things he had done. She hadn't been repelled then, but now she had seen him get in a fight twice.

Jon rolled over and got his rosary. On Monday nights, they said the first part of the rosary, the part with the crucifix; then they said a decade all other nights of the week, with a night off on Sunday.

Just after the third Hail Mary, and just before the Glory be to the Father, they heard the car engine in the street.

Jon ripped the sheets off and went to the window. He stood to the right side of the window and opened the blinds a slit. The engine sound was coming from the left.

"It's a police car. They're shining a spotlight on the trees across the road."

The spotlight hit the window like a flashbulb going off.

He groaned.

"Jon!"

"It's okay, Teresa. It's okay."

He had his hand on his forehead, and his eyes were squeezed shut. "Jon," she said again.

"It's okay. The spotlight just wiped the visual purple out of my rods."

"Jon! This is no time for a dissertation on eyeball anatomy."

In his aviation physiology classes, Jon had learned about the ear and balance, hypoxia, and the effects of g-forces. Normally, Teresa, with her nursing education, knew more about the body than Jon did. Recently, Jon had had lectures on the anatomy of the eye and how the workings of the eye related to flying at night. He delighted in those rare moments when he could demonstrate superior knowledge of medical or body-related issues to his nurse wife.

"Sorry. Flash blindness. It'll be better in a moment."

As if on cue, the spotlight on the window went out.

"They just want us to know they are protecting us."

"How about if we call it harassing us?"

Jon knew she was afraid, angry, and ready to pounce on anything he said.

Teresa sat on the side of the bed, and Jon knelt on the floor in front of her, kissed her knees, took her hands, and interrupted with "Glory be to the Father."

"Phooey," Teresa said. "You just love to ruin my mads, don't you, Jon Zachery?"

He helped her up, and they peeked in on the babies. Both angel faces were peaceful.

*   *   *

The next morning as he drove to work, Jon listened to the local radio station. During the morning news, the announcer reported the twenty-sixth monthly Negro church burning. Additionally, a new synagogue, ready for the services, had been dynamited during the night. The synagogue had to be condemned as structurally unsafe. A reward of five thousand dollars had been posted. Jon recalled driving by the new synagogue his first day in town.

He wondered if the Mississippians were working down Lieutenant Amos's list. *Negroes, Jews, Catholics ...* He wondered if Captain Morgan's promise from the Meridian police chief would protect his family. He wondered if he'd cut it as a Navy jet pilot.

Part II

Lieutenant Refly Redmond, Instructor Pilot:

"A naval aviator, he wears wings. He is something. You are nothing. It is not likely you will ever not be nothing."

22

Jon stood in front of the base CO's desk.

"Zachery, you keep your mind on flying." Captain Morgan punctuated his words with his cigar waves and jabs.

"Zachery, keep your mind on flying." Thirty minutes later, Commander Pabst, the CO of VT-7, the squadron to which Jon was assigned, punctuated his words with an accusatory finger.

Jon agreed to keep his mind on flying, but flying was ten days to two weeks of lectures and demonstrations down the road.

One of the differences with flying the prop jobs of Saufley Field was that jet cockpits came equipped with ejection seats. A number of emergency procedures ended with the "Pull Ejection Handle" step. Jets exposed pilots' bodies to high altitudes, which required breathing oxygen, and to high g-forces, which could cause blackouts. Before entrusting a student aviator with an expensive jet, the Navy insisted he understand how to cope with these threats to flying safety.

Basic jet training included a lot of material to learn, and it came fast. As he pulled under the carport, he felt pleased with a full first day of work at Naval Air Station Meridian. He had worked at what he came to do rather than clean, paint, and build a fence.

In the mudroom, he hung his hat and car keys on the hooks on the wall.

"Honey, I'm home."

"In the babies' room," Teresa called.

She was changing the baby's dirty diaper.

"Whew," Jon said to Jennifer, who sat on her twin bed with one of her industrial-strength cardboard books. "Your brother is a stink bomb."

Jennifer looked up at her daddy, nodded, and went back to her book.

"It's good to see you, Mrs. Zachery," Jon said as he held his nose, leaned over the changing table, and kissed Teresa.

"Well, I'm happy to see you too, Mr. Zachery," Teresa said, "but delay in getting boy babies diapered is not a good idea."

"Yes, ma'am," he said.

Dealing with a dirty diaper and having completed a normal day at work felt like something to appreciate after the weekend they'd had, even if his daughter preferred *Lowly Worm* to him.

Jon and Teresa both started asking each other about their day.

"Age before beauty," Jon said. Teresa was three months older than him.

She shook her head as she continued to work on the baby, but even from behind, Jon could see her smile. After five years of marriage, he didn't have to say the joke. She got it when he thought, *Cradle robber*. And maybe she felt the same way about having normal things to deal with.

"Clarissa called," Teresa said.

It took Jon a moment. "Clarissa, Clarissa Johnson from church on Sunday."

"She wanted to let us know she got back to Chicago safely." Teresa handed the repackaged baby to his father. "I was so embarrassed. I forgot about her with what happened Monday morning. I didn't say anything about those men and the sign, but she apologized to me. She said she lied to me, and it took her a day to get the courage to call me."

Teresa headed for the bathroom to take care of the diaper.

"Clarissa lied?" Jon asked as he trailed after her.

Teresa explained, and she told Jon how afraid Clarissa said she had been.

"She sure didn't look like she was scared," Jon said. "I was totally impressed with how calm and composed she looked. The girl had guts, and I admired her for it."

"She feared she'd never get out of Meridian, that she'd be killed and buried somewhere where no one would find her to ship her body back to her momma and poppa."

Jon followed Teresa into the hall, and Jennifer trailed him. Jon knelt and picked up his daughter.

"She doesn't like to be A-L-O-N-E," Teresa said. "She hasn't let me get out of her sight all day, and she wouldn't take a nap unless I stayed in the room with her until she went to sleep."

"Well, we all need a couple of quote normal unquote days between us and Monday morning."

Edgar Jon started squirming. Jon humphed. "The boy has a dirty diaper, and then he's hungry. I guess that's our normal," Jon said.

"Dinner's almost ready," Teresa said.

Jon started heading for the kitchen but stopped. "Teresa, did you ask Clarissa if she's coming back to Meridian?"

"I didn't ask her that question," Teresa said as she washed her hands, "but she did say she is never doing anything like last Sunday ever again."

Jon stood in the hallway, and thoughts of Clarissa Johnson, Negrophobia, colored people who know their place, and Captain Morgan and his cigar paraded through his head. Then Teresa dried her hands and went into the kitchen. He followed with his children in his arms.

23

Clarissa entered the apartment at 6:20 p.m. on Thursday, spaghetti day. Even after seven months of rooming with Dorothy, seeing her at the stove on the kitchen side of the room made her smile. Dorothy Dolman, Dodo, looked like the image on the pancake syrup bottle had come to life: a red bandanna knotted over her hair, an apron tied around her thick trunk, and a warm, all-embracing smile shining between her puffy cheeks.

"Wash up and make a salad, Rissa," Dodo said. "Then we be ready to eat."

Clarissa deposited the bag with her tennis rackets in the closet and hung her jacket.

"How'd your quiz go today?" Clarissa asked.

Clarissa helped her roommate with her studies. Without the help, Dodo would be failing half her classes.

"Who knows. Papers'll be handed back tomorrow."

Dodo stirred sauce in a skillet. Clarissa started tearing lettuce.

"You ready to tell me about Meridian?" Dodo asked.

"I told you I don't want to talk about it."

"Pretty bad, I guess, huh?"

She had fended off Dodo's inquiries every night that week. She knew the girl wouldn't quit.

"You can be awfully aggravating, Dorothy Dolman, you know that?"

"Sure I know. My momma told me that all the time."

Clarissa sighed. "I've seen people look at me with hate, with contempt. But before it was like it came in manageable doses. I don't know if that makes sense."

Dodo nodded.

"In Meridian," Clarissa shook her head, "it was so concentrated. Billy dropped me off right in front of that church and drove away as soon as I closed the car door. And every white person on the sidewalk, everyone walking across the street from the parking lot stopped walking and looked at me. Three people were climbing the steps to enter church, and it was like they must have Negro-detecting radar or something. They turned and looked at me too. I never felt so alone. They all hated me. I wanted to turn and run after the car. I don't know how I convinced my legs to start walking. I was so afraid I'd faint or my legs would give out. I don't even remember climbing those steps and walking down the aisle. Somehow, I got into a pew. Billy talked me into going with him. I went, but I'll never do anything like that again."

"What about Pretty Boy? How you two gettin' along?"

"We're not, and we won't ever, and I don't care how persistent you are. I will not talk about him."

Suddenly, there was a pounding on the door. "Clarissa, Clarissa, open up."

The pounding resumed, and Clarissa hurried to pull the door open.

"They killed Dr. King." A distraught Billy stood with his hands open, palms up, tears streaming down his face. "They shot him."

"Rissa, see if Emil or Ray's home," Dodo called. "They got a TV."

Emil and Ray lived a floor up, and Billy followed Clarissa up the stairs. The boys had the TV on, and they watched from their ratty sofa covered with an army blanket.

Clarissa listened to the announcer drone about what they knew and what they didn't know, and the camera never moved from the upper level of a two-story motel. Apparently, Dr. King had been staying in one of the rooms in the camera's field of view, and he'd been on the walkway in front of the room when he'd been shot.

Clarissa walked out of the room, and Billy stopped her when she was halfway down the stairs.

"Where're you going, Clarissa?" Billy asked.

"For a walk. I need to get out."

"I don't think that's a good idea."

Clarissa resumed her descent.

"Wait. I'll come with you."

Clarissa stopped and faced him. "I do not want to be with you." She started down again and didn't look back.

24

John Calhoun looked across the kitchen table at his son. He was not the sharpest knife, but he'd kill anyone if they said so. He was twenty-two, but John thought of him as a boy. With blond curly hair and a face a notch beyond handsome, he wouldn't let himself think *pretty*, even though the word fit. He looked just like his momma before she got fat and sloppy.

The sow. That was how he thought of her. After Rafe was born and he started growing, so did she, and she grew the fastest. He thought about putting her away when Rafe turned four. But his first wife died birthing Arlene. He didn't wait long to marry sixteen-year-old Sue Ellen. Two good things about her were that she got pregnant right away and she produced a boy. On the other hand, there were the bad things, besides being a pig. Finally, he decided against putting Sow Ellen away to get a third wife. After two straight losers, he'd probably be unlucky again. Wives carted along a lot of crappy baggage.

John Calhoun glanced into the living room, where he knew Sue Ellen sat on the sofa by a lamp, holding a folded-over trash magazine in her left hand while her right fed chocolate into her face.

"Sue Ellen," John Calhoun said.

She waddled through the doorway and went to the stove for the coffeepot and filled John's cup. She held the pot up to Rafe. He shook his head no.

John Calhoun watched her replace the pot on the stove. She didn't seem to be afraid of him anymore. It had been a while since he called her Sow Ellen or hit her. It'd be a mistake to wait until she crossed the line and he *had* to hit her. He stared at the doorway until he heard her flop down on the sofa and then the rustle of the little paper cup the chocolates sat in.

He turned to the boy. "You still gettin' along okay with your pardner?"

"Yeah, Paw."

"So tonight, you see any niggers getting stirred up over the King killing, you call me, hear?"

"Yeah, Paw. I will. I know what you want."

"Watch for whites too. What about that Navy guy on Fortieth? You hear anything about him?"

"No, Paw. I drive by there every night. We're s'posed to, and I do a time 'r two extra."

"They git visitors? You see extra cars?"

"No, Paw, ain't seen none a that."

John Calhoun thought about the Navy guy. Short little bastard, Rafe had said, but he charged after Ford when they spiked that sign to their door. A fighter, Rafe said. Killed a bunch of men in Nam. But what the hell kind of man would charge Ford with nothing but his bare hands? *Little fart was prob'ly lucky Chevy turned chickenshit 'n ran.*

"Word is," Rafe said, "Bollinger moved his wife and two daughters up to Ohio somewheres."

"That so?" John Calhoun tipped his chair back. "Go by his place coupla times tonight. That be a problem with your partner?"

"No, Paw. Billy lets me drive. Wherever I want's okay with him."

"Better git goin', boy."

"See you in the mornin'."

After Rafe closed the door, John Calhoun called Sam Germaine.

"John Calhoun here," he said. "Lunch tomorrow, noon, okay?"

He listened.

"Hell yes, it's important. You think I'd drive all that way for shitty coffee?"

He slammed the phone down and looked toward the living room. He heard the crinkle of candy paper and ground his teeth.

25

TERESA GOT UP FROM THE sofa as Jon turned off the TV. Twenty-eight hours after Dr. King was shot, the authorities didn't have a clue as to the identity of the killer. *Maybe they know who shot him but haven't told us for a reason,* Jon opined.

Teresa was afraid it would be a murder case with no solution, no one to punish. White people, some of them, admired Dr. King. Jon admired him even though he disagreed with the man's stance on Vietnam. Colored people though—he was a savior to them. *As if I can understand how Negroes would feel,* she thought. *As if I can understand how they would look at Dr. King. As if I can understand how they would feel about whether the assassin were identified and caught or not.*

Jon just stood there, looking at the dead TV.

"What is it, dear?"

With his back to her, his shoulders rose and fell as he took a deep breath before facing her. His brow was wrinkled, and the corners of his lips were curled up, but he wasn't smiling. A hurt soul looked out through his blue eyes.

Teresa went to him and put her arms around him.

After a moment she dropped her arms and looked up at him with her left eyebrow elevated.

He smiled and kissed her raised eyebrow.

"Ah, Teresa. We were watching the clips of rioting in LA, Boston, and Detroit, and I thought the Negroes were stupid for burning and destroying their own neighborhoods. Why don't they pillage white sections of town? They showed Chicago. Black Panthers caused those Chicago riots, the reporter said. I knew Clarissa would not be part of what was going on there."

Jon shook his head.

Teresa put her hand on his forearm and waited.

"Then," he said, "I thought if anyone had a right to riot, it was Meridian Negroes. But, as far as I can tell, they haven't made a peep. Remember what the Welcome Wagon lady said?"

"Our colored people know their place. That?"

"That."

*   *   *

Teresa awoke with a start and looked at the electric alarm clock. She turned over.

"Jon?" After they made love normally, he wasted no time falling asleep. "It's midnight. Are you all right?"

From the night-light in the hall and the rectangular halo around the street-side blinds, she could see him staring at the ceiling with his hands cupped under his head.

He started putting his hands down.

"Careful, Teresa, my arm's asleep. I don't want to knock out your front teeth."

At least he could try to be funny. "What's bothering you?"

"Why I decided to stay in the Navy. Deciding the protestors were wrong, that Dr. King was wrong about Vietnam, deciding I had to fly and go back to Vietnam, I don't know. All of it seemed so clear. I had it all in place."

"Jon, all any of us can do is to look at the things in front of us, to pray, and do the best we can with our decisions. You did that."

"It just doesn't feel good. The only other time in my life I felt like this was during my first year of college when you said we should date other people. I was sure it was stage one to a kiss-off. It discombobulated me."

"Didn't it occur to you that maybe the reason we came to Meridian was not so that you could learn to fly and bomb North Vietnam? Maybe the reason was so that we could meet Clarissa."

Teresa pulled her nightgown off, dropped it on the floor, and climbed on top of him.

"What are you doing?"

"You Midwesterners," she said. "You need even the simplest things explained."

26

HARRY SAT IN THE PASSENGER seat of the DeSoto, holding the barrel of his Thompson. He checked his switchblade in the watch pocket, his forty-five stuck in his belt on the left, and the four spare magazines on the seat next to him.

He looked at Amanda Sue. Both hands were on the wheel, and she was sitting forward a little, her eyes searching ahead, the sides, and the mirrors. She was driving fine.

"Take the next left," Ford said from the backseat behind the driver.

"Okay," Harry said. "Garage light on the left there, Ford. You get that, 'n Chevy the one two houses up on your side."

Amanda Sue stopped, and the boys got out.

"Lights, 'Manda Sue," Harry said.

"Oh, yeah."

"Brake lights too."

Harry watched Ford break the lightbulb above the driveway, and then he trotted toward the Bollinger house. On the other side of the street, Chevy swung his stick at the garage light and missed and cussed. He swung and missed a second time.

Chevy, Jesus.

Harry flicked on his flashlight. "Put your wrist over here." He set his watch to match hers. "One minute past one," he said. "Drive by the Bollinger place at six minutes after. Drive slow, five miles an hour. If you don't see us, kick it up to the speed limit 'n come by again at eleven after. We will be there the second time whether we get Bollinger or not. Got it?"

"I got it, Harry."

Funny, he thought, *how some people measure up when the going gets tough.* He looked around toward Chevy. *Dark. Great, the dipwad finally got the job done.* Harry got out and hustled, with the Thompson at port arms, to where Ford waited at the corner of Bollinger's dark house.

Harry pulled the flashlight out of his pocket and handed it to Ford. Ford flicked it on and headed for the back of the house, and Harry took a step after him when Chevy ran into the back of Harry and staggered him.

Harry stood still. He didn't look around. If he did he might hose a full magazine into the stupid bastard.

A loud *skrunk* violated the silence. Harry hurried to the rear of the house and got there as Ford pushed the door open and entered. In the dark room, Ford paused to get his bearings and sweep the kitchen with the light. Harry moved past him through a doorway and pointed his Thompson down a dark hallway.

"Who the hell's there?" came from the end of the hall. "I got a gun."

Harry almost hosed off a burst when Ford grabbed his arm and pulled him into the kitchen. A light flicked on in the hallway. Ford turned off the flashlight and flattened himself against the wall next to the door. There was enough light from the hall for Harry to see Ford's grin.

From the hallway, Harry heard the ratchet of a pump-action shotgun, and he crouched with Thompson stock under his elbow. *Shit.* He couldn't fire without hitting Ford.

A skinny man with a high forehead stepped into the doorway from the hall. He wore a white T-shirt and blue pajama pants. Harry was in darkness. The man didn't see Ford or him, but he did see a man standing in the busted-open back door. The man's eyes got big. He raised a shotgun and pointed it at Chevy. Chevy raised his hands in front of his face. Harry shifted the machine gun to his left hand and pulled his forty-five.

Ford grabbed the man's shotgun and pushed the barrel down. He grabbed the man by the throat with his other hand. Harry heard the click. *Dud?* The shotgun fell to the floor, and the man raised both his hands to try to break Ford's grip. Ford got both hands on the man's throat, and he shook him and shook him.

"Let him go, Ford," Harry said.

Ford stopped shaking the man but held him by the throat.

"Let him go. He's done for."

Ford dropped the limp body to the floor, and the man's head and shoulders lay in the hallway. His mouth was open—his eyes too, but they weren't seeing anything.

Harry felt frozen, like a statue that could see. He shook his head.

"Chevy, git your gloves on. Ford, get a rug or blanket."

Harry picked up Bollinger's shotgun and half-pumped the chamber open. He smiled and tossed the gun to Chevy. "Not loaded."

Ford pulled the body through the hall into the living room and started rolling it in a quilt.

"Chevy, look through there. See if that's the way to the garage. Put the gun in the car, and wait there for us."

Chevy went through a door at the end of the hall, opposite from where Bollinger had been sleeping. A light flicked on. "Car's here," Chevy said.

Ford hoisted the rolled-up body onto his shoulder and headed for the garage. Harry checked his watch. Four past one. It felt like it had been hours since he sent Amanda Sue off.

Harry checked the rooms off the hallway. Girl's bedroom, a boy's, bathroom, master bedroom. No luggage in any of the rooms. Ford came down the hall, and the dark hulk of him looked as if he might get stuck. He had a suitcase in each hand.

"On a shelf in the garage," Ford said.

Harry opened both suitcases on the bed in the master bedroom and started opening dresser drawers. When he found the man's underwear, he dumped the drawer contents into a suitcase and threw the drawer on the floor. He ripped open the closet and started taking suits, trousers, shirts, all still on hangers, and dumped them across a suitcase. He took two pairs of shoes off the closet floor and put them in with the clothes.

"Close 'em up, Ford, and put them in the backseat of his car."

Harry looked through the closet and found a jewelry box on the top shelf. He dumped the contents in a pillowcase. Bollinger's wallet, watch, and car keys were on the night table by the bed. *Nothing else worth a thief's time.*

Ford was waiting in the hall near the entries to the kitchen, living room, and garage.

Harry looked at the tabletop TV. "Think you can get that in the backseat a his car?" Harry asked.

Ford nodded.

Harry pulled Bollinger's wallet out of the pillowcase and removed forty-two dollars from it as Ford carried the TV into the garage.

Harry followed Ford into the garage and checked his watch. Nine minutes past.

Harry took Bollinger's keys and handed them to Chevy who was behind the wheel of Bollinger's Pontiac.

"Okay, Chevy. Here's the money from his wallet. Not much." Harry shrugged, turned out the light, and opened the garage door. Chevy backed the car out, Harry closed the garage door, and Amanda drove up.

Harry got in his DeSoto. "Right on time," he said.

Chevy backed the Bollinger car into the street and drove off.

"Let's get back to Jackson," Harry said.

Amanda Sue drove and watched, and Harry went over the mission. The driver worked out. Ford did his part. *Jesus, the guy was strong.* Bollinger flopped around like a rag doll in his big hands. Chevy, well, Chevy was Chevy. Harry. Harry screwed some things up. Harry should have used the forty-five inside. The Thompson was too unwieldy in the kitchen. And if Bollinger had had a loaded shotgun, they'd have had a royal screwup. Harry should have stayed where he was in the hallway to cover it and not let Ford pull him into the kitchen. That gave Bollinger the opportunity to take the initiative.

There was a thought that Harry's screwups had been worse than Chevy's. It was trying to elbow its way into his brain. He looked at Amanda Sue. She was charged up, not something he could see, but he felt it radiating off her. She was going to be something when they got back to the apartment.

Hell, I might get raped, Harry thought.

27

At Meridian Naval Air Station, student pilots absorbed survival lore through their pores like wrong-way sweat. The lore included:

- Half the instructor pilots were screamers.
- Screamer IPs still gave good flight grades—sometimes.
- Just don't let the bastards get you down.

The basic jet training syllabus began with the transition phase, thirteen flights. The first eleven training hops appeared on the schedule as Tr-1 through Tr-11. The twelfth was written as Tr-12X. X denoted a check flight, a completion-of-phase exam to determine if a student had mastered the elements of jet flying and could be trusted to fly solo. One of two grades was possible on a check flight: up (passed) or down (flunked).

A student soloed in a jet for the first time on Tr-13.

"I guess the Navy doesn't want us to be superstitious," Jon said one Saturday afternoon as he and Tutu stepped sideways around the grill to get away from the grease smoke.

"Not so," said Tutu. "Naval aviators are a superstitious lot. We even have a prayer."

"So I have to ask you to tell me? Okay, I'm asking."

Tutu's face donned solemnity. "Yea, though I fly into the valley of death, I will fear no evil, 'cause I just don't got no sense. But I do have a rabbit's foot and a St. Christopher medal hanging on my dog tag chain."

Initially, Jon was lucky. For his first ten hops, Lieutenant James Milson sat in the rear instructor seat. A good instructor, a nice guy, and not a screamer, he invited Jon to call him by his first name. Getting overly familiar with an IP didn't seem right, like calling a priest by his first name. James insisted though.

Tr-11 had to be with a different instructor, and the Navy and the law of averages gave him a screamer for that hop. Still, Jon received good flight grades. After he debriefed, Lieutenant Milson found him in the student pilot locker room.

"You'll do fine on the check," he said. "Just don't get Refly."

IPs didn't say things like that. They were establishment guys who spoke the party line. Still, many of them thought Refly went too far with his approach toward students.

"That's like saying don't hit into a double play," Jon said.

"Don't hit into a double play then."

James didn't control the schedule though, and a student didn't ask for specific instructors to fly with, or to not fly with.

There it was.

Date	Takeoff	Flight	Pilots
12 May	0930	Tr-12X	Zachery/Redmond

Lieutenant Robert Redmond had three nicknames: Red, Redass, and Refly. He wasn't a screamer. He had his own way to make a student pilot's life miserable. There were stories about him that included all three of his nicknames strung along with a few other epithetical accompanists. Still, Jon thought Refly couldn't give a down, an unsatisfactory grade, to every student he flew with. Jon had done well at Saufley in the T-34 aircraft. He had done well with James Milson and with the screamer on Tr-11. With Refly, he didn't really need to do well, just average. Even with a couple of below-average grades, he could still pass the check ride.

During the preflight briefing in his office, Refly did everything he could to psych Jon out. When Jon arrived, Refly looked up from his study of an open manila folder on his neat desk, pointed to a gray metal folding chair against the wall to the left of the door and in front of his desk, and dialed four numbers on his black phone. He drummed his fingers on top of the folder.

"Roy, Red." Refly leaned back in his swivel chair. He had probably called Lieutenant Commander Leroy Fransen, the training officer. "I've got those stats you asked for on Tr-12 downs."

"One of your questions, Roy," Refly said. "If a student does well in primary training, does that lessen the probability he will have problems on the Tr-12 check? I'll give you all the stats, and I've broken out the numbers a couple of different ways. I think students who do good in primary have more problems passing Tr-12. That's what I think the numbers show."

Refly had a lot of statistics, and he took his time with the discussion.

It seemed bizarre that he would stage the whole thing, but the comment about students who did well in primary having trouble with Tr-12X, that had to be aimed at him. Jon almost smiled but knew that would be a big mistake. The rumor mill promulgated a number of Refly stories. Jon had heard that half the time he didn't say anything in a post-flight debrief. He just looked at a student with disgust and disdain slathered on his face as he filled out the grade sheet, and then he handed it over and walked away.

In the rumor mill's favorite story, Refly asked an ensign what he was.

"Sir, a student naval aviator, sir," the academy grad had responded.

The student was a couple of inches shorter than Refly, and Refly had stepped very close to the student and looked down on him. With a soft, totally controlled voice, he'd said, "A naval aviator wears wings. A naval aviator is something. You are nothing. It's not likely you will ever not be nothing."

Refly's phone call droned on.

Jon looked at his watch. The instructor acted as if they had all the time in the world, that they were not twenty-five minutes late for starting the brief. He considered saying something but decided that would be pushing things.

"Okay, Roy, I'll have a yeoman bring the report to you. I just wanted to cover the gist of it with you before you got the paper."

"You ready?" Refly asked, with the phone on the way back to the cradle. He spoke softly, much quieter than he'd been speaking into the phone.

"Uh, yes, sir."

"Technically," Refly's voice was very reasonable, friendly even, one Navy lieutenant speaking with another, even though Jon was only a lieutenant (jg), "this is Tr-12. Consider it Tr-13. Consider yourself to be alone. Consider me to not even be here. Let's go."

Jon started to stand up but sat back down.

"I can't do that, sir. We have to cover ejection procedures and passing control from one cockpit to the other. I also want to cover bird-strike procedures."

Without waiting for him to respond, Jon went over those items. After he finished the safety procedures brief, Jon was sure that Refly had expected him to just walk out of the room to sign out the airplane from maintenance. If he'd done that, he was sure Refly would have given him a down on the spot for failing to cover the required safety items on the preflight briefing checklist.

As he preflighted the aircraft, Refly never said a word. After Jon strapped in, he ran through the engine start procedures and informed the backseat what he was doing over the intercockpit communications system, the ICS. Refly never responded or acknowledged. Before Jon called for taxi clearance, he asked Refly if he was ready to go. Not a peep from the backseat.

"Mr. Redmond, I have to know we can communicate before we can taxi out to the runway." Silence from the backseat.

"Mr. Redmond," Jon keyed the radio instead of the ICS—it was a common student mistake, one that elicited a lot of ribbing in the ready room. "If you don't answer me, I'm not calling for taxi."

"You went out over the radio, you idiot," Refly said.

"Oops. Sorry about that, Mr. Redmond. Now, over the ICS, are you ready for me to call for taxi?"

Silence. Jon got angry. He thought about just shutting the plane down and walking back to the hangar.

Finally he responded, "All right, Zachery. No more screwups on the radio or the flight is over. Call for taxi."

"Aye," Jon said over the ICS and immediately keyed the radio and called for taxi.

The early part of the flight progressed without a hitch. Forty-five minutes into Tr-12, Jon began to think he might not get a down, despite Refly in the backseat. He had one more evolution to complete: practice landings.

The air station maintained a secondary airfield called the Remote, where students could practice landings without clobbering the traffic pattern at the main base, McCain Field.

Jon flew over the Remote at 2,500 feet. He kept to ten degrees of left bank angle. High bank angles hid other planes behind the up wing.

Below, a T-2 was on short final. It touched down with a double cloud of white smoke from the wheels, climbed, and turned to the left to set up for another touch-and-go. It was the only plane using the Remote, not the usual six or more. *Almost peaceful down there,* Jon thought, and he was about to enter the landing pattern when he caught sight of another plane on final approach.

Coming in too steep. Too fast.

The plane plowed into the dirt just short of the runway and threw up a cloud of red dust. The edge of the concrete chopped the landing gear out from under the T-2 jet trainer like a scythe mowing through weeds, and the aircraft slid on its belly a thousand feet and stopped with the nose pointed about forty-five degrees left of the runway heading.

It happened so fast. One moment the world was in order. A T-2 trainer doing practice landings, the check flight going well—so far, and between eye blinks, a crash.

Jon keyed the ICS mic. "Uh, do we need to call back to base about the accident, Mr. Redmond?"

"Fly the plane."

Okay.

Jon scanned the sky for other planes, checked the flight instruments, and looked for airplanes again.

Down on the runway, the crashed plane was still running at full power, blowing the knee-high grass alongside the runway. Then the agitated grass became calm as the engine was shut down. Lights flashed on top of the crash truck parked beside the runway at the far end of the field. The truck belched a black diesel cloud and headed for the wrecked plane.

Jon knew he had been looking down at the crash for too long. He thought of Lieutenant Amos.

"The way the Navy teaches you about flight safety," Amos said, "they take a simple safety message, paint it on a Burma Shave sign tacked to a stick with a pointy end, get a student to hold the stick with the pointy end on top of his skull. Then they pound the message into your head with a sledge. Five times a day. Five days a week. Five weeks in a row."

Amos liked to boil a safety lecture down to shaving cream signs: "Don't look inside," "Look out," "Burma Shave."

Jon checked the sky for planes, thinking Refly would have been on his case if he saw him staring at the crash. He wondered if Refly was staring at the crash too.

Another check for planes.

"He was doing a practice power-off landing. Dumb shit. Hope he's a VT-9 instructor," Refly said.

Refly and Jon were in VT-7. VT-9 was the other training squadron on the base. Aviators were competitive. And pack animals. Screwups reflected not only on the individual, but on the pack, on the squadron too.

Practice power-off landings were specifically forbidden by base policy and were feloniously stupid. If you lost power in the jet, you were expected to use the ejection seat. A power-off landing could be executed, but the likelihood of walking away from it was low. Test pilots proved it could be done.

Test pilots, however, were exceptional "stick and throttle jockeys." Blue Angels sat at the top of the aviator ability ranking system. Test pilots were just as good at punching a jet through the sky, but many of them lacked one essential ingredient to win a spot with the Blue Angels. After donning a tailor-made flight suit, a Blue Angel candidate had to make a girl's heart go pitter-patter. Many test pilots were afflicted with "too tall," "not tall enough," "real plain-looking," or "he's some kind of ugly."

Among the general population of naval aviators, one other ability category fell out of the continuous competitive and winnowing process imposed on Navy pilots: a Good Stick. Every squadron had a couple of Good Sticks. They were the guys who brought their planes aboard the carrier on the first landing attempt, no matter how crappy the weather. They got the best bombing scores on the practice range and won training dogfights. Blue Angels and test pilots all came from the select population of Good Sticks. Pilots wanted to be known as Good Sticks. Pilots wanted to be able to do things in an airplane that Blue Angels, test pilots, and Good Sticks could do.

In the past, pilots screwed up practice power-off landings quite frequently, especially those who thought they were Good Sticks. Accident statistics led to the "no practice power-off landings" policy.

The maneuver was in the book in case a pilot had a really bad day: lost power, pulled the handle, and the ejection seat failed to fire. An instructor-pilot lecturer told Jon's class that if they were having one of those kinds of days to consider an alternative. He said, "Rather than worry about the power-off landing, spend the time bending way over and kissing your ass good-bye."

After Refly's "dumb shit" comment, Jon looked back down at the runway. The crashed-jet canopy was open. The guy in the front had climbed out. The backseat guy just sat there, maybe hurt or trying to figure out how to explain the accident. The fire truck stopped. Two men in silver fire suits ran to the disabled aircraft.

"Zachery! Get your head out of your ass. While you're watching the show down there, we could run into some dumb son-of-a-bitch solo who is just as fixated on the crash as you are."

Jon thought he had done a decent job of the flight to that point. He hadn't violated any operating rules. Acrobatics was a part of the transition phase of training, and he did those pretty well. He hadn't gotten lost.

Refly said, "Back to the field."

Jon knew. Refly had found his excuse to give him a down, and he got the plane headed back to McCain Field.

Refly would say Jon got so focused on looking at the accident that he had stopped flying the airplane, that he couldn't be trusted to safely solo. And Jon was pretty sure Refly's "dumb shit" comment was intended to suck him in. It worked. When Refly made the comment, Jon's eyes went down to the crash site.

So many things could disqualify you in flight training: medical conditions, inability to handle night flying or flying in instrument conditions, inability to handle the speed at which things happened in a jet. Refly.

Not fair, Jon wanted to say.

He pulled his mind back to flying. As he scanned for other traffic, he noticed a few things he had never paid attention to before. Before, there were procedures to comply with, IPs to keep happy, planes to watch for, and no time for just looking around. But then, from two miles above, he noticed that Mississippi was attractive: all green, mostly pine trees that fed the paper pulp mills. A few ponds or small lakes looked like drops of blue slopped off the overloaded palette of the painter who had done the study in green. A couple of red lines sliced through the forests, dirt roads allowing the red clay a peek at the sky along a thin line.

There was haze below, but looking straight down, it didn't affect what he could see. At altitude too it was clear, and one could see a long way. Up to the north, over Columbus, Mississippi, maybe, a huge thunderstorm towered over the earth, the top ripped off into the anvil shape.

The airfield at Naval Air Station Meridian was named after the World War II carrier admiral. Clouds covered McCain Field, and Jon descended to get under them. Bases at 5,000 feet. *No problem.* In back, Refly was quiet.

After Jon landed, taxied to the line, shut the engine down, and opened the canopy, Refly climbed out and walked to the hangar.

Jon stayed in the cockpit. On his first flight in the T-2 trainer, he had felt so awkward and constrained in all the paraphernalia. The oxygen mask felt especially weird and confining. It didn't feel natural. Then, on flight number twelve, it seemed proper to have the oxygen mask strapped to his helmet, his lap belt, and shoulder straps securing him to the ejection seat.

It occurred to him that he was where he wanted to be. He wanted to be there, flying jets, not just for some kind of patriotic reason. He wanted to fly, forever maybe. He sure didn't want it to be over because of Refly.

The power someone like Refly has over you ...

"Hey, Zachery, you asleep in there?" James Milson stood next to the jet, looking up at him.

Jon rechecked that his ejection seat was safe and climbed down.

"Nah. Actually, I was thinking that I had a pretty good flight."

They started walking around the plane, doing the post-flight inspection.

"Before you go in the hangar," James said and put his hand on Jon's arm, "step back and think about your flight with Refly. Make sure you learn every lesson from the experience. The worst thing you can do is to worry about how unfair it is. Understand?"

They started walking toward the hangar.

"Don't go in with the wrong attitude about this, Jon." James looked worried. "This is really important. What happened on your Tr-12, well, it happened. What happens next depends on your attitude. Understand?"

Jon didn't understand, but there were times when it was better to just keep your mouth shut than to ask questions. James had made a special trip out to meet him, to try to help. And to mention attitude.

When Jon got to the ready room, the duty officer handed him his grade sheet. A down. It would have been a surprise if he'd marked the up box. Surprise or not, it still felt like a kick in the stomach. There was only one mark on the sheet. Headwork, down. And the comment was "Got focused on incident on runway and stopped flying the airplane."

That was technically correct, Jon thought, *but it had been just a moment. And he had been trying to set me up from the moment I arrived for the brief.*

"Wrong attitude," Jon could almost hear James saying.

"Lieutenant Redmond says you're to put that in the completed grade-sheet basket and then report to the training officer," the ensign SDO, squadron duty officer, told him.

The door to his office was open, and Lieutenant Commander Leroy Fransen told Jon to come in and sit. Commander Fransen studied Jon for a moment, and then he asked, "What do you think about your Tr-12?"

"I learned one big lesson today," Jon said. "You can do almost everything perfectly, but screw one thing up and it is, at best, a bad hop. You, and others, might even wind up dead."

The look on his face told Jon the training officer had expected some other response. He questioned Jon as to details about the big lesson. Jon told him about the crash at the Remote and about getting focused on watching that and not paying enough attention to flying the airplane.

"You know that was a VT-7 crew in that plane?" Lieutenant Commander Fransen asked.

"They okay, sir?"

"They weren't hurt. The student is probably going to get a letter of warning in his record. The instructor is getting a Feenab. Know what that is?"

Jon didn't.

"Field Naval Aviator Evaluation Board. They will probably recommend he lose his wings."

Both of them kind of chewed on that thought for a moment.

"What did you think of Lieutenant Redmond?" he asked.

Jon looked him in the eye. "I don't think I'd have learned the lesson with any other instructor pilot."

"But," he said. "Is there a but?"

Jon shrugged. "In the entire domain that defines a horse's butt, he has staked out a unique corner."

For just an instant, a frown cloud darkened Fransen's face, but then he laughed and shook his head.

"Zachery, you little son of a bitch, get the hell out of here."

Jon's XO on USS *Manfred* used to say that to him quite often. Being called an SOB and being told to "get the hell out of here," and thinking that what you heard was respect, well, you had to be sure you weren't into heavy-duty self-delusion. Jon didn't think he was.

28

Jon sat on a bench in the student locker room and looked up when James Milson pushed in through the spring-loaded door. "You pulled it off," James said. "You'll get a refly of flights ten and eleven with a different instructor for each. Tr-10 on Monday, 11 on Tuesday, and then, if those go okay, Roy Fransen will give you your safe-for-solo."

"I'm ready to redo the twelve check now."

"Just stick with the program. So far you've only flown with three instructors here. It'll be good for you to have some other pilots see how you do. Understand?"

"Understand? I'm not sure. But thanks. I'd have blown it without your tip about attitude."

"Turns out Refly thinks the need for so many students in the jet-training pipeline is about to end. The president's announcement means we're going to be getting out of Vietnam and won't need as much cannon fodder. He also thinks the older students—and you're four years older than the average—ought to be the first ones to go. I think Roy was halfway inclined to listen to him. I don't know what you said to Roy, but he apparently thinks you're okay."

Jon checked out with the SDO and went to the gym. Sometimes he needed to hit something.

In 1966, *Manfred* returned from deployment to Vietnam and was sent to the Long Beach Naval Shipyard for four months for equipment upgrade and repairs. Jack Wallis, one of the new officers who reported aboard during that time, boxed at the Naval Academy. He taught Jon how to use the speed and punching bags. He asked Jon to get into the ring. Jon didn't want to box with him or anyone else. If one didn't need to protect himself, if one didn't intend to hurt someone, there wasn't a reason to fight. So he worked the speed bag, and Jack got others into the ring.

Now, as Jon pounded the speed bag in the Meridian gym, Refly worked inside his head. Anger built, and like a drunk having to hit bottom before he could start getting better, the anger had to peak before it could start burning out.

Jon's teeth ground together. Fury escalated. The bag was going fast, and his fists had the rhythm. He was zoned and about set for the jaw crusher, when someone started working the bag next to him. He lost the rhythm, and he hit the bag with a ferocious right intended to rip the bag from the hook.

"Zachery, let's go a couple." It was Refly. His hands had the speed bag going while he smiled at Jon and waited for a reply.

Jon saw only downside. *Refly must be good,* he thought, *or there'd be no invitation. Payback, maybe, for the accidental-on-purpose radio call?*

"I don't box, Mr. Redmond. Never have. I just work the bag. I really don't know anything about boxing."

"Well then, Zachery, time you learned." Refly gave his bag a good rap. "Come on. We'll use the big gloves. They're so soft it'll be like a pillow fight." He put his gloved hand under Jon's upper arm and pulled him toward the ring.

They both took their T-shirts off, and Jon took his teeth out. Refly told him to hike his shorts up higher, went over the rules, and gloved him.

Jon looked around. All twenty people in the gym gathered by the ring.

Refly motioned "Come on" from his corner and started for the center of the ring. Jon let out a breath of resignation. Just as Refly had instructed, he held his hands up.

Refly tapped Jon's gloves with his left, and about a microsecond later his looping right caught Jon over his ear. Jon's arms dropped. A left jab snapped his head back.

He managed a forearm against Refly's looping right, and instead of landing flush against his ear, Refly's glove scraped it. Jon's ear felt as if it had been set on fire, but that didn't matter. For the moment, Refly was off balance. That mattered.

Jon stepped into him, grabbed him about the waist with his right arm, pivoted on his left foot, stepped his right hip into him, and threw him to the mat. Refly hit hard—partly on his shoulder, partly on his back—and his head bounced off the mat. Jon backed to a corner but kept his eyes on him. Refly was stunned for a moment; then anger burned in his brown eyes.

"Boxing, not wrestling, asshole."

"Sorry. Told you I don't know how to box. I'm obviously not in your class. I'm done."

"Like hell you are. Get to your corner. I need a minute. Then we're going another round."

"Mr. Redmond—"

"Another round!" he snarled.

The way he walked, his hip must have hurt.

Jon put a glove up to the side of his head. Was Refly intentionally going after his ear? A busted eardrum would ground him for a long time.

Refly radiated malevolent fury from his corner.

Jon had his eyes locked on to him. Refly signaled, "Come on."

Jon charged, hands down at his side.

Refly was surprised for a second. Then he moved forward.

Refly led with his left. Jon counted on that and sidestepped it. The right—Jon expected that too—and parried with his left and hit him on the nose with his own good right.

Refly was dazed, and Jon caught him right on the waistband with another hard right. He let out an *oof* and bent over. Jon nailed him with a right uppercut on the nose, and he went over backward.

Refly was stretched out on the canvas with his arms above his head. Blood streamed out of his nose.

"Somebody call sick bay," Jon said.

29

John Calhoun wasn't much on waiting. Sitting in his kitchen late at night though, with Sue Ellen sleeping in her end of the house with her door closed and not disturbing the quiet, he waited for the feeling that the ghosts or spirits of his mam and pap were in the room too. That wasn't waiting.

His eyes were open but saw the room the way it had been: the pump with the pitcher of priming water next to it at the end of the sink, the icebox where the fridge sat, and the coal-oil stove in the place of the gas range. The round table and the eight chairs were the same. Then he would see Mam and Pap. One night Mam would be at the stove, another at the sink, but at some point, as he sat and watched, Mam would come over to where Pap sat at his place at the table, and she would place her hand on Pap's shoulder or his arm. And they would look at each other.

His pap had died twenty-two years before, and Mam went the day after. John didn't know how many times he'd seen Mam and Pap do that touch and do that look before they died, but he figured he'd seen it a thousand times since.

There was a tap, tap at the back door. John got up, pulled the door open, nodded, and waved Ike Larsen in. "Hungry?" John asked.

"I could eat."

John indicated Pap's chair for Ike to sit in. "I'll get Sue Ellen up to fix you sumpin'. He'p yourself to the jug."

John pulled Sue Ellen's door open and wrinkled his nose. She'd farted. He turned on the ceiling light, and she started awake.

"I got comp'ny," John said. "Get up 'n fix 'im sumpin' to eat."

Sue Ellen raised up on an elbow. "They's ham and tater salad in the fridge. Turn the light out."

John crossed the room in a stride and slapped her. She was trying not to cry as she held her hand to her cheek. John drew back to hit her again, and she threw the sheet back, swung her feet to the floor, and started fumbling for her slippers.

"Don't need 'em," he said. She reached for her robe at the end of the bed. "Don't need it." He grabbed her arm, pulled her up, and pushed her toward the kitchen.

The stopper was still in the jug on the table. John pulled the corncob and poured two fingers into the two juice glasses with the tiny blue, red, and yellow flowers painted on.

"How?" John said and lifted his glass. Ike lifted his.

Sue Ellen set a plate heaped with potato salad and a thick slice of ham in front of Ike. She put a knife and fork next to the plate with a cloth napkin.

"You want anything else?" John Calhoun asked Ike.

"Coffee'd be good."

Once she had the fire going under the pot, John Calhoun told her to go to bed.

Ike waited until the woman was gone. "What about Bollinger? What's your boy say?"

"Police don't know what to make of it yet. Car and clothes gone, but back door busted open and stuff stolen. His family is in Ohio. Family don't know why he would have left. But why would anyone kidnap him? He's not rich by a long shot. Paper ran a story about the disappearance and mentioned when Bollinger got his window shot out and how he mouthed off the next day. But nobody knows nothing right now."

Ike nodded and swallowed. "Things is going pretty good. We get these one, two people think they gonna change things, and we smack 'em down. Things is going pretty good."

"One thing. A Jew businessman posted a $5,000 reward for information about the synagogue bombing. Story ran in the paper. I'd like to do sumpin' about him."

Ike shook his head. "Five thousand isn't going to buy 'em a squeal."

"Hell, some a these folks, five hundred would."

"Keep an eye on the guy, what's 'is name?"

"Greene."

"We got things in balance right now. The church burnin's out in the counties, hell, we can do those until Judgment Day and nobody gives a good goddamn. Let's ever'body know we're around, and we're gonna be around. Stuff in the towns and cities, we just need to be mindful of what we get for what we risk. For now, sit tight, just watch him."

John got up from the table and got two mugs of coffee.

"John," Ike said, "your boy Rafe, he stayin' clear of the action?"

"He don't like it that way, but he's clear."

"Does us more good where he is than a passel of church burnin's." Ike sipped. "How you related to those Henley car-name boys again?"

"My daughter Arlene married Darnell Henley, and Chevy and Ford's momma was Darnell's sister."

"How close are you to them boys?"

"Not very. Loan 'em a truck or a tractor now and then."

"You or Rafe talk to 'em direct about Bollinger?"

"No. Only thing Rafe knew was to watch the house. Chevy and Ford do talk to Rafe when they here."

"Now on, work it so they don't see each other no more. We got to minimize these links between our boys."

"And only you 'n me knows the links," John said. "'Ceptin' I don't know all a them."

Ike gave a lopsided smile, finished off his coffee, and stood up. "John Calhoun," he said and left.

30

Jon soloed on Thursday of a tough week. At 0600 on Friday morning, he was asleep on three chairs in the back of the ready room. The duty officer's sudden "Morning, Skipper" woke him. Jon sat up, yawned, and stretched.

There were a lot of differences between the aviation Navy and the destroyer Navy. Both communities though used the term "skipper" the same way. Skipper, an informal term of address for a commanding officer, included two-way respect of one warrior for another.

Jon saw the skipper bent over the duty officer's desk, reading the logbook. Abruptly, he stood up straight.

"Call Zachery," the skipper said. "Get him in here."

The duty officer pointed to Jon at the rear of the room. The CO turned slowly. It reminded Jon of the forward, twin-barreled, five-inch turret on his destroyer, slewing to a target.

"Come with me," the CO said. He charged out of the ready room, down the hallway, and into the administration area.

His was the middle of three offices forming the rear wall of the large, open space filled with desks and filing cabinets. The XO's office was to the left when coming in from the passageway. Refly's office was to the right. His door was closed.

"XO," the skipper bellowed.

The XO hurried out of his and into the CO's office. Jon followed, wondering what was going on.

The CO flopped the large green duty officer's logbook on his desk and pointed out a couple of entries to the XO. "Refly assigns watches, and he gave Zachery the midnight-to-0400 watch every night this week. Zachery flew every day. Clear violation of the twelve-hours-at-work squadron policy. Cancel the flight schedule. We're going to have a back-to-basics safety stand-down today. Refly's office is closed. Get him in here."

As the XO started out the door, the CO said, "Close it, XO."

"You violated squadron policy about crew rest." The skipper pointed a condemning finger at Jon.

"No, sir. I didn't violate the policy. No more than twelve hours at work. I did not violate that policy."

"What the hell are you talking about? The logbook shows you had midnight to 0400 every night this week. And you flew every day before today."

Jon stepped forward, flipped pages of the logbook, and pointed at an entry near the top of the left page. Then he moved his finger to another entry near the bottom of the opposite page. He turned more pages and pointed out entries.

"See, Skipper? I logged out with the duty officer every day at 1145. I showed up for my midwatch at 2345. Every day. It's in the log."

"We've got enough dropouts and medical downs to stand the nighttime watches." The skipper shook his head. "Okay, Zachery, you played it so you observed the letter of the law. But clearly that's not what was intended. You should have said something."

"Skipper, after the fight with Lieutenant Redmond, you told me you did not want to see or hear from me again unless you flew with me."

The skipper was ready to fire another verbal shot at Jon, but he stopped. "I saw the completed flight schedule from yesterday. You only logged 0.8 flight hours on your solo. How come?"

"Well, sir, the early part of the week, I was handling it pretty well. When I was on a destroyer, we stood midwatches ten nights in a row. But on my solo, I got out in the area, did a couple of acrobatic maneuvers, and then I had a real sinking spell. It caught up with me. I came back and landed."

The skipper stood behind his desk and glared at Jon. Then he slumped into his chair, as if he were a blowup CO doll and half his air escaped. He swiveled the chair and muttered profanities.

After a few moments of looking at his back, and after the profanities had run out of steam, Jon asked, "Am I dismissed, Skipper?"

He spun around. "Hell, no. What you did, you painted yourself into a corner. Sometimes the letter of the law—" He shook his head. "Christ almighty! Dismissed my pimply, hairy ass. Get the hell out of here."

Jon was halfway though the outer admin office when the skipper hollered his name.

"Yes, sir."

"We're going to have seven, maybe eight, hours of classroom lectures today. You fall asleep and your ass is grass. Understand?"

Often, "your ass is grass" was followed by "and I'm the lawn mower." But the skipper didn't need to say it, and Zachery didn't need to hear it.

"Yes, sir," he said and got the hell out of there.

*   *   *

The last agenda item of the safety stand-down was an all-officers session in the base theater with the CO at 1530.

Jon sat in the middle of the third row in the center section of seats.

"Word is that Refly stuck you with the midnight-to-0400 duty officer watch every night this week. That right?" Chuck Arbeit asked as he lowered the spring-loaded seat next to Jon.

The brain that made Chuck want to speak was not connected to the one that wanted him to avoid embarrassing blurts. Jon wondered whether he even possessed the latter, but he was the closest thing to a friend he had in VT-7. Tutu was in VT-9, the other squadron on the base.

Jon shrugged.

"Midwatch every night, and you flew every day until today. Did you bust squadron policy?"

Chuck didn't give him much chance to answer. "Payback for the busted nose. Right?"

Jon liked Chuck but wished he'd shut up or find something different to talk about.

"It's a real long story. Changing the subject," Jon said firmly. "How's Marci doing?"

Marci Arbeit had logged six months of pregnancy. Chuck thought he needed to know about having babies and that Jon should be his ID, instructor daddy. *Chuck never embarrassed himself by what he blurted out, just me and everyone else within earshot,* Jon thought. A couple of weeks prior, Jon told him about Teresa's C-sections, hoping to shut him up. It did but also freaked him out. An even more freaked-out Marci called Teresa.

"Be nice to Chuck," Teresa told Jon. "They're just young, just having their first baby."

Chuck punched Jon in the arm. "She's bought bigger bras, twice!"

A guy behind them hooted. "Eat your heart out," Chuck said to the hooter.

Jon shook his head and hoped sitting next to Chuck burned off purgatory time.

"Hey, Zachery." A student pilot named Herb plopped down next to Chuck. "You got called in to the skipper's office twice this morning. What was that about?"

The XO called, "Attention on deck!" so Jon didn't have to answer.

The XO had herded the students into the front rows of the center section of seats. Instructor pilots and squadron officers occupied the section of theater seats to the left.

Everyone stood, generating disorderly sounds of seats springing up, rustling, and feet shuffling. After a moment, orderly silence reigned until the CO clumped up the wooden steps to the stage and across the wood floor to the podium.

"Seats," the CO said.

Eyes down and gripping the sides of the podium, the skipper waited for the getting-seated noises to subside. Then he looked up and glowered, first at the instructor side and then at the student-pilot section. In a protracted silence with a large audience of young men, someone always tried to be funny by making a noise with a fake clearing of the throat or a belch. Jon thought the skipper expected something like that, and then he would pounce. That day, common sense in many and survival instinct in the few Chuck Arbeit–like combined to avoid defiling the sacred quiet.

"I got to work this morning," the skipper said, "expecting to find the squadron humming along, doing its business, pumping student naval aviators through the training pipeline. What I found was something very different. What I found was that my squadron was out of control. So I canceled the flight schedule and devoted the whole day to a review of procedures and policies."

"You know what happened?" Chuck whispered to Jon.

The XO heard him and aimed a glare at Chuck. Jon faced the skipper, but he felt the XO's eyes on him too.

"Last week," the skipper went on, "one of my instructor pilots attempted a practice power-off landing. Squadron policy specifically prohibits practice power-off landings for a very good reason. People who try the maneuver crash most of the time. That instructor lost his wings. He is no longer a pilot."

There was a buzz of voices. The skipper waited. The noise ceased.

"This morning I found out that another one of our instructors assigned a student pilot the midwatch every night this week. Our mission is to push students through the pipeline. If a student is standing the midwatch every night, it is difficult for him to complete syllabus hops without violating the twelve-hour workday policy. In this case, the student found a way to manage his situation so he didn't violate policy, but he was not getting enough rest to fly safely. The instructor who put him in that position did not lose his wings, but he is no longer assigned to the squadron. By Monday he will be off the base."

Jon squirmed in his seat. In a way, he was responsible for getting the flight schedule cancelled and for the safety stand-down. *Does everybody know that?* It would be just like Chuck to blurt something.

The skipper leaned forward and aimed righteous fury at the instructor seating. Weighty silence filled the theater.

"So we've had two instances of unsatisfactory performance by an instructor pilot. The first was a clear violation of safety policy. The second an abuse of a position of authority to put a student in a situation that compromised safety. Both those instructors have been fired. Both those instructors have orders off this base."

The skipper shifted his gaze to the students.

"The real indicator that the squadron is out of control came from you students. This morning, one of the instructors found an eight-foot black snake in his locker."

A buzz of voices started in the student section. Jon willed Chuck to be quiet, but he was talking to Herb.

"Knock it off!" the skipper shouted. "Knock … it … off! I've got one more thing to say to you students, so listen up. It's not easy to fire an instructor, but it's a piece of cake to fire a student. You all would be well advised to think about that."

The skipper allowed his indignant silence to own the theater for a moment.

"Flying is serious business. I will not have stupid pranks like the snake in the locker. This morning and all day today, this squadron has been out of control. As of now, it is back under control."

The skipper's eyes swept the students and the instructors and came back to the students.

"Back," he said and stabbed the top of the podium with a finger. *Thump.* "Under." *Thump.* "Control." *Thump.* "You do not want to be the first one who makes me think otherwise. Safety policy is not arbitrary, not just for some. It is for the XO and me, as well as for each and every instructor and each and every student."

The skipper nodded to the XO, who called the squadron to attention.

As the skipper strode out, Jon thought about the second time he'd been summoned to the CO's office that day.

It was 0900. Zachery stood at attention in front of the skipper's desk.

The skipper wanted to know if Jon put an eight-foot-long black snake in Red Redmond's locker.

"No, sir," Jon said.

"Do you know who did?"

"No, sir."

"What do you know about that snake?"

"Skipper, I don't know anything about it."

Jon told the truth. He didn't know anything about the snake. He had an idea, but he wasn't about to lob his speculation in front of his commanding officer.

The CO stood behind his desk. He looked like he was moving heavy stuff around inside his head.

"So," the skipper said, "the snake? You weren't getting even with Refly?"

Jon shook his head. "I don't know anything about it, sir."

"Get the hell out of here, Zachery!"

It was 0902. The meeting seemed longer than two minutes.

As the skipper marched up the aisle at the end of the workday, it occurred to Jon that the CO might be under the gun. His instructor pilots had broken rules. If he couldn't control his instructors, his leadership would be questioned. His boss wouldn't know about the snake probably. He would know about the power-off landing crash. And he would know the skipper fired Refly.

Jon entered the lobby of the theater and saw the XO gesture, "Come here." Jon followed him out to the parking lot, where the CO stood by his car.

The skipper waggled his finger in front of Jon's face. "I do not want any more grief from you. I don't even care if it's not your fault. But every time something goes wrong, you're in the middle of it. Just one more thing and you're history." He glared at Jon for a couple of seconds, and for the third time that day, he said, "Now get the hell out of here."

31

The CO had canned Refly, but it didn't improve Jon's position. He was hanging on but barely.

Tutu and many of the other students moved confidently through the program with never a doubt that they'd finish. Things occasionally popped up and doomed even the confident ones. A fluke medical issue always lurked in the background. Bad luck nailed some.

A portion of the student pilots had to work harder than others. Last were the hangers-on. A poster with a kitten dangling from a rope by a single claw hung on the locker-room wall, kind of a patron saint for the hangers-on to pray to. A student-pilot's face told where he fit: confident, a work-harder-than-others type, or a hanger-on.

Jon thought about the poster as he joined the line of cars exiting the theater parking lot. The poster held out two options to a viewer: determination and motivation, or amplification of despair over inevitable failure that niggled in the belly.

At times Jon thought that trying to understand the complexities, the contradictions, and the absurdities of life made his head hurt. The cure for those headaches was to find some enduring simplicity, a chunk of bedrock to hang on to.

When he had been in boot camp, a petty officer had given a lecture to Jon's company.

"You are in the naval service," the PO said. "It is called *service* for a very good reason. You are here to serve. How do you serve? It's simple."

The PO held up his right hand in a fist and extended the index finger. "God." He extended the second finger. "Country." Successive fingers brought "Navy, family." The thumb represented "Self."

If Navy life ever got that simple, it sure didn't stay that way long. Jon could never accept that Teresa would be number four on any list like that.

Teresa. The lecture she and the other wives received about not worrying their student-pilot husbands—maybe it was time he did something like that for her. She worried about him flying. He decided she didn't need to worry about the fact that he was hanging on by a kitten claw as he pulled under the carport.

Jon walked into the mudroom as Teresa pulled a casserole from the oven. After she placed the dish on the stove top, Jon turned her around and kissed her.

Teresa had an oven mitt on one hand, a hot pad in the other, and her left eyebrow levitated. "What's the matter?" she asked.

"Nothing. Why are you asking that?"

The phone rang. Teresa pulled off the oven mitt, answered the phone, listened a minute, and then frowned. "Excuse me! I don't care who you are. If you want to talk to anyone in my house, you will call back after I hang up. And you *will* have courtesy and a civil tongue in your mouth." Then her voice got all nice and pleasant. "Otherwise, I will just hang up again. Good day, sir." *Click.*

"Who was that?" Jon asked.

Teresa was staring at the phone, and she held up a finger. It rang again.

"Zachery residence. This is Teresa. How may I help you?" Pause. "Why certainly, XO. Just a moment, please. He just came in the door."

She held the phone away from her mouth. "Jon, the exec from VT-7 would like a word with you, please."

Pleased with herself, she was, Jon thought.

"Lieutenant Junior Grade Zachery, sir."

"Zach—Mr. Zachery. Skipper's office. Right away. Please."

"Sir, it's a forty-five-minute drive back out to the airfield. Just so you know, sir."

"Speed limit." The XO's voice strained at the leash he had on it. "Quick as you can. Please."

Something was strange. The XO didn't use verbs.

There could be only one reason to call Jon back to the base on Friday afternoon. He was going to be booted out of flight training. The action word wasn't missing from that thought.

"What is it, Jon?"

"I think they're going to boot me out." He stopped talking and shook his head.

"Wait right here."

"XO said I should get out there right now."

"He'll wait one extra minute," Teresa said and walked back to their bedroom.

She returned with her rosary in her hand.

"You take the first bead on this side, and I've got the first one on this side. We're going to say one Hail Mary. When you come back, no matter what happens, we'll finish the rosary. I'll go around my side, and you go around the other till we meet in the middle."

Jon started to say he should get moving, but Teresa stopped him.

"Sometimes you tell me that you and the Navy married me. Other times you act like you want to protect me from Navy life. We are in this together. We face things together, and we trust in God."

"Hail Mary," she started, and Jon entered the prayer too.

Four minutes later, Jon backed out onto Fortieth Street and pointed the car toward the base.

Teresa was not number four on his priority list. "No sir, ma'am," he said aloud.

As he drove, he thought about what he might do. Clearly, he was going to be booted out of flight training. After they kicked him out, he would still have five years to serve: Swift Boats and the riverboats, the PBRs, in Vietnam. If he couldn't fly, he'd like to go to the boats, but they were selective. A lot of people volunteered for them. They probably wouldn't want a flight-training reject.

It would be 1973 before his obligated service was up. He'd have fourteen years in by then. Not that he'd stay for twenty, or that the Navy would even let him. Maybe he could get back to destroyers, and maybe he wouldn't get seasick. Maybe he had outgrown that and his Two Buckets nickname. Before Captain Peacock showed up, the bridge of a destroyer had been a great place to be. Not like the cockpit of an airplane, but a very solid second place. Probably, though, they wouldn't even let him fill out a dream sheet. The Bureau of Personnel would probably send him to some no-load job in some godforsaken place. Welfare and recreation officer at Adak, Alaska, in the Aleutians. Everybody joked about being sent to a job like that.

But what happened? he wondered. *All I did was drive home.*

At 1813 on Friday afternoon, there were plenty of student parking places close to the hangar. Jon hustled to the CO's office on the second deck.

The CO was at his desk when Jon entered the admin area.

"Grab the XO, Mr. Zachery, and then come in," he said.

The XO slouched into a chair. The CO pointed to another chair.

"You want me to sit down, sir?"

"Yeah, I want you to sit."

Jon had expected a quick reaming and a "Get the hell out of here forever."

The skipper eyed Jon. He had the elbow of his right arm on his desk. He held up his index finger. "According to the XO, Mrs. Zachery is a heck of a fine woman." He held up a second finger. "It's a good thing it's a forty-five-minute drive to get here from town."

The CO sat back in his swivel chair and rubbed his hand across his forehead; then he rocked forward again. "XO and I talked for most of the time it took you to get here. He told me about speaking with Mrs. Zachery. There's a right way and a wrong way to call someone's home. I think that was her message to the XO. It made me think. What I've been doing is, I've been too worried about how things make me look to my bosses instead of just getting the job done the best way I know how."

The CO held up a hand with finger and thumb just barely not touching. "I was that close to just shit-canning you, based on a couple of things, but mostly because I just don't need extra grief right now. But we talked about you, XO and I. We got your grade sheets out, and I talked to all the instructors you flew with—not Refly, of course." He paused for a second before he went on. "Everybody says you have the makings of a good pilot."

In Jon's mind, a picture of the CO's finger and thumb almost touching gave way to an image of Adak, Alaska, derived from a movie. During one rainy afternoon when they couldn't fly during primary flight training at Saufley Field, the students had watched a black-and-white movie of flight operations at Adak during World War II. A good part of the hour-long flick comprised shots of takeoffs and landings in absolutely abysmal weather conditions.

"Monday," the CO said and held up an index finger, "you start the precision acrobatics phase. XO will fly one of those hops with you, and I'll fly another."

"Mouth, Zachery," the XO said. "Baby robin."

It took Jon a moment to figure out what he'd said. "Sorry, XO. I was—I was thinking about Adak actually."

"Ha" came from the skipper as he held up two fingers. "Second thing. A few minutes before the XO called you, I had a final session with Refly. The reason I called you out here, someone put a timber rattlesnake in Red Redmond's car. It was in a burlap sack, so it only scared him when the rattles started after Red got the car moving. Red got some scrapes and scratches from bailing out of his moving car."

"And then?" the XO asked Jon.

It was probably in his childhood that the XO was mistreated by a verb, Jon thought.

But he had just enough sense to know that he was feeling a little too exuberant, coming back from the brink of extinction of Jon Zachery, fledgling naval aviator. Wiseacre comments were bouncing on the tip of his tongue like a diver on a springboard, looking to execute a quadruple twisting octaflugeron, but he swallowed them and shook his head. "Don't know, sir."

"Red's car plowed into the back of my Thunderbird," the CO said.

The XO smirked. "Mouth. Baby robin."

"If I ask you to get the snakes stopped, could you do it?"

"I might be able to, Skipper, and, uh, about your car—"

"Insurance will cover it. Stop the snakes. Now get the hell out of here."

Before Jon got to the door leading out of admin, the CO called, "Oh, Mr. Zachery."

"Yes, sir?"

"Have a nice weekend, and please pass my respects to Mrs. Zachery."

At his car, Jon turned the key in the door, and then he stopped. He was seeing the CO's thumb and finger doing "This close." It dawned on him. If Teresa hadn't hung up on the XO, he'd be going to Adak. And he'd go alone. The Navy didn't send dependents to that godforsaken island.

* * *

At 1908, Jon blew in the door. Teresa was sitting at the kitchen table, reading. He threw his arms around her and kissed her hard, dislodging his front teeth.

He got his teeth back in place. "The CO and XO said you are a fine hunk of woman."

"What?" Teresa's face was trying to smile and frown at the same time.

"They're right, of course. I seem to recall telling you the same thing a time or two."

He kissed her again.

Jon called Melody's house and asked for Greg.

"I'd appreciate it if you'd knock off the snakes. Will you do that, please?"

"What makes you think it was me, Buckets?"

"Come on, Tutu."

It was quiet for a long moment. "Okay."

"Thanks."

"No problem, Buckets. What are friends for?"

"Did you get those Refly retribution reptiles by yourself?"

"Melody's cousin, Carl Castle, contributed."

"Melody has a cousin Carl Castle?"

"No. Actually his name is Jake, but you didn't think I was going to let you out-alliterate me, did you?"

"I should have known better. It won't happen again, and for supper on Sunday, no snake steaks." Jon hung up.

That night they finished their rosary the Teresa way.

32

It was 10:45 p.m. Overcast and a chill moist wind sliced through her thin jacket. Clarissa walked beside Billy, with plenty of distance between them. She was on the street side. More and more she felt like she had to protect him, like he was her little sister. Parked cars lined the street, and beyond those, cars and taxis and vans whizzed by.

Up ahead of them, maybe ten yards, Clarissa saw two long legs ending in work boots extended over half the sidewalk. The legs' upper torso was hidden in the shadow of a doorway. A hand wrapped around something in a brown paper bag was also visible. Billy stopped.

Clarissa grabbed Billy's arm and pulled him forward. The man never stirred when they hurried past his feet.

"I don't understand you, Clarissa. You say you don't want to go back to Meridian this summer because the first time scared you to death. You're braver than I am, which may not be saying much. What I did, I took a white boy with me into my own church. They were going to be mad at me, but they weren't going to hurt me. You went into a white church, sat through the service, and came out after just like we planned it. You were so cool. I was amazed."

Clarissa didn't say anything. "Well, then," Billy said, "what did you think of the meeting?"

"I was surprised to hear about so many towns in Illinois and Indiana where coloreds 're treated just as badly as they are in Mississippi."

"See, that's why we have to do something. We have to continue pushing Dr. King's dream. Otherwise it'll die and things'll never get better."

"At least they identified the assassin and tracked him to Atlanta."

"I don't know whether to believe any of it. At first it was a guy named Galt, now supposedly James Earl Ray. Catchy name, isn't it? Sounds made up to me. If they actually catch someone and put him in the electric chair, maybe I'll believe the government was really interested in catching the murderer."

"So all of you at the meeting are going to do something like we did at the end of March. And you have churches in eight towns picked out." Clarissa shook her head.

"People who go to church already have God in their hearts. We just have to remind them He's there."

"In March, in Meridian, only one person in that whole crowded church had God in her heart, and that was the woman who sat with me. Her husband just went along with her. You weren't in that church. You didn't feel the hate, and, Billy, I don't want you to feel it. Don't go back down there."

"I have to go, Clarissa. And I'd really like you to come too. Next time, you, me, and Albert will go in and sit together."

"I went with you to the meeting," she said as wind gusts pressed their slacks against their legs and swirled papers in the air, "but I'm not going back to Mississippi."

Clarissa had her hands in the jacket pockets, and she hunched into the wind. She could tell Billy was thinking of putting his arm around her. *Don't you dare.* She gritted her teeth, concentrating on telepathizing a strong message to him.

"Here we are," Billy said. "Want me to walk you up?"

"I make it up that flight of stairs by myself several times each day. And, Billy, I skipped a Bobby Kennedy rally to go with you tonight. I should have gone to that meeting. That's where we're going to change things. Good night."

33

Jon touched a match to the charcoal. Soon the leaves of the towering oak above him danced in the rising heat. He stepped back, in the interest of preserving arm hair and eyebrows.

Gazing into the flames, he thought about his expectations of Meridian and how it had actually turned out.

Welcome Wagon lady: no welcome there.

They'd sat with Clarissa. The white pickup welcomed them.

He'd applied for aviation out of a sense of duty, of patriotism. Refly trashed that.

Where would I be now, if Teresa hadn't pulled my bacon out of the fire?

"Napalm?" Greg Haywood asked.

Jon hadn't heard his car arrive. "Wasn't I supposed to use the whole can of lighter fluid?"

"Actually, Jon, a can that size, I think it's supposed to last the summer."

"So, you are counseling me about moderation?"

"That's me." He thumped his chest. "The voice, yea verily, a model of moderation."

Jon looked up at the tree, just to make sure he hadn't set it afire. The tree was okay mostly. Next time though, he'd use less lighter fluid.

"Mr. Model of Moderation, care if I say something about the snakes?"

Tutu shrugged.

"I appreciate what you were trying to do, but you know, this wasn't like on *Manfred*, with Commander Peacock. On the ship, it was the whole wardroom that was threatened. Here it was just me. That's different."

"Bull." Greg glanced around behind them at the open kitchen window. Teresa and Melody were in there. He dropped his voice to a whisper. "Refly would have railroaded you out of flight training. Everybody knew he wasn't going to quit until he did you in. I gave the Navy time to straighten Refly out. It didn't happen."

"But it did. Our skipper found out what he was doing Friday morning."

"A day late."

"The rattlesnake was after he was fired."

"I didn't know that at the time. Besides, after going to all the trouble of getting those snakes, I didn't want to waste one." Greg's face lit up. "I set that up pretty good, didn't I? Black snake first, then the rattler in his car. Genius, eh?"

Jon tried not to smile. "Yeah, genius, but I don't think you needed to do that, with either of the snakes, I mean. You didn't even know him."

"I knew what he was doing to you though. Word gets around. Even in VT-9 we knew. Your squadron acted like it didn't know. That was enough to make it my fight."

*   *   *

Jon and Teresa placed their rosaries on their bedside tables.

"I'm worried about Greg," she said.

"Tutu. Why are you worried about him?" Jon asked.

"Melody is going to break his heart."

Teresa surprised Jon often with her observations of things he never saw. He thought dinner with Tutu and Melody had been a pleasant affair.

"Break his heart? What do you mean?"

"Melody told me she doesn't want to leave Meridian. The way she said it, I think that's more important to her than Greg."

Jon found Teresa's hand under the sheets.

"You know what Greg is doing?" Teresa asked.

"Tell me."

"He wants both Melody and you in his life, and that's a problem for Melody. She's okay with being in our house, but she doesn't want any of her friends or acquaintances to see her with us. We're the people who sat with the colored girl in church."

Teresa was right. It seemed so clear, after she pointed it out.

"He's twitterpated over Melody, alright." Twitterpated, *Bambi* movie speak for horny.

"Twitterpated," Teresa affirmed. "We're going to have to give them some room, stop having them over for dinner for a while."

Jon didn't want to think about backing away from Tutu. He had been there beside them through everything that had happened since their first Monday in Meridian. Backing away from Melody would be okay. With Tutu or Teresa present, she was fine, but he wound up alone with her a couple of times. He could never think of a thing to say. It had been that way that evening. Teresa and Tutu had put the babies to bed while Melody and Jon did the dishes. The atmosphere in the kitchen had been palpably uncomfortable, and it made Jon sweat.

"I don't know what he sees in her."

"Melody is a wonderful person," Teresa said. "She has something she is trying to sort out right now. She has one foot in the past and one in the present. She knows she needs both feet on one side of the line or the other, but she can't bear to step out of either."

"Now I'm worried for him too."

"That's why, from now on, we're praying our nightly rosary for the two of them."

"For how long?"

"As long as it needs to be."

They lay side by side, and the silence felt like an extra sheet to Jon.

"Teresa," he said as she said, "Jon."

"You first." Teresa straightened her nightgown and pulled up the sheet.

"Should we try again to get you some help with the housework? I worry about you. I still think you haven't totally gotten over your second C-section."

"I don't want to get into that again. Talking to Melody, the good ones are committed to local families. She also said that the good ones would be reluctant to work for a Navy family that would only be here for a couple of months. I'm doing okay. I'm more worried about you. You don't get enough rest."

"Sleep is—"

"It is not overrated, Jon Zachery." She rolled onto her side. "No matter what load you have to carry, you just stick out your chin and keep on going. That, that Refly guy, when he stuck you with the midwatches, you didn't say anything to anybody at the squadron. You just absorbed what he did to you and flew, and all while you were trying to watch out for me too. And it did catch up with you. You got tired on your solo flight and came back early. You have to promise me you won't box yourself into a corner like that again. Promise?"

"There's another corner I want to talk about."

"Don't you go and try to change the subject, Jon Zachery! Now you promise me you'll take care of yourself. Promise you'll get enough rest." She punched him in the shoulder. "I mean it!"

"Alright, Teresa. I promise." He rolled onto his side to face her. "Now can I talk about the other corner?"

"About me getting pregnant again?"

They had talked about the subject a number of times.

"The church's position on birth control is crystal clear," Teresa always said. "There is no point in talking to a priest about it only to have him tell us what we already know."

Teresa's parents were another matter. After Jennifer was born, Jon had told the Velmers about Teresa's ordeal. She had been in hard labor all night, but there were difficulties with the birth. Jon was called and told she was scheduled for an emergency C-section.

He'd raced to the hospital and found her on her side on a gurney in a hallway. She was moaning and sweaty, and her contractions seemed to be tearing her insides apart. Then, later, when the nurse wheeled Jennifer out of the operating room, Jon thought Teresa had died and that he would have to raise his daughter by himself. He told the Velmers almost all of it.

After Teresa's ordeal with Jennifer, the Velmers were convinced that it was stupid for him to get her pregnant a second time. Even a St. Ambrose hick should be able to see his lust endangered their daughter's life. Six weeks after Jennifer was born, Mr. Velmer spoke to Jon on the phone. The conversation was pretty much one-sided. The language was obtuse and indirect, but Jon knew that Mr. Velmer thought Jon should sleep in a separate bedroom.

After she got pregnant the second time, Jon felt as if he had killed her.

Teresa laughed at him for worrying. Her parents hadn't laughed though. Teresa's mother had always been frosty with Jon. Teresa had married beneath herself. Teresa's mother never said it, not that Jon heard, but she shouted it clearly with her thoughts.

Jon had gotten along fairly well with Mr. Velmer, but the second pregnancy soured that relationship too, until Edgar Jon was born. A male grandchild thawed things with Mr. Velmer.

"See?" Teresa said. "I told you they'd get over it."

"Not your mother," Jon said.

Teresa laughed. "That's just Mother."

But Jon couldn't stop worrying about it, even if Teresa could.

Chuck Arbeit went to church in town, and he'd convinced Jon to give the in-town church another chance. The priest who had the service the morning Clarissa Johnson showed up was the associate pastor. According to Chuck, they'd like the pastor himself.

Teresa told Jon, "God will take care of us. He won't give us anything we can't handle."

Jon's faith was different. God was up there, no disagreement on that point, but ever since He'd kicked Adam's fig-leafed-over butt out of the garden, He expected people to take care of a whole bunch of things themselves.

It wasn't just her parents. Teresa's doctor made it clear that another baby would endanger her life. *But sleep in a separate bedroom!*

He had to try something.

"Teresa, Chuck said we'd like the pastor, Father Allbright."

Teresa said, "Jon."

Maybe he could convince her to go with him to see Father Allbright some other time.

34

Harry saw the red neon "Elmer's" sign on the roof the two-story, which was set back off the pavement a ways. "On the right, 'Manda Sue," Harry said.

Harry loved the purring grumble the DeSoto made coasting down from road speed. Even slowing, it was one hell of a car.

Amanda Sue turned off the pavement and immediately hit a hole, which bounced Harry off the seat. He hit his head on the roof and bit his tongue.

"Jesus, goddamn" started a string of curse words as the jouncing continued and he hit the roof a second time.

"Stop the goddamn car, 'Manda Sue."

She jammed on the brakes, and Harry was thrown against the dash. Anger filled his head with white heat, and he snarled and was about to slap her when dust boiled in the windows. He started coughing and waving his hands in front of his face. Harry held his breath until he put his handkerchief over his nose and mouth.

The dust settled, but he could feel it on his arms and tingling in his hair. He blew his nose and looked over at Amanda Sue. She cringed up against the door. Harry started laughing. Then she sneezed, and he laughed even harder. Finally, the humor evaporated, and Harry blew his nose again.

"See if you can get us parked without killing us or tearing the car apart," Harry said.

Even inching along, the ride was rougher than hell, and Harry shook his head, remembering Crazy.

They'd called him Crazy Goddamn Gilbert, or Crazy Gil. Sometimes just Crazy.

One summer night, fifteen-year-old Gil stopped by fourteen-year-old Harry's house and took him for a ride. Crazy Goddamn had a six-pack under his legs on the floor of his dad's pickup, and he drove them to where a two-lane gravel road crossed the railroad tracks next to the trestle bridge over Cowmire Creek. He stopped the truck on the wrong side of the road just before the tracks.

"What're you doing, Crazy?"

Gil didn't say anything. He pulled a beer from between his legs, used his church key to pop a big and a little hole in the top, took a swig, and handed the beer to Harry.

"Hey, how come I get sloppy seconds?"

He opened another beer, guzzled, and pushed the light switch in to the "parking" position, and from the light of the instrument panel, Harry could see him grin and sat up straight. "Uh, Crazy ..."

"Relax, for Christ's sake, Harry. It's a great night. Look at all the stars up there. A million, a billion, a gazillion, what d'ya think? Maybe there isn't even a number big enough to count 'em all."

He tipped his head back with the can to his lips, and Harry heard a *gulk, gulk* sound from his throat. "And we got beer." He belched. "Listen. Hear the cicadas? That's like the string section of an orchestra. The bullfrog, that's like the bass, and an owl, why, we got woodwinds. A regular symphony orchestra, and only you and me out of the whole world can hear it."

Harry hadn't noticed the night sounds. His ears had to push the grumbling from the engine, which wasn't idling smoothly, into the background to hear the bugs, birds, and frogs out there in the dark. He'd never have considered that noise to be music, especially not something highfalutin like a symphony. But that was Crazy Goddamn Gilbert for you. Harry didn't know how many violins there were in an orchestra—a pot-load though. It certainly was a pot-load of cicadas grinding out their music, as Crazy would have it. *And the frog, and the owl.* Harry smiled. "A person never knows what the guy will come up with next." That's what they said about Gil at the barbershop. Then he heard the train whistle from the right.

"Throw the beer out," Gil said.

"What?"

"Throw the goddamn beer out, Harry. Now, goddamn it. Do it. I don't want beer spilled all over the inside of the truck."

Harry's mouth hung open. Gil grabbed the beer out of Harry's hand and threw it out his window. He took a last swallow of his own and tossed it.

Gil put the truck in low gear and revved the engine. He stared intently past Harry. Harry turned to see what he was looking at.

"Sit back. Sit back, goddamn it! Sit back!"

Harry sat back against the seat. Keeping out of Crazy's way, he turned his head and the blood in his veins stopped moving as his heart idled through a couple of beats. Then his heart really pumped.

Way down the track, where the rails made a ninety-degree turn, a light was bouncing up and down on the trees.

Gil popped the clutch. The pickup jerked forward. He turned the wheel sharply to the right. Harry almost fell against his shoulder.

The truck was on the tracks, headed right for the dancing light. Harry thought the bobbing light was growing larger very quickly, but he couldn't see clearly as they jolted across the ties.

Crazy shifted into second. He grinned. Shifted into third. Screamed loud and shifted to fourth.

Harry felt something let go. He smelled urine, felt the warm on his legs, and felt the truck slow down.

Gil had a determined look on his face as he downshifted, and Harry felt heat from the light of the train on the side of his face. *Jesus, God!* The train was that close. And he was slowing down!

Gil jerked the wheel left, and the pickup jounced hard a couple of times. Harry felt as if he were bouncing between heaven and hell, like a shuttlecock in a celestial/bestial game between angels and devils. Then they stopped.

"Yeeeeeeehah!" Crazy was flying, but Harry was sick. Wind from the passing train rocked the pickup.

Harry opened the door, fell out onto his hands and knees, and puked. His throat felt like he had vomited a log. The puking passed before the train did. Still on his hands and knees, Harry raised his head and watched the dark train cars rip past, and he felt the breath of the train like a series of punches that turned into *phwoof, phwoof, phwoofs* of air as the train passed.

It almost felt as if he were coming back to life. He heard *clickety-clack, clickety-clack*. Towering dark silhouettes of steel and wood boxes hurtled past his eyes. Gravel bit into his palms and knees. He tried to spit the sour stink of beer vomit off his tongue, but the smell of it and urine hung in his nose.

Then it was like total silence reigned on earth, but two sounds came from another planet: *clickety-clack* receding and Crazy Goddamn Gil laughing his ass off.

Harry walked home. It took almost an hour.

The next morning he became Harry Peepee instead of Harry Peeper. By the afternoon he was Little Harry Peepee. For the first time, Harry considered killing someone. The ride down the railroad tracks was forgivable, but the name-calling was not. Before he had decided how to, and two days after he had puked beside the railroad tracks, Crazy rolled his dad's pickup into Cowmire Creek. A broken moonshine jug was in the cab of the truck with Gil's broken and drowned body.

The morning after Crazy Gil died, a boy greeted Harry with his nickname, and a lightning-fast fist to the boy's mouth stopped the name at "Little." Suddenly, Harry became known as a mean SOB. Once you were defined as something that had seemed so desirable, why would you ever want to try to change peoples' minds about who you really were?

Harry'd been a mean SOB until he joined the Army, and then he listened to Barney.

"The Army ain't so bad," Barney said the second week of basic. "You just gotta know the ropes. Stick wit me. We get us in the motor pool and stay the hell away from jungle rot and gettin' shot."

Barney Brick was short for goldbrick. Because he listened to Brick, nobody in the Army ever considered him to be a mean SOB.

But I am one now, he thought as Amanda Sue shut off the engine.

After they entered, Harry pulled Amanda Sue with him, and they stood with their backs against the wall while Harry's eyes tried to adjust to seeing through gloom and cigarette smoke.

At one time, Elmer's had been a two-story home. Elmer still lived above. The bottom floor walls had been ripped out, except the ones cordoning off the kitchen at the right rear of the building. A long bar with stools ran from the edge of the kitchen wall the rest of the length of the building. A pool table with a fluorescent light fixture hung above it occupied the left end of the place, and six round tables filled up the rest of the floor.

Chevy and Ford waited at one and watched them.

Harry nudged Amanda Sue toward their table.

The twins had their eyes on Amanda Sue. Harry's imagination flicked a picture through his brain of Chevy with his tongue hanging out. Amanda Sue was eating it up, even though she loathed Ford and couldn't stand the smell of Chevy. Looked like Dudley Do-Right, she said. She sure liked men to look at her. She sure forgot about being afraid after she made him bite his tongue.

Harry sat on his chair with room between his belly and the table so he could draw his forty-five if he had to. He nodded to Ford and then to Chevy as Amanda Sue sat between him and Chevy.

"Any problems disposing of the baggage the other night?" Harry asked Ford.

"No," Chevy said. "We took care a the business."

Harry looked back at Ford, who nodded toward his brother.

"Okay, Chevy, then," Harry said and slid a slip of paper across the table. "Address of a guy named Greene. Need you and Ford to scout the place. Work out an escape route. Next month, before we do the next church, I want you to take me by the place and show me the escape route you work out."

Ford picked up the paper.

"That all we doing?" Chevy asked. "He's the guy posted the reward about the Jew church. Whyn't we do him like Bollinger?"

Harry shook his head. "Things are a little hot right now. Nigger church, Jew church, and Bollinger. We'll take care a Greene when the time's right. The guys in Jackson'll tell us when."

"Greene needs doin'. He's in Meridian. What the hell we need the Jackson guys tell us when?"

Jesus.

Sam said to keep the twins on a leash, but he didn't want any traceable connection back to Jackson people. Dancing that fine line between keeping peanut-brained Chevy interested but held off enough to satisfy the guys in Jackson, it just pushed things to the limits. Harry took a deep breath, trying to figure out something to say.

"Why the hell can't we go to them Jackson meetings? Then we'd know ever'thing same time as you."

"Let it alone, Chevy," Ford said.

Harry let a smile curl up a side of his mouth, and he nodded his thanks to Ford.

"Nothin' else to talk about now. We'll be goin'," Harry said and stood.

"We scout Greene, his house is close to that Navy Catholic," Chevy said. "Maybe we should pay him a visit."

Harry leaned on the table. "Chevy, look at Ford. Look at him, goddamn it. He keeps his mouth shut and does what he's told. He's helpful. You're mostly a pain in the ass."

35

Chevy cast a quick look at Ford, wishing he hadn't brought up the Navy Catholic. You just never knew when Ford would say something. Chevy didn't want Harry to know he and Ford had run away from that little guy in his underwear. It was bad enough cousin Rafe knew.

"C'mon," Harry said, and Amanda Sue followed him out.

Chevy watched her butt until the door closed on it. Then he chugged his beer.

"C'mon," he said to Ford.

"Shouldn't."

"Gonna."

As they walked out to the pickup, Chevy smiled at Ford's *shouldn't*. Ford always came along.

Chevy drove the pickup, jouncing and bucking through the hard-baked clay parking lot, paying no mind to how rough it was. The pickup took it all in stride. Ten minutes after he bounced onto the blacktop, he turned onto Fortieth Street.

"We should scout the Greene place," Ford said.

"Tomorrow."

Chevy let the truck coast against the engine as he crested the rise just before the Navy Catholic's house. He scooted forward on the seat and pulled the thirty-eight out of his pocket.

"Shouldn't," Ford said.

Chevy grinned as the truck rumbled and grumbled as it coasted and slowed. The Navy Catholic's house was dark. *Maybe we'll make 'em turn a light on,* Chevy thought. He stopped under the streetlight just past the house, set the brake, and got out. He fired at the light, missed, swore, and fired three more times. The light went out, and bulb fragments tinkled on the hood of the pickup.

Chevy got back in the truck, dropped the pistol on the seat, put the truck in gear, and started down the road slowly.

"Navy guy ought to be mindful we ain't forgot him."

Ford didn't say anything. Of course, he often didn't.

"Harry don't need to know. Goddamn him," Chevy said. "Treats us like his dogs, like niggers."

Chevy was quiet for a block. "One thing I say for Harry. He got fine taste in women. Unka Darnell says a person ought to give a fellow his due, even if you don't like him much."

His brother liked Harry—a lot more than he did anyway. "Knows what he's doin'. Figures things," Ford said once.

"'Manda Sue. Uh uh uh uh uh," Chevy said. "The way she ties the tails a her shirt under those boobs a hers. Like that just ain't enough to hold 'em up. I mean, don't it make you want to reach across and say, 'I kin hold those for ya'?"

That made Ford squirm on the seat.

36

A noise woke Jon.

A car with a bad muffler. The pickup! It was in front of the house. A *pop* sounded, and then three more. The light halo around the street-side blinds blinked out.

Jon threw the sheet off, started for the closet to get his shotgun, and then stopped to grab a pair of Bermuda shorts from the chair. He pulled on his tennis shoes, and his shoestrings slap-slap-slapped the floor. He yanked open the closet, grabbed the shotgun off the top shelf, and knocked a full box of shells clattering to the floor.

"Jon!" Teresa yelled, and a wail from Edgar Jon blew apart the night.

Move!

Jon scooped five shells off the floor, stuck two into the double-barrel, tried to stick the other three into a pocket, dropped one, and snapped the gun shut.

Teresa said, "I'm calling the police."

"No," Jon shouted.

He hurried into the living room with the thumb of his right hand ready to cock the left hammer. About to jerk open the front door, he remembered the *pop*.

Shoestrings flapping, he raced through the living room and the kitchen and opened the door onto the carport. He could hear the bad muffler sound of the pickup in the distance, but he couldn't see anything. It was pitch-black out.

The muffler sound was swallowed by distance, and he stood listening to his heart thump.

Back inside, Edgar Jon was quiet.

Jon unloaded the shotgun and propped it against the wall in the hall outside the children's room. Teresa was nursing Edgar Jon, and Jen-Jen was standing beside the rocking chair with a thumb in her mouth and her left hand hanging on to the short sleeve of Teresa's nightgown. Kneeling on one knee, Jon gathered Jennifer into his arms.

"It's okay, Jen-Jen. Daddy was a klutz. Daddy dropped something and woke Edgar Jon. That's all."

Jennifer stepped back from him and took her thumb out of her mouth. "I *scah-oat,*" she said. Then she grabbed Jon around the neck and held on for all she was worth.

Jon patted Jennifer's back as she squeezed his neck. Teresa caressed Edgar Jon's head as he nursed. He met her eyes.

He saw things on her face that they shared: fear and anger that their babies had been frightened awake again. Then he discerned the anger that was aimed solely at him.

He figured he deserved it. The way he'd handled the situation with the pickup—she had every right to think he was too stupid and too clumsy to handle a gun.

Jennifer let go of Jon's neck, leaned back, and looked earnestly into his eyes. "Gaham cacker."

Jon agreed. A graham cracker was in order. A "Sorry" was in order for Teresa, but it was one of those times when "Sorry" would make it worse.

By the time the babies were asleep again, it was 0240. Teresa wanted Jon to come back to bed, but he went out to the carport with the shotgun.

At 0330 he climbed into bed, and despite a number of mosquito bites, which itched something fierce, as soon as his head hit the pillow, he was gone to where it'd have taken dynamite to awaken him.

37

It was better to be lucky than good.

Naval aviators seemed to have a saying for everything. Jon had never believed that one. On the morning he was scheduled for his completion-of-basic-instruments-phase check flight, at least for a time, he became a believer.

Better to be lucky than good. Jon hadn't heard that saying on his destroyer. Aviators used it a lot though. The plane crash short of the runway during his flight with Refly had a different message: if you did something stupid, no amount of luck could save you from catastrophe. As he drove out to the base for his early-morning brief, he resolved to avoid being an idiot in an airplane and not rely on luck.

It was 0442, a pleasant, balmy June Mississippi morning. He drove down the road leading from the administrative area out to the airfield with his arm resting on the open window, and the breeze poured over his skin like warm bathwater. He wasn't really worried about the five o'clock brief for his final flight in basic instruments. Most of the students in his class hated instrument flying, especially the way they did it in training. The instructor pilot flew in the front seat. To simulate flying in clouds, the rear cockpit, the student's seat, had a canvas cover attached with Velcro to the inside of the canopy. It was called flying under the bag. Jon didn't hate the bag. He liked it, though he was sure if any of his fellow students heard him say that, he'd get strange looks.

The bag locked him into a little world all his own.

Under the bag, nothing existed but him and the flight instruments. He liked the challenge of having to manage them all at the same time: altitude, heading, airspeed, vertical speed indicator, the clock, and, of course, the fuel quantity gauge. As you looked at one gauge, the others were all trying to get away from your control.

Before going under the bag in an aircraft, the students trained in flight simulators. The students hated the sims more than the bag. In the sims, it felt like the simulated airplane sat atop the point of a needle, and it took a lot of work to keep it flying level. Often, despite air-conditioning in the room, a student left a sim session drenched in sweat. Flying an actual airplane in a real cloud was easier, a piece of cake.

One of Jon's instructors had told him the main thing about instrument flying was subtlety and finesse. It was holding a fine bone-china teacup with pinky finger sticking out and sipping without slurping. "Finesse, Zachery," he said. "Make smooth, small corrections. You're not trying to kill snakes with the stick."

When he said that, Jon thought the IP was making a reference to what had happened with Refly. But it was an expression the instructors used quite often.

"Killing snakes" meant "you're being spastic with the control stick."

Aviators' speech, Jon thought, *was mostly pithy bodacious exaggeration.*

The basic instrument phase had gone well. Jon smiled, thinking about his instructor and how much he'd learned from him. And he thought about Refly and how close he'd come to being booted out of flight training.

Suddenly, a *whoosh, whoosh, whoosh* sound pulled him from his reverie.

"Holy Mary, Mother of God!" he said out loud.

He was driving on the grassy shoulder of the road and to the right of some Burma Shave–like safety signs. After the last sign, which read,

"Arrive Alive," he pulled back onto the road. The edge of the blacktop blended smoothly with the grassy shoulder, but his heart wasn't beating smoothly, or with the elevated pinky on the teacup level of finesse either. It was hammering, as if trying to bust ribs and smash its way out of his chest.

But at least he was awake. He was wide awake, very wide awake, and lucky, very lucky! He took a deep breath, waiting for his heartbeat to slow down into normal territory.

The last three weeks had gone by quickly, and Jon was moving rapidly through the flight-training syllabus, flying almost every day, occasionally twice. The slowdown Refly had predicted wasn't happening. If the pace kept up, he would finish Meridian in less than the forecasted six months.

The precision acrobatics phase had been practice for basic instruments. In PA, the students were in the front seat, but the emphasis was on flying acrobatic maneuvers with great precision: hit entry parameters precisely, pull on the stick to establish the precise g level prescribed, control turn rate precisely, and complete the maneuver precisely on heading, altitude, and airspeed. Student pilots learned to concentrate on their flight instruments and, at the same time, kept track of what their airplane did relative to the horizon. They practiced loops, barrel roles, wingovers, Immelman turns, and half Cuban eights. Besides teaching the students how to control an airplane in four dimensions—time included—the maneuvers had practical application. Portions of the acrobatic maneuvers were required to deliver bombs or to dogfight with another aircraft.

Jon found PA fun and a nice transition to flying under the bag, where the precision and the elevated pinky were so important. He thought it was a good way to train for flying in instrument conditions. Sometimes it almost seemed as if the Navy knew what it was doing. In BI phase, or basic instruments, they did a lot of the acrobatic maneuvers they had practiced in PA. Only in BI, they did them under the bag.

At work he went through PA and BI. At home, he got up at 0130 every morning and took his shotgun out into the mudroom. Mosquitoes owned the carport, so he moved his white-pickup vigil inside. Teresa wanted him to call the police after the streetlamp had been shot out, but he refused.

He was sure it wouldn't do any good, and he really didn't want to call any attention to himself, or his family, with the police or with the squadron CO.

After he'd flown a PA hop with the skipper, he'd told Jon he had flown a nice hop. "But," he said, "keep your nose clean, and keep your mind on flying."

So he couldn't go to anyone on the base, and he couldn't go to the police in town. The skipper would find out. But after that night when he'd dropped the shotgun shells and convinced Teresa that he was not capable of protecting her and the babies, he was determined to try to get out of the mode of being reactive to the white pickup truck.

The two policemen who responded to the railroad spike in the door had said something about the two men coming after their bar closed at 0200. Both times they'd come, that he was aware of, was around 0200. So Jon got up at 0130 and stayed up until 0250. That week, however, he'd gotten stuck on the early brief every morning. In one way it was great. By 0830, he'd be done debriefing the hop, and if he didn't have a second flight, the day's work would be done. But the week of early mornings had caught up with him, just like it had with Refly and the midwatches.

Then, after arriving at work, completing the briefing, and strapping in to the airplane, the instructor downed the airplane for a bad radio.

Jon figured it was just one of those Fridays when all the airplanes seemed inclined to break to get an extra day of rest in the hangar. Sometimes airplanes had a mind of their own.

With Friday afternoon available, Jon called Teresa and asked her to go with him to see Father Allbright. She agreed, probably because she thought the priest would finally nail the issue down as firmly for him as it was for her. Normally, Jon didn't like to ask for help. Teresa put it this way: "We have a flat and no jack. You'd try to lift the car with your bare hands and have me put the spare on rather than ask someone for help."

She scolded him for trying to do too much on his own with his shotgun watches. That got him to thinking about their other problem, how his lust endangered her life.

Mutually exclusive issues hovered over their bed. He loved her more than his life, and the expression of that love inexorably, inevitably, led to passion. His passion threatened her life. Birth control was wrong.

He couldn't resolve the impasse, so he'd ask for help. Maybe Chuck was right about Father Allbright. Maybe there was a way to love and live with Teresa that didn't make him feel like he was playing bedroom Russian roulette with her life.

38

Clarissa gave up on sleeping and pressed the button that illuminated the dial on her watch. Quarter till five. The *We won, we won!* in her head refused to shut up, but it was okay, better than okay. Actually, it was *hal-ee-loooo-eee-yah* glorious. Bobby won, but she had helped. She helped Bobby Kennedy win.

She sat up and pushed out of the sleeping bag. The van would take her back to Chicago that afternoon. She could sleep then.

From the night-light in the hallway, she could make out the lumps that defined the sources of the snores, whistles, and a *phwoo*. She was going to have to step over people to get out to the patio, and she had to get outside. Her euphoria could blow the roof off, could fill space and eternity from the earth to the stars.

Sliding the door open slowly and quietly, she stepped out onto the patio, and the concrete chilled her bare feet, a matter of passing interest. Stars, zillions in the slice of sky she could see between the edge of the eave and the towering weeping willow she saw only as star-blotting blackness. She took in a deep breath and felt as if she were breathing twinkles of starlight along with cool clean air.

Bobby had to win the Nebraska primary. He had to or the campaign might end. It would be just a fluke that he had made it as far as he did. For a week, she had phoned, rung doorbells, carried signs, attended rallies, and passed out leaflets. Averaging two hours of sleep a night and living on soda, pizza, and doughnuts blew her conditioning program to bits. But Bobby won, and if her contribution was pimples and pounds, it was a small price to pay. Bobby won, and it felt like he was separated from the White House by only a matter of time. Everything else was a done deal.

The sliding door opened and then closed behind her, and Clarissa couldn't see who had come out until the person moved out from the shadow of the house.

Anita Freeman, college freshman and hostess to eight girls from Wisconsin and Illinois, hugged Clarissa. "I was stupid to think I was going to be able to sleep."

"I was exhausted," Clarissa said, "until my head hit the pillow. I gave it forty-five minutes. Your mom and dad ever come home?"

"No. They wanted Bobby to win so bad, they may celebrate through today and all night again."

"Would you like something to drink? A soda?"

"No soda, and nothing, thanks."

"Let's sit." Anita led the way to two of the four wooden lawn chairs.

"I am so glad I had this experience. And I couldn't have afforded to come if your parents hadn't allowed us to stay with you."

"You all worked hard. Dad was impressed. He said, 'If I ever run for office, I'm going to have college girls run my campaign.'"

"Your parents did their part. It just feels so wonderful to have worked so hard on something so very important and have it work out."

"I heard that you went down to Mississippi this spring and sat in on a church service. Was it as awful as I've heard?"

"It was the most awful, scariest thing. I thought I would die down there. The worst part of it was that I didn't feel like I made a difference at all by scaring myself so. If I went back, it would be just the same, or worse. President Bobby Kennedy will change things down there. Clarissa Johnson couldn't do a single solitary useful thing."

39

Jon's eyes opened Saturday morning. It was light outside. He decided to smile.

Feeling as if he could move a mountain, he raised his arms above his head, stretched, and arched his back until his muscles came close to pulling something apart. After he let out a held breath, he let go of everything, including the strength to move a mountain. Getting out of bed might be too hard, he thought, and considered staying right there for another week or so.

Teresa had let him sleep in. He sighed. It was time to get up and allow her to grab a piece of Saturday morning to enjoy.

Jon found them in the kitchen. Edgar Jon was in his infant seat on the table. Teresa maneuvered Gerber's on a tiny rubber-coated spoon into his open mouth.

Jon kissed Teresa on the cheek.

"Sleeping Beauty has whiskers," she observed.

Jennifer was in her high chair. "Good morning, princess," Jon said.

"Gaham cacker," Jennifer said and held up the fragment that remained, but she didn't hold it up for very long, as if it occurred to her that show-and-tell could be mistaken for an offer to share.

Jon got a mug of coffee and took over with Edgar Jon. Teresa headed for the bathroom.

Jon looked out the window to the backyard. The sky was blue, with no clouds visible. Birds tweeted happy songs. Jon wrinkled his nose at Edgar Jon. He knew what his next job would be, as soon as the baby food jar was empty.

Even the impending dirty-diaper change felt like something proper, maybe, to have in the house that morning. Maybe because it was a problem for which a real solution existed.

That afternoon, he and Teresa had an appointment to see Father Allbright at the church in town. Jon had wanted to visit a priest about birth control. Teresa didn't. Finally she'd agreed to go with him. But then, with the visit looming, disquieting concern elbowed its way into his brain. Talking about sex with a priest no longer sounded like a good idea.

Edgar Jon fussed and waved his arms.

"Sorry, little man, I know you're doing all the work down there. You have your mouth open, and all I have to do is shovel it in."

As he fed the baby, he thought about discussing the white pickup with Tutu. He really didn't want to put his personal problem on him. Since the white pickup came to spike the sign on the front door, it had not returned, as far as he knew, until the streetlight was shot out. Shooting out the streetlight wasn't as big a deal as the spiking. The white pickup was probably just trying to keep them scared, trying to make sure they knew that it was still out there, reminding them to not do anything else to support civil rights efforts. Probably.

He'd left Tutu alone, as Teresa suggested, but talking to him at work about the white pickup, to see if Tutu agreed with his assessment—there was nothing wrong with that.

* * *

It was 1500 on Saturday afternoon. The rectory housekeeper led Jon and Teresa to the pastor's office.

When Chuck Arbeit told Jon that he would like Father Allbright, Jon had been skeptical.

"Father Allbright's different. Just go and listen to one of his sermons. You'll see," Chuck had said.

The previous Sunday, he and Teresa had gone back to the church in town. Watchful for any hint of animosity, Jon scanned the faces of ushers, people filing in, and those in the pew they entered. He saw nothing but pleasant, polite little smiles when he made unavoidable eye contact. Jon thought the Welcome-Wagon-lady usher recognized them, but he smiled and nodded, the same way he greeted all those entering the church. It wasn't crowded that Sunday, so the ushers remained in back and the congregants found their own seats.

Jon hadn't expected to be warmly welcomed. He expected to find some vestige of the hostility they felt the last time. Could the congregation have forgotten who they were and what they'd done? Had they been forgiven? Whatever the reasoning behind the treatment, Jon felt relieved.

He told Teresa before they left for church, "If they act like they don't want us there, we'll leave. We can make noon Mass on the base."

The reception had been passively pleasant and normal, and Chuck had been right about Father Allbright's sermon. It wasn't the my-soul-is-holier-than-yours-so-you-should-pay-attention kind, and it wasn't simple-minded grade-school catechism either. It stirred thought. To Jon, Father Allbright did a good job of bringing God in heaven down to earth, where people had mud between their toes and practical problems. Jon was impressed with the homily and glad they gave the church a second chance.

They did not give the parish babysitting service another chance, however. Teresa discovered a high school senior girl named Jackie two houses down the street from them. Jackie had watched Jennifer and Edgar Jon the previous Sunday, and she had them that Saturday afternoon too.

Father Allbright rose, shook hands with Teresa and Jon, and indicated two dark leather-covered chairs.

He was about fifty, six feet tall, narrow shouldered, with a small potbelly. Without his vestment armor, his body appeared to be soft. His face, however, was hard angles: pointy chin, thin sharp nose, and high flat forehead. His black hair was thin on top, thick on the sides.

Chuck Arbeit had said that neither of the priests had mentioned the colored girl who'd crashed the services the last Sunday in March. Jon wondered if the priest would mention Clarissa. After the obvious strong reaction he and Teresa felt, ignoring it seemed strange. Could the man who delivered the sermon just a week ago be like the rest of the white people in town and look at something but choose not to see it?

"How may I help you?" Father asked. He sat with his hands folded on his desk. The air in the gloomy room felt and smelled as though it had been stuck inside too long.

Jon began to sweat, and he knew he should not be there. He should not have brought Teresa. But it was too late for that.

"Father, we—I want to ask you about birth control. Is there anything we can do besides abstinence and rhythm?"

Father regarded his hands on his leather blotter for a moment. When he raised his head, his eyes stared through Jon.

"Y'all are in," it sounded like a single word, like *yawlerin*, "the Navy. You move around, and you ask this question everyplace you go."

Jon sat forward in his chair, and his embarrassment, his conviction he was wrong to come, wrong to bring Teresa, and the shame that had built in his gut as soon as he opened his mouth about lust to a man of God—all of that blew up in a spike of anger.

"Was that a question, Father?"

He felt Teresa grab his hand and squeeze it. The look on her face said, "Don't say anything else. Please?"

"My concern is with the salvation of your immortal souls." Father Allbright paused. "First I need to know if you are now engaging in immoral birth control."

Jon stood and took Teresa's hand and pulled until she got to her feet. "I'm sorry, Teresa. I'm sorry I brought you here." He said to Father Allbright, "And I'm sorry I wasted your time. We can let ourselves out."

"Sit back down," Father Allbright demanded. "You need to answer the question."

"No, Father," Jon said. "I am not answering your question, and I am not sitting down."

Out in the parking lot, Jon went to the passenger side of the car, as he always did, to hold the door, but Teresa wouldn't let him help her into the car. He didn't know how many of God's sins he had committed, but he knew he had committed a boatload of Teresa's.

Jon got behind the wheel and sat there. What he really had wanted from the session was for the priest to say that practicing rhythm was okay. Teresa didn't want to talk about rhythm or any other methodology. He looked at her. She stared straight ahead. He thought, *She probably hoped the priest would convince me once and for all to quit poking at a subject when the answer was crystal clear.*

"I want to go home," she said.

After a frosty ride back to Fortieth Street, Teresa dismissed the babysitter. Jon sat in the car, and in the rearview mirror he watched Jackie walk down the street toward her house.

He thought about how he'd been ripping through life. Stuff was happening over here, and he handled it. Another thing happened over there, and he handled it. His family, the Navy, flying, Meridian—he handled it all. Or maybe it only seemed like he handled it. Maybe it all went so fast he couldn't tell if he handled it, or *it* handled him. Then he'd run smack into Father Allbright.

His world had been spinning fast, and then the brakes were jammed on and pieces flew off the world and hurtled into the blackness of outer space. He had the feeling he wouldn't ever get some of those pieces back.

After a few minutes, he went in, put on old jeans, and got his ax. There was a stump in the backyard. Turning the oak stump into toothpicks wasn't exactly therapeutic. It didn't cure anything, but being out there with the stump was better than being in the house.

That night Jon slept on the couch.

Great plan to avoid sleeping in separate bedrooms, Zachery, which led to several other thoughts of the nonsleep-conducive sort.

40

Jon wind-sprinted up to the edge of the hangar and stood with his hands on his knees, breathing hard near the sidewalk-wide awning in front of the ten reserved parking spots so the VT-7 and VT-9 heavies could walk to the hangar dry, in case it rained. It wasn't raining. A few puffy, cotton-ball clouds hung to the east. Not a breath of cooling breeze stirred. Standing still, the sun felt like hands of heat, resting on his shoulders.

On the ramp, four planes pulled out of their parking spots and filed toward the takeoff end of the runway. Jon walked to the edge of the parking lot to watch them. Airplane number one turned right, and the others followed like baby ducks in a row. Four planes meant a formation flight. Formation phase was the last part of training at Meridian.

Above, the sky was the blue that always cheered Teresa.

Teresa. The sofa. Teresa wasn't keeping him on the sofa. He kept himself there.

He had walked out on Father Allbright. Even if the priest was wrong in what he thought and said, he was a priest. You did not walk out on a priest. Teresa had not totally forgiven him, but she forgave him more than he forgave himself.

Getting back in bed with her with the Father Allbright issue unresolved was not a good idea. So he whacked on the "take that" stump in the afternoons and slept on the sofa at night.

On the runway, number one ran his engine up and started to roll. Five seconds later number two followed. Automatically, emergency procedures in case the plane in front of you lost power popped into Jon's mind. Number three started moving. Then four. The engines made a noise like tearing a never-ending sheet of butcher paper near a microphone.

Lucky stiffs, Jon thought.

The day before, he had completed his basic-instrument phase check ride. On the grade sheet there were a couple of above averages, which was pretty good for a check ride.

The next phase was navigation by radio instruments, RNav, basically flying airways using TACAN or automatic direction finder (ADF) to steer by. A radio station broadcasted a signal, and in the cockpit, the ADF needle pointed at the station. The stations were located on navigation charts. TACAN was like an ADF, but in addition to a needle pointing at the ground radio station, TACAN included a mileage readout.

RNav lectures and sim flights were scheduled for Tuesday, Wednesday, and Thursday. On Friday, he would begin the RNav flights. RNav was a short phase, only six hops. Before he went to run, he found out he was scheduled for a cross-country over the weekend to knock out all six.

It was a RO2N. On some airways navigation flights, one flew to a remote base, refueled, and returned the same day. On others, one remained overnight. A one-night stay was an RON, two nights an RO2N.

After the RO2N, the last leg of the cross-country would be the flight-training phase completion check flight. RNav seemed pretty easy compared to the precision acrobatics and basic instrument phases. Mostly, RNav was flying straight and level and trying to measure the effects of crosswind. If one could figure that out, one could compensate and keep the TACAN or ADF needle where it was supposed to be.

The hardest part was the approaches. TACAN and ADF approaches were sometimes complicated with simultaneous arcing turns and descents. During an approach, the rate-of-descent gauge was important, but so were heading, airspeed, altitude, and TACAN or ADF needle position. An instrument approach was where all that basic instrument training came together, where it really meant something to be able to control all those different gauges in a precise fashion. If a pilot controlled the gauges precisely, he would wind up safely looking at the runway after flying through the clouds. If he gooned it up, he would have to wave off and go around again, or he would die if he flew into an obstruction or just dropped too low.

Ground controlled approaches (GCAs), on the other hand, were a piece of cake. There, a ground controller watched on radar and gave heading and altitude calls. So the Meridian students didn't practice those very much. However, they practiced the TACAN and ADF approaches a lot.

After RNav, Jon had the formation-flying phase to do. That meant at least another five or six weeks in Meridian. After Meridian, he'd go back to Pensacola for two months and initial carrier qualification (CQ). After that was advanced jet training.

Students thought it was bad luck to think too far ahead. He pushed the future out of his head.

The four-plane formation he watched take off was reduced to dots against the blue. He turned for the hangar and wondered how and when to tell Teresa he would be gone over the weekend.

41

Fosgrove's Feed and Farm Equipment was just inside the eastern city limits of Columbus, Mississippi. A long, tin-roofed, wood slat–sided shed housed the feed and seed storage. A tin-covered overhang extended beyond the front of the building. The parking lot was pocked with holes pounded into the gravel. All the parking places in front of the store were occupied. Harry parked to the right, against a chain-link fence that had been run into no small number of times. Behind the fence, old and new red, green, and gray hay balers, wagons, combines, plows, disks, and tractors sat amongst the waist-high weeds in the lot next to the long shed. Before he got out of the car, he touched his switchblade in the watch pocket of his dark pants and then reached under his unbuttoned short-sleeved shirt to put his hands on the grip of his forty-five under his belt on the left. Shoes, pants, shirt, gun, and knife—those were what he wore every day.

Harry twisted the knob and pushed the door open. A bell jangled.

A large office occupied the width of the front of the store. A square doughnut-shaped customer-service counter filled the center of the room. Two men stood inside the doughnut. Desks and filing cabinets lined both sides of the room. To the right, a man and a woman sat at two of the three desks on that side.

Behind him, he felt Amanda Sue come in and almost smiled. She was working out just fine. She could drive, and she was learning how to cover his back. His mind had to dance over the bedroom. Even going into something new and worrisome, his mind twitched on that.

Behind him, the door closed, and the bell jangled again. The men behind the service counter looked briefly at Harry and went back to the farm equipment catalog they had open. The man from the desk got up, gave Harry a "come on" signal, and led them to a door that opened onto a long open storage bay. Stacks of seed and feed on pallets lined both sides of the shed. There were enough dirty windows to allow gloom inside with the musty, moldy smell.

The man led them all the way to the end of the shed to another door. He opened it, stepped aside for Harry, and left without saying a word.

A big-shouldered, thick-necked, head-shaved, black-T-shirted man sat at the end of a long table and stared at Harry. The man didn't say anything. Raw-wood walls compressed the room. A single bare bulb dimly lit the bare concrete floor.

"Jimmie?" Harry asked.

"Come in. Close the door."

"I'm Harry."

"Know who you are. Sit."

Harry sat opposite Jimmie. Amanda Sue took the first of three chairs on the side to Harry's left.

"Army grunt!" Jimmie smirked.

Harry gritted his teeth. Then he saw the Marine Corps symbol tattooed on Jimmie's left forearm.

"Jarhead."

"Peeper. The hell kind a name is that? Should we call you Mr. Peeper?"

Harry wished he'd sat next to Jimmie. If he had, he could have shown Jimmie his switchblade. He was thinking about the forty-five.

Amanda Sue banged her fist on the table and jumped up. "I did not ride all the way up here to this shit hole so you guys could sniff each other's assholes."

Jimmie smiled. "Oh, sit down," he said to Amanda Sue and shifted his gaze. "Word is you got a temper, Harry. You were thinking about pulling a gun, weren't you?"

Jimmie pulled his right hand from under the table. He pointed his forty-five at the ceiling, let the hammer down, and placed the gun on the table.

"You pissed me off, so I wouldn't look for a piece in your lap," Harry said. Jimmie smirked.

"This whole business is pissing me off. You know me, but I don't know who the hell you are," Harry said.

"Other word about you is you're a good sergeant. We'd like to keep you. Thing is we're changing how we do business. You want to come along with us?"

"What was wrong with the way it was? Hell, I knew everybody. Everybody knew me. Everybody knew what was going on. Once a month we'd meet in Sam's garage. Now Sam says I'm not to see him or contact him again. I work for you, he said. I don't like not knowing anybody and not knowing what the hell is going on."

"You and me are going to get to know each other. Tonight we're going to boost a car, paint it, and swap out the plates. Tomorrow morning we're going to hit a bank together. Amanda Sue will drive. You done a bank before?"

"Why the hell we into robbin' banks now?"

"You, me, coupla us going to be working full-time for the Klan. Need money to live on, don't you?" Jimmie's eyes bounced from Harry to Amanda Sue and back again. "You done a bank before?"

Harry shook his head.

"Nothing to it. We'll brief the mission after we get the car. Now you follow me. I'll lead to where we're holing up tonight. You're in, right?"

Harry looked at Amanda Sue. Her eyes were sparkling. Her mouth was open a little. She either wanted to rob a bank or climb all over Jimmie.

"In."

"Good."

"What're you carryin'?" Jimmie asked Amanda Sue.

"Thirty-eight." Harry had gotten her the gun and taught her to fire it.

Harry watched as Jimmie looked her over. Other men would be checking out Amanda Sue's boobs. He was sure Jimmie was evaluating how she wore the revolver in a shoulder holster under an open-in-front button-up blouse over a T-shirt. Jimmie nodded. He said to Harry, "Tomorrow night I'll tell you a couple of things we'll be doing over the next month."

Jimmie stood. Amanda Sue pushed her chair back.

Harry met Jimmie's eyes. "You act like banks are easy."

"Pick the right one, and if you're not stupid, they are. Know how to use your Thompson?"

"Some."

"Let's go then."

Harry watched Amanda Sue follow Jimmie out the door. He thought Amanda Sue was beginning to act like a hard-ass and wondered if he needed to do something about that.

42

Teresa watched Jon from the window behind the sink. He stood in profile with the ax above his head. His left hand gripped the base of the handle, his right was halfway to the double-bladed head, and he glared at the stump with vicious and murderous intent. He took a deep breath, started the weapon down, and slid his right hand down to join the left for two-handed power.

Whunk.

The blade sank into the wood and peeled a sliver of wood from the edge of the stump. He swung the ax again but at a slight angle off the vertical and cut the base of the sliver and sent it sailing eight feet into the yard.

Teresa knew she had to let him work things out on his own. If she pushed him, it would take them backward, not forward.

"Men have the same brains as an amoeba," Rose said once. "The only time they are not thinking with their penises is just after they got laid and they are hungry."

He raised the ax and brought it down. *Whunk.* Raised it. *Whunk.*

Rose's gross exaggeration sounded like how Jon described aviator speech, which was ironic given Rose's opinion of a Navy pilot's mental age. But there was an element of truth in what she said too, as there was in an aviator's bodacious exaggeration.

Bodacious. Jon had used the word to describe aviators' speech. But it fit the way Rose spoke too. And there was a thought. Rose, a naval aviator, as if the Navy would ever allow a woman to pilot one of their precious jets.

However, Jon had a brain much more complex than an amoeba's. He had a conscience. He gave himself penances much harder than any priest in a confessional had ever given him.

Whunk. Whunk.

*   *   *

Since they'd walked out on Father Allbright, Teresa had not had a delicious sleep. Delicious sleep happened when her head touched the pillow, and her mind surrendered to exhaustion, and her body sank into the mattress, as if it had decomposed into molecules, and her guardian angel winnowed away her tiredness like chaff. Since the walkout, she slept every night. Her muscles and her bones demanded it even as her mind wanted to pester her with what he'd done to cause the difficulty between them, but it was a long way from delicious sleep.

When Jon came in from his stump, he apologized.

"Teresa." He was shirtless and mopping sweat with his T-shirt. "I was stupid and I was naive to drag you to see Father. I'm sorry. I was wrong to walk out on him. I am sorry about my temper. I do not have your faith that God will take care of us. And I don't know what to do about that yet. But I am sorry I brought anger and animosity between us. Nobody did that but me. You have enough to worry about without me making your life harder. I'm sorry."

She would have hugged him, but he stopped her, took her hand, and kissed it.

"You are huggable always," he said. "I am not."

He meant that there was more to it than sweat and stink. He wasn't fishing for "Oh, Jon, you are huggable." It had taken years to learn that about him. When he offered himself up like he did with his apology, he was dealing with truth as he saw it, and truth was defined in hard, cold black and white. And the worst thing she could do was to treat what he said as anything less than that. She had to allow him the space to follow his first step back with a second driven by his will.

"It looks like you made a square of the stump." She asked him, "Are you trying to make a square peg out of a round bole?"

She could see he was stunned, and it surprised her too. Normally, she didn't crack jokes. The thought just popped into her head, and she voiced it.

Jon frowned. "Bole, I've got to look that up," he said.

Jon laid his big dictionary on the kitchen table, found the entry, and laughed but quickly clamped a hand over his mouth. It wouldn't do to wake Edgar Jon.

"If you have to look it up in the dictionary, it really isn't a joke, is it?"

"I knew it was a joke. I didn't know how funny it was till I looked it up." Jon did an imaginary tip of a hat. "That was clever."

He walked to the sink, looked out the window at the stump, and said, "Round bole." His shoulders shook, and he snorted snot out his nose as he kept his mouth covered with his hand. He mopped his face with his tee, turned, looked at Teresa, and started laughing again.

After the shower, he told her about the stump.

The stump was Jon Zachery. He had a stupid naive side, a hot temper side, a lust side, and a not-enough-faith side. He was whittling away at those, he said.

Then he told her about his RO2N over the weekend.

"If I do the RO2N," he said, "I can knock out six flights over the weekend. It could take two weeks to do that during the workweek. It'll get us out of here sooner.

"The white pickup, it was a couple of months between them tacking the sign on the door and shooting out the streetlight. I think they are just warning us to stay away from the civil rights people. The Navy wants us to do that too. But I am going to ask the legal officer on the base to call the police in town and ask them to watch the house over the weekend. I am pretty sure they haven't driven by for a while. And I'll ask Tutu to watch over you."

The white pickup. Jon healed the anger between them, but immediately fear of the white pickup took its place to ruin her sleep.

When Jon headed for the sofa, she told him to come back to bed. It was a comfort having Jon back with her, even if he was all the way on his side, and even if he didn't have his hand touching her. When he had been on his deployment to Vietnam, he said he fell asleep each night reaching out to touch her from halfway round the world. He said he didn't think he would ever get to the point where it wasn't a blessing to actually be able to have his hand on her as he fell asleep.

"When I am not with you and I fall asleep, quite often I get this feeling that I'm falling off the world, and I jerk awake. When I have my hand on you, I know I will not fall off the world."

Men. No, they were not just lust and hunger. He loved her. She saw that lying awake beside him, listening to him breathe slow and deep. He probably hadn't slept well for a long time either.

What would I name the sides of my stump? she wondered. She only came up with a name for one side: safety and security. Her imagination tried to offer specific names for what worried her, but she resisted and clung to a worry for safety and security, for herself and for her—their—babies.

Jon didn't fear anything. All by himself, he charged into the middle of a fight, barehanded and outnumbered by boys or huge, scary men—it didn't matter. He wasn't afraid.

If she had a stump, its name would be fear, and it would be petrified wood.

Jon had a not-enough-faith side to his stump. Maybe she had one too. Her faith covered the pregnancy issue for her. Why couldn't it cover the white pickup?

43

Cyril sat across the round table from his momma's poppa, John Calhoun. He mopped sweat from his face. He hadn't been in the house before that he could remember, though his momma told him he had been there when Momma's momma died.

"Sumpin' ta drink, Cyril? Coffee?" John Calhoun eyed him for a second, and then he nodded toward the cob-stoppered jug.

Cyril shook his head no but said, "Yes, sir, coffee please."

"Sue Ellen."

She waddled in from the living room, poured a mug of coffee, placed it before Cyril, turned, and started walking away. John Calhoun spun around on his chair and slapped Sue Ellen's upper arm.

"Sugar 'n milk. Why in hell I gotta say it?"

Cyril tried to swallow, but he was out of spit. He watched her trundle toward the fridge but felt John Calhoun's eyes on him. He put his hands around the mug, but it was hot. A pitcher of milk, a sugar bowl, and a spoon appeared on the patch of table he was looking at.

"Cyril." Cyril looked up. "Milk and sugar. You like your coffee that way."

"Yes, sir." Cyril loaded his mug and stirred.

"Sumpin' ta tell me?"

"Yes, sir." Still out of spit.

"Shit, Cyril."

"Yes, sir. What I come to say is, that Navy guy sat with the nigra a handful a Sundays back, well, he ain't been to church since. Till last Sunday, that is. He come back."

"What'd he do?"

"Well, nothing. Jus' the same as others do."

"You see him come, see him go?"

"No, sir. I didn't see those. But I know the usher, Ollie. He seen 'em come, seen 'em go. Walked in like nobody's bidness. Walked out the same, Ollie said."

Cyril watched John Calhoun rub his chin and look off at a corner of the room behind him. John Calhoun sat like a statue for a long time.

"Drink your coffee" startled Cyril. He jerked and spilled some onto the table. Taking a red bandanna from his pocket, he mopped up the puddle. John Calhoun stared at him, and he gulped a mouthful of wet sugar.

Wish I'da asked for corn, Cyril thought.

John Calhoun uncorked the jug. The jug looked tiny in his big hands as he filled Cyril's mug back to the brim.

Cyril drank off a slug as John Calhoun stood and started pacing from the table to the back door, from the back door past the sink, the door to the living room, the fridge, the pantry to the far wall, and back again. Cyril drank when John Calhoun's back was to him, and he felt the shine invade his brain with a strange, cool numbness that crowded his fear into a corner of his head.

John Calhoun turned on his heel at the back door, walked to the table, and sat back down. "Need you to run out to see the twins."

"Tonight?"

Cyril looked at the jug.

"No." John Calhoun stared at Cyril for a couple of seconds. "Yes."

Asking his momma's poppa, John Calhoun, what he was *noing* and what he was *yesing* flitted through Cyril's thoughts, and that added a new worry. Sometimes John Calhoun knew what people were thinking.

"Yessir," Cyril said and went to do what he didn't want to.

44

On Friday morning Jon and his instructor, Lieutenant Frank Morrison, launched on the first of three legs flying to and then north up the east coast. They RONed at the third stop.

On Saturday morning, they planned to fly a fourth leg to Quonset Point Naval Air Station, Rhode Island. Frank would spend the afternoon and night in the BOQ, and Jon was going to stay with George and Samantha Justice.

Jon had met George Justice at Purdue. George had been a chief petty officer and the senior man in a group of seventy-five Navy men attending the university on a program called the Navy Enlisted Scientific Education Program, or NESEP.

George's boyish face didn't seem to belong under his white hair, but Jon lost that initial impression quickly. What registered and stuck was that Chief Petty Officer George Justice was outgoing, confident, and in charge. Everyone called him CJ, for Chief Justice.

Just before classes began in September 1961, Jon was promoted to third-class petty officer with two years in service. CJ had nine years of service. At Halloween that first year, Dale, the only NESEPer younger than Jon, dropped out of school. Navy leadership became concerned about losing one of the younger members. Generally, the service expected to get a total of twenty years from career personnel, and with guys like George, they wouldn't get a lot of payback for the investment, since time in college counted as part of the twenty. With George, the Navy could expect seven years of commissioned service after he graduated. With Dale and Jon, the Navy expected fourteen or fifteen years.

After Dale left, CJ—either on his own or maybe he was ordered to—began to look after Jon to make sure he wouldn't quit too.

Samantha Justice was a superb match to CJ. She always looked elegant, her home was nicely furnished, and her girls looked as if they had been brought to life from the pages of children's wear catalogs. At Purdue, Samantha had earned a nice income working out of her home. She designed and furnished display and model homes for some of the builders in Lafayette and West Lafayette, Indiana, and she sold her landscape and still-life watercolors. She threw parties in the basement of her home once a month. Being a CJ special project, Jon had an invitation to dinner every other week.

If it hadn't been for CJ, Jon was sure he would not have married Teresa. He wanted to be an officer when they married. He planned to wait until he had graduated from college and from Officer Candidate School before proposing.

Jon and Teresa started dating the summer between their junior and senior years of high school, and she didn't date anyone else when he went into the Navy. Jon knew she was the only one for him, and he thought she felt the same way about him. But after his freshman year at Purdue, Teresa suggested they each date other people. She didn't want to stop seeing him but wanted both of them to date other people to make sure they didn't have doubts or reservations about their commitment.

To Jon, it was a kick in the stomach. He didn't have a clue as to what it meant. The only thing he could think of was that it was a precursor to an announcement that she was going to marry someone else, that her mother had finally turned her away from him.

After one of Samantha's Sunday dinners, Jon and CJ were sitting on folding lawn chairs on his patio. Despite a powerful inclination to keep his mouth shut about such personal business, he brought up the situation with Teresa and dating other people. CJ took a pull on his bottle of beer, let out a sigh, shook his head, and said, "Christ."

"What?"

Without looking at him, Chief Justice said, "Stand up."

Jon stood.

"Put your drink down and turn around," he said.

As soon as his back was turned, CJ kneed him in the butt hard enough to lift his feet off the patio. He told Jon to call Teresa right away and make a date with her for next weekend. On the date, Jon had to propose and give her a ring.

When Jon thought about that conversation, it created a cold hollow feeling in his belly. If he hadn't brought up the issue, if he hadn't listened to CJ, Teresa would have married someone else. Even during the times when the relationship got a little frosty, it was nowhere near as bad as contemplating life without her.

Flying to Quonset Point on Saturday morning was uneventful, but during a TACAN approach and then a GCA, Jon worked up a sweat as he fought severe turbulence to keep the airplane close to glide slope and on speed. Normally a GCA was easier to fly, but even that was tough, as the plane bounced and the heading wandered and the airspeed varied from a few knots fast to a few slow, and the plane seemed to have a mind of its own and did not want to get down and onto the glide slope.

"One-half mile. Above glide slope. Take over visually or execute missed approach," the GCA controller said over the radio.

"I got the airplane," Frank said and shook the stick.

Jon let go of it and blew out an exasperated breath into his oxygen mask. He pulled the bag away from the Velcro tabs and looked out at blue sky. The plane didn't seem to be bouncing as badly with the bag down.

Frank was crabbing into a crosswind and, at the last second, rolled and ruddered the plane to align it with the runway. Jon could feel Frank working the controls to counter the effects of the wind. Jon thought Frank was working about as hard as he had on the GCA.

With the plane slowed to sixty knots, Frank said, "Piece a cake," over the ICS.

Frank switched to ground control frequency and checked in, and then he came back up on the ICS. "You probably thought that turbulence was severe, didn't you?"

Jon didn't answer.

"And the crosswind," Frank said, "we're still ten knots below the airplane limit. Turbulence, crosswinds, you're gonna see these things, and you have to be the boss of them."

Frank turned off the runway onto a taxiway. "Debrief, Zachery. The TACAN and GCA approaches, you were high on both of them. You probably think it's safer to be high than low. But if you are high and you are trying to land on a carrier, it means you won't get aboard. High is not safer than low. You have got to fly your approaches right on."

"Yes, sir."

"Thermals off the end of the runway happen in daytime. You find thunderstorms over the field or carrier at night. Gusty winds. It all happens. You still got to fly that damn plane."

The major lesson from the entire RNav phase seemed to be that there were no excuses for not flying a good approach, Jon thought as Frank parked the jet. A line crewman installed landing gear pins, and Frank shut the engine down, opened the canopy, unstrapped, climbed down, and invited Jon to hustle it up.

Jon climbed out, peeled off his torso harness, unzipped the G suit, and put them on top of his helmet in the backseat. Frank was coming around the left wingtip, having just completed inspecting the airplane as Jon closed the canopy.

"Most of the big pieces are still on the airplane, Zachery. Means you did a halfway satisfactory job."

"You did the landing. That's when the big pieces fall off, isn't it?"

"Getting cocky, are we, Zachery?"

"Oh no, sir," Jon said as Frank looked at his watch.

Frank said, "0930. Good. Breakfast beer. One of the nice things about going on a RON, I can have a beer for breakfast."

During instrument training at Meridian, Jon had observed a number of instructor pilots like Frank—married, with kids. They looked forward to those opportunities to get away, to be kids again themselves for a couple of days. Even though his relationship with Teresa was still a little tense, he didn't think he'd ever be glad to be away from her and their kids, and especially not with the white pickup still out there. When he considered the threat from the white pickup to be small, his argument seemed logic-based. From the perspective of hundreds of miles away and Teresa alone to handle it by herself, with two babies to look after, it didn't feel like such a small worry.

"Jon, we'll be okay," Teresa said Friday morning. "It's just two nights."

Jon knew she awoke every morning with that don't-worry-your-husband lecture in the front of her mind. Flying was a demanding business. It *demanded* total concentration. That lecture had infuriated Teresa, but it had also stuck deep. If Jon was killed in a plane crash, he knew that for the rest of her life, Teresa would ask herself if she had given him extra burdens and interfered with his concentration on flying his airplane.

A punch on the shoulder pulled Jon back to NAS Quonset Point. Frank pointed at the base operations building. "I think those people over there want to say hello to you, and I want to howdy a can a beer. Let's go."

Base ops was located across an expanse of concrete from their jet. There was an elevated concrete porch in front of the one-story building three steps above the level of the ramp. George Justice stood on the porch with his three daughters. The youngest Justice, five-year-old Sally, was hopping up and down and waving. Jon waved to her, which made her happy. The other two girls held hands, and their father, George, stood behind them.

Jon looked at George in khaki trousers and a polo shirt. Even in civilian clothes, he was Chief Justice, CJ. Even if he'd come in uniform as Lieutenant (jg) Justice, he'd still be CJ.

45

The waitress smiled at Ike and slid the platter in front of John Calhoun. John Calhoun didn't even look at her. He just picked up his knife and fork, broke an egg yolk, sawed into a pork chop, speared two fried potato slices before the chunk of meat, sopped up yolk with the forkful, and stuck the load in his mouth.

"Top you off, sir?" she asked Ike.

"Please," Ike said. She poured from a carafe. "Thank you, Leah."

Leah blushed. She was about forty, a bottle-assisted redhead, and skinny. Her name was embroidered on the top of her apron. She started turning away.

"Hey," John Calhoun said and pointed to his mug.

She topped off him too, cast another glance at Ike, and swished away.

John Calhoun looked at Ike and shook his head while chewing with his right cheek puffed out.

"Why you shaking your head? That Leah, I'm sure she finds me fetchin'."

"Even with that black curly-haired wig and those glasses, you still draw up well short of fetchin'."

"Don't you ever lighten up?" Ike asked. "You ever laugh?"

"Gave it up."

Ike didn't joke much, himself, just when it served a purpose. He thought he understood John Calhoun, but every once in a while, it didn't hurt to test his assumptions.

He watched the other man gnaw on the bone of his first pork chop.

"Before you start on the second, you want to tell me why I'm here?"

John Calhoun dropped the bone, wiped his mouth and hands on his paper napkin, and slurped coffee.

"Bollinger. I wanted to do him. Sam said shouldn't. I come to you, and you said do 'im. Now we got this Navy guy name of Zachery. He sat with the nigger girl at the Catholic church end a March. He never came back to the church in town after we tacked a sign on his door. But he come back to the church last Sunday. We thought Bollinger was up to something, I think Zachery is too. I talked to Sam. He said shouldn't. I'm asking you."

Ike cupped his hands around his mug.

"Zachery. Got a wife and kids, right?"

"Gotta squash the nits too."

"Yeah, but I'm thinking we coulda done better with Bollinger. Coulda grabbed him, made him tell what was going to happen, then kill him."

"That what you want, we grab Zachery?"

"We don't need to stir up the Navy. May be another way."

Ike pulled a notebook from his shirt pocket and paged through it.

"That Sunday in April, Plymouth picked up the nigger girl. Indiana license number goes to a guy named Wexall. Address in Chicago, probably a college kid. I got somebody can check him out."

"Hell, already got the hole dug for Zachery."

"Well, fill it back up. I need to tell you, you can't have an open hole layin' around a long time, then somebody disappears and so does the hole?"

"Go ta hell," John Calhoun said.

"There's that famous John Calhoun sense a humor."

* * *

Jimmie arrived at Rosie's Diner in Pamooka, about twenty miles south of Meridian, at 3:00 p.m., four hours before his meeting with Ike Larsen. He parked his panel van so that he had a view of the entrance to the restaurant through the windshield, and then he went inside, ate a steak, drank coffee, used the restroom, bought a coffee to go, and went back to the van.

Jimmie set up a folding chair behind and between the driver and passenger seats, and then he strung a black curtain with a view hole in it in front of his perch. He settled back with his coffee to wait and watch.

Ike was just the guy they needed running the Klan in Mississippi, but he was a ruthless bastard. Trusting him felt like a bad idea.

Cars and customers came and went. Jimmie saw no one who looked like scouts for Ike or a threat. Jimmie didn't know what kind of vehicle Ike would arrive in, but he'd for sure see him walk into the place. Five after seven came, but Ike didn't. Ike was always already there, waiting for him at their previous meets. Strange thing, Ike late. Jimmie decided he should leave.

He pulled the keys from his pocket, pushed the curtain aside, and moved up to the driver's seat. As he was fumbling the key into the ignition, there was a knock on the passenger-side window.

Jimmie's heart rate kicked into high gear. He dropped the keys and started reaching for the forty-five in his belt. Ike was standing there looking at him through the window.

"Unlock the door," Ike said.

Jesus Christ.

Jimmie reached over and pulled the lock button up. Ike opened the door and climbed in.

"We'll meet here," Ike said and slammed the door.

"Ike, um—"

"Natural for you to worry some. We got a fight on our hands. Any one of us can go under. You, Jimmie, are the best man I ever worked with. I wouldn't toss you under no bus."

Just like that, Jimmie was ready to trust him, but a part of him pushed back, wanted to be careful, wanted to come eight hours early the next time.

"Business now." Ike scooted his legs around the edge of the seat so he faced Jimmie. "John Calhoun gave me a line on one a those Northerners came to Meridian in April and brought a nigger girl to the white Catholic church. Usher got the license number of the car picked that girl up. Belongs to a guy named Albert Wexall. Registered in Indiana, but he got a Chicago address. Could be a college kid.

"John Calhoun said back in April when the nigger girl came to the church, nobody sat with her until a Navy guy name of Zachery walked in. Usher tried to squeeze Zachery in to 'nother pew, but Zachery pushed the usher out of the way and Zachery 'n 'is wife sat with her. After the service and everybody left, usher said Zachery stayed and talked with the girl. Usher said Zachery wrote something on a card and gave it to her. Since that Sunday in April, Zachery hasn't been back to the church. JC figures Zachery goes to church out to the Navy base, but last Sunday, Zachery came back. Remember that Bollinger guy in Meridian? He sent his wife and kids away. We figured he was cooking something up, and we took care a him. We shoulda found out what he was cooking."

Ike made a *tsk* sound.

"Do it better this time, eh, Jimmie?"

Jimmie nodded.

"JC wonders if those Northerners are planning something with Zachery. Want you to go to Chicago, find this Wexall, find out what you can about him. See if you can get a line on what they might be planning and if there's any link to that Zachery fellow. You wanna do it yourself or take someone?"

"Harlan," Jimmie said.

"Harlan's good." Ike got out of the van.

Jimmie watched him cross the parking lot and enter the diner.

46

As CJ drove through the main gate, Jon turned and smiled at the girls in the backseat. The oldest, eleven-year-old Sarah, sat in the middle with a large book open in her lap, reading to her sisters.

"Perfect angels," Jon said.

"Spoiled rug rats," CJ growled, "always wasting what little good behavior they have on strangers."

"I'm telling Mommy," Sally piped.

"No, no. Anything but that!" CJ said to the windshield as he peeked at the rearview.

Jon turned back around to the front and wondered if he'd ever have a comfortable, easy relationship like that with his children.

They came to an intersection, stopped at the sign, and turned right.

"So, how's sub school? You still happy about going back to the boats?" Jon asked.

CJ had been on diesel boats before coming to Purdue. Submariners talked about being on boats, not submarines. After graduation, he would have preferred going back to them, but the Navy had other ideas then. The submarine Navy had transitioned to nuclear propulsion by that time, and the junior officer corps in subs consisted of young men trained in managing a nuclear plant. So CJ went to his second choice, which was a destroyer, though a newer class of ship than the *Manfred*. A year after he graduated, the sub Navy realized that their highly educated junior officer corps was over-smart and under-endowed with common sense and basic leadership skills, and a number of submarine billets were opened for experienced diesel submariner officers. Lieutenant (jg) Justice epitomized what the Navy was looking for.

"Judas priest!" Jon turned to see what CJ was staring at through the passenger-side window.

Six people milled around in front of a Navy recruiting station in a glass-fronted office in a strip mall. Two of them had signs: "No Nukes" and "No War." The sign carriers were girls, a blonde and a brunette. Both wore tight jeans and loose, colorful tops. Two of the boys had spray-paint cans and were drawing peace symbols to go with "No Nukes" on the windows of the recruiting office. One tall, skinny young man with a purple sweatband, somewhat organizing his long black hair, hurled a rock through the glass window in the top half of the door.

A Navy lieutenant in whites and with his right arm in a sling opened the glass-busted-out door. Another of the young men hurled a bucket of red paint on him.

"Stop."

"Not a good idea."

"Stop and let me out, Chief. Then get the girls out of here."

CJ checked the mirror and braked to a stop. Jon bolted out, slammed the door, and ran at the stone thrower. Stone Thrower was cocking his arm with a second missile when Jon plowed his shoulder into the middle of the guy's back and knocked him down. Jon grabbed the back of the shirt of the spray-paint guy to the right of the recruiter's office door, pivoted, and flung him into the spray-paint guy to the left of the door.

Something hit Jon on the head—not hard, just an annoyance. He turned to his left. In an instant, his vision went away. All he saw was black studded with bright stars. His head hurt.

Move!

He dove to his right, rolled over, and came up into a crouch with fists in front of his face.

Blonde Sign Girl didn't have a sign anymore, just a one-by-two held like a bat. She swung, but he ducked it easily. With the stick cocked back, she came at him again. Before the swing developed, Jon stepped closer to her, grabbed the one-by-two with an upraised left arm, and was ready to deliver a fist, but a spray-paint guy grabbed her shoulder and pulled her away.

"We gotta get outa here!" Spray-Paint Guy said as he pulled the girl away.

She wanted to take another whack at Jon with her fists. Jon had her stick. "Get in the car." The guy shoved the girl toward the curb.

Jon's left arm hurt. He couldn't see well with his left eye until he wiped blood away.

The six protestors were piling into two cars. He started toward them when someone grabbed his arm. Jon turned toward the new threat.

It was the lieutenant. He held up his good left hand. "Whoa up there. Let 'em go. Let's take a look at you."

Jon was still running on a lot of juice, and he had his right fist clenched, the stick in his left hand.

"Now don't you go whuppin' up on a cripple." The officer raised his right arm a couple of inches in the dull, dark-green cloth sling. Then he winced. "Damn, shouldn't a tried to be a comedian. C'mon inside. We need to look at your head."

He was six feet tall, and most of the paint had hit him right at his slender waist, run down his trousers, and splattered his white shoes. He looked like Tab Hunter, and he had Tab's hair too.

Jon dropped the stick, and it clattered onto the sidewalk. The lieutenant took Jon's arm and led them into the recruiting office. A young man, probably eighteen or nineteen, was sitting on a chair in front of a desk, and a second-class petty officer was wrapping some gauze around a cut on the prospective recruit's arm. The kid looked up at Jon as they came through the door, and his mouth fell open.

"What?" Jon snarled at the kid.

"Now, don't y'all go frightenin' our prospects away. We got a tall quota to meet this month."

Jon glared at the lieutenant.

"Cripple, remember?" Then he laughed.

It infected Jon. Tension evaporated from his limbs, and, suddenly he felt tired.

"Sit down," the lieutenant said.

There were four desks in the room. Only one was occupied with the petty officer and the young man. The lieutenant led Jon to a desk with "Butt Ugly" on a two-inch-high brass nameplate. Jon sat on the chair in front of the desk.

"I'm Steve Elkins, or that," he pointed at the desk sign, "if you prefer."

"Jon Zachery. I'm Navy too. A lieutenant (jg)."

"Figured you were Navy or Marine."

Jon stuck out his right hand but then realized Steve's right was crippled and pulled it back just as he was reaching for Jon's right with his left.

"Sorry."

Steve smiled, and his left hand patiently waited for Jon's to come out and meet it.

"Petty Officer Foster, soon as you are done with Mr. Simmons, bring the first-aid kit into the bathroom. Then call the police."

"We're done here." Petty Officer Foster was a second-class aviation electronics repair technician. He was slender, about five foot seven, and his whites were immaculate.

The prospective Navy recruit stood up. He didn't look like he needed to shave yet.

"You need to stay, Mr. Simmons," Lieutenant Elkins said.

"I didn't see nothing."

"Fine. But you have to stay, and you have to be the one who tells the police that. Sit."

The bathroom—"head" in Navy talk—had a commode, a deep sink, a regular bathroom sink, and a medicine cabinet with a mirror above the regular sink. In a corner, there was a bucket, a broom, and a dustpan. A mop hung from nails in the wall. Next to the mirror, there was a paper-towel dispenser.

The image looking back at Jon wasn't pretty. There was a gash above his left eyebrow, and the left side of his face was covered with blood.

Aw, crap! Teeth are missing.

47

CJ AND SAMANTHA HAD INVITED five couples from his sub-school group to a potluck dinner.

The potluck was a regularly scheduled monthly affair, and when Jon called about flying up, CJ told him about the potluck. Jon said he didn't want to interfere with their event, but CJ insisted he come and RON.

"RON. Always good for Navy guys to learn new acronyms," CJ said, "even from jet pukes."

So he'd come for a visit. The encounter outside the recruiter office took up the rest of the morning and past lunch. There were police interviews and a visit to the medical clinic on the base for stitches and checkout by a flight surgeon. Fortunately for Jon, there was one doing weekend reservist duty.

Jon apologized to Samantha for complicating her Saturday. "Not a big deal," she said. "Everything's set for tonight."

Pretty quickly after the party started, Jon and the guys ran out of things to talk about. Submariners were as hard to talk to as women.

The Justices had a small bar, two stools wide, in a corner of the basement rec room. He sat on a stool with a plate of food in front of him. The men in the group would bring a paper plate and sit with him. Jon never saw CJ take a bite, but his barstool mates would sit down and say something. Then CJ would talk, and the guy would eat and listen. After ten or fifteen minutes, the guy would thank him and get up."

CJ would respond with "It was nothing" in French, Spanish, Italian, German, or Japanese. A couple of minutes later another man would sit down.

Samantha held court at one of two card tables. The ladies, three at a time, sat longer with her than the men with her husband. When something needed to be done with the food, napkins, or paper plates, a woman from the table would get up and tend to the need. That seemed to be the signal for a new lady to join Samantha.

As Jon watched the social interactions, he thought that everyone was taking something away with them when they left CJ and Samantha. The Justices seemed only to give. They didn't get anything in return.

The last couple departed at 2220. Samantha closed the door, put her arms around CJ's neck, and kissed him. Jon watched and smiled. After a second, he felt a nudge from jealousy. It had been a long time since Teresa kissed him like that.

Jon went down to the basement rec room and started gathering up plastic drink glasses and paper plates. He knew where they kept the garbage bags, and he got a new one out and started loading it with the detritus of the party.

"Stop." Samantha stood, arms akimbo, on the bottom step of the stairs from the kitchen. "That's not how we do things. Stop. Right this instant. We're going to sit on the patio. Now you march on out there. Would you like something to drink?"

"Coffee, and instant's fine. I can make it."

"March."

Jon marched ahead of her up the stairs and out on to the patio as she turned on the kettle for the coffee. He sat on a lawn chair next to CJ.

CJ said, "We always take a few minutes and just sit after a party. Don't you remember from Purdue? Anyway, it's like work during the evening. So we like to take a few minutes and unwind. The mess will still be there."

Samantha came out with a cocktail glass for CJ. "Kettle's on, Jon. Just be a moment."

CJ took a sip and said, "Thank you." Samantha smiled at him, and then the kettle whistled.

Jon got up. "I'll go, and can I get you something, Samantha?"

"Sit."

"Best to not mess with Sammie." He took another sip.

"You didn't drink anything during the party, did you, Chief?"

"Nope. I learned a long time ago that it's too easy to get caught up in the feeling of the party and to lose track of how much you are drinking. So I only drink when I know I'll be in control of it, not the other way around." He sipped. "You get caught up in all the frivolity, and you don't even taste what you are drinking. It goes down like water, except that what it does to your brain, water won't do."

Jon recalled the time he'd pounded down drinks like he was drinking water. Hong Kong, 1966. He had been sicker from the booze than he ever had been from seasickness. He was glad it was dark on the patio. The recollection made him blush.

Samantha came back out and handed Jon a mug of coffee.

"I put an ice cube in it. It should be okay." She sat next to CJ and took his left hand in her right, took a sip of her white wine, and placed the wine glass on the small table next to her.

Chief Justice raised his glass. "A toast, Jon Zachery, to the real hostess with the mostest!"

"The mostest." Jon lifted his mug.

"Another reason why he doesn't drink during a party. See how he behaves with one sip of booze in his belly."

"Ah, Sammie, not booze. This is the good stuff."

"Another one?"

"No, my dear. Truly good stuff is truly good the first time, but it's sneaky. It would like you to think that a second glass will be even *gooder*, but invariably it disappoints, and so it tempts you to try a third."

CJ handed his glass to Samantha. "How's the head?" he asked.

Jon put his hand up to the bandage. "Okay. It doesn't hurt, but I'm wondering how my flight helmet is going to work over it."

"So stick around for a day or two," Samantha said.

"We can't. If I can't fly tomorrow, the instructor will take the plane back. It needs to be there for the schedule on Monday. I'll go back commercial, if it comes to that. But it won't. I'll be okay in the morning."

Samantha took a sip of her wine and said, "Ah, the adequate stuff." She placed the glass carefully back on the table, and it was as if silence had been pulled down onto the patio, like pulling down a window shade. CJ had his back to the house. Light spilled out of the family room, and Jon couldn't see his eyes. He could feel them on him though.

"You know you scare the life out of Teresa when you do something like you did today," Samantha said.

It didn't seem to be a question.

"What were you thinking when you jumped out of the car and took on six people?" CJ asked.

"I saw the guy with the rock. I saw the lieutenant with his arm in a sling." Jon shrugged. "I wasn't going to let him face that by himself."

"Teresa told me about your encounter with the antiwar kids in California, in '66," Samantha said. "She told me about the guys in the white pickup truck. What happens to you in those situations?"

How do you tell somebody about Al Schwartz?

"Sounds like you go berserk or something," Samantha said.

"Samantha—yeah, that's it. I just go berserk."

"Oh, horse feathers," Samantha said. "I said it sounds like you go berserk. You don't go berserk. What is it? What comes over you?"

"When I was in grade school, I got beat up. Guy I worked for, his brother, actually, taught me how to take care of myself. He said, 'You get in a fight, take charge of it.' That's where it comes from."

"You learned this in grade school?" CJ asked. "I sure didn't see it in you."

"Nothing to see really," Jon said. "I don't look for a fight."

"I don't know about that," Samantha said. "Seems to me you could have avoided all three of those incidents."

"No, I couldn't avoid them. Today, if I'd been with my two kids in the car, my first responsibility would have been to take care of the kids. I'd have done that. But the situation was different. CJ had the kids. I had to help Lieutenant Elkins."

"This is the second time you've tangled with antiwar protestors," Samantha said. "Do you hate them?"

"No, I don't hate them. I don't go looking to start trouble with them."

"I still think you could have left those kids alone today," Samantha said.

"Signs and spray paint, I agree. Rocks and throwing a bucket of paint on a wounded guy crossed a line."

"Oh, so it's like—"

CJ cut in, "Sammie, I'd like another shot of the good stuff, please."

After she went inside, CJ said, "You scare the crap out of Teresa when you charge into those situations. Sammie was trying to get you to see that."

Jon took a deep breath and let it out. "Yeah, Chief, I see that, afterwards anyway."

"What do you see, Jon?" Samantha asked as she set a tray on the table.

"I should have stopped with berserk."

"Except that would have been a lie," Samantha said.

"Right," Jon said. "That's why Catholics need confession, because we lie so much."

"That encounter with those protestors in California, that's what drove you to apply for aviation. That's not a lie, is it?" CJ asked.

"A shot of truth serum for you, my dear." Samantha handed CJ a glass. "And a double for the Catholic."

Jon sipped and coughed. Straight Scotch.

They talked about protest, JFK's inaugural address, the Revolutionary War, *The Rise and Fall of the Third Reich*, and a booklet written by Supreme Court Justice Abe Fortas about protesting within the constraints of the law.

There was a pause in the conversation. The sound of a car driving by the front of the house reached them. CJ rattled the ice cubes in his glass. Jon sniffed at a sweet flower smell. "Honeysuckle?"

"Yes. Brings a few hummingbirds around," Samantha said.

"This is one little bird gonna hum off to bed," CJ said. He kissed Samantha. "If you're still going to six o'clock Mass, Jon, keys 're on the hallway table. We'll have breakfast for you when you get back. Good night."

Samantha tried to shoo Jon off to bed too, but he insisted on helping her clean up. As they did, she told him a story about when they'd been in Japan, their first assignment after Purdue. There had been no house for them on the base, so they rented a house in a Japanese town. To heat the water for the bathtub, they had to go outside and build a wood fire under the tub. She'd done that one night and then gotten the two older girls in the tub for a bath, when Susanna had an accident. She had expelled a couple of floaters into the tub. So, it was drain, sanitize the tub, and start the whole process over again.

Samantha is quite a woman, Jon thought. *There probably isn't much that the Navy, or the world, could throw at her that she can't handle.*

※　　※　　※

Jon was in the Justice kids' bathroom. He stopped brushing his teeth, put his hands on the sink, and hung his head. He looked up and saw the blue plastic toothbrush handle sticking out of his mouth. It was better than looking himself in the eye.

While they had been cleaning up after the party, he and Samantha talked. The talk had been easy and natural, never an absence of things to say. With Teresa, at times, it seemed as if it had all been said. And if he forced it, more often than not she would say he had told her that before.

Talking with Samantha had felt good. They didn't talk about fighting. That subject seemed to have been, if not settled, discussed enough for that night. They spoke as equals, and that seemed worth something extra to Jon since he looked up to her. When the cleaning was done, she hung the dish towel on the handle of the oven. She turned, saw Jon looking at her, and stopped. After a moment, she turned and left the kitchen. She didn't say good night.

What did she see on my face?

Just before she hung up the towel, he had been thinking that Samantha really took care of CJ, and it wasn't clear if he appreciated it. Maybe he took her for granted. He tried to take care of Teresa, but she didn't appreciate what he did any more than CJ appreciated Sammie.

He brushed his teeth until his gums bled. Then, in Sally's room, he pulled the pink-ballet-slipper comforter on the twin bed up to his chest. Sleep was not going to happen for a while. What had Samantha seen on his face? It must have been bad, the way it just stopped her in her tracks. The Scotch had not been a good idea.

He and Teresa were going through a rough time, and he was away from her, for two nights. *What the hell's the matter with me?* He awoke once in a panic from the dream where he was falling into darkness, falling off the earth, and he had nothing to grab, nothing to hold on to, and he flailed his arms against the bedclothes.

When the alarm went off, his tongue felt as if it were covered with caterpillar fur, and the taste in his mouth could have come from eating Cheerios with cider vinegar.

48

Cyril had to two-hand the jar of shine to his mouth. His hands were still shaking after he sipped and set the glass back down on the sticky table. Coming to the twins' cabin in the daylight was bad enough. He hoped he'd never have to come out there at night again.

"You come to tell us something?" Chevy asked. "Or you just come for a drink?"

Cyril looked at Chevy, then at Ford across the table from him, and then back to Chevy.

"Tell somethin'." Cyril tried to one-hand the jar, but he sloshed some, put both hands on the jar again, sipped, and shivered.

"Momma's poppa, John Calhoun, wants you to fill that hole back up."

"Fill it," Chevy said. "We just dug it, to put that Navy guy in. This mean we ain't doin' him?"

"John Calhoun said fill the hole. That's all I know."

Chevy scratched in his ear. "That it. Just fill the hole? He doesn't want us to do anything else to the Navy guy?"

"Just fill the hole."

Chevy's face bloomed a big smile. Cyril didn't know what there was to smile about. Chevy pulled a thirty-eight revolver from his pocket, opened the cylinder, held it up to the coal-oil lamp, and rotated the cylinder.

"Better not," Ford said and scared the hell out of Cyril. He'd forgotten about Ford.

The boys were looking at each other in that way they had that made Cyril think they could read each other's thoughts or something.

Cyril didn't say anything. He just left. His pickup was mighty anxious to feel the civilized blacktop of the Jackson-Meridian highway under its tires.

*   *   *

When she was upset, Teresa often dreamed that her intestines were tied in a complicated knot. Alexander appeared and raised his short sword. She always woke up with the sword descending. But she felt the weapon slice on her C-section scar. Disgusted, angry, and worried about being awakened by the stupid dream, she threw back the sheet, put her feet on the floor, and rubbed her belly.

It was 0145.

She stepped into her slippers, went into the hall, and listened at the door to the babies' room. Quiet. Sometimes Edgar Jon would be awake and just lying there quietly. When she opened the door he'd see her. If that happened, the quiet would be gone. Still, she had to see them, had to see that they were safe. Cracking the door open as quietly as she could, the dim light from the nightlight showed Jen-Jen asleep on her side, facing the doorway. She had to open the door to see over the top of the baby bed to see Edgar Jon. He was sleeping too. And he was breathing.

She let out the held breath, and some of the tension melted out of her. Easing the door shut, she went through the living room toward the kitchen. The hallway past the bathroom to the kitchen, even with a nightlight, was a route she still avoided. It seemed to be okay to use the hallway to go to the bathroom, but, irrational or not, she did not like to use that hallway to go from the bedroom to the kitchen, especially when Jon was not in the house.

Oh, Jon!

The call from that Navy recruiter's office had been such a shock. She'd been relieved when he called after they had landed. No need to worry about a crash, at least until Sunday. But he'd gotten into another fight with some protestors, needed stitches, and lost his teeth.

Teresa thanked God often that Jon had returned from his 1966 cruise alive and without a Purple Heart, and she prayed he'd never get one of those. Back in the States though, if they gave the Heart for injuries sustained in fights with protestors, he'd have the ribbon with a star on it for the second award.

Teresa opened the refrigerator door and studied the apple juice, orange juice, and iced tea all in Tupperware containers on the shelf next to the milk. None of them seemed appealing enough to warrant brushing her teeth again. Closing the door, she went to the sink, ran a glass of water, and took a sip. "*Ptooui*," she said to the sink and dumped out the water.

At the kitchen table, she pulled a chair out and sat in the dark. The night-light in the hall threw a bit of its glow into the kitchen. They had replaced the streetlight on the corner four days earlier, and light from it seeped around the blinds over the living room windows. The streetlight held at bay the blackness, which was capable of hiding nightmare villains. It comforted.

The knot in her stomach was gone, replaced by an icy hand around her heart. Tears started down her cheeks.

She imagined Jon in his tuxedo on their wedding day. *You make me so afraid for you!* She saw him with his officer's hat the day he was commissioned. *Why do you do these things?* She saw him holding two-week-old Jennifer. *It's not your fight!*

The white pickup was her fault. That thought was mixed up in her head too. She had gotten into the pew with Clarissa and brought those two men to their house. She was to blame for the pickup returning to remind her how she had endangered her own babies and made Jon spend his nights watching for them.

She got a Kleenex from the box on top of the refrigerator and blew her nose, and as she was walking to put the tissue in the trash under the sink, she heard the menacing rumble of a car or truck engine from the street in front. The icy hand around her heart squeezed. She stood statue still, waited, and listened. The deep-throated grumble moved slowly past the front of the house. It stopped.

Her breathing stopped.

There was a *pop* sound. She heard, "Shit!" Then another *pop* sounded.

The streetlight went dark, and she could sense nightmare beasts closing in on the house.

Fear tingled the skin of her arms and back.

She was frantic to grab the babies and run. *Run where?* her thoughts screamed back at her. *Run how?* Her feet were rooted to the linoleum.

The engine grumbled louder. The sound moved. Finally, when it faded away in the distance, she ran to the babies' room. They were both still sleeping peacefully.

What do I do now? she wondered. *Call Tutu?* He came by at 2100 to check on her. *He'd come again if I called.*

She looked through the blinds in front, but it was pitch-black. No engine sounds. But they could be coming back for her out of the darkness.

Rose had said once, "After you've said, 'My, what big teeth you have,' then it's okay to holler Wolf."

She went into the bedroom to call Tutu, turned on a light, and saw her rosary next to the phone. As her fingers caressed the tiny crucifix, she thought, *God, in you I trust.* She repeated the thought three times and moved her fingers on the Hail Mary beads under the crucifix. *It would be nice,* she told herself, *if there were terrorful mysteries of the rosary.*

49

Jon preferred attending early Masses. Because of the babies, and Teresa, they went midmorning. Early Mass attendees were older and quieter. Moments of silence occurred before early services, and sitting in that church stillness had always seemed healing and restorative to Jon. That Sunday, however, the silence just provided opportunities to dwell on the night before. During the conversation on the patio, both CJ and Samantha had disapproved of what he'd done at the recruiting office. Then he'd looked at Samantha in an inappropriate way. He worried, during the service and the drive back, about what he'd find when he returned to the Justice home.

He hadn't expected a happy kitchen, the girls lined up on a bench in the breakfast nook, patiently waiting for CJ's pancakes on the griddle, and for CJ to greet him as if nothing untoward had happened the night before.

Just after Jon entered the kitchen, Samantha walked in and hugged CJ's back.

"Mommy, you'll make Daddy burn the pancakes." The oldest, Sarah, watched out for her sisters and herself. There were still four pancakes on the grill. CJ held the spatula in his left hand and turned to give Samantha a frontal hug and a kiss that was not perfunctory.

Sarah sighed. "She makes him burn the pancakes *all the time!*"

Watching CJ and Samantha, Jon experienced another spike of jealousy. Teresa would have gone to Jennifer and Edgar Jon first.

The three girls stared at the kiss. Jon thought they liked what they were seeing, that they might even be made to feel secure by it.

The Justice family seemed so comfortable with each other and so happy with their Sunday morning. Jon felt as if he were observing it through a slit in a curtain, as if it wasn't seemly to be watching them.

"Uncle Jon's on a spaceship," said Susanna, the middle daughter.

Sarah giggled.

Samantha still had an arm about CJ's waist. "I said good morning, Jon."

"Oh, sorry." He glanced quickly at Samantha, just long enough to note her eyes sparkling and to feel something electric between them. He quickly looked away.

"You made Uncle Jon blush, Mommy." It was Susanna again.

"Alright, you rug rats and exalted, blushing houseguest, let's get this breakfast under way," CJ said. "Serving wench, get the houseguest a cup of coffee while I serve the princesses their royal pancakes. The unburned royal pancakes, I point out."

Jon sat next to Princess Sally. Samantha placed a mug of coffee in front of him. He took a sip. It was weak. That was how CJ made coffee.

* * *

Before CJ drove Jon to the airfield, he dropped Samantha and the girls at the base swimming pool by the Officers' Club. Jon knelt on a knee to hug Sally and Susanna but stood to hug Sarah. Samantha wore a midthigh-length terrycloth robe that covered her two-piece swimsuit. Embracing her made him sweat.

She kissed Jon on the cheek. "Tell Teresa we missed her."

Jon moved up to the front seat as Samantha herded her daughters toward the pool entrance.

As they drove to the airfield, it was silent, one of those lip-locking, tongue-gluing silences like the ones that followed a Teresa "talk to me." Jon knew he had to say something, but everything he considered seemed contrived, fake, forced, and false. He wondered if Samantha had said anything to CJ.

"How's it feel, Jon, being an old married man with kids among the bachelor student pilots?"

Jon sat up straight and tried to get some thoughts organized.

"It's a little funny for me too, you know," CJ said, "being with all these egghead college science and engineering types. But that's why I'm here, to put some age and experience into the nuclear sub officers' corps. It's not quite the same with the aviators, is it?"

"Well, no. Right now it's just about flying an airplane. Leadership, age, experience, none of that matters. Only the flying matters. I think that's how the Navy looks at it. Fitting in with others in the program is hard. We have Jennifer and Edgar Jon, and the other students, well, they have whatever bachelors worry about during off times."

And then it wasn't hard to talk anymore. It was like being back at Purdue, like during the second semester when Jon got to know him pretty well. CJ had mother-henned him, watched him to make sure he wouldn't drop out, as almost a third of the class had.

Jon would have stayed the course with the program without CJ's attention. The Purdue scholarship was a once-in-a-lifetime opportunity. Even a goober farm boy from St. Ambrose, Missouri, population 277, knew that.

As they rode, CJ talked about sub school, and Jon talked about flying. Then Jon felt time slipping away. He had one issue he wanted cleared up.

"CJ, um," Jon said and then was stuck searching for a way to put his question.

"Go ahead, ask."

"You don't think I should have charged into those protestors at the recruiting office?"

"As far as I'm concerned, you're the one who has to decide that."

"Last night both you and Samantha disapproved."

"We were trying to give you a few things to think about. And it worked both ways, you know. The conversation gave me plenty to mull over."

There was a thought. CJ got something to think about based on what Jon, the junior NESEPer at Purdue, said?

They drove up to the gate in front of the Quonset Point Naval Air Station, and Jon and CJ nodded acknowledgment of the sentry's salute to the officer sticker on the station wagon windshield.

CJ stopped in front of the base operations building, and Jon got out.

"Thanks, Chief," Jon said through the open passenger door. "Thanks."

Mother Hen smiled, nodded, and said, *"De rien."*

50

Clarissa descended the gently sloped ramp from the concourse to ground level and the crowded main lobby of the San Diego Airport. Someone was supposed to meet her with a sign. She stepped to the side and surveyed the crowd. There, a brown-skinned young woman was holding a black Magic-Markered sign with her name. She was five two or thereabouts, had black hair pulled back into a ponytail, and wore a bright-yellow blouse. *Nineteen or twenty*, she thought.

Clarissa worked her way through the press of people moving right and left between her and the sign. The sign girl noticed her, pointed to the sign, and mouthed, "You?"

Clarissa nodded, and the sign girl smiled.

"I'm Juanita," Sign Girl said. "You checked luggage, yes?"

Juanita led the way to the crowded luggage carousel. She pushed between two men, and then pulled Clarissa beside her. Both men frowned at them. Juanita either was oblivious or didn't care. Clarissa smiled uneasily and wished she could be so confident and assertive.

"You were in Nebraska, yes?" Juanita asked.

"Omaha."

"Oh, that must have been glorious. It just didn't seem like Bobby could win Nebraska, like the system finally realized he could be president, so they had to stop him, you know. But he did win. That's when I started to believe he could be president. And you were there." Juanita shook her head from side to side. Her eyes sparkled.

"It was glorious," Clarissa said. "And when it became apparent that he'd won, I felt like I was the winner as much as Bobby. We worked so hard for him, and it felt like such a big thing. I know it wasn't big, what we did, but hopefully we did help in a small way."

"Oh, Clarissa, such modesty. We are so happy you have come out to help us organize."

"I came out to work."

"You can tell us what you did in Omaha. We have enthusiasm, but we are chickens running around."

"Aren't you connected to the campaign?"

"We aren't connected to anyone."

"I know someone who is in LA with the campaign. I met him in Omaha. I'll call him, if we can figure out a phone number."

"See. I knew you would know what to do. I am so glad they sent you to us."

They *didn't send me,* Clarissa thought. After Bobby lost Oregon, and the George Wallace campaign gained a scary amount of traction, Clarissa called Oscar, the young man she met in Omaha, and offered to help in California. "Good," Oscar said. "There is a request for help in San Diego. You have to get there on your own though." The plane ticket put a major dent in her money for the fall semester.

Daddy would have a fit about the money. Momma would have a fit about her running off alone again.

But if Bobby lost in California, if George Wallace wound up in the White House, what then?

51

Jon knew it would hurt. The edge of the pads in the front of the helmet sat right on top of the cut on his forehead. The helmet was designed to fit tight, not to accommodate stitches and a bandage. Before he left the Justice house, he removed the gauze pad over the stitches and replaced it with a Band-Aid. Still, with the helmet on, he could feel the knot in each one of the three stitches pressing into his head. An hour into the flight, it would be agony. He had a couple of hours to figure something out.

At 1445, Jon's instructor, Lieutenant Frank Morrison, arrived at base operations. Jon had filed for a 1600 departure. It took fifteen minutes to brief the lieutenant on the flight, winds aloft, and weather at their destination.

After the first flight, they planned to meet another T-2, and the two instructor pilots would switch students. The last flight in a phase, the check ride, had to be with a different instructor.

Jon didn't consider himself a salty naval aviator. He only had 58.6 hours in his logbook, but he was seasoned enough to have ritualized the get-ready-for-flight process. A sacred part of the ritual was a stop by the head after the brief was completed. They did that and then walked across the broad concrete ramp to where their plane was parked.

"Teaching point, Zachery. As an aviator, you're going to be getting check rides from now till you hang up your G suit. You get to the fleet, some of the guys who give you the checks are going to be your friends. Check rides are business. It's not personal. You perform, you're okay. You show the check pilot you can't do the business, he'll keep your wife from becoming a widow. It doesn't have anything to do with you. It has to do with your performance. Nothing personal at all."

Jon appreciated Frank. Not every instructor took time to explain things beyond the syllabus.

About ten feet away from the airplane, Jon stopped. It had suddenly occurred to him how what Frank said about check flights fit with Teresa's "Don't bother your husbands with trivial matters" lecture. He recalled his check flight with Refly. Refly had tried to psych him out. He had to work to keep Refly out of his head and flying in there.

He was fretting about a lot of things: Teresa's disapproval, CJ's disapproval, the Catholic Church's disapproval, the Welcome Wagon lady's disapproval. For the next two hours, all those frets were trivial matters. The T-2 jet, the laws of physics, and his ability to pilot an airplane—those three mattered.

"The hell you doing, Zachery?"

"Saying hi to the airplane, Lieutenant. Airplane says hi to you too, sir."

"You're a piece a work, Zachery."

A Follow Me truck pulled up, and a lineman got out to help them get started and clear the ramp. After preflighting the airplane, Jon got his gear out of the backseat and started suiting up.

Frank grabbed Jon's helmet. "What's with this?"

"Got a hacksaw from the crash truck guys. Two flights with the helmet pressing on my stitches would have been agony. Distracting. So I cut the rim of the helmet away."

"Government's probably going to dock your pay for a new helmet. Damn if you aren't a piece of work." Frank laughed. "C'mon. Let's get the hell outa here."

Frank climbed up in front, and Jon started setting up his office for under the bag in back. After post-engine start checks, Frank turned on the radio, and Jon copied the clearance. Frank taxied to the end of the runway, got the tower's okay to take off, and positioned the aircraft on the runway.

"Ready to take control?" Frank asked over the ICS.

"Compass reads one five nine, one degree off," Jon said. The compass should have read one six zero, runway heading, but sometimes a compass was off a degree or two. Not a big deal. But you had to know that when you did an instrument takeoff. "Ready to take control."

The aircraft rolled forward just a little and then stopped again, with the heading indicator now showing one six zero, right on runway heading. Jon smiled into his oxygen mask for having called him on the one-degree heading difference. Frank was just checking to make sure he was paying attention.

"You have control," Frank said.

"I have control," Jon said and wiggled the control stick, ran the engine up, and checked the gauges. "Good to go in back."

"Let 'er rip, Zachery."

Okay, airplane, Jon said to himself—ships were female, no question about that, but a jet had to be male—*instrument takeoff. No screwing around now. Let's nail this thing.*

Jon took his feet off the brakes, and they started moving. He tapped first the left and then the right brake to keep them on heading. Then the rudder became effective.

The thrust in the T-2A just barely exceeded the coefficient of static friction. At least it felt that way under the bag, as if the airplane wasn't really sure it had it in it to accelerate to flying speed. Eventually, though, the plane seemed to say, "Oh, what the hell, let's go flying."

Five knots below takeoff speed, he started to pull back on the stick, pinky elevated, as if he was drinking tea with her Ladyship. It was easy to ham-fist it and over-rotate, which was not a good way to start a flight. That afternoon though, the airplane and Jon did okay. And they were flying.

The wheels clunked into the wells. "Three up and locked," Jon said.

Frank gave two clicks of his mic. The flaps were coming up, and Jon adjusted the attitude to keep the plane on climb speed.

"Two Victor one three seven, switch to departure on two eight four point six. Have a good one," the tower directed.

"Thanks, tower. Two Victor one three seven switching to two eight four point six."

After Jon checked in with departure control, Frank came on the ICS and asked what he'd do if he lost his radio. Jon gave him the VFR and IFR procedures. That was the last he heard from Frank until they got to their destination, and Jon hit minimum altitude for the TACAN approach.

"I have the airplane," Frank said before Jon could initiate the wave-off procedure. Jon passed him control and pulled down the bag. You could see forever. The bottom half of the sun was gone, as if the earth had bit away half of a huge orange cookie.

Jon patted the edge of the canopy as Frank squeaked the jet onto the runway.

Squeaking a landing was pulling back on the stick just before touchdown so that the landing was gentle. On a carrier, a Navy pilot didn't squeak it on. Navy jet pilots drove their airplanes onto the deck in what some referred to as a semi-controlled crash. Every landing was supposed to be practice for landing on a carrier. Air force and cargo-plane pukes squeaked landings.

For a Navy jet jock, Frank lands like a puke, Jon thought but had just enough sense to keep it to himself.

Aside from Refly, Jon had been lucky with the instructor pilots with whom he flew. Even the screamers taught him valuable lessons, "words to live by." Even Refly taught him things he needed to know. James Milson had been good that way too, but Frank was unique in how much he shared his accumulated flying wisdom.

52

"Another important lesson about flying, Zachery—you listening?" Frank talked around a big bite of a double cheeseburger with the works, and he made sure Zachery, his own mouth full, acknowledged with a nod.

Jon would probably never fly with Frank again, and Frank seemed intent on dumping everything he'd learned about flying into Jon's brain bucket. Frank was beginning to repeat himself, but Jon wasn't going to interrupt him when he was on a roll. Jon thought about the flight they'd just completed. He had hoped to encounter turbulence so he could show Frank he could handle bumpy air.

"Damn it, Zachery." Jon looked up as Frank stuffed the last of the burger in his mouth under his angry eyes. "You catch any of this? Hell, I'm pouring my soul out and you aren't even here mentally. You have a girlfriend back in Quonset Point?"

Jon blushed furiously and choked down a big mouthful of burger. He took a long drink of fountain 7Up and held up a thumb. "Stay in shape." He raised a finger at each point. "Don't fly hungry. Hit the head before suiting up. Get enough sleep. Take care of all other physical distracters, like I did with the helmet."

Frank smirked. "There's a remote chance you might make a satisfactory aviator out of yourself, Zachery. I've got one more for you. Word is, you have the makings of a good stick. You study, you work hard, you focus, but you're a lone ranger. How are you going to figure out where the airfields are that have burger bars open on weekends if you don't go to happy hour with the squadron? There's other stuff you pick up that might be even more important than burger bars. Happy hours do a lot for aviators. Oh, sure, to some they're beer-guzzling, let-your-hair-hang-down bashes. But there's the important stuff too, if you work it right."

"It's the drinking. It's too easy to get caught up in the drinking and lose control. That's what I don't like about happy hour."

"You don't have to swill the booze. Hell, drink Coke." Frank pointed to Jon's cup. "Or that. But next Friday," he aimed his finger at Jon, "happy hour, be there."

"Hey, Frank" came a voice from the door.

It was the crew from the other VT-7 aircraft. The instructor was Lieutenant Randy Wolford. He and his student, Marvin Maxwell, went up to the counter and placed an order.

Jon had met Marvin in Pensacola during preflight ground training. PT was a big part of the program in Pensacola. Marvin always finished the cross-country runs first. They called him Streak. Jon beat him on the obstacle course though. There were two obstacles where upper body strength was a big help, and Jon went up those like a monkey.

Randy walked over to Jon and stuck out his hand and introduced himself. Jon shook, and then he noticed Marvin standing awkwardly behind Randy. Marvin's eyes were aimed at the floor.

Randy turned to Frank. "This won't be a check ride for Marvin. Do another RNav-5 for him, okay?" Randy gestured "follow me" to Jon and went to another table.

Jon started briefing Randy on the planned flight and the weather, when he asked Jon what happened to his teeth.

"It's a long story, Mr. Wolford. Can I tell you about it after we get to Meridian?" His eyes glanced up at the Band-Aid on Jon's forehead. "Like I said, long story," Jon said.

Randy shrugged. Jon completed the brief, and Randy went up to the counter to get his burger. Jon went to the pay phone in the hallway outside the burger bar and called Teresa. He was still talking to her when he got a rap on the back.

"Come on, Zachery. Hell, you'll see her in two hours, if you get a move on, that is."

"Sorry, Teresa. Gotta go."

Randy was zipping up as Jon walked over to a stall.

"Jesus Christ, Zachery. We don't have time for you to take a dump. Come on."

Jon said, "Yeah, Mr. Wolford, we do." And he closed the door to the stall.

When Jon walked past the burger bar, Frank and Marvin were still briefing. Frank was taking his time explaining something to Marvin. Randy stood on one foot with his other resting on the toe of his flight boot as he leaned on the wall next to the door leading out to the flight ramp. His arms were crossed. He shook his head at Jon, unfolded himself, and led the way out the door to the ramp.

"How'd you get the Band-Aid on your head?" Randy asked.

"It's a long story, Mr. Wolford."

"So get started."

"I'll tell you after the flight," Jon said.

"Don't go getting all pissy on me, you little son of a bitch."

Jon stopped and turned toward him. "Mr. Wolford, you're an instructor and a check pilot. I'm a student naval aviator, a nothing. I know that as soon as I wake up in the morning. You don't have to work so hard to give me that message. Now, are we going to go do the check ride, or do you want to just give me a down right here?"

Jon didn't look away from the IP's glare. Suddenly, Randy's expression changed.

"Son of a bitch! Redass Refly Redmond's all-time favorite student! I'd forgotten."

"Yeah," Jon said, "I'd forgotten about Refly too." Jon started walking for the airplane again, mindful of the necessity to watch for danger from all directions.

Just short of the left wingtip fuel tank, Jon stopped with the toes of his flight boots near a seam in the concrete, and he pointed at the seam. "We leave Refly and all other crap on this side of that seam, okay, sir?"

"Anybody ever tell you you're a piece of work, Zachery?"

"No, sir. Never." Jon took a deliberate and exaggerated step across the seam in the concrete. "Hello, airplane," he said.

* * *

When Jon got to the ready room in the VT-7 hangar at Meridian, the ensign duty officer handed him the grade sheet for the flight. Every item was marked average except for a below-average in headwork. There were no comments on the headwork grade, but Jon knew why Randy dinged him.

He'd implied Randy was like Refly. He had pissed his check pilot off before they even got to the airplane. Not good headwork, but Jon had just absorbed a bunch of wisdom from Frank. Then Wolford blew in the door and seemed intent on poking a massive hole in Frank's wisdom.

The main thing on the grade sheet was that the RI-6X flight-completed box was checked. He passed the check ride.

Still to go at Meridian were a couple of acrobatic flights, a couple of night flights, and the formation stage. With a bit of luck, they could be back in Pensacola in early August.

* * *

Teresa was unusually quiet during the drive home from the base, and Jon wondered if Samantha had told her about the look. The two had talked a couple of times over the weekend.

Jon blithered. He talked about CJ and Samantha, the girls and Sunday pancakes, the party and CJ's sub-school classmates, and how much he enjoyed flying with Frank and how much he learned from him. He avoided mention of Randy Wolford, the incident at the recruiter's office, the Scotch, and the look. As they neared their house, it occurred to him that he had repeated something he'd said earlier about Sarah Justice, and Teresa hadn't called him on it.

They crested the rise, and Jon saw it. The streetlight was out.

"Teresa?"

"After we get the babies to bed."

Getting them to bed didn't take long. They were both already in pajamas and happy to be reunited with the bed they had been pulled from an hour and thirty minutes earlier.

Jon and Teresa sat at the kitchen table, and she told him about her night.

"That's it, Teresa. We have to move you and the babies to Missouri until I finish here. It's just another month."

"No, Jon. I'm not going. We're staying together."

"Teresa, you know I really can't protect you. I can't be on watch all night. You told me that. And even if the police drive by, it doesn't really protect us. They'd have to sit in front all night. They won't do that. Missouri is the only thing that makes sense."

"No, Jon. No." Teresa wiped her nose with a Kleenex. "I'm sorry I got mad at you about Father Allbright."

"Father Allbright? Teresa, I'm the one who needs to apologize about that."

"Whether you do or not, I do most definitely. God put us together. When troubles come, He means for us to face them together. I'm sorry I got mad and stayed mad."

"Teresa, I—thank you." He took her hand. "Now it's my turn."

He started rattling off apologies, and after a handful, she interrupted.

"You had those all lined up. That's what you do, isn't it, line things up? I didn't see it until last night. I thought you just wanted to ignore what happened and move on, pretend it didn't happen. Like Meridian and Clarissa Johnson. But last night I understood. When you work on the stump, you are working to get a jumbled mess lined up, put straight again. Right?"

After they talked, they said a decade of the rosary, Joyful Mysteries that night, and then went to bed. Teresa fell asleep quickly. Jon lay awake and thought about how lined up his world felt then. If Teresa was not upset with him, the world was okay. Even though the world was still full of protestors with whom he disagreed; hard-nosed, cantankerous instructor pilots; and moral thousand-piece jigsaw puzzles—as long as Teresa wasn't angry with him, the world was okay.

Teresa.

It was better to be lucky than good.

"*Whoo, whoo,*" an owl called from the woods across the street from their house.

Jon smiled and fell asleep with his hand on Teresa's hip. He didn't fall off the earth that night.

53

Monday to-do list: front teeth.

Jon arrived at the base dental clinic at 0745, checked in with the second-class petty officer manning the desk, and took a seat.

The waiting room was fairly crowded, with sailors mostly. A lieutenant had wings on his khaki shirt, probably an instructor from VT-9 since Jon didn't know him. There was a no-wings ensign, obviously a student, and Jon. Sailors filled the rest of the waiting room.

Jon took a seat and thought about the white pickup. Shooting out the streetlight was probably just a warning, a "Remember, we got eyes on you" sort of thing. If those two men really intended to harm the Zacherys, they wouldn't bother with warnings.

"Lieutenant Zachery, Lieutenant Zachery, phone call, sir," the petty officer at the desk called. He held the phone out in Jon's direction and went back to looking at someone's dental record.

"Hey, Jon. Duty officer. Skipper wants to see you right away."

"My front teeth got smashed over the weekend. I'm at the dental clinic. Can you see if it can wait?"

"The skipper's yeoman said right away."

As soon as Jon walked into the VT-7 admin area, the first-class yeoman, YN1, got up and stood in the CO's open door. "Skipper, Mr. Zachery's here."

Jon entered the CO's office. He had a phone to his ear and pointed to the chair in front of his desk. "That's right, Captain. Zachery's got a Bronze Star, a Navy Commendation Medal, and a Navy Achievement Medal … right, all with a combat V."

The CO listened for a moment. "Yes, sir. The Bronze Star. Zachery was put ashore with the Marines as gunfire liaison officer. June 1966. The VC attacked. At night. Twenty-six KIA. Marines credited Zachery. Captain, how about if I send the citation for this and his other medals up with him?"

The CO put down one piece of paper and picked up another. "The Navy Commendation Medal. This is a good one too, Captain. Okay, sir, 0930 I'll have him there."

Jon wondered what was going on.

After hanging up the phone, he hollered, "YN1, two cups a coffee, please."

"Black or with stuff?" the skipper asked Jon.

Jon told him, "Both black, YN1."

The skipper met Jon's eyes. "So tell me what happened on Saturday."

Jon started relating the incident, and after a few lines, the skipper leaned forward and held up his hand to stop him.

"Smile, Zachery."

The CO immediately picked up the phone and dialed five numbers.

The skipper explained to Captain Morgan about Jon's teeth. There was a bit of discussion. Then the skipper said, "If I may suggest, Cap'n, the bandage on the forehead is a positive. But the teeth, if he were a hockey player, okay, but not a hero-student naval aviator."

Jon was taking a sip of the weak coffee when he heard, "… hero-student naval aviator."

"Well, how about if we have Zachery keep his mouth shut for the photo?"

The skipper listened for thirty seconds longer. Then he said, "Right on it, Cap'n."

He hung up. "You need to hustle right up to the dental clinic. See Commander Hawkins. He'll fix you up with some choppers so you can smile pretty. From there you see Captain Morgan. Hustle."

"What's going on, Skipper?"

"Dentist, then Captain Morgan. The captain will explain. Hustle, Zachery! Get the hell going."

*   *   *

After Commander Hawkins finished gluing in temporary teeth, Jon stopped in the head and smiled at the mirror. The new white incisors glistened against the backdrop of the less radiant, more off-white enamel.

Commander Hawkins explained that the temporaries wouldn't stand up to eating or drinking. It was just an expedient ordered by Captain Morgan for a photo shoot. And, no, Commander Hawkins didn't know anything more about the photo shoot.

Jon did not want to get tangled up in some kind of public affairs hoop-de-rah thing. He wanted to see the dentist about new teeth, and he wanted to talk to Tutu about the white pickup.

Reacting when the pickup chose to visit was not a satisfactory way to handle that problem. Maybe he and Tutu could bounce some ideas around. Maybe together they could come up with something.

For the moment, he had hoop-de-rah to deal with.

In Captain Morgan's office, a yeoman brought in a silver tray with a coffeepot, sugar bowl, cream pitcher, and two cups sitting on saucers. He placed the tray on the side of the captain's desk. Captain Morgan put cream and two spoonfuls of sugar in his. Jon declined.

"So here's the deal, Zachery. It hasn't been decided what to do about you saving the injured recruiter from the protestors."

"Captain, I think that's going a little overboard. One guy threw a rock. I'm sure he was aiming at windows, not at Lieutenant Elkins."

"Lieutenant Elkins says you saved him. He says you knocked the rock thrower asshole over teakettle and then took on two guys spray-painting his windows. After you charged into the middle of the six of them, they lit out of there."

"Two of them were girls, Captain."

"Lieutenant Elkins says in Nam, he and his backseater had to punch out just off the coast of North Vietnam after they got hit. He got pulled from the water by a helo, but his backseater was captured. He says he knows what a rescue looks like. He says that when the protestors saw him standing in the doorway to his office, an arm-in-a-sling cripple, they seemed to get braver. Then you showed up."

"It wasn't that big a deal, sir."

"Well, as I started to say, it hasn't been decided yet what to do about this incident. Do we publicize it, or do we just put it aside? While the powers that be are deciding, we're going to move forward as if we'll publicize and make Jon Zachery a hero-student naval aviator."

Jon shook his head.

Captain Morgan laughed. "Having trouble with the concept? It's better than being labeled a civil rights agitator, isn't it?" He didn't give Jon a chance to answer. "You got a Bronze Star and the other medals from your destroyer tour. We don't seem to have any heroes. The press is bad, and it's getting worse. Damn Cronkite.

"Still, it may be decided to let it slide, but we have to be prepared to publicize. I need you to talk to my public affairs officer. He is talking to the PAO on the admiral's staff in Pensacola, and the admiral's staff is talking to DC. This is going to be decided at a pretty high level. So we proceed as if we have a story to tell. If the powers decide to let it slide, we let it slide. Not a big deal. Just cost a few of us a little time. So when the PAO takes your picture, you smile pretty, hear? His office is down the passageway on the right."

The door to the PAO's office was open. Lieutenant Bernie Bradford sat behind his desk, introduced himself, waved Jon to a seat on a sofa next to a second-class yeoman, and launched into an outline of a Create a Hero Student Aviator project. Bradford radiated enthusiasm, the noncontagious kind. While he was spouting outline points, he rose and went to his window, turning his back. Jon glanced at the YN2, who shrugged.

The PAO completed his verbal outline, turned, and faced Jon. Jon wished he could think of something to say.

Lieutenant Bradford blinked and started rattling off potential titles for the article: "Hero Student Aviator," "Rock-Throwing Protestors," and "Wounded War Vet" stewed in combinations and permutations with "Attacked" and "Saved."

"The title's one of those," the PAO said, staring at the YN2. "You wrote those down, didn't you?"

The YN2 held up his left hand as he continued to write on a yellow legal-sized pad with his right hand. "It was coming kinda fast, sir. But I'm getting it down."

Bradford turned and stared out the window behind his desk again.

There was a lot of him packed around hips and lower belly. His shoulders were narrow, and his head was small. From the back, he looked like an albino pear in his white uniform. He turned back around.

"Christ, YN2, aren't you done yet?"

The YN2 stabbed a period onto the pad with a flourish.

"I gave you the outline. I gave you titles to pick from. Now you just need to hang meat on the bones of the story." He checked his watch. "Have it done in an hour."

The YN2 went to his desk.

"Okay, here's the plan," Bernie said. "Not you, YN2. You keep writing. Zachery, we need you in a white shirt with your hero ribbons. Base exchange. You'll have to buy a shirt and ribbons."

"I don't have enough money for that."

The way Bradford was looking at him, Jon wondered if his fly was open.

"New plan," Bradford said. "It's even better. I'll go to the exchange." He eyed Jon. "Medium size. Zachery, you stay with the YN2 and make sure the facts in the article are true. When I get back, we'll suit you up and take your picture." And he darted out the door.

"You ever get run over by him?" Jon asked.

"No, sir. When he's on mission, I know to stand aside."

While Lieutenant Bradford was gone, Jon decided Pear would be a good name for him. The YN2 finished the article. Jon suggested: "Recruiter with Purple Heart Attacked by Rock-Throwing Protestors." He didn't want "student aviator" included in the title with or without "hero." The yeoman answered the phone. It was the PAO attached to the admiral's staff. He wanted the article, so the YN2 read it to a yeoman who took notes in shorthand.

As the YN2 hung up, Lieutenant Bradford blew in the door. "Status report, YN2," he said as he hung his hat on the coat tree in the corner next to the wall full of filing cabinets.

"Article's done, LT," the yeoman said. "I read it to the admiral's PAO. Photog's set up in the conference room. Cap'n Morgan's yeoman says a plane is ready to fly the pics to DC soon as they're developed."

"Satisfactory work, YN2," Pear said.

54

Jon asked the VT-9 squadron duty officer if Greg Haywood was around.

"Flying. Back in twenty."

Jon turned away to find a seat.

"You're Zachery, right?" the SDO asked.

Jon stopped and nodded.

"Word is you took on six doped-up hippy protestors on Saturday. That right?"

"I don't know if they were doped up or not. Two of them were girls."

"Word is you hate those commie protestors."

"I don't hate—" Jon shook his head and walked to the row of chairs at the rear of the ready room.

There were two other students to his left. One was looking at a Grandpa Pettibone cartoon in a *Naval Aviation News* magazine.

Grandpa Pettibone was a grizzled old aviator cartoon character who had seen it all, but, *dad burn it,* he still got outraged when the whippersnapper generation did some bonehead maneuver with an airplane, like the power-off landing attempt Jon had witnessed. The other student was looking at a copy of *Approach,* a magazine dedicated to aviation safety. Both students were looking at Jon. He flashed them a gap-toothed smile, and they raised their magazines.

At 1510, Tutu entered the ready room, and Jon followed him to the student lockers.

Tutu peeled off his flight suit, sniffed an armpit of the coverall, wrinkled his nose, wadded the suit into a ball, dropped it on the deck, and said, "Jesus, Jon, you draw protestors like vultures to roadkill."

"Yeah. Got that going for me."

Tutu grinned, reached out his big paw, and ruffled Jon's hair.

"The white pickup came back."

Tutu's face clouded over.

"They shot out the streetlight. Teresa didn't call you because they drove away after shooting the light. Teresa said she thought they just wanted to frighten her, not really do anything."

"Ah, man, I wish she'd called."

"She thought about it, but it was late Saturday night. By the time you could've gotten there, they were long gone."

Two blathering students charged into the locker room before Tutu could say anything. He finished dressing, gathered up his dirty clothes, and they left. In the parking lot, Jon and Tutu stopped next to his Corvette.

Tutu said, "The only thing you really have to go on is that one of the policemen said that the guys in the pickup had probably stuck that spike in your front door some time after their bar closed. Melody has a cousin." Tutu grinned. "Yeah, the snake guy. I'll talk to him and see if he's got some ideas on some bars we can check out."

"Tutu, uh, I didn't mean for this to become your problem. There's just no one else to talk to. But I don't want to get you into this."

Tutu reached out to mess with his hair again. Jon pushed his hand away.

"Hey, not to worry, Two Buckets. I'm just going to talk to Jake."

"Just talk, okay? But promise me you won't do anything else. You just have two hops left, right? Don't mess that up."

Tutu held up one finger.

"You just have one more flight?"

He nodded once.

"Tutu, hey, I'm sorry I brought this up. I shouldn't have even mentioned this to you. I'm sorry."

"Two Buckets, relax your brace. Don't worry. I'm not going to do anything stupid, but I am going to talk to Jake."

Jon watched Tutu walk toward his Corvette. He shook his head.

Talking to Tutu about the white pickup was just as smart as taking Teresa to see Father Allbright.

*   *   *

Teresa got ready for bed after the weather on the ten o'clock news. Jon liked to watch the sports. The St. Louis Cardinals were looking good. Bob Gibson was still mowing them down. In a way, it was funny. Growing up, his dad had rooted for the Cardinals, and he had rooted for the other team. Now, being away from his dad, he could root for what he regarded as the home team.

After the sports, Jon turned the TV off and got the shotgun and shells from the shed in front of the carport.

"Jon!"

Teresa stood in her nightgown in the doorway to the bedroom from the hall.

"What would you have me do, Teresa? The pickup came back. You told me. If they came back, I think we have to assume there's a reason."

"You can call the police."

"We talked about this. You didn't call them when it happened because you didn't really see it. If I call them now, they would just laugh at me, at us. But I believe you, Teresa, and I am going to do my best to take care of you and the babies."

"I just wish you didn't have the gun in here."

55

"Clarissa, Clarissa." Dodo pulled the covers off her roommate. "You goin' to be late for work."

Clarissa moaned, pulled the quilt up over herself, and rolled onto her side.

"You ain't got outa bed in three days. You gotta get up." Dodo shook her. "Don't go to work. Just get up. I'll fix you breakfast."

"Leave me alone."

Clarissa heard her leave, mumbling. She pushed herself up. She felt terrible, with a splitting headache and an upset stomach, even though there was nothing in it. Sitting on the edge of the bed, she leaned over and put her face in her hands and waited for the dizziness to pass. She knew she needed to eat. More than that, she needed to drink.

But it didn't matter. Nothing mattered.

California at first had been like Omaha. Work, work, work. And like Omaha, it had been turning into such a glorious comeback after Oregon. Clarissa sang her "Hall-lay-loo-eeyah" piece for the girls she was staying with as they ate pizza and watched the news. Spirits were soaring. Then Bobby had been shot. Just like that, the world went from the joy of heaven and salvation to hopeless despair and damnation. She had hurried to the bathroom and threw up. She remembered cleaning pizza puke from the rim of the commode with toilet paper, but she couldn't remember anything after that until Dodo met her at O'Hare.

Now standing in her Chicago apartment, she waited for the dizziness to pass enough so she felt safe walking to the bathroom. She got there and wondered why she'd come. In the mirror, a disheveled, stringy-haired, sunken-cheeked, bloodshot-eyed reflection looked back at her.

She became aware of a foul taste in her mouth and got her toothbrush. She fought a gag response when she put a Crest-loaded toothbrush in her mouth. After she brushed, her mouth felt better, for a moment. Then the bile taste returned, and she went back to bed.

Sometime later—Clarissa didn't know when—Dodo came into the bedroom.

"I called your momma. She be here this afternoon," Dodo said. "Now I gotta go back to my job."

56

Jon watched Lieutenant Bradford stride into the ready room, mission and purpose written large and clear on his face. Hands on ample hips, he eyed the scattered students for his target. Pear's eyebrows leaped up, hovered for an instant, and then settled low, abetting the sudden bloom of his ferocious frown.

"Zachery." Bradford pointed his index finger and then crooked it once in a "You come with me" gesture. "We have a disaster!" he emoted to the room, spun on his heel, and stomped out.

Besides the duty officer behind his desk, eight students had distributed themselves over the chairs, as if someone had calculated an arrangement that resulted in the maximum distance between each one. A sailor stood at the grease board, adding a line to the flight schedule. Ten pairs of eyes shifted from magazine or task to the back of Pear and then to Jon Zachery.

Jon hoped the hero business would just fade away, a real fade, not the MacArthur kind. When he said "fade away," what he meant was "you and I both know you can't get along without me," but no such luck. *General MacArthur and First Lieutenant Amos—there's a pair for you,* Zachery thought. *But a fade, not a disaster. And what's the disaster?*

At 0630 that morning, the squadron skipper informed Jon that the Navy had decided to publish the article. It was going through a final editorial review, however, and he needed to stand by in the ready room in case there were questions.

Jon took a chair in the back row in the ready room with a book, *The Age of Reason Begins*, Volume VII of *The Story of Civilization* by Will and Ariel Durant. Through his book club's bonus awards, he could afford the book. He had read it before but wanted to read it again. He was especially intrigued by the "Note to the Reader" in the front matter.

According to the Durants, Faith and Reason were mortal enemies. In the period from roughly 1550 to 1650, murderous nationalism rose and murderous theologies declined. Murderous theologies. The Inquisition qualified. *The Catholic Church, a murderous theology.* That thought always stopped Jon.

He thought about Meridian and what was playing out in the town between white people and Negroes. It didn't seem to be either nationalism or theology, but the threat of murder was sure there.

Growing up in all-white St. Ambrose, Missouri, the townspeople used only one word to talk about Negroes, the other N word.

Up until the St. Louis Browns left town, Jon's dad had followed them. He took Jon to see a game once. His dad wanted to see "Mr. Paige" pitch. It hadn't occurred to Jon before, but his dad called him "Mr.," as if he was a regular person. Regular, you know, white.

Satchel was Mr., but his dad called other colored people the regular St. Ambrose name.

He read the "Note to the Reader" again. Murderous nationalism. Jon wanted to get back to Vietnam before the war ended. He wondered how many young men, since that rise of murderous nationalism began, had prayed, "Please, God, don't let the war end before I get there."

Then Pear staged his ready-room entrance and exit.

By the time Jon got to the passageway, Lieutenant Bradford was almost to the admin office, and Jon ran to catch up. Jon opened the outer door to admin in time to see the PAO pull the CO's door open and charge into his office.

"A disaster, Skipper!" Pear blurted. "It's all blown up on us! It's megatons of disaster!"

The XO and the training officer sat on chairs to the left of the door. The XO turned and frowned up at Pear.

Seated behind his desk, a brief moment of surprise was shouldered off the CO's face by outrage. "Jesus, Bradford! What the hell's the matter with you, busting in here like this?"

Just then, the first-class yeoman who ran the admin office pushed around Lieutenant Bradford. "Skipper, Captain Morgan's on the phone."

"Christ, XO." The skipper pointed at the PAO. "Get him out of here." Then to Lieutenant Commander Fransen he said, "We'll do this later, Leroy."

The skipper grabbed the phone. "Yes, sir."

The XO had Lieutenant Bradford by the arm and was propelling him toward the outer door of admin.

"Wait, XO. I know what the call is about. I should be in there," Lieutenant Bradford said.

"Out!"

Lieutenant Commander Fransen followed the XO and Pear. "What a goddamn zoo," he said. He looked at Jon, as if it was his fault.

Outside the door to admin, the XO spun Lieutenant Bradford against the wall and waved his finger under Pear's nose.

The CO's door was open. "Yes, sir," he said three times, and then he hung up.

"YN1," the skipper yelled. "Get Zachery—" Then the CO saw him, and he shook his head and waved Jon into the room.

Jon stood in front of the desk and saw the CO's intense repressed fury in his angry eyes. "You just can't keep out of trouble, can you?"

Jon had no idea what he was talking about, but saying anything didn't seem like a good idea.

"Damn, damn, damn," he said and sat behind his desk and immediately stood up again. "YN1!" he yelled louder than the first time. "Get the XO and the PAO back in here!"

Jon moved out of the doorway so the two could come back in. The CO pointed the PAO to a chair.

"You sit down, and I swear to God, if you open your mouth before I ask you a question, I will rip your beating heart out of your chest and squeeze it bone-dry in front of your face before your eyes go dim!"

Jon saw the XO start to smile, but he quickly clamped a lips-pressed-together scowl onto his face to match the skipper's anger. The YN1 came in and placed a mug of black coffee on the corner of the skipper's desk.

The skipper let out a breath. "You don't have some medicinal brandy to go with it, do you, YN1?"

"Actually, Skipper—"

Surprise blazed over the skipper's face. "Thanks, YN1. Um, no."

The skipper apparently hadn't expected the YN1 to admit he had booze in the office.

"Okay, Mr. Bradford," the CO said, "you have a picture to show me?"

Pear started to stand, and he said, "Oh, yes, sir, Skipper." His enthusiasm motor had gone from zero to sixty in a second, but the skipper pointed at him, and he abruptly shut up, sat back in his chair, and raised his hand to his heart.

"The photo, XO. Please."

The skipper took an eight-by-ten photo out of the manila folder the XO handed him. He looked at it for a moment. Then he showed it to the XO.

Lieutenant Bradford edged forward on his chair. "See. Disaster! This was in a San Francisco paper this morning, and it's as bad as the South Vietnamese general executing that gomer in Saigon!"

An image of that photo flashed into Jon's mind: the gomer kneeling, the muzzle of the general's revolver just a foot or two from the man's head when he fired, the matter expelled out the exit wound caught on film, the VC's mouth open, almost as if to say, "Ow! Goddamn!"

The skipper was holding the photo, and he and the XO turned and looked at Jon.

"You said you only fought guys," the skipper said.

"I knocked one guy down, threw another one to the sidewalk, and one of the girls hit me with her sign. She got me twice. That's how I got the cut on my forehead. I never fought with her. One of the other protestor guys grabbed her, and then they all ran for their cars. I never fought with either of the two girls."

The skipper handed him the photo. There was Jon Zachery, an ugly, gap-toothed snarl with kill lust slathered all over his face, his right fist cocked and ready to fly at the profile of a young blonde girl with a horrified look on her angelic face. There was a caption under the photo: "Berserk naval officer attacks peaceful demonstrators."

Jon shook his head. "It wasn't like that, Skipper."

"The picture shows what it was like, Lieutenant Junior Grade Zachery," Pear cut in. "Also, I found out he got his Navy Commendation Medal for shooting a girl! The VC he shot was a girl. It's just a disaster!"

"Jesus!" the XO said.

"The NCM, tell me about that again," the skipper said.

"Sir, my ship was anchored in the Saigon River. We were doing H and I, harassment and interdiction."

"We know what H and I is." Pear's voice dripped scorn.

The skipper's chin sank to his chest for a moment, and then he charged around the desk, grabbed the front of Pear's shirt, hoisted him to his feet, and dragged him out to the passageway outside the admin office. He ordered the PAO to stand with his back against the wall.

The skipper stormed back to his office and slammed the door behind him. He said, "You were saying, Mr. Zachery?"

"Uh, yes, sir. H and I, Saigon River, lookouts spotted some trees and brush drifting toward us. We were talking to the PBR, the riverboat guys, and they told us that the VC were known to put a swimmer in driftwood to get close to a ship so the swimmer could attach a mine to it and sink it. So, the XO, our CO was ill at the time, and the XO was running the ship. The XO sent a crew and me out in a motor whaleboat to see if there was a swimmer in the driftwood. There was. It was dark, and with the spotlight, I couldn't tell that the swimmer was a girl. The XO had told me to not take chances, and there were three sailors with me in the boat. I thought there was danger the swimmer could trigger any explosives he—she—had and take us all with her. I shot her. She did have a satchel of explosives tied to her."

"Bother you?" the XO asked.

Jon looked him in the eye. "If she had triggered her explosives and hurt any of the sailors with me, that would have bothered me."

"That's it?" The XO was clearly disgusted with Jon. "Used to be a peaceful job. Then you!"

"I don't go looking for trouble."

"Sure finds you." The XO glared at Jon. "Magnet-ass."

The skipper sat behind his desk. "Alright, XO," he said. "Don't make me park you at parade rest next to Pear."

Jon was surprised to hear the skipper call Lieutenant Bradford "Pear." It seemed like a junior officer thing to call someone a derogatory nickname. Jon's nickname had been Two Buckets on the destroyer because he got seasick. His aviator—rather, his student naval aviator—nickname was, apparently, Magnet-ass.

"At the risk of telling you something you already know," the skipper said, "a magnet-ass is a guy who routinely brings his plane back from a mission full of shrapnel holes, while everybody else in his flight comes back unscathed."

"Fly too low, too slow. Fly stupid," the XO piped in, "blame magnetic ass."

The skipper held up a hand to shut him down. "Get the YN1 to see if he can get that crippled recruiter Zachery rescued on the phone. We have to make sure we have all the facts right before I call Captain Morgan back."

The XO left, and the skipper said," Okay, Zachery, if you go anywhere, tell the duty officer."

Jon went back to the ready room, called Teresa, and explained about the picture the skipper had shown him. She listened to it all, and then she said, "Oh, Jon!" in a tone of voice that made him think of a painting of the Blessed Virgin with a tiny sword stuck in her heart. "Oh, Jon." It was also Navy wife speak for "I wish you weren't such a magnet-ass." At least Rose would have put it that way even if Teresa never would.

After hanging up, Jon didn't bother checking out with the duty officer. He went to the gym and worked the speed bag. Then he ran. Back in the ready room, no one had asked for him. He went to the other training squadron, VT-9, and asked for Tutu. He had been scheduled to fly his final hop, but the flight had been canceled. He'd gone home.

57

When Ford and Chevy needed money, they borrowed a stake bed truck from John Calhoun to haul a load of pulp to the mill. They liked to check in with their cousin Rafe once a week also. It was handy having a cousin on the police force. Rafe was at home when they returned the truck.

"Still pretty hot," Rafe said as Chevy handed him the truck keys. "That Jew synagogue the same weekend as that last church that got burned really got folks in a tizzy. We're doing all kinds of extra patrols."

"What? Folks in a tizzy 'cause a Jew church blew up?" Chevy asked.

"No, Chevy. Those church burnings out in the counties, nobody worried over much. They're in a tizzy 'cause now stuff is coming to town. Those two shotgun blasts into living room windows a couple months back. The Jew church on the edge of town and the same week with another burning in Newman County, and now Bollinger's disappeared—that's what gets the folks het up." A funny look came over Rafe's face.

"What?" Chevy asked.

"Pap says I shouldn't talk to you boys anymore. Security, you know?"

As Chevy drove the pickup out of John Calhoun's dirt driveway, he said, "Security. Don't talk to Rafe. And what's with these townspeople? You'd think they'd appreciate somebody blowing up a Jew church in their town. We oughta tell 'em we saved them from another invasion of Northerners too."

As usual, Ford didn't say anything. That bothered Chevy sometimes, but that day, he had money in his pocket, and he continued a monologue about the ungrateful bastard townsfolk in Meridian until he saw the bar ahead and grinned.

"Elmer's."

"Better not," Ford said.

"Just going to get something to eat. Harry said we had to lay low for a bit. Didn't mean we couldn't eat. An 'e was talkin' about bars after the sun goes down. Still light out."

Ford looked out his passenger-side window and shook his head as the truck jounced through the holes of Elmer's parking lot.

"Come on, Ford. It'll be okay. Just grab something to eat, and then we'll go back to the place. And one beer." The paper money in Chevy's pocket was as real and heavy as a gold ingot.

* * *

At 1530, Tutu passed the city limits sign. He cast a casual glance over at Elmer's parking lot. There were three cars and a black pickup parked in front of the bar. Then he saw it, and he sat up straight. A white beat-up pickup was parked to the side of the lot up against a line of trees and brush. It had to be the one.

Tutu's heart rate kicked up a notch. He pulled into a two-pump gas station with his Corvette facing Elmer's. An attendant came out, wiping his hands on a red rag.

"High test," Tutu said.

"Reckon so." The attendant was almost as tall as Tutu but skinny as a rake handle.

Tutu put the top up while the young man filled his gas tank, checked the oil, and scrubbed bug cadavers off the windshield. At another time,

Tutu would have been aggravated with the slow motion, but not then. He mulled over the advisability of going home to change into skivvies. They might be in there till 2:00 a.m. The operative word though was *might*.

After he paid, Tutu pulled forward and parked by the phone booth at the edge of the station's ramp. He was hungry, but he didn't want to risk missing the white pickup leave the parking lot.

He was glad he had the Hemingway book about hunting in Africa in the car. It could be a long night on stakeout. He found his place. Papa wanted to bag a sable antelope, but it was an elusive beast.

* * *

It was 2100, the babies were down, and Teresa was exhausted. Jon hadn't called since 7:00 p.m., and there was no telling what was going on out at the base. Sometimes the emotions just sucked the energy out of you. Yesterday Jon was a hero, and this morning he had caused a disaster.

Even the rosary had no comfort, no power to leach the poison out of her muscles and bones and soul. She sat on the side of the bed and resigned herself to another of those nights where a knotted stomach would keep her from sleeping. And if she did sleep, Alexander's sword would jerk her awake.

She was about to put the rosary back in the drawer of the bedside table, when she remembered the terrorful mysteries she'd put to the rosary. Terrorful mysteries had helped so much that night. Terror and the mystery of what to do about it overwhelmed her, but that night, after she prayed the rosary with her mysteries, she had been able to sleep.

Picking up the rosary again, she started with the first "Please help me hold it together" mystery.

* * *

"Christ, Zachery, what are you still doing here?" The skipper had just come in from his night flight, and he saw Jon sitting in the back row of chairs in the ready room. "Aw, hell, I told you to stay close." Then he turned to the squadron duty officer. "Any messages for me, SDO?"

"No, sir," the ensign replied.

The skipper turned back to Zachery. "I'm not flying tomorrow, and neither are you. In my office 0645. Go home."

"Sir," Jon said and stood up. His mind was empty, but both anger over having been forgotten and relief for the same reason were outside and thinking about coming in.

*   *   *

The rap on the window of his car startled Tutu awake, and he sat up straight. Two policemen were standing beside his car. He sat up straight. The younger one was next to the car and had a billy club in his hand. Standing back a few paces, an older policeman watched.

Tutu handed over his license and registration and got out of the car when told to do so.

After the younger one had patted him down, the older policeman asked, "Watcha doin' heah, Navy? Get into some shine? Sleepin' it off?"

"No, Officer. See, I met this girl at the club on the base last Friday night. She gave me her number. I called her, and she was supposed to meet me here. While I was waiting, I fell asleep."

"You been here a spell. Del runs the station there." The older policeman hooked his left thumb back over his shoulder, indicating the dark station behind him. "Says you parked here since about four. Near ten now."

"Yes, sir. Well, like I said, I called this girl. She said she'd be here in fifteen minutes. I remember looking at my watch after twenty minutes. Then I guess I fell asleep." Tutu manufactured an abashed look. "Guess she didn't show up."

The older policeman pulled a small notebook from his shirt pocket and wrote on one of the pages.

"Give him his papers back, Rafe." To Tutu he said, "You can go. But, just so you know, I'm goin' to be watchin' for ya."

"Yeah, and maybe you should leave our Miss'sippi gals—"

"Rafe, goddamn it." The older policeman pushed the young one toward the patrol car parked by the gas pumps. Over his shoulder he said, "Mr. Haywood, you git."

Tutu opened the door of his car, but he took a moment to look at the parking lot in front of Elmer's. The lot was full of cars. He couldn't tell if the white pickup was still there or not.

The speed limit was thirty. Tutu drove at twenty-nine and a half.

Well, that worked out pretty well, he thought. *Falling asleep. Getting rousted by the cops. You dweeb, Haywood!*

*   *   *

When he got home, it was 2245, and Teresa was in bed. She was awake. He could feel a chill radiating off her. He stood next to the bed, trying to figure out the right thing to do.

"What?" she asked in a voice with saw teeth at the edges.

"Uh, I have to go in early tomorrow."

"Of course." And she rolled away from him.

He slept on the couch, again, and got up for his shotgun vigil.

58

YN1 was alone in the admin office. He pointed to the two-carafe coffeemaker. "Pot's there."

The skipper's and the admin officer's doors were closed. The XO's door was open, and he was working through a stack of papers on the blotter atop his gray metal desk. Jon got a Styrofoam cup and took some coffee back to the Naugahyde sofa positioned against the wall next to the door into admin.

Jon didn't know the YN1's name. Many people in the Navy were known by their job or rank.

He considered telling the YN1 that the CO had told him to be there at 0645, but after thinking about it a moment, the YN1 would know. He was one of those guys who knew everything.

The YN1 was sorting messages into stacks. He was about five ten, not skinny, but certainly not fat. He had black, thick, close-cropped hair with a part on the left. Jon thought it had been to obedience school. It made him want to reach up to straighten out what wind or a hat had done to mess his own fine hair, which was so susceptible to disarrangement from the least of stimuli.

The YN1 stood up and took one of the piles of paper into the XO's office. The XO groaned.

"Jesus, YN1! "

"It's not so bad, XO. It's worse most weeks."

"Balls!"

A bit of student naval aviator wisdom: Aviators drew flight pay, not to compensate them for the extra risk associated with their job, but rather to get a pilot to do paperwork.

As the YN1 exited the XO's office, the CO jerked open the door to his office.

"XO, need you in here, please," the skipper hollered.

The skipper stepped out of his doorway and into admin as the XO hurried out of his office.

"They want you on the phone, XO," the skipper said.

The XO stopped within arm's length, question and concern on his face.

"Go on, XO. Don't keep them waiting."

The skipper whispered something to the YN1. He got a flat pint-sized bottle out of his bottom right-hand desk drawer, followed the skipper into the XO's office, and closed the door.

In the skipper's office, the XO was standing in front of the desk with his back to Jon. "XO, sir," he said into the phone. He listened for a few seconds, and then his shoulders slumped. "Yes, sir," he said in a small voice. "No, sir." He stood up a little straighter. "Yes, sir." He listened, and then he turned and looked at Jon. The XO was angry. He turned his back again. "Chickenshit, sir!"

The XO took the handset away from his ear, looked at it, shook his head, raised the handset back to his ear, and listened some more. "Yes, sir ... Yes, sir ... Yes, sir." He hung up the phone, and then he lifted the handset again and said, "Go to hell!" into it, but Jon was certain he made sure there was a dial tone there first. "Goddamn all heavies," the XO said as he hung up the phone again.

To Jon, it was strange hearing the XO cuss *heavies*. Almost every officer a lieutenant (jg) met was a heavy. The XO qualified as a heavy twice: as a lieutenant commander and, in his position, as the number-two man in the squadron.

For a moment, the XO leaned on his arms with his hands on the front of the skipper's desk. Then he stood up straight, picked up the phone, dialed one number, and waited, probably getting an outside line; then he dialed another number.

"Betty," he said, "it has hit the fan. Jim's been fired. I'm acting CO. I was on the phone with a captain from the admiral's staff … Hang on." He laid the phone on the CO's desk. His eyes hit Jon like a slap, and then he pushed the door shut.

The XO's eyes made Jon perspire. He had sweat on his upper lip and was clammy all over. Wiping his lip with a handkerchief, he stood up and pulled the backs of his trousers away from his thighs.

The picture—could all this be happening because of that picture Lieutenant Bradford brought in yesterday?

The door to the CO's office opened, and the XO motioned Jon inside. He didn't invite Jon to sit.

"Zachery, you have to go to Pensacola. You're getting an admiral's mast on Friday at 1000." He was using complete sentences, and that threw Jon for a moment. But then what he'd said sank in. Jon started to say something, but the XO held up his hand. "Destruction of government property, destroying your flight helmet, that's what you are going to be charged with, as well as conduct unbecoming an officer. Getting into a fight at the recruiting office, mainly, but also flying two flights after you had been injured without getting properly checked out."

Jon waited to make sure he was done speaking. "Okay to say something, XO?"

"I'm CO. Acting. Skipper was relieved."

"What? Why?"

"Was on probation. Landing accident, Red Redmond. Two instructors, two safety policy violations. PAO disaster. Last night, maintenance incident. Injured sailor. Last straw. Skipper relieved. Going P'cola. Admiral's staff."

"The skipper! God, I'm sorry."

"Sorry! Too damn late! YN1'll cut orders. Drive tomorrow. Admiral's mast Friday. Get the hell out of here."

Admiral's mast was the ultimate form of non-judicial punishment, NJP. The commanding officer of a military unit, whatever his rank, could hold a hearing, or mast, to determine if a subordinate in his command had committed a violation of the Uniform Code of Military Justice. Maintenance of good order and discipline was a CO's main responsibility. NJP was his main tool.

Jon's first CO on the *Manfred* had told him about it. He said it was his heaviest peacetime responsibility. At mast, he was judge, jury, executioner, and attorneys for both defense and prosecution. He said he worked hard to make sure he got at the truth before he ruled on a case. But he also said he was afraid that one day he might face a situation where the good of the Navy demanded one verdict, and the truth demanded another. He worried about that every day.

And in the same flash of recollection, Jon knew. The truth didn't matter. He had already been judged. It was a hard, clear, cold fact.

The XO was beginning to get mad because Jon wouldn't drop his stare.

Jon started sweating again and said, "No."

"What?" the XO almost shouted.

"I do not accept admiral's mast. I demand a court-martial."

"You can't do that!"

But Jon could see from the look on his face that he knew otherwise. In the military justice system, an accused had the right to refuse mast and demand a trial by court-martial. At sea, a sailor could not refuse NJP, but on shore duty he could.

"And I want Commander Harrington as my defense attorney," Jon said.

"Hell, you get the court-martial, he'll be with the convening authority."

"I'm going to insist, and also on a change of venue. I won't get a fair trial here or in Pensacola. If I have to go to Pensacola to tell the admiral I refuse mast, no problem. But I do refuse mast."

"Jesus Christ, Zachery. Haven't you done enough? Skipper canned!"

He wasn't going to call him Skipper. That was a term that connoted respect, and at the moment, that was something Jon begrudged the man—and the Navy, for that matter. "Acting CO, I didn't get him canned. I gave them an additional excuse maybe, but if all they were waiting for was an excuse, they were going to find it sooner or later."

The acting CO was getting angrier, but he didn't stop Jon.

"The destruction of property charge, I went to the maintenance officer on Monday, told him what I'd done, and offered to pay for a new helmet. He told me not to worry about it. He said I got two syllabus hops completed by doing what I'd done. If my instructor had to deadhead the plane back, the cost of the fuel and rescheduling those hops was way more than a helmet. And there would have been the price of a commercial airline ticket." The maintenance officer, Lieutenant Commander Smizer, had also said, *Hell, Zachery, you're a friggin' hero. We're not going to pull some chickenshit thing like charging you for the helmet.* But Jon kept that to himself. Monday had been his day to be a hero.

"You talked to Lieutenant Commander Smizer?"

"I did, and I did get checked out medically by a flight surgeon. Who said I didn't? Did you talk to my instructor? It was Lieutenant Morrison."

"No. On leave. Randy Wolford. Wolford said he asked you about the bandage on your head, but you wouldn't tell him what happened."

"XO, Lieutenant Wolford wasn't there on Saturday. And I don't think he had time to talk to Lieutenant Morrison about it."

"Doesn't change anything. Still going to admiral's mast."

"No, XO, I told you, and I mean it. I want a court-martial."

The XO didn't seem to know what to say, and he didn't correct Jon about his job title. He just glared at him as he did a kind of mental or moral tag-team wrestling match all by himself. Jon felt a little sympathy for him. He'd come in to work, fat, dumb, and happy with his life as VT-7 XO. Before he even had a second cup of coffee, the skipper was fired, and he had a major mess to deal with.

"Mongolian goat rope," the XO muttered and turned his back to Jon.

Jon watched him clenching and unclenching his hands. He had explained what had happened, and still the XO didn't want to do anything. He didn't want to rock the boat. The little bit of sympathy Jon felt for him didn't last very long, and he left him looking at the wall.

The YN1 was back at his desk.

"YN1, I need Commander Harrington's number, please," Jon said.

59

Sometimes trying to hold it all together was just too much. Sometimes taking care of two babies and worrying about Jon flying was too much. Sometimes living in Meridian, with Jon keeping his shotgun in the house and watching for the white pickup truck in the middle of the night, was too much. All the time it was so awful not having anyone to talk to.

Teresa said, "Rose," as she brushed her hair, but her image could never render complex, charged situations into bedrock simplicity the way her friend could. The mirror didn't begin to fit the bill.

Jon had pulled into the carport at 0945. He'd come into the kitchen as Teresa was about to start giving Edgar Jon a bath in the kitchen sink. Without changing out of his khakis, Jon had taken over the bath. Teresa wasn't sure if she should be pleased or if, in his attempt to be helpful just then, there wasn't further reason to be angry with him.

She thought of how Jon had been with Jennifer when she had been an infant. He'd been terrified at the thought of giving her a bath, afraid he would drop her or squeeze too hard as he held her soapy and slippery little arms. But he'd watched intently as Teresa bathed their first baby, and he'd listened to Rose. Now, with the second, he was so comfortable with all those fundamental baby-need chores.

While Jon carefully supported Edgar Jon in the sink and worked the washcloth tenderly over his floppy little body, he began telling Teresa about what was happening regarding the incident at the recruiting office on Saturday. When he got to the part about the admiral's mast and the court-martial, horror and terror assaulted Teresa's brain, and at the same time she felt a physical blow to her stomach.

Court-martial, he'd said!

Teresa always stayed close when Jon bathed the baby, even though she didn't have to be. She was there to hand him a towel, or a diaper, or a clean outfit. But that day, something just exploded in her head, and she had to get out of the kitchen, get away from Jon, get away from the maddeningly calm way he talked about a court-martial.

She slammed the door to the bedroom behind her, sat on the bed, and put her face in her hands. Spasmodic sobs shook her and turned her inhales into a series of choppy air-sucking gasps.

Through the bedroom door, she heard, "Mommy." Teresa got a Kleenex from the dresser, and when she opened the door, Jennifer grabbed her knees.

For just an instant, Teresa was angry at her daughter, angry that she couldn't have just a minute to try to get this tragedy into some kind of perspective, but it flitted away. Her hand caressed Jennifer's head.

Then Jon was standing in the hallway. He had Edgar Jon in the bath towel with the little pocket sewn into the one corner over the baby's head like a hood, just as she would have done. He knelt on a knee.

"Come on, princess," Jon said, taking Jennifer's arm and gently unpeeling it from Teresa's leg. "Mommy needs a minute."

He pulled the door shut.

When Teresa woke up, Jon was kneeling beside the bed. A rosary was in his hands. Jon held up one finger. His lips moved as he said the last Hail Mary. Teresa's angry heart just melted. Waking up and finding him like that, it was hard to remember why she'd been so mad at him.

His face was so easy to read. He was pleading with her to not be angry with him.

Teresa rolled onto her back and stretched her arms above her head. It had been so delicious to get a half hour of peaceful sleep. Then the ups and downs, the swings from hero to court-martial, started flooding back. What would happen to her, to the babies?

And why does he have to go charging into the middle of trouble when normal people would steer clear of it? And his solution to our problems is to bring a shotgun in the house! His shotgun didn't keep our lives from just falling to pieces. The thoughts popped like a string of Chinese firecrackers.

She saw a look come over his face, as if she'd slapped him.

He left the bedroom door open. In a moment she heard him reading to Jennifer.

She knew she should have called him back, but she couldn't. Jon's voice carried in from the living room. He read as he always did for Jennifer. His inflections intended to make the story fun. Fun. "Jon" and "fun" didn't fit together really well. Teresa got out of bed, gathered her things, and headed for the bathroom. Sometimes it was afternoon before she got in the shower. With Jon home, she could get in there before noon. At least she had that blessing.

* * *

While Teresa was in the shower, Jon recalled how Teresa periodically told him that he reverted to being a three-year-old. "It's like I'm the mother of three infants," she said more than once. Jon was pretty sure she didn't really mean it. Maybe she was jealous.

There was seriousness to Teresa that came from the depths of her soul. The seriousness prevented—or inhibited, at least—her ability to have fun. Her aversion to drinking lived down there, in those depths. There were times when something kind of tough happened and Jon would crack a joke. He intended it to take the edge off the bad thing, whatever it was. Teresa always took those bad things personally, even the smaller ones, like getting in the shortest line at the checkout only to have the machine run out of paper. He knew it made her mad, rather than cheer her up, when he cracked a joke in the face of some adversity. But it was his way of dealing with troubles.

Pain and bad luck—it's like they are entirely different things to men and women, Jon thought. *Or maybe it's just that way to Teresa and me. When I crack a joke in the face of adversity, it's as if I ruined something in the pain or in the bad luck that Teresa needed to extract pure and unsullied.*

*   *   *

When Teresa got to the kitchen, Jon had a cup of coffee in one hand and Edgar Jon on his shoulder. As soon as he saw her, Edgar Jon reached out his arms and lurched toward his mother. Jon dropped the coffee and caught the baby. The mug didn't break, but coffee splattered over Jon's shoes and legs and a good bit of the floor.

"Uh-oh," Jennifer said.

Jennifer's "uh-oh" was so cute sometimes, but not then. Teresa started for the tiny mudroom off the carport to get the mop, and Edgar Jon cranked out a yowl.

"Teresa," Jon said and handed the baby to her. Then he cleaned up the mess.

When he was finished she said, "You want to go run, don't you?"

Jon had told her that when he felt out of sorts, it was as if poisonous stuff was infecting him all over, and the way to get it out of his muscles was to sweat, really sweat.

"I'd like to, but I'm supposed to stay close to the phone. I'd like to work on the take-that stump."

He had renamed the sides. The east side of the square he shaped was called Dad, the west was the Navy, the south was protestors (the antiwar kind), and the north was perversely named Meridian. Another flicker of anger lightning sparked along the edges of Teresa's soul.

Men are such Neanderthals! she thought. *Just go chop a stump to pieces and every tragedy in the world can be dealt with.*

"Go chop on the take-that stump. I'll listen for the phone."

It wasn't long before she heard the *whunk* from the backyard. One of Jon's favorite movies was *Shane*. In the movie, Van Heflin, the homesteader, and Alan Ladd team up to chop out the roots of a stump. Teresa had asked Jon if that was his *Shane* stump.

"*Shane* is a great movie," Jon said. "The stump could be a symbol of evil, I think, or it could be a symbol for an old way, dying out, but the old guys refuse to let go. The boss rancher and his brother are depicted as old-maid men and never shown with women. The old way is dying out, but they just can't let that notion take root. Whichever it is, evil or old way, the homesteaders are definitely meek. So Jesus's promise that they get a piece of land too is in there. In *Shane*, the Van Heflin and Alan Ladd characters sweat and strain and get that stubborn stump out of the ground. An obvious metaphor for how the meek homesteaders need to approach the problem of dealing with the ranchers. See? A great movie. The real world isn't so simple, even though I'd like it to be."

"You see all that in a stupid cowboy movie?" she asked.

He shrugged. "I need to sweat. An ax helps me do that."

Whunk. She remembered the time she brought a glass of water out to Jon as he worked the Meridian side of the stump.

After Jon had guzzled the water, she said, "I worry you are going to hurt yourself with that ax."

It was two-bladed, and to Teresa, it looked like a vicious weapon.

"I'm careful. The summer before our freshman year of high school, I worked several nine-hour days by myself with one just like this, clearing some forest for Heiny Schwartz. I'm careful, and I know how to use it."

Jon went in the house and got a black Magic Marker that they had used to label some of their self-packed moving boxes. He drew a line in the center of the stump, and he swung the ax and buried the blade inside the line.

"Beginner's luck," Teresa said.

"I swung an ax a lot that one summer," Jon said. "Then we blew the stumps out with dynamite."

"You worked with dynamite before you were in high school?"

"Heiny worked with it. I was just there watching him."

Whunk startled Teresa.

Axes, dynamite, the Navy. What's going to happen to us, Jon?

Whunk sounded again from outside, but inside nothing chipped away at the black and gray stuff filling and solidifying in Teresa's soul.

60

Tutu was elated. His final hop at Meridian was in his logbook. He had gotten good grades. After getting his wings, he wanted to fly single-seat fighters. If he could continue to knock down good grades, chances were good he'd get his first choice of type of airplane to fly.

He pictured himself on the deck of an aircraft carrier: just returned from a flight over North Vietnam, having bagged three MiGs, two with sidewinder missiles and one with guns. The whole flight-deck crew mobbed and cheered him as he climbed out of his single-seater, nobody in a backseat to hog some of the glory. F-8, *the* plane to fly.

F-8s were still some ways into the future.

It was too early to call Melody; she didn't like to be called at work except at noontime. He'd be back home by then. What he'd like to do was celebrate with Jon, Teresa, and Melody. *I'll talk to her,* he decided.

In the locker room, Tutu stuffed gear into a green canvas bag. Two students, a new guy he didn't know and Al, entered talking. Tutu didn't pay attention to them as they suited up for a flight, but he looked up when he heard, "Zachery."

"Hey, Al, what were you saying about Zachery?"

"Greg. You just had your last hop, right?" Al asked.

"Yeah, but what about Zachery?"

"Word is he's getting a court-martial."

"Court-martial! Jon Zachery? What the hell for?"

"Don't know." Al closed his locker. "It's weird. What's that Sinatra song about riding high one day—"

Tutu tore out of the door and ran to the VT-7 ready room, where he startled the drowsy duty officer. Jon had gone home.

As Tutu drove off the base, he recalled the Monday stories. Zachery had taken on the antiwar protestors and had sawed his helmet to complete his flights. The little fart was something else. Some of the students wished they could think of stuff like sawing the helmet.

He was coming into town when a stake bed truck with a battered white pickup right behind it drove in front of him toward the highway to Jackson. Without pausing to think about it, he followed the two vehicles. West of town, the truck and pickup turned right off the highway and onto a dirt road sliced through the pine forest.

Tutu turned around and noted his speedometer reading as he passed the dirt road where the two vehicles had turned. Seventeen miles. *Better to be lucky than good,* he thought. Finding the white pickup was something, but the real issue at the moment was Jon's court-martial.

As he drove back toward Meridian, Tutu thought about how his squadron mates looked at Jon's squadron, VT-7. Most of the students in VT-9 were six feet tall or taller. The Navy seemed to have assigned all sub-six-footer students to VT-7. In VT-9, they considered the other training squadron on the base to be for short guys and screwups. VT-7 was not as good a squadron as VT-9.

On Monday, as the rumor mill cranked out Jon Zachery stories, the VT-9 students squandered a bit of admiration on the little guy. That a little guy from the screwed-up squadron—and the latest rumor was that the VT-7 CO had just been fired that Tuesday morning, which pretty much confirmed that VT-7 was screwed up—could do what he'd done, well, you just had to admire him. The rumor mill resurrected the Refly boxing match and the story of Jon taking on the KKK his first weekend in town. By the end of the day, Jon Zachery was an honorary tall guy.

A day later Jon was getting a court-martial. Tutu hadn't had a chance to talk to him. The ace private investigator had been busy with stakeout duties.

* * *

Jon was in the backyard with his shirt off and whacking at the take-that stump.

"Hey, Jon."

He had the ax over his head, lowered it, and turned. Tutu was coming from the carport.

"Hey!" Jon said, turned back to the stump, lifted the ax, brought it down hard, and sliced off the point of the square where the Meridian side and the Navy side met. The next time he worked on it, he'd square it off again.

"Jon, I heard about the court-martial. What the hell happened?"

Jon picked up his T-shirt to mop his face and to hide what might be showing there. It felt like a long time since someone had been on his side. Tutu was on his side. His face said so.

"So, uh." Jon cleared his throat. "The issue is a San Francisco paper published a picture of me in the fight I had with the protestors on Saturday. The picture was taken after one of the girls hit me with her sign stick. Caught me on the forehead and split the skin. I had a grimace and a snarl on my face, and I looked like I was going to hit this girl with my fist. I gotta admit, the picture looks bad."

"A picture." Tutu waved his hand, as if brushing at a gnat. "How bad can a picture be?"

"The picture is bad enough the way they used it, and they've got other things they're charging me with."

"What about those kids destroying government property?"

"I talked to the base legal officer, Commander Harrington. He said the six protestors included two college kids from San Francisco visiting

East Coast family. Four were locals. Before the West Coast kids went back home, they hatched the scheme to demonstrate in front of that recruiter office. According to the commander, we know the names of all the kids. But the Navy has decided not to do anything about it. They don't want to give any newspapers another excuse to publish that picture."

"The Navy doesn't want to punish them, but you get a court-martial?"

"The commander says from what he's seen of it, there is no real case against me. Even the crappy little thing they were going to hit me with for destroying my helmet."

"So, no court-martial?"

"Probably not, according to the commander."

"What about flight training? They aren't going to boot you, are they?"

"It's kind of hard to see what they're going to do right now. The squadron has a lot going on. Our skipper got fired, new guy taking over. They can't be too worried about one little no-account magnet-ass student naval aviator. That's what the XO says I am. I apparently have a magnet in my butt that attracts trouble."

"Christ, Jon." Tutu put his big paw on Jon's sweaty shoulder.

61

Bang!

Jon's eyes popped open. His heart was pounding.

"Jon!"

He tore the covers off. Teresa grabbed his arm, but he pulled away and ran to the closet for the shotgun. But Teresa had asked him to leave the gun in the shed. He had done what she asked.

Bang!

It was right outside.

For an instant he was mad at Teresa but angrier with himself for listening to her.

"Mommy!" Jennifer's scream raised the hair on the back of Jon's neck. Then Edgar Jon cut loose. Teresa went for the babies, and Jon stood by the side of the window and cautiously lifted a slat. There was a four-door '59 Ford in the street in front of the house. From the streetlight, Jon saw four silhouetted heads in the backseat.

He heard one say, "Gimme another one."

The car started forward, rolling slowly. A guy, a kid, had his arms and head outside the rear window of the Ford. He worked a cigarette lighter.

A fuse sparked. Then he tossed something in the yard of the next house up the road.

"Let's git the hell outa here!" a voice said.

Bang!

Kids, high school kids, he thought. He watched until the taillights disappeared up the road, and then he went to the babies' room.

Teresa had a baby in each arm, wailing Edgar Jon and big-eyed Jennifer, and she made *shh* sounds and swayed from side to side.

"Just high school kids," Jon whispered. "Just firecrackers."

Teresa's angry face shattered. Tears rolled down her cheeks.

"Jennifer, will you go to Daddy, please?"

Jennifer thought about it for an instant, but then she reached out her arms. Jon took her into the kitchen, got her a glass of milk, and talked to her about firecrackers.

"Gaham cacker," she said.

"Yes, princess." Jon smiled. "A much better kind of cracker."

Jon left Jennifer at the kitchen table with her treat and went to check on Teresa.

Edgar Jon was winding down. While he was nursing, he did a couple of his snuffle inhales. Teresa looked up at Jon with a hard look.

Just when you think things can't get any worse, stand by. It was another of those ubiquitous sailor sayings, like the luck one, though it probably wasn't exclusive to seagoing types. It sure seemed to fit Meridian.

Jennifer was asleep on his lap when Teresa came into the living room.

Teresa hissed, "Put her to bed."

When he got back, Teresa was at the kitchen table. He got a cup of coffee and sat across from her, knowing he was going to catch some kind of hell.

"Jon, we can't keep going like this. At least I can't. And it's a terrible thing to do to Jennifer and Edgar Jon."

There was no safe ground to go to with the conversation. He sat ready to absorb whatever she threw at him.

"Sometimes you act like a kid, playing cowboys and Indians."

He hadn't expected that.

"You can't fight everybody. You are married, and you have two children." She sounded like Samantha Justice. "You have to grow up and walk past some of this, this stuff that you just charge right into the middle of. Our first Sunday night here, you did that, and with the recruiter's office too."

Why is she bringing these things up now?

"You've been trying to do all this yourself, watching for the white pickup in the middle of the night, then going out to fly. It's too much. You are not superman. I don't want to lose you."

That surprised him. He thought she was mad. *How do you figure?*

He went around the table. She stood, stepped into his arms, and cried as he held her.

Inadvertently, I've done something right. Better to be lucky than good.

He wondered if there'd be any luck left after the sun came up.

After they got in bed, Teresa slept. Maybe her tears had washed the worry out of her for the moment. Maybe she was just worn out.

Jon lay next to her and thought about Adak, Alaska. Even if he didn't get either a mast or a court-martial, he couldn't see a favorable way out of the mess he was in. He couldn't see them letting him continue in the flight-training program. Neither could he see them letting him out of his obligated service. Adak, Alaska, was probably his future.

After the five years of purgatory, there'd be a big time gap between college graduation and applying for an electrical engineering job. Would he be able to find the kind of job he wanted? His mind hopped from worry to worry, and nowhere it landed did it find anything comforting, or that even made sense.

He thought of getting out his rosary. He thought about calling Chief Justice in the morning. He thought about the take-that stump, but he felt more like blowing it up.

He recalled how afraid he'd been the first time he helped Heiny Schwartz with a stump.

As Jon bored a hole in the stump with a hand auger, Heiny got a stick of dynamite from the truck.

"Jon, catch," Heiny said and tossed the stick.

Jon jumped up, frantic to catch the dynamite. Heiny thought it was the funniest thing he'd ever seen. It took a while for him to stop laughing.

Jon finished boring the hole, and Heiny tamped three sticks of dynamite into it and inserted a blasting cap and fuse.

When it went off, the dynamite hurled stump shrapnel a long ways.

Heiny laughed at Jon's fear of dynamite without a blasting cap inserted, but he respected the explosive too. They had a blasting cap fail to detonate in one stump. Heiny stayed well clear of the loaded stump for weeks. Then he'd laid a single stick of dynamite atop the stump and blew it up. Heiny made Jon watch from a safe distance. He also made Jon promise to not tell his wife what he'd done.

Several times that night, Jon awoke to the annoying sound of a mosquito buzzing above his ear.

62

Thank you, God, for Jennifer, for making her like one of your angels. She often had that thought about their daughter.

Jon went off to work, though work didn't seem like a proper name for where he headed. She thought of living in the LA basin the year before. The *Manfred* had moved to the Long Beach Naval Shipyard for repairs. She and Jon—and Jennifer too—lived there for two months before they were blessed with a clear day and saw mountains to the east of San Bernardino. The smog hid the towering mountains so effectively and persistently that without that freak clear day, she'd never have known they were that close. The future, Jon's, the babies', hers—it felt like that. It was out there in front of them, but she couldn't see it. *Maybe it's better I don't see it,* she thought.

Then Edgar Jon awoke with one of his ultra-cranky yowls. Interrupted sleep upset his tummy quite often, and his diaper filled with chemicals that attacked his poor little bottom. He was a mess clear up to his armpits. The bathwater seemed to hurt him as much as the contents of his diaper had, and he yowled nonstop. When she got him bathed and wrapped in a towel, she asked Jennifer if she wanted "breftus."

"I he'p." Jennifer looked up at Teresa with big bright eyes.

Most of the time, Jennifer was intent on breakfast as a first item of business in the morning, but that morning she seemed to understand that her mother had to take care of the little maker of big noise. It was fairly easy for Teresa to orchestrate little chores for Jennifer to be "he'pful" with.

Even as Edgar Jon wailed through the bath and getting dressed, Teresa recalled bringing Jennifer home from the hospital and that first day with her in the apartment in Chula Vista. Teresa's mother had been there, and Jon had been there too, but there had been moments when it seemed as if Jennifer and Teresa were the only two people on the face of the earth. The bond she felt with her daughter had seemed that strong, and she felt it again. But then Edgar Jon's persistent noise pushed into the forefront of her brain on the heels of a bit of Catholic guilt.

Teresa Zachery, she scolded herself, *stop daydreaming and take care of your baby!*

Besides, it was not a good idea to waste time in getting a fresh diaper on a baby boy. When she moved to the rocking chair in the living room to nurse him, Jennifer got one of her books, sat on the floor, and began paging through the book. While Edgar Jon nursed and gradually cranked things down toward the calm and peaceful end of his emotional scale, Teresa smiled down at Jennifer. Jennifer was the exception to the rule that ages two and three were "terrible."

She shifted Edgar Jon to the other side, and he seemed to be a moment or two from being totally calmed down. He would probably go down for a nap. Generally, he wore himself out, making noise. Teresa smiled down at angelic Jennifer. She was thinking that, finally, she had the morning under control, when the phone rang. Teresa considered letting it ring, but it could be Jon with news of what was going to happen to them.

Before she'd fallen asleep the night before, Teresa had decided that the Navy would never let Jon continue in flight training after what had happened. And when she'd realized that, a measure of peace had descended over her. At some point in their foreseeable future, they would leave the Navy, and leave Meridian sooner rather than later, maybe even in a few days. She'd started thinking about how their life had suddenly gone from a future with promise to no future at all, but then that bit of peace had floated into her thoughts. During Jon's two years on the *Manfred*, she'd gotten to admire a number of the wives of the officers from the wardroom. She liked how they'd supported each other during Jon's deployment to Vietnam, and although she had never expected Jon to want to stay in the Navy, when he did surprise her with that decision, she hadn't been disappointed or angry or afraid. She'd even looked forward to continuing to associate with the extraordinary women so many of them were. But there had been a lot of things that made life so very hard too. Waiting for sleep last night, she'd gotten it all into balance, and she'd come to peace with the idea that there was no future for them in the Navy.

The phone startled Edgar Jon, and he lost the nipple. Teresa helped him find it again, and then she got up.

"Hello," she said in a voice carefully governed to the minimum amplitude possible and injected with baby-soothing serum.

"Teresa!" Jon was excited, and he was loud, and Edgar Jon started and lost the nipple again. He waved his arm around like he was ready to crank it up again, but she got him reattached and quieted as Jon bubbled. "There isn't going to be a court-martial or a mast. They're dropping the whole thing!"

Teresa felt as if she'd been slapped by the news, and she tensed. Edgar Jon immediately howled.

"Jon, call back in ten minutes. I have to get Edgar Jon settled." And she hung up.

Before Jon called back, she had the baby asleep in his playpen, and she had gotten what he'd said into some kind of perspective. She had worked hard to accommodate the notion that there was no future for them in the Navy, that they would be leaving in disgrace. She had just gotten to where she accepted what was in front of them, and now that was jerked away. Somehow, the loss of the disgrace and the disaster seemed to be worse than the disgrace and disaster had seemed. She wanted to scream.

Before Jon's second call, Teresa had expunged most of the pressure that wanted to blast a scream past the lump in her throat. When he called, the excitement was gone from his voice. He wasn't sure what to do. As far as the Navy seemed to be concerned, the whole business with admiral's mast and court-martial had never happened. A part of him wanted to drop out of the flight-training program and serve out his time in whatever no-load job they gave him. A part of him wanted to continue flying jets.

The sudden changes made Teresa feel helpless. To go to sleep contemplating nothing but ruin in front of them, to wake with another heart-pounding jolt in the middle of the night that scared the babies as much as it did her, to get an hour of sleep, if she was lucky—*Lucky! Hah!*—to wake again to a very distressed Edgar Jon, and then to hear it was all just dropped. Everything was okay.

Last night, they had faced a disaster. This morning, *Oh, sorry, it was a mistake.* But they didn't even say that. The Navy never apologized. She was only a junior officer's wife, but she knew that much about the Navy. The pope was infallible in matters of faith and morals, but the Navy, well, the Navy was infallible in all matters!

By the time Jon called back, she'd decided that she and the children were just along for the ride. There was nothing she could do to change anything. So Teresa was going to take care of what she could control, her babies. The rest was up to God, His sometimes-infallible pope, and the always-infallible Navy.

"Whatever you decide, Jon." She wished she'd just left it at that. But she'd added, "It doesn't matter."

But it did matter, and she knew how that last little sentence would hurt Jon. After she hung up, she thought, *I have to get to confession on Saturday.* Then she went to let her babies know they had a mother who loved them.

63

Ike sat behind the wheel of his pickup, three parking spots away from the phone booth at the edge of the parking lot of the Flying A Truck Stop. A pole light provided entertainment for a cloud of bugs and dropped a circle of illumination over the phone.

The phone rang. Ike didn't move, but his eyes did, from side to side. At the tenth ring, he got out, opened the door of the booth, lifted the phone off the hook, stood still, and listened to see if anything came out of the quiet.

Ike put the phone to his mouth. "Rise," he said.

"Again," came from the earpiece. It was Jimmie.

"Goin' okay?" Ike asked.

"Pretty good. Harlan's working out. Tall, skinny, beard, and ponytail, he looks like he belongs in this group of doper hippies Wexall runs with. Harlan meets 'em coupla times a week. Always brings a baggie of good stuff with him. They like Harlan, especially Wexall."

"You make it sound like he's queer."

"Word is he's got a boyfriend, but apparently he likes girls too. But what he really likes is Harlan's free dope."

"You got any idea about how much longer this might take?"

"Shouldn't be but another week. Harlan's going to take Wexall to this fishing cabin up in Wisconsin in a couple of days. He'll wring something out of him there."

Ike hung up the phone and stood still and listened. When he turned he rubbed his chin like he was thinking rather than very carefully looking around.

*   *   *

Billy sat on the top row of the three aluminum bleacher benches next to the tennis courts. Clarissa had just demolished her opponent with aces, with demonic lunges and dives to make unmakeable returns, and with vicious shots aimed at the girl. The girl wouldn't come to the net to shake, but she did invite Clarissa to go to hell.

"Already been there," Clarissa said.

When he had watched her before, she played well but almost apologetically. He told her once, "You look like you are trying to get the best out of your opponents, not beat them."

She just smiled and said, "I love playing tennis," as if winning had no part of the game.

This was a different Clarissa. After she came back from California, Dodo had called and asked him to come over and help coax Clarissa out of bed. She cursed him until he went away. Then Dodo called Clarissa's parents. Dodo told him that Mr. Johnson had torn the covers off her, pulled her out of bed, and told her to take a shower or he'd scrub her like he did when she was a baby. The Johnsons stayed for three days, and before they left, Clarissa had started running and eating. Dodo told him she was playing tennis that afternoon, and he'd gone to watch. She knew he was in the stands, but she grabbed her bag, slung the strap over her shoulder, and started walking at a fast pace toward her apartment.

He ran and caught up with her. "Slow down, Clarissa, please."

But she didn't. "Were you mad at that girl, Clarissa?"

Looking straight ahead, she marched on.

"You probably feel like everything that mattered was taken from you," he said.

She stopped and faced him. "You have no idea what was taken from me," she said through clenched teeth.

I tried, he thought and watched her stomp away. He wondered if the rip in his heart would ever heal. He had never given his heart to anyone before Albert. Each year of high school, his anguish and self-disgust grew worse. He dated girls, kissed a few, but after the prom his junior year, he never asked a girl out again. What he felt stirring inside him for other boys seemed like a sin, and he considered confessing it. But the idea of giving voice to his torment appalled him.

Then, during the freshman year of college, he studied with Albert. He knew Albert was shallow, lived for kicks, took nothing seriously, but somehow, in seeing how Albert lived and managed those heavy issues, he saw that it was okay to feel how he felt. Albert made it okay to love him. After that first night they spent together, Billy felt as if he had stepped out of hell and onto earth for the first time in his life.

But now Albert was gone. He'd moved out to take up with some unwashed, long-haired dope fanatics.

Billy turned and started walking back to his apartment.

64

On Thursday, flight operations were suspended at the air base for a double change of command. In VT-9, the executive officer fleeted up to the position of commanding officer at 0900 in an abbreviated but formal ceremony in front of the assembled squadron. At 1100 the former commanding officer of VT-9 assumed command of VT-7.

In the afternoon, both squadrons held a series of "back to basics" sessions for the enlisted and officers. For the VT-7 officers, their last event was an address by the new CO, Commander Dan Major, which concluded at 1545. After the CO had dismissed the officers and they began to file out of the theater, Jon followed the crowd and waited in the lobby for the XO.

When the XO appeared, Jon asked him for a minute. They walked to the side.

Jon looked him in the eye. "I want to DOR, XO."

The XO's face manifested a sequence of emotional transitions: surprise, astonishment, and then pissed off. "Stay," he said.

The XO made a call on a wall-mounted phone, and then he grabbed Jon's arm and propelled him outside to his Ford station wagon.

Neither of them spoke as the XO drove from the admin area of the base to the airfield. Halfway to the airfield, the Burma Shave-like safety signs flashed by the car.

Jon said, "XO, where are we—"

The XO flashed an angry look and cut him off. "You fought this thing. People went to bat for you. The skipper took a grenade for you! You won. Now you want to quit?" He shook his head as he glowered at the road.

After the XO had parked the car next to the hangar, Jon had to run to keep up with him. The admin office was empty, but the administration officer's office was open, and a light was on inside. The former CO was sitting behind the desk and working on officers' fitness reports.

From the doorway, the XO said, "Skipper, I got Zachery."

The commander held up his hand. "XO, you've got a new skipper now."

"New CO, not new skipper."

"Ah, XO, mutiny. Let's see, isn't there an article in the Uniform Code of Military Justice against mutiny?" Commander Pabst shifted his gaze to Jon. "And you, not mutiny with you. You just want to abandon ship, that it?"

"Skipper asked a question, Zachery!"

"XO, please. Call me Jim, or Commander Pabst, whichever you prefer. Will you do that for me, please?"

The XO was obviously reluctant to do so, but he nodded.

Commander Pabst smiled. "Thanks for driving him out here. You'd better get back to the club. I'll bring Zachery."

Calling him commander sounded wrong. He should be the skipper or the CO.

Commander Pabst waited until Jon met his gaze. "What's going on, Zachery? Why do you want to drop out?"

"XO said you took a grenade for me. That right, sir?"

"Zachery, you know, better than most maybe. A grenade winds up in the trench with you. Most of the time, someone will jump on the grenade."

Commander Pabst clasped the fingers of his hands together on the desk blotter in front of him. "There's no organization in the American military I admire more than the Marines. There's the elites, the Green

Berets, the SEALS, but for an overall branch of the service, the Marines are something special. We have a couple of Marine instructor pilots who've done a year at Chu Lai. At the club one night, we got to talking about Marines and North Vietnamese. We talked about a grenade in the trench. We even talked about a situation where one of your own does something stupid and drops the grenade. The Marines said it wouldn't make any difference to a Marine or a gomer. In both gomer and Marine trenches someone would jump on the grenade. The difference, the Marines told me, is that the North Vietnamese, or the VC, would jump on the grenade so that his buddies could go on killing Marines. A Marine, they said, would jump on the grenade to save his buddies. So, Zachery, what do you think? You think the Marines are right?"

Jon shrugged.

"Organizations sometimes find a grenade in their trenches too," Commander Pabst went on. "The difference between an individual and an organization is that an individual will jump on the grenade to save a buddy. An organization will grab the closest individual it can to throw on the grenade to save itself.

"We thought we had a PR opportunity, and it turned out to be a grenade. And me, I was already standing on the edge of a cliff with both feet on a banana peel." Commander Pabst sat back in the admin officer's chair and grabbed the point of his chin in his hand. "You didn't tell anyone else you wanted to drop, did you?"

"No, sir."

"So, Zachery, what's at the root of this? I have trouble seeing you as a quitter."

"It's Teresa, sir. I just feel like the Navy—like this situation has really jerked her around. We have two small babies, and we've been attacked in our house. I know she doesn't feel safe there. Last night, kids threw cherry bombs in our yard. Just firecrackers, but after all that happened … and I go from having career prospects to admiral's mast to, oh, it's all okay again. I just don't want to expose her to any more of this."

"When the Kluxers first stuck that note on your door, I know there was discussion about moving you and your family onto the base. But there's a waiting list for base housing, and even the BOQ is full until we get the new building complete. And Captain Morgan said he had assurances from the police that they'd watch out for you. They have, haven't they?"

"The police have driven by, yes, sir."

"The kids with the firecrackers, did you know they were dependents from the base here?"

"No, sir."

"Yep. Apparently Captain Morgan ate some humble pie in front of the mayor and chief of police. Mississippians don't celebrate the Fourth. It's a day of mourning for when Grant shelled Vicksburg. The kids' parents caught a heap of crap from Captain Morgan."

Jon thought about it.

"Besides the note on the door and firecrackers," Commander Pabst said, "anything else happen?"

"No, sir."

The commander stared at Jon a moment. "Have you seen *Cat on a Hot Tin Roof*?"

Jon nodded.

"Big Daddy used the word 'mendacity' in the movie," the commander said. "A good word, that. I think I have a nose for mendacity. At captain's mast I've heard every kind of cockamamy story the fertile mind of a sailor can come up with to justify their violations of the Uniform Code of Military Justice. And, Zachery, I smell mendacity now."

"Nothing else happened, sir."

Commander Pabst shook his head. "I've only talked to your wife once," he said, "and I'll tell you I was impressed. She's a tough lady, probably tougher than you and me combined. Give her some credit for her strength.

"This is what I want you to do. You have real potential to be a good pilot. Think about that. You've got a good head on your shoulders. Not everybody has these tools. Talk with your wife about this. In the morning, see the XO and let him know if you still want to drop out. If you do want to drop, I'll respect that decision, right after I kick your ass. Now wait out there in admin while I finish this last fitness report. Then I'll take you back to the club."

65

TUTU WAS AT BASE OPS at 0600 Friday morning. His helo-pilot friend Charlie showed up at 0601. Charlie and his crew were going out on a two-hour training hop. Fortunately, there weren't many rescue missions for the helicopter crews to fly, and at times they flew to meet their minimum flight times.

Charlie had no problem with including Tutu's reconnaissance mission. It was something to do besides just driving the helo around the area before they practiced auto-rotations at the Remote.

After Charlie gave Tutu his safety brief, Tutu handed him a chart of the area that he had marked with where he thought the white pickup truck had turned off the highway. Charlie studied the chart, folded it, and stuck it in his navigation bag.

"Shouldn't have a problem finding it. We're going to fly at two thousand feet. If we have to, we'll go lower. But we get shot at out here when we fly low."

"I'll get a gun and shoot back," Tutu said.

Charlie said, "Jet jocks!"

After they got airborne and cleared the airfield, they turned west and flew right to Tutu's road. They were sure it was the right one. It led to several shacks, and a few of them had a vehicle parked nearby. Tutu got a good look through the binoculars but didn't see a white pickup.

After the reconnaissance portion of the flight, they went to the Remote. Charlie and the copilot each completed six auto-rotations to a low wave-off, and then they returned to the air station.

Tutu was disappointed. He had hoped to pinpoint a specific house or shack. After lunch, he planned to borrow Charlie's motorcycle, go down that red clay slash of a road they'd seen from the air, find the white pickup, and convince the yahoos who drove it to butt the hell out of Jon Zachery's life.

* * *

Jon was at the XO's office at 0605.

"Daylight been burned," the XO said, kind of ambling the words out à la John Wayne in *The Cowboys*. "So?"

"Stay, if you guys will have me."

His face hinted a smile. "TO," he said.

"See the training officer. Is that what you meant, XO?"

"Said it. Plain as day."

Jon turned and started for the door.

"Zachery. Teresa, right?"

Jon stopped, turned, nodded once, and left.

The XO was right. Jon had convinced himself he should just quit flying, serve his time in whatever purgatory they assigned him, and be a civilian. But Teresa told him she had heard his voice when he called Chief Justice about flying up to see him and Samantha.

Teresa said, "When you were talking about flying, you were pumped up, excited. If you quit, you're going to miss it the rest of your life."

Jon thought Teresa would be happy and relieved, and she had been angry with him for a long time. He was tired of feeling like he couldn't do anything right around her. But when they talked about flying, their relationship was like it always had been.

Teresa and Jon got along very well most of the time. They had spats, and when they started coming out of them, Jon always thought he saw how they had gotten into anger and out of love. *Next time,* he always told himself, *I'm going to see her side before we get angry.* But his resolution got lost on the way to the bedroom. Their reconciliations wound up there. Not last night though. Jon didn't want to get her pregnant again. Maybe that would help him remember to see Teresa's side.

As he walked down the passageway toward the TO's office, he thought that celibacy and reconciliation were most unnatural companions.

The training officer had his door open.

"TO, XO," Jon said and pointed back along the passageway.

"Zachery, if you don't use sentences with adjectives, adverbs, dangling participles, and a verb at least every other sentence, I will kick your butt."

Jon was feeling pretty good. Flying made all the difference in the world. Feeling good often led to wiseass remarks, but it was no time for frivolity.

"Sorry, sir."

The training officer said Jon was going to move into the formation phase.

"Can I ask a question, sir?" Jon asked. "What happened? What changed so that I can stay in flight training?"

"You can't ask that question. Any others to ask?"

* * *

Jon stood at the bar, sipping 7Up. Teresa was almost done being angry with him, but he had mandatory happy hour. He wanted to be home. "Crap," he mumbled.

"Talking to yourself, Zachery?"

It was Lieutenant Wolford, his RNav-6 instructor pilot.

"What'll you have, LT?" the bartender asked.

"Johnnie Walker Black, on the rocks."

Wolford looked at Jon's drink. He was standing right next to the barred-off waitress station in the center of the bar. Plastic cups filled with lemon and lime slices, olives, tiny white onions, and cherries were right next to him. He grabbed a maraschino, dropped it in Jon's soda, pushed a bill across the bar, took his Scotch from the bartender, smirked, and left.

On Monday Jon had been a hero, on Tuesday a goat. The VT-7 squadron CO had been fired, and here it was Friday, and Lieutenant Wolford was pulling Jon's chain with the cherry. It was just a big bunch of aviators and wannabe aviators laughing and scratching at the O Club. Life was good. It was normal out. He recalled what the policeman, Junior McCauley, had said when he asked him about playing football.

"Some days the fox gets chicken, some days just feathers. Sometimes the farmer gets the fox."

A hand grabbed Jon's left arm. It was the XO. He nodded in the direction of a table with the new CO and the VT-7 department heads sitting around it. Two chairs to the CO's left were vacant. The XO propelled Jon toward the one right next to the CO.

"Permission to join the mess, sir," Jon said.

That set the maintenance officer to laughing and coughing at the same time, and he expelled cigar smoke like the little engine that could, *chugga-chugging* up the hill. The rest of them at the table laughed more at Lieutenant Commander Smizer than at the comment.

"Shoe!" the XO said, baroque gilding of disdain decorating his word. The rest of the Navy wore black shoes with khakis and blues. Aviators wore brown shoes with khakis. To aviators, those who wore black shoes with khakis were Black Shoes, which in the way of things came out Shoes. It was handy having another pejorative other than puke.

"Black shoe Navy destroyer decorum, Lieutenant Junior Grade Zachery, I regret the necessity to inform you, is wasted on brown-shod aviators engaged in the more relaxed and easygoing, but no less hallowed tradition of happy hour." After his soliloquy, the training officer smiled at Jon.

All the department heads were looking at him. Smizer took a puff on his cigar.

Jon turned to the XO. "Happy hour. Yuks. Air. Not breathe. Chew."

Lieutenant Commander Smizer started coughing again.

The training officer said, "Zachery, one of him," he pointed at the XO, "is enough."

The XO grabbed Jon's drink, took a sip, grimaced, and spit the soda back into the cup. He poured beer from a pitcher and handed Jon the new cup.

Just like that he was one of the boys and accepted by the heavies. They did some talking, some laughing, and the training officer told a Refly story.

Then the CO asked about Teresa, and Jon got three sentences into telling the CO about her when the XO yelled, "Eject, eject!"

The XO pointed at Jon. "Mouth diarrhea."

"That," the training officer interpreted for him, "means your time in the token student naval aviator chair has expired. Or, in other words, get the hell out of here, Zachery."

Before Jon got up, the XO was there with another token student.

* * *

Greg Haywood looked at his reflection in the mirror in the head at the O Club. His image wore a I'm-a-poor-little-whupped-puppy message as plain and clear as if it were shouted from a neon sign. It hadn't been neon, but the sign had spooked him, and he hadn't been afraid of anything since his freshman year in high school.

Back then, his dad had always wanted to play tackle football with him. His dad was six feet three inches of hard muscle. When Greg tried to tackle him, if he didn't get stiff-armed, it hurt.

"You hit like a girl," his dad had said. "C'mon, this is boys' tackle, not girls' touch."

His dad always stiff-armed him the same way: his right arm clutching the football, his big left hand right in Greg's face. He recalled the time it changed.

His dad came at him, just like the other times, but just before the hand smashed into his face, Greg zigged to his right. One of his dad's fingernails scraped a line of fire across his cheek and ear just before Greg slammed his shoulder into his dad's chest, standing him up and turning him. Greg's dad wound up on his back, his head in the direction he'd been running. The football was about ten yards away, in that direction too.

"Can't breathe," his dad wheezed.

Greg was sure his dad was breathing. Greg had been hit like that before. After, it hurt to breathe deep. He picked up the football, keeping an eye on his dad to make sure he wasn't faking. He gave his dad a wide berth in case it was a really good act. After laying the football on the ground just over the goal line, he came back to his dad.

It turned out his dad had two broken ribs and was grounded from his airline-pilot job. Since that football game with his dad, he hadn't been afraid of anyone or anything again—until the sign.

He'd borrowed Charlie's Harley and ridden out on the highway to Jackson. Using the odometer and what he remembered from the helo flight in the morning, he found the turnoff. He followed the dirt road away from the highway, but after two-tenths of a mile, he came to a chain with a faded, whitewashed, crudely lettered signboard: GO AHED. TRESPAS.

When he first read the sign, he thought about going around it. But the hairs on the back of his neck stood up. The sign rooted him in place, and he sat astride the bike as it grumbled and vibrated between his legs. There was room to go around the tree to the left, but the longer he looked at the sign, the less resolve there was trying to move him forward. The bike noise kept him from hearing threatening sounds. That added to the worry.

As Greg looked at himself in the mirror, he thought, *I need somebody with me.* With that settled, he left the head and saw his helo friend walk in the front door.

"Get you a free VT-9 beer?" Greg asked.

"Don't drink horse piss," Charlie said. "How about a Jim Beam and Coke?"

"Why don't you grab that table?" Greg pointed.

As the bartender was fixing the drink, he thought, *Brown sugar water and Absorbine Junior! What a taste combination. And he turns his nose up at beer.*

There was a sign taped to the squadron keg: ~~VT-9 ONLY.~~

That was crossed out and underneath was scrawled: HELL, HAVE A BEER.

My day for signs, Greg thought. He drew a beer for himself and carried the two drinks back to the table.

Greg lifted his beer. "To helos and motorcycles."

"And from a jet puke!" Charlie sipped and put his drink on the table. "How was the ride?"

"Great. One of the guys in the squadron just got married, and he wants to sell his bike. I'm going to buy it this evening, but I appreciate you letting me take a ride this afternoon."

"You tell Melody you're getting a bike?"

"Nah. She won't mind. Want to ride tomorrow morning?"

"Sure. There's a route to the east I like to ride."

"I was thinking west."

"West. You want to go after those guys you were looking for today? Count me out. You'll get shot back in those woods."

"Who's going to be shooting at you, Greg?" Jon Zachery stood behind an empty chair.

"Hey, Jon. What're you doing here?" Greg asked. "You don't come to happy hour."

"Well, the CO and XO pretty much said I had to come. No room for lone rangers in naval aviation, they told me. 'Navy flying is formation flying.' That's what they said. I'll have my form-one flight midweek. But what were you talking about guns and getting shot at?"

66

Jon hung up the phone in the kitchen as Teresa came in from putting the babies down.

"Did you find the right McCauley?" she asked.

"Yep. I'm going to meet him at Chip's Diner tomorrow at seven. I'm buying breakfast."

Teresa was looking at him funny. "What?" he asked.

Teresa headed for the sink and the dinner dishes, but he stopped her. "Teresa, what was with that look?"

She put her arms around his neck and gave him a kiss that dislodged his teeth. Then she smiled and started running water into the sink.

At happy hour, Jon had had a couple of sips of the beer the XO had pushed on him. On the way home, he had worked three pieces of gum pretty hard. When he kissed her hello after he got home, all she said was, "Juicy Fruit."

Some guys got lie detector tests after happy hour. Jon got a taste test, which apparently he passed.

"I didn't taste like beer?"

"That was nice."

"You're happy I called Junior McCauley about the white pickup?"
She nodded.

After Jon got home from the base, he told Teresa about Tutu's plan. Tutu thought he'd found where the white pickup guys lived. He told Jon how the sign had caused him to, the way he put it, "turn around, you know, the discretion and valor thing." So he was going to try to talk his helo buddy into going with him on Saturday morning and go back. This time though Tutu was taking a forty-five-caliber handgun and going around the chain and the sign.

His helo buddy, Charlie, had no intention of going along with Tutu's scheme. That wouldn't have stopped Tutu. He'd have gotten someone else to go with him. Or he'd go alone, and he wouldn't stop at the sign the next time.

Before Jon left the club, he made Tutu promise to leave the situation alone. Jon got the navigation chart that Tutu'd marked with the location of the turnoff the white pickup had taken. Tutu had done more, much more than Jon had asked. Jon thanked him a couple of times. Instead of "You're welcome," Tutu messed up Jon's hair.

While Jon drove home, besides chewing gum, he thought about the problem of the white pickup. Even though he thought as hard as he chewed the gum, he didn't come up with a solution. After he got home, he read a book to Jennifer and held Edgar Jon as he talked to Teresa about Tutu. Just before he got the kids up to the table for dinner, he remembered Junior McCauley. Junior was the policeman who had accompanied the owner of Binford's Real Estate the day after the first visit by the white pickup.

After they ate, Jon called the first McCauley listed in the phone book. They directed him to Junior. In the morning, over breakfast, the white pickup was going to be Junior's problem. At least Jon hoped so.

When Jon walked into the diner the next morning, the smell of grilled ham steak made him wish he'd brought one of Edgar Jon's drool bibs.

Junior only wanted coffee. He wasn't able to exercise much because of his knee. He didn't want to get fat, he said.

"Just coffee for me too, please," Jon said to the waitress.

Junior had sympathy for his taste buds. "Order something."

"Coffee's fine."

Jon interpreted the look on the waitress's face as *Oh, this'll be a good tip.*

"Your nickel," Junior said.

Jon told Junior about the streetlight being shot out twice and that he was sure the white-pickup guys had done it.

"Maybe it's just a warning, you know," Jon said.

The waitress slid a mug in front of both of them. Jon looked down at the brew. It looked weak.

Junior shook his head. "No. I wouldn't count on that. They haven't forgotten about you. That's how we need to look at this." He shook his head again.

Jon explained to Junior about Tutu following the white pickup. Junior turned and looked out the diner window to the parking lot. He was worried.

"Maybe I shouldn't have bothered you with this, Junior."

He put on a serious look, distinctly different from the worried one. "No, I know you couldn't talk to anyone else about it." He looked Jon in the eye. "I got it," he said.

67

Saturday afternoon at 1600, Jennifer was standing on a chair at the counter by the sink, helping Jon. She was trying to stick a fork into the potatoes and almost managed to penetrate the skin. Jon helped her help and then wrapped them in foil. The teeth-grating *bzzt* of the door buzzer played "shave and a haircut." Jennifer made an O with her mouth. At the *bzzt, bzzt*, she grabbed the edge of the counter and hopped to the floor.

"Unka Tutu!" she said as she raced for the front door.

Jon was almost as excited and pleased as Jennifer. He missed the weekend dinners they'd shared with Tutu and Melody. He wasn't expecting Tutu though.

Jon opened the door. Mount Rushmore rose majestically from the sidewalk. The mountain bellowed, "O say can you see … "

Tutu had a jaw-dropping costume. He really looked like Rushmore, and the four presidents' heads, Halloween masks, were arranged just like on the real mountain.

"What so proudly … " came from the top of Tutu's considerable lung power. Well, that was too much and Jon started laughing.

"And the rockets' red glare … "

Teresa stood in the doorway. "Jon," she admonished. She had Edgar Jon in her arm. First, she placed Jennifer's hand over her heart, and then she took Edgar Jon's little hand and held it over his heart.

Jon snapped to attention and put his hand over his heart. The singing mountain mesmerized Edgar Jon.

"... home of the brave."

"Tutu, you—" Jon started but got trampled by "On the shore dimly seen ..." with even more volume than he'd used in the first stanza. And they all stood, or were held at attention, until the second "... home of the brave" dribbled off into a silence as deep and stunning as the sudden loss of power on a ship. Mount Rushmore stood massive, immovable, and mute.

Jennifer still had her hand over her heart as she turned and looked up at Jon. He shrugged.

"So, Tutu—" Jon said. "And where is that band—"

Teresa lost it then. She started laughing. "Greg, stop. Stop."

Mount Rushmore stopped, and Jon looked down at Jennifer. "You can put your hand down now, princess. We've just gone from sacramental to sacrilegious."

She still had her hand over her heart, and she looked up at Jon and asked, "Sack a mental?"

"Yeah, mental."

"Oh, Lord!" Teresa said. "Is all this to celebrate the Fourth? Where's Melody?"

"Hey, Two Buckets." Mount Rushmore was indignant. "Don't just stand there, laughing like a dorky dweeb. Get me out of this thing."

Jon went down the steps to behind Greg.

"I don't see how to get you out, Tutu."

"Lift George off."

George rested on a platform that appeared to have been constructed of slats like those supporting a plaster wall. The rectangular frame of slats went over Greg's head and extended from shoulder to shoulder. The George mask was supported by a Styrofoam head, which fit onto a peg to hold it in place. Jon went around to the front of him, stood on the first step, and lifted George. The backs of the heads were painted gray, with some black stripes imitating crevices and vertical features. It was all very mountain-like. George's head only weighed a couple of ounces, and Jon put him on the sidewalk. Teddy and Abe came off his left shoulder pretty easily too.

After the mountain was relieved of its presidential burdens, Greg said, "Undo the Velcro in back, Two Buckets."

"He didn't say pweeze, Mommy," Jennifer said.

Appropriately admonished by a child, Mount Rushmore said, "Pweeze," and like Sancho Panza after a day with the windmills, Jon finished getting him devested.

They got Greg's mountain rig into the passenger seat of a new Ford pickup.

"Traded the Corvette. To haul my motorcycle," Tutu said to Jon. Then he turned to Teresa. "I'm not ignoring your questions. This was for a pre-Fourth of July party we are having at the apartment building. We started at 1000. Apparently people down here don't think the Fourth is a celebration of independence."

"I was about to start the grill. You want to stay for dinner?" Jon asked.

"No. Melody and I are going to dinner and a movie. I just wanted to show you my costume. Pretty cool, huh?"

Jon spread his hands and shook his head slowly.

"Renders you speechless. Understandable," Tutu said.

Greg explained how he got the parachute riggers to help him. A set of king-sized sheets, wooden slats, foam the riggers used in making custom-fit flight helmets for the instructor pilots, starch, spray paint, and his creative and artistic genius were the raw materials.

Tutu got a goofy grin on his face. "Melody and I are engaged."

"Oh, Greg, that's wonderful." Teresa hugged him.

"Happy for you. Congrats." Jon shook his hand.

"Thanks," Tutu said. "Gotta run. The mountain thought it should come visit you guys, especially you, Jennifer. You got a hug for Unka Tutu?"

She did.

With Teresa holding Edgar Jon and Jennifer in Jon's arms, they waved from the sidewalk in front of the house as Tutu backed his pickup out of the drive.

"You're worried?" Jon asked.

"Maybe I'm wrong. Maybe Greg won't get his heart broken."

* * *

It was 0545 on Sunday. Jon swung his legs out of bed, stretched, scratched, and yawned. It probably wasn't the first good Sunday morning in Meridian, but it felt like it was.

He hadn't worried about the white pickup the night before. After he had told Junior McCauley about Greg seeing the white pickup and the road the truck had taken, Junior had said, "I got it." It was like being in a two-seat plane and passing control to the other pilot. Junior was in charge. He had control, and Jon slept well.

In skivvies and barefoot, he padded into the kitchen and was about to get the coffeepot started, when he felt someone watching him. He turned. Tutu stood in the carport, looking in the windowed door.

Jon unlocked the door and invited him in. Tutu walked over to the table, pulled out a chair, sat, put his elbows on the table, and rested his face in his hands.

"What's the matter, Tutu?"

"Coffee," he said without lowering his hands.

Jon got the pot out of the cabinet and spooned grounds into the basket.

"Greg, what's the matter with your hand?" Teresa was standing in the doorway with a robe over her nightgown.

Greg dropped his hands to the table and looked at them. Teresa took his right hand. The middle finger was swollen and purple.

"Greg, that's probably broken. We should get you to a hospital—the base, I guess."

"That one's been broken before. It got itself stepped on in high school football."

"Jon, why don't you get some clothes on so you can take Greg out to the base."

"What happened?" Teresa asked Greg.

"The movie."

In the bedroom, Jon grabbed clothes, shoes, and socks. He got dressed in the living room, where he could hear Greg.

"It was *In the Heat of the Night*. I didn't even know what was playing. We were just going to the movie, you know? There were only four other couples in the theater. I thought that was strange, but well, every once in a while, strange things happen here.

"Anyhow, I could feel that Melody wasn't liking the movie. I asked her if she wanted to leave. She said no, so we stayed. I thought it was going to be something we'd talk about after, but then we came to the scene where Sidney Poitier slaps the white grandfather-looking dude who raises orchids. I said something like, 'Slap him again, Sid.'

"Melody slapped me as suddenly as Sid slapped Orchid Guy. Then she pulled her ring off and stuck it in my shirt pocket and left. In the lobby, she called her dad to come get her. She wouldn't even look at me. The orchid grandpa in the movie, he looks just like Melody's grandfather."

"Oh, Greg, I'm so sorry." Teresa put her hand on Greg's wrist, well clear of the finger.

Jon put a mug of coffee in front of Greg and pointed at his finger.

"My new pickup needs a new driver's side window." Greg rubbed his forehead. "Twelve hours. I was engaged for twelve hours."

Jon took a thermos of coffee and drove Greg out to the base in his pickup. After they got to the infirmary, Jon called base transportation to take him to the chapel so he could go to Mass with Teresa.

68

Immortal. Invincible. Even greater, Jon Zachery felt like a Navy jet pilot!

He had just driven out through the main gate, when the bulletproof balloon of euphoria started building. It grew from a spot the size of the tip of his little finger to the right of his heart and expanded explosively and caught all the humiliating things that had happened to him since he had come to Meridian, along with every old shame, sin, and disappointment, and shoved all those things up until they lodged like an apple in his throat. The throat lump capped the emotional gusher, and for a moment, he held in the scream.

Then he cut it loose. "Yeeehah!"

Form one, his first flight in the last phase of training at Meridian, still affected him—his watch hands pointed at 1430—an hour after he had climbed out of the cockpit.

Puffy white clouds floated above, but they were just too lethargic to expend the energy to build up a thunderstorm, even though the July heat and humidity were present in abundance. Jon, however, had energy to spare.

The car windows were open as he drove home from the base that Wednesday afternoon. The wind whistled past the window and brushed his arm on the sill. He had never felt so fired up after a flight during the other phases of training.

The flight had begun as the most humiliating experience he'd had in an airplane. The two instructor pilots flew the two planes to the training area and took turns playing the lead—or being the target, as they called it. On a student's first formation hop, the instructors got a fair amount of stick time. They flew the planes when it was their turn to be the target, and they spent a lot of time demonstrating how to fly a steady position on the wing of another plane.

Jon was in the lead airplane, and his instructor flew so Jon could observe. The instructor in Number Two flew the jet into the proper position, the tip of the lead airplane wingtip fuel tank lined up with the helmet of the pilot in the front seat.

"Now watch," Jon's instructor said over the ICS, the intercockpit communications system. "The student has just taken control. Now the PIO starts. And he's outta there."

Jon recalled the lecture about PIO, pilot-induced oscillation. A pilot got into PIO by getting out of sync with the airplane. If a pilot got a little low on the lead airplane, he pulled back on the stick, but it was easy to pull too much and wind up high. Then he had to correct for that. Generally, bigger and bigger corrections were required, and PIOs got dangerous very quickly. Student pilots had to overcome the tendency to get into PIOs.

Number Two had started in rock-solid position, placed exactly in the proper position on the lead airplane. Then control had passed to the student, and almost immediately the airplane started sliding low. Then it abruptly started coming back up, but too fast and too far. Then it went down, then up, then down, and the excursions were amplifying until the instructor couldn't stand it anymore and recovered.

Two moved back into position. Lead and Number Two were sculptured airplanes locked in space on invisible wires 15,000 feet above the Mississippi pine trees.

"He's going to try harder the second time," Jon's instructor said. "Watch."

This time Two's excursions were more dramatic than the first time, and the IP quickly took control. Number Two stayed off the right side for a couple of minutes. Jon was sure the instructor was talking to his student.

"You see this happen to Two, Zachery, and you probably think it won't happen to you, but it will. You can see it, and I can talk to you about it, but you're going to do the same thing. Wanna bet a beer on it?"

That was just what Jon had been thinking. He wasn't going to let it happen to him. *No, sirree.* But he said, "No, sir, no bet."

Jon's IP laughed as Number Two moved back into position, locked in for a moment, and then the excursions started again. After Two's instructor recovered, he assumed the lead, and it was Jon's turn.

"Okay, Zachery, don't ham-fist it. Pinky elevated. Sipping tea with her Ladyship, right? Ready?"

The airplane was lined up perfectly. The wingtip was lined up with the helmet of the student in the front seat of the target.

Jon's heart was beating fast. He said, "Ready."

"You got it."

"I got—" But he didn't have it. *It* had *him*. From rock steady, as soon as the IP, the instructor pilot, gave him the stick, the lead airplane started rising. Then Jon was rising, the lead was rising again, and then the instructor took control.

The IP moved them back into position. There it was, the exact sight picture needed, wingtip on the white helmet of the student pilot in the front seat, and it wasn't moving. It didn't even tremble. The two planes were locked together.

"Now, remember," the IP told Jon. "Let your hands fly the airplane. If you see the motion, think about which way you are moving. Think about what you do to correct it. Then tell your hand what to do with the stick. You are just going to get into a PIO again. You get behind what's happening. Your hand on the stick, it knows what to do without thinking about it. Let it fly the airplane. Okay, ready?"

Jon sucked a lungful of oxygen. "Ready, sir. I got it."

"You got it."

Jon's hand was flying the airplane, and he probably held position for two or three seconds. Then he lost it again.

"Damn, Zachery. I thought you were going to set a new world record with your third attempt at formation flying. You spazzed. What happened? You start trying to think again? Probably squeezed the life out of the stick too, right?"

He had. When he started losing control, he had gripped the stick hard enough to squeeze juice out of the black plastic grip.

Each student got three sets of three attempts at flying formation. After Jon's first set, he felt as if he was beginning to get a handle on the up-and-down excursions, but then the in-and-out dimension became a problem. On the second try of the second set, he focused intently on the in-and-out dimension, and the vertical got away from him again. Finally, during the third set, everything clicked. Jon was not able to lock his plane into a rock-steady position, as his IP did, but he flew formation. The instructor didn't have to take control.

As he drove home, Jon relived the flight and savored the feeling. But real aviators were cool under pressure. They might be pumped, but they acted cool.

There were stories about pilots being cool. Some of them might even have been true. In one story, a pilot called the tower. "Be advised, tower, my engine is out, I'm on fire, and one of my wheels fell off."

"Are you declaring an emergency?" the tower operator asked.

"It's not that serious," the cool pilot replied.

And there was a saying: *It's better to die than look bad.*

Be cool, and it's better to die than to look bad. An aviator's total life philosophy could be wrapped up in one short sentence.

Aviators didn't seem to want to think about that other side of the coin and the eternal consequences of the alternative to looking bad. So aviation squadrons had a safety officer to help pilots and aircrew deal with the tails' side. The VT-7 safety officer had talked about being and acting cool. He said, "Unrestrained cool leads to hubris—and if you don't know what hubris means, look it up in a dictionary, and those of you students who got a real education, please give the full-ride scholarship jocks some help and show them what a dictionary is—and hubris leads to complacency, and complacency kills."

"Complacency Kills." Those were the current words on the last safety sign alongside the road to the airfield.

Jon thought about how close he had come to being booted out of flight training and how close he had come to quitting.

Teresa told him that if he quit, he wasn't going to be miserable for a few weeks. He'd be miserable the rest of his life. She did not want to live her whole life with a miserable, grumpy poop who was an old man at twenty-six, and who would suck the joy and light from her life, and who would be a rotten father to their babies.

Jon didn't know whether she had decided, they had decided, or he had decided that he would not drop out of flight training, but that's the decision that was made. When he got up at 0445 the morning after the decision, he was euphoric, not quite to the extent he'd just experienced, but clearly euphoric. At first he didn't understand why. It just happened sometimes, but somewhere in the midst of shaving he figured it out. He had been feeling pretty miserable over how the Navy had betrayed him. But looking at his half-shaven face in the mirror, he understood. Betrayal by the Navy was a minor aggravation compared to the thought that he'd never fly another Navy jet ever again.

From the moment he'd started preflight training at Pensacola, he was sure he was different from everyone else in his class. They were there because they wanted to fly. Jon was there because of the first encounter he had with antiwar protestors. They threatened the life he wanted for Teresa and him.

He had also applied for Swift Boats. At first it didn't matter which one the Navy sent him to. The most important thing was to serve in some capacity, when so many people his age were burning draft cards and running away to Canada.

But that Wednesday morning, he finally became like all the other student naval aviators. He was there because he wanted to fly.

Driving home he was intensely aware of the afternoon air, so thick with humidity he could almost squish it through his fingers. The skinny pine trees, sprouted out of the iron-red dirt along the embankment next to the road, reached up toward the white puffs dotting the incredible blue lid on the world. The smell of the pine perfumed the air and masked the things that didn't fit in the picture his mind was building. The wind *whooshed* by his open windows, and formation-phase flight number one kept playing in his mind.

He wished he could fly again the next day, but the Fourth was the start of a four-day weekend on the base. Even though he didn't think a long weekend stacked up favorably against the opportunity to fly a couple of more hops, Teresa could very well have another opinion about that.

Besides, Tutu was coming up the next day. He was now living in the BOQ in Pensacola, but he still had to check out of his furnished apartment in Meridian. Jon really wanted to see how he was getting along.

Jon had talked to him after he got to Pensacola. He was grounded because of his broken finger, but Tutu acted like it was nothing. He talked about his motorcycle, as if it was more important than flying, and Melody wasn't mentioned, as if in punching his window and breaking his finger, he'd just erased her, like chalk from a blackboard.

69

"Clarissa Johnson, you scare the liver out of me," Dodo said.

"You're the one nagged me to get out of bed." Clarissa placed knives and forks beside plates as she set the table.

"I wanted you to get out of bed and eat something, not go off on another of your crusades."

Dodo sprinkled chopped basil leaves over the chicken breasts in the skillet, and Clarissa sniffed and smiled as her taste buds anticipated "Dodo-bird." The first time she prepared the dish, Clarissa had asked her what she called it. "Chicken," Dodo said. Clarissa told her it was an elegant dish and it probably had a fancy name in a recipe book, *pollo-*something French or Italian. "Chicken," Dodo said again. Clarissa tried a few name variations for her roommate's creation and settled on Dodo-bird.

"And you're trying to dissuade me from my calling by tempting me with Dodo-bird. The way to a man's heart is through his stomach. It doesn't work that way with women."

"Clarissa, honey, there ain't no way to a man's heart. Women have a heart. Men got a blood pump. But that's a matter for some other night.

Right now, your calling ought to be to make your momma and poppa proud of how well you doin' in school."

"Poppa told me he didn't care if I stayed in school or what I did. Momma and he didn't go through all the trouble of raising a colicky, ear-infection-champion-of-the-world girl baby to sleep herself to death. There's plenty of things worth doing in the world. 'Pick one,' he said, 'and do it.'"

"I heard him say it. I didn't hear him say go back down to Mississippi with that Billy."

*   *   *

Jimmie slipped into the booth across from Ike.

"Saw John Calhoun leave five minutes ago," Jimmie said.

Ike didn't say anything for a minute. "John Calhoun's got a Jew businessman in Meridian posted a reward for info about the synagogue bombers. Greene's 'is name. Greene just bumped the reward from five to twenty thou. John Calhoun thinks we oughta take Mr. Greene down."

"Not yet, I reckon."

Ike nodded.

"We got the Chicago situation figured," Jimmie said. "Harlan got in tight with Wexall, fixed him up to sell marijuana and LSD, if he'd get back with his boyfriend. Told Wexall he was going to do a sit-in with some kids going to a place in the Missouri Bootheel. Harlan asked Wexall if he knew anybody ever did a sit-in. Wexall told Harlan about the March trip to Mississippi and told him what they were planning.

"Three of them driving down to sit in on the July 14 Catholic services in Meridian, Wexall said. Two niggers and Wexall. They're gonna spend Saturday night in a motel in Memphis, drive on to Meridian the next morning."

"Harlan know which motel?" Ike asked.

"Not yet, but he will."

Ike grinned.

70

Jon flew his second formation flight and climbed out of the cockpit, discouraged. He thought he would pick up where form one flight ended, feeling so high he almost didn't need an airplane to fly. Instead, form two demonstrated with clear and unmistakable evidence that he had a lot to learn. When he had the up-and-down dimension relative to the lead airplane under control, the in-out dimension got away.

"Formation flying is hard work," his IP said. "Every student goes through the same thing. Some of it is just gutting your way through. Each hop you're going to get a little better. In week or so, you'll solo."

Jon didn't believe him, but the third flight was better than the second, and the IP turned out to be right. His ability improved on each flight. By his seventh flight, rendezvousing on the lead airplane in an expeditious but controlled manner and holding position once he joined had become not quite mastered, but comfortably managed, skills. The Navy seemed to think students didn't learn anything from comfortable situations though, and he was scheduled to solo. His IP flew one plane. Jon flew formation on him without an instructor in the backseat to save him from mistakes.

After the flight, as they walked back to the hangar, the IP said, "Damn fine solo flight, Zachery. Damn fine."

Jon looked at him. "Thank you, sir."

"You didn't run into me once. Just a damn fine flight."

On July 18, Jon flew his first night formation flight. When it was over, his flight suit was drenched in sweat. The next night he flew solo in formation. It was the scariest thing he'd ever done. Still, it was another damn fine flight. On the nineteenth, he flew twice, both solos. The second hop was another night solo.

That night, Jon was on his back in bed when Teresa came in from the bathroom.

"You look rather pleased with yourself," she said. "Night flying that much fun?"

"No. Not fun. Actually, it's hard work. Real hard work. One of the IPs said night flying is the price we have to pay for the privilege of flying in the day."

"So what are you so pleased about?"

"For one thing, I just have ten more flights to do. God willing, the creek don't rise." He rapped his knuckles on his head. "We could be out of here by the end of the month."

"I think there's more to it than that." Teresa bent and kissed him. "I think Jon Zachery thinks he's a good stick."

"I'm much too modest to think that."

"Modesty and naval aviators—there's two things that really go together."

71

AMANDA SUE PERCHED IN THE dark atop a large sack of soiled linen behind Harry in the passenger seat of the delivery van they boosted from Memphis Fine Linen Service. The light coming off the back of the two-story motel didn't reach across the lot where they parked.

She watched as Harry leaned forward to see the rooms in which they were interested. Jimmie sat behind the wheel and in his way. She could tell that irritated him. He didn't like the role Jimmie assigned him, and he didn't like being on a mission and not being in charge either. Harry fretted, but she was excited. Taking up with Harry had exceeded what she had expected. *Church burnings, knocking over two banks, and now this,* she thought and smiled, wondering what her college roommate, Charlene, would think of her.

Amanda Sue looked behind Jimmie. She could see light glowing around the bottom of the window in room 117, the bottom-floor room with the two boys in it. The white kid's 1961 Plymouth Valiant sat in front of their room. The colored girl was in 204.

"Girl's asleep, at least," Amanda Sue said.

Harry was about to snap at her, when Jimmie spun around.

She couldn't see his face, but she was afraid.

"'Manda Sue." Jimmie's voice was quiet, calm. "You've been waiting a long time, I know. You watched the place while Harry and I got the van. You done good tonight. The white boy and white girl that got the rooms for them, you got their license number. That was good. What's bad is, I can't think when your mouth is going."

Jimmie turned back toward the motel. She looked too. Up against the building, the blacktop had paint-striped parking spots. About half were filled with cars. She saw nobody on the walkway in front of the upper-floor rooms and no one before the lower-floor rooms. Not a soul stirred in or around the parked cars.

Three dim lights illuminated the ends and middle of the sidewalk in front of the doors on the bottom level. The top level had only two lights. The one close to 204 was out.

Jimmie didn't turn when he asked, "Harry, you ready?"

"What? Yeah. Let's do it."

Jimmie did turn to look back at Amanda Sue.

She nodded and then realized it was dark and said, "Ready."

"Go." Jimmie started the engine, opened his door, checked that his shotgun was behind the driver's seat, and picked up the crowbar.

Harry took his Thompson, held it down along his leg, and walked behind the van to the corner of the motel. He looked out toward the highway and gave a thumbs-up.

"Go," Jimmie said again.

Amanda Sue opened the side door. It didn't make any noise. They'd greased the upper and lower tracks.

Amanda Sue and Jimmie walked across the lot. He positioned himself with his back against the wall between the window and the hinged side of the door to 117. He nodded to her.

She knocked on the door, and her heart skipped a beat at the noise.

She knocked again. "Mr. Wexall. I'm the manager. We have a problem in room 204. Please open up." She knocked a third time. "Please open up, Mr. Wexall. I'm the manager."

The door opened a crack onto the security chain.

"What's the problem?" asked the man.

She stepped to the side, Jimmie hit the door with his shoulder, and it flew open. Wexall slid across the linoleum floor in boxer shorts and hit the far wall. He started to stand up. Jimmie swung the crowbar and hit him on the jaw. The white kid spun onto the foot of a twin bed and bounced to the floor. He lay on his back with his hands above his head, his lower jaw displaced.

Amanda Sue closed the door as Jimmie ripped the covers off a naked colored boy. *They were right about colored boys,* she thought. Then Jimmie swung the crowbar again. The sound it made on the colored boy's face made her stomach queasy. The colored boy fell out of the bed and landed facedown.

Jimmie pulled the wooden handles of his garrote out of his back pocket and started bending over the colored boy, but he stopped and turned to Amanda Sue.

She was frozen in place, eyes big, mouth open.

"Go," he said through clenched teeth. "Go, goddamn it."

Amanda Sue opened the door and looked at Harry at the end of the building.

"Still good," she told Jimmie.

She walked, not too fast, just the way Jimmie said, to the van, got in, and moved it so the open sliding door faced 117. She left the motor running and went back inside and into the bathroom. She wrinkled her nose at the thought of touching the wet towels jammed onto the one small towel bar.

"Towels, damn it," Jimmie said. "We're falling behind. Move your ass."

Amanda Sue threw a towel toward the colored boy and wrapped one around the head of the white boy. There wasn't too much blood from him, a trickle leaking out of his mouth.

Jimmie tore the covers off one twin bed, wrapped the colored boy in it, hoisted him onto his shoulder, took him to the van, and dumped him inside. Jimmie checked with Harry. Still thumbs-up.

Back inside 117, Amanda Sue was looking at the second twin bed. That bed hadn't been slept in.

"Queers." Amanda Sue shook her head.

Jimmie slapped her across the face. "Move."

Amanda Sue fell onto the made-up bed and put her hand to her cheek. Jimmie was getting ready to hit her again, and she jumped up, pulled the case off the pillow of the stripped bed, and started gathering wallets, coins, watches, and clothes. She put the keys to the Valiant in her pants pocket. Each boy had a small bag, and she took all the toiletries out of the bathroom and dumped them in the bags. Jimmie stood in the middle of the room and scanned the tops of the nightstand and the TV. He pulled the two drawers out under the TV and closed them again. Last, he checked the bathroom.

"Clean," he said and hoisted the white boy onto his shoulder. Amanda Sue followed him out and closed the door.

She tossed the bags in the van and went to check the fuel level in the Valiant.

Jimmie pulled the van to the end of the building, where Harry stood. Amanda Sue started the engine in the Valiant, got out, and followed Jimmie up to the second level. She did her manager act again.

When Jimmie shouldered-open the door to 204, it didn't hit the colored girl. He had the crowbar cocked to hit her but just stood there looking at her. The girl stared back. Two statues. Amanda Sue felt time stop. There was a light on. The girl's lips moved, just a little. Amanda Sue thought about the *Mona Lisa*. She had seen it with her aunt in Paris. The colored girl was as unmoving as the painting and as placid.

Then the girl lowered her chin to her chest. Time ticked. Jimmie swung.

Cleaning out her room went by in a blur for Amanda Sue, and they were ready to go.

Jimmie eased the van door shut. "How much gas in their car?"

"Three-quarters."

"Give Harry the Valiant keys. Then get in the van."

Harry led the way southeast out of Memphis.

Amanda Sue waited for Jimmie to say something, but he just stared at the taillights in front of them.

"When you hit the colored boy, the sound it made, I thought I'd—"

"Don't," he snarled.

72

Piece-of-shit car!

Harry was hunched forward at the wheel. The jiggling and jouncing from the rutted dirt road didn't bounce his head around as much if he sat forward. But he was tired of sitting forward, tired of the shitty shocks, and just plain tired. He checked his watch. Thirty hours since he had woken up from two hours of sleep, sitting in his car. His eyes burned, and his mouth tasted like he'd sucked on one of the twins' armpits.

The odometer didn't work in the Valiant. They were supposed to meet Chevy and Ford 2.6 miles from the Jackson-Meridian highway. All Harry knew was that he'd been driving forever on the damn tree-lined, two-rut dirt road at five miles an hour after three hours of two miles an hour below the speed limit all the way from Memphis.

Then he broke out of the trees on one side. To the right, the wall of pines continued without interruption. To the left was an open area of stumps spotting the undulating deforested red dirt, like some giant had scythed a swath through the trees. According to Ford, the area was going to be replanted next week. The bulldozer Ford promised sat in the middle of the area next to a mound of raw, red dirt. *Ford,* Harry thought. *Nice to have one guy to count on.*

The white pickup was parked next to the trees. Ford and Chevy sat on the bed, their legs dangling. Harry stopped behind the pickup, got out, and opened the trunk with the key as the van with the "Adelbarger's Electric of Columbus" sign duct-taped to the door parked next to the Valiant.

"Lend a hand, would ya?" Harry said to the twins.

Amanda Sue stepped down from the passenger seat and slid the van door open.

Ford and Chevy walked over and looked at the three bundles of sheets stacked two on the bottom and one on top. Blood stained the far end of the top bundle.

"Throw those in the trunk," Harry said.

Chevy pointed at the man in the van driver's seat. "Who's he?" he asked Harry.

"Chevy," Harry said. "Just once, shut up and do what you're told."

Ford pushed Chevy aside and grabbed a leg through the sheet and started pulling.

They all heard the moan, and Ford dropped the leg.

"Shit," the van driver said. He got out and came around to the open door. Ford moved out of his way.

The driver reached inside to grab the shoulder of the top bundle and knocked off his ball cap.

"Shit," he said again and grabbed the top bundle and rolled it out the door.

Another moan came from inside the sheet.

The driver grabbed the legs and dragged the sheet-covered body to the other side of the Valiant. He pulled his forty-five, slid the action back to make sure a round was chambered, and cocked it.

"I wanna do it, Jimmie," Amanda Sue said as she grabbed his arm.

She was wearing an unbuttoned white blouse over a V-neck T-shirt. She reached inside the blouse and drew a thirty-eight revolver from a shoulder holster.

The van driver moved aside. Amanda Sue bent over and started peeling the sheets away from the head.

"More splatter if you unwrap her," Jimmie said.

"I wanna see her face," Amanda Sue said.

"Wait," Jimmie said. He picked up his ball cap, told her to put it on, took a sheet from the van, and draped it over the front of her.

"Do it," Jimmie said.

Amanda Sue's pistol clicked as she pulled the hammer back. The colored girl opened her eyes.

Those eyes looked inside Amanda Sue. She tried to swallow, but her mouth was dry. The pistol in her extended arms started shaking.

The van driver grabbed her pistol, with his thumb over the hammer.

Amanda Sue hurried to the edge of the trees and bent over. The cap fell off, and she puked on it.

Harry pulled his own forty-five and stepped forward.

Jimmie stopped him and nodded toward Amanda Sue. She spit, wiped the back of her hand across her mouth, and reached for her gun.

Harry watched her assume a two-handed stance and fire five rounds into the colored girl's face. Amanda Sue's right hand with the gun hung at her side. She looked down at it. A wisp of smoke curled out of the barrel. Her lower lip quivered, and then she looked up at the van driver, and a triumphant smile lit her face.

"You're splattered some," Jimmie said and turned away from her. "We dicked around long enough. Get the Valiant loaded."

Jimmie pulled driver's licenses and student IDs out of his shirt pocket. He tossed those in the trunk of the Valiant. He studied a three-by-five card. "Jon and Teresa Zachery," he said and stuck it back in his pocket.

"Okay," Jimmie said to Ford, "you good to go here?"

Ford nodded.

"You know to be careful when you crush the Valiant before covering it up. You get the dozer stuck or turn it over, we're all screwed."

"Careful," Ford said.

"Okay, Harry, I'll drop you and Amanda Sue at your DeSoto out by the highway."

He handed Harry an envelope. "Don't open it till later. Directions for the next meet."

Harry looked at the envelope and shook his head.

Since that last meeting with Sam, he hadn't liked the way things were going. He felt separated, cut off, exposed. *We used to get together,* he thought. *Talk, drink some beer, and Sam would give us the target, how to hit it, and how to get away. After, we had a place to go back to. But, goddamn, they were doing some stuff. These three civil rights—there just isn't a word ugly enough for them.*

"Harry!" Jimmie was in the driver's seat. "Move your ass."

Amanda Sue brushed past him. She opened the sliding door and climbed into the back of the van.

73

Jon decided to watch the ten o'clock Saturday night news. He'd flown every day that week, including night hops on Thursday and Friday, and hadn't watched TV or read the paper since the previous Sunday.

He'd hit a good streak and Xed off syllabus hops at a good clip. Two flights to go. If he could complete those by Wednesday, he could schedule the movers to come on Friday, and before the sun set that night, they'd be on their way to Pensacola.

The set warmed up, and the anchor narrated a story about three college students from Chicago who had disappeared from a Memphis motel a week ago. The announcer read off the names. Jon didn't pay attention to the first two, but the third was Clarissa Johnson.

Jon knocked on the bathroom door. Teresa opened it, irritation evident for an instant. She spit out the toothpaste and rinsed her mouth.

"What's wrong?"

"It's Clarissa. Clarissa Johnson. She's missing."

* * *

Sue Ellen sat in the living room with her romance novel. John Calhoun and Rafe talked at the kitchen table. She heard snatches of their conversation: "Jew businessman," "green," "Navy guy," "dynamite," and "third a August."

"Sue Ellen, coffee."

"I'll get it, Paw," Rafe said.

"Sit. Get in here, lard-ass."

Sue Ellen turned her head toward the doorway to her left. "It's right there on the stove."

She turned a page as John Calhoun tore around the doorjamb and grabbed a handful of her hair. She screamed and put her hands to her head, as if she could hold it on as he threatened to tear out a handful. She stumbled, following him into the kitchen.

He let go, and tears ran down her cheeks. She didn't cry or whimper. That would make him act even uglier.

She got the coffeepot from the stove and poured Rafe's cup first and then his. All the while, she could feel those hot, hate-filled eyes on her.

"Go to bed," John Calhoun said. "Git."

She trundled back into the living room, picked up her book and box of chocolates, and headed for the back of the house. In the bathroom, she dumped the book and candy in the trash can and looked at her puffy fat face. She couldn't even remember what she had looked like twenty-four years ago, when John Calhoun carried her in though the front door, dumped her onto the throw rug just behind the door, lifted her dress, and tore off her panties. Before they were married, during that week of courtship, he'd told her about how his mam and his pap used to be with each other. That's what he wanted for the two of them, he said, but that had been a lie. All he wanted was sex, rough and frantic. Having a boy baby made him happy, but he'd come after her again without letting her heal.

She looked into the reflection of her eyes but saw his. There was a new meanness, a new depth of sin in those eyes. He was going to kill her.

The next day was Monday, and he was going to be in Jackson all day. *Please, God, let him take the pickup, not the car.*

* * *

Tuesday evening Jon walked into the kitchen from the carport.

"Major bummer, Teresa," he said. "The base is clobbered with hurricane evacuation planes from Pensacola. A hurricane is due to coast in at Jacksonville tomorrow, so the Navy scrambled all the flyable planes out of Florida. We caught a lot of them here. My hop, the last one, was canceled, and for the rest of the week, there won't be any syllabus hops. Lots of those planes need work before they can fly back home."

Teresa turned from the sink and kissed him. "Will they waive that last flight?"

"I asked." Jon said. "The training officer said no part of the basic training syllabus can be waived. 'You get to enjoy our company another week, at least,' he said."

"You really did complete a lot of hops this month," Teresa said. "Even with another week, we'll still get out of here in less than six months, which is the standard time, right?"

"Did it ever occur to you, Teresa Ann Zachery, that sometimes people don't want to know there's a silver lining in—*mmmph*."

She stepped back, and he got his teeth back in place. "You were saying?"

He picked her up. "Was someone saying something?"

"Later, silly. We have to feed the babies."

"Oh, fine. One minute you say, 'Oh, look, that cloud has a silver lining.' I say, 'Well, by golly, you're right.' Then you say, 'Sorry, it's just shiny lead.' Man."

74

Something was wrong. Jon didn't know what. Lights from the streetlamp in front haloed the blinds. It read 0107 on the electric alarm.

Then 0108 arrived with a tiny click that seemed to turn his ears on.

A car in the street. Not moving.

Someone ran across the front yard just outside the bedroom window.

"Halt, police!" came from the direction of the carport.

The running feet stopped, and a loud *brrrp* ripped the night.

Automatic weapon!

Jon threw the sheet back and stopped with one foot on the floor. The shotgun was in the shed. *Move!* He raced to the front door and was about to pull the door open when he heard it: a hissing, spitting combination of a cornered snake and treed cat sound. It was the sound he and Heiny Schwartz heard when they lit the fuse to the dynamite.

The image flashed in his mind of that first time. Heiny had held a lighter under the end of the fuse for what seemed like a long time, and it startled Jon when it finally lit. But Heiny managed to look cool about it. He stood right there next to the fuse, hissing and spitting, shook his head, and said something like, "Didn't think I was going to get the darn thing going." And he had a grin on his face. Jon looked down at the spark climbing the coiled fuse, and he wondered if the spark could jump to one of the touching coils, and then they'd have a lot less time to run. When Jon looked back up, the look on his face made Heiny laugh out loud. Then he suddenly stopped laughing and said, "Run like hell, Jon."

And Jon ran flat out, and he could hear Heiny laughing behind him. When it blew with a *whoomp,* Heiny hollered, "Hit the dirt!" and Jon dove into the space between the two rows of just-picked corn and wound up with dirt in his mouth and Heiny standing over him, still laughing. Then the sky started raining splinters, wood slivers, and dirt clods.

"We kin use one less stick on the next one," Heiny said and started laughing again as Jon spit dirt.

But nothing was funny this morning. Thinking about Heiny wasted time. He unlocked the dead bolt and pulled the door open. A hail of tiny, sharp, stinging things assaulted his face, arms, and chest. As he ducked back, he heard the *brrrp* sound again.

He saw a shoe box just in front of the door. The box contained a bundle of sticks of dynamite with a ball of fire sparking on a fuse cord. Jon grabbed the box and quickly backed into the house. No machine gunfire that time. He grabbed the fuse just behind the sparkle and yanked. He checked to make sure the blasting cap had come out too. Then he threw the fuse over a body sprawled facedown in the yard with a pump shotgun in its right hand, and he dropped the shoe box beside the door.

"Get in the car." It was a woman's voice. It came from the street.

Jon peeked around the corner of the brick wall next to the front porch, and he caught a glimpse of a man standing near the rear fender of a car. The man aimed a shoulder weapon at him. Jon jerked back as brick chips flew from the wall to the left of the door. Then he looked at the body lying in the grass a few feet from the sidewalk, just below the steps up to the door.

"Jon!" Teresa was in the hallway between the doors to the two bedrooms. She held a sleepy Edgar Jon in her arm. He rubbed his eyes and was about to howl. Jennifer stood next to Teresa, her eyes big, and something grabbed Jon's heart. But there wasn't time for any of that.

"Get them in the bathroom. Now!" Jon barked.

He hoped she would obey and peeked around the corner. The man with the Thompson submachine gun started walking around the rear of the car toward the house. Jon leaped out the door. His feet landed just to the house side of the body, and he rolled over the body, as he'd been taught to do with a parachute landing. There was a *brrrp,* and bullets dug up grass and made the body twitch. Then the gun went silent.

Jon grabbed the shotgun from beside the body, ratcheted the pump action and ejected a shell, fumbled a bit to find the safety just in front of the trigger guard, and got the gun to his shoulder as the man by the rear of the car worked a round from a new clip into the chamber. Jon fired, and the recoil punched his shoulder. The shotgun pellets must have hit the man in his left side. He dropped the weapon, spun, and fell behind the car. Jon chambered a new round and watched to see if the man would get up again.

"Harry? Harry?" the woman called.

Pop, pop came from Jon's left. The driver stood with the door open behind him—no, her. There was no overhead light on inside the car, but there was enough light from the streetlight. The driver's arms were stretched out and pointed at him. *Pop* sounded again.

Jon fired at the driver, and a big fist seemed to smack her back against the driver's door. Then the door sprang her forward and sprawled her facedown on the pavement. He worked the pump and ejected the spent shell.

He wondered how many shells were in the magazine and looked in the dark grass for the shell he had ejected but couldn't find it. Working the pump action back just a tweak, he felt to make sure he had a round in the chamber. Once again, it was the middle of the night, and he was crossing the front yard barefoot and with nothing on but skivvies. Keeping the shotgun aimed at the rear of the car, he glanced at the downed woman every step or two, but she wasn't moving.

The blasting cap popped behind him and scared him, bad, and then he heard sirens, lots of them, but they were blocks away and coming from behind the house.

Coming around the rear of the car, he kicked something with his bare toe. Off to the right, someone crashed through the brush, and he fired at the noise and almost ejected the spent shell. The sound in the brush continued moving away.

The thing he had kicked was the Thompson. He picked it up, went around the car to where the woman was sprawled facedown, and rolled her over. Her throat was a bloody mess. He picked up a revolver lying on the pavement. It felt wet and sticky. Back in the yard, he put the shotgun by the body of a policeman. The spent shell was in the chamber. He checked to make sure the safety was off. Then he grabbed the policeman's right wrist to feel for a pulse, but he figured he was too pumped to feel it. He rolled him over and felt his chest to see if he was breathing. It was wet too. Several bullets had chewed up the left side of the face, but Jon knew him.

Officer McCauley was dead.

Jon clamped his teeth together and muscled control into his brain. He looked at Junior and the placement of the shotgun, decided that was okay, and rolled Junior onto his back, away from the shotgun. *Okay.* Then he hustled up the steps and into the house and placed the shoe box of dynamite sticks on the top step.

The sirens were getting closer. He had his story straight except for the bullet-chipped bricks by the front door. He had to get that part straight. There was no time to check on Teresa. The sirens were close.

Jon thought about the last Sunday in March when Boy Policeman had come to the house. He stood beside Junior's body and raised his sticky hands toward blackness above him. Hopefully, this all wasn't going to end with him getting shot by a boy-cowboy policeman. Even that thought didn't hold back the sudden weariness that sucked strength out of his arms and legs. He clamped his jaws and raised his tired arms higher. The sirens were almost on him.

*   *   *

By the time the police left at 1145, Jon's brain buzzed like a bowl of electrified oatmeal. He had gone over the events with four different two-man interrogation teams and one FBI agent. All seemed to have a script they followed and a technique of snapping back to points in the questions previously covered. From hearing the car engine until the first police car arrived, Jon figured he had told his story at least ten times. He wanted to get with Teresa. She had been questioned too, but they finished with her pretty quickly. Through most of the gunfight, she had been in the bathroom with the babies.

There had been times since coming to Meridian when Jon felt as if life was a bullwhip, and he and Teresa were hanging on to the end of it as Zorro popped it again and again. They had had some testy times. Jon wanted the shotgun in the house. She hated the gun in the house. Jon acted like a kid playing cowboys and Indians, she told him. He took the gun out of the house.

If Junior hadn't been there, we'd all be dead. If I'd had the shotgun, we'd have had a chance without Junior. Those two thoughts were in Jon's mind, but what would Teresa think?

As soon as he closed the front door behind the last policeman, Teresa came out of the children's room with Edgar Jon in her arms and Jennifer trailing behind. Jon had barely seen her since the police arrived. He wasn't sure what to do or say. So often it seemed, the wrong words came out of his mouth.

At the same time, they moved toward each other. She cried on his shoulder. Teresa wasn't angry with him, and to Jon, that was all that mattered. They didn't say anything.

Finally, Teresa stepped back and wiped her tears with her hands. "What are we going to do, Jon?"

He thought about asking her where her faith in God was, but he stepped on the impulse. It worked when she said it. It would be awful if he did.

Part III

An altar, on a hill,
in the land of Mariah.

75

Harry grimaced when he raised his left arm, grabbed the coal-oil lamp, and moved it from the center to the side of the round table so he could see Cyril. Cyril had saved his life a month ago, and he'd sustained it since.

After he'd been shot, Harry crashed through brush for ten minutes and came out onto a street running roughly north/south. Two houses away from where he left the woods, a four- or five-year-old Ford pickup truck sat parked in a driveway. The truck wasn't locked, and Harry hot-wired it, drove to a gas station next to Elmer's Tavern, and called his emergency number from a phone booth. John Calhoun answered, and Harry started telling him what happened. Not far into his story, John Calhoun stopped him and gave Harry a phone number. "Call the number. Tell Cyril John Calhoun said to call him. Now I gotta go. They coming for me."

According to Rafe, John Calhoun called Cyril, and then he went out onto the front porch to meet the FBI agents. Rafe got away through the woods in back. It was a hard run to Elmer's, but he found Cyril and Harry already there.

Harry sat in the passenger seat of the pickup he'd boosted. Rafe drove it and followed Cyril to a veterinarian who treated the wound. "Left arm's never going to come all the way back," the vet said before he closed the door on the three.

Then Cyril led them to a hunting cabin across the state line into Alabama. Once a week, Cyril brought them food and medical supplies.

"Damn Chevy," Cyril said. "He been in a coma a month and wakes up with his mouth running. He gave up everything. Tol' 'em where Bollinger was buried. Tol' 'em where the Northerners was planted. Shit. If one a the twins had to die, why couldn't it be big mouth Chevy?"

"What about my momma, Cyril?" Rafe asked. "Any word on what happened to her?"

"She disappeared. Nobody seen or heard from her."

Harry waved his hand, as if Rafe's momma wasn't worth talking about. "What about who tipped the police on us? They were waiting for Chevy and Ford at Greene's, and they were waiting for me at the Navy guy's."

"Nobody's got any idea who ratted," Cyril said. "But what I heard was the cops knew about Greene, not about the Navy guy."

"Well, I sure as hell got ratted out," Rafe said. "Night sergeant sent me home as soon as I showed up that night. 'You got the night off,' he said. I never got a night off before."

"Shut up, Rafe," Harry said. "They didn't know about the Navy guy, you said. Then how come that cop was waiting there?"

"Cops don't know what he was doing there. He was supposed to be covering the street north of Greene's house in case Chevy and Ford tried to escape that way. Course now they can't ask Junior McCauley about it. Had twenty-three bullet holes in him."

"So McCauley just happened by, which was bad luck, or he was tipped. But if he was tipped, why only one cop there and a bunch at Greene's?"

"Don't know the answer to any a that, Harry. I can't really be asking questions about something like that," Cyril said.

"It was the FBI got Rafe's daddy, you told us," Harry said. "You hear anything about them catching any other Klansmen, like Sam Germaine in Jackson?"

"A guy named Ike Larsen got arrested. That was in the paper, but nothing about anybody in Jackson."

"What about you, Cyril?" Harry asked. "They question you again?"

"They questioned me the day after the big shoot-out, but nothing much more 'n you'd expect being a kin a the twins. After Chevy started talking, they worked me hard. Six hours." Cyril stared at Harry. "This gonna haf to be the last time I come out here."

Harry rubbed his chin with his left hand. "You get the stuff?"

"Well, um, couldn't get no Thompson."

"The rest though?"

"Yeah, Harry, all the rest. Even put in a .30-06 and two extra pump twelve gauges. Ammo."

"The girl stuff too?"

"It's all in my pickup, Harry, but you gotta un'erstan'. Things just real tight right now, you know."

Harry fired his forty-five under the table and blew Cyril and his chair over backward.

Rafe jumped up and put his hand on his pistol.

"Don't pull, Rafe. I don't want to have to shoot you too. Sit."

Rafe's eyes grew big. He breathed deep and fast. Harry's black eyes seemed to burn atop his black-bearded face.

"Sit, I said."

Rafe sat and shook his head.

Harry brought his pistol up from under the table, let the hammer down, set the safety, and stuck the weapon back under his belt on the left side.

Rafe's mouth was open, and he couldn't look away from Harry.

"Sorry about Cyril. Had to do it. You going to be able to get over it?"

Rafe didn't answer.

"You worried I'm going to shoot you too, Rafe? Here's how it is. You got nowhere to go. You need me, and thing is, I need you too."

Rafe closed his mouth, and his Adam's apple bobbed.

"Only thing you can do, Rafe, is be an outlaw. We gonna start you off right. Tomorrow, I'll teach you how to steal a car. Then I'll show you how to rob a bank."

Harry needed operating money. He had some in a bank in Hattiesburg, but not enough to risk trying to get. *Need to do two or three,* he thought and decided Alabama would do. Florence maybe. Tuscaloosa maybe. Both maybe. After that, if he needed more money, he'd find one in Tennessee. Three should give him plenty, especially since his debt to Cyril had been paid off. In Tennessee, Rafe's usefulness would expire—assuming, of course, it lasted that long. The dumb-butt didn't seem to realize that his own momma had ratted him out. That was the only thing that made sense, if he thought about it.

"Question for you, Rafe. How big you want your boobs to be?"

"What?"

"Yep, unless Cyril lied about bringing everything. You're going to be a blonde. Real looker too, with your pretty-boy face. So what do you think about the boobs? How big you want 'em?"

76

THE DAY AFTER THE SHOOT-OUT, student pilots were doubled up in the filled-to-capacity BOQ to make two rooms available for the Zachery family. Jon only had one flight to complete, but Captain Morgan and the VT-7 CO worried about Jon's mental state. Jon insisted he had a handle on things and that he could complete his remaining flight, a solo, safely. The VT-7 CO flew with Jon two days in a row before becoming convinced and allowing Jon to complete the syllabus at Meridian.

They moved back to Pensacola in mid-August.

Flying at Pensacola was spectacular. At P'cola, students flew the T-2B. The twin-engine B version had much more power than the old pig single-engine T-2A. "The T-2B goes like a scalded ape," Jon heard when he checked aboard VT-4, the training squadron at NAS Pensacola. "Bat outa hell" would have made more sense, but that had probably been rejected as trite and used by earth-bound mortals. The B was a flying hot rod though.

During takeoff in the A, after pushing the throttle forward, Jon felt as if he had time for a cup of coffee before getting to liftoff speed. After he got airborne, he had to wait to reach the "raise the flaps" speed.

In his first B flight, Jon pushed the throttles forward and liftoff speed came so quickly that he jerked back on the stick, and he felt the instructor pilot push on the controls to keep him from raising the nose too high. Then his IP nagged him to get the gear and flaps up. In the A, he worried about reaching minimum speeds—in the B, exceeding maximums. On his first two hops, he thought that things sure happened fast in the B. By his third, he thought, *Things sure happened slow in the A,* and he loved the "Scalded Ape," a major kick to fly.

The syllabus included four flights to master the basics of the B. Then Jon moved into the air-to-air gunnery phase, another evolution where the pace of things seemed to be just barely within human ability to manage. A plane towed a large target banner on a steel cable over an area of the Gulf of Mexico designated for gunnery. Four students flew a precise pattern, circling the tow aircraft, and took turns firing painted bullets at the target. After the flight, IPs counted paint smudges on the banner and gave the students their scores, which routinely ranged from zero to a handful. The program emphasized flying the pattern properly and managing the gun-arming switch with one hand and driving the plane with the other. The Navy did not emphasize scoring hits. The competitive juices of the students did, however. The students in Jon's group who had red- and green-painted bullets scored hits on their first gunnery flight. Jon notched his first blue hits on his fourth. He didn't score on all his subsequent flights but did on the G-10X, the completion of phase check flight.

During the debrief of the G-10X, the IP told the four students, "I want you yahoos to think of something. Nine, ten months ago most of you never even flew before. Today you showed the Navy you could be trusted with a live gun in your airplane while whistling around the sky at four hundred knots. You can fire at a target in a *one-second* window of opportunity without being a danger to the good guys you're flying with. Proving you could do that was a hell of a lot more important than scoring hits. You have come a long way, but you aren't even halfway through the program. That should give you an idea of how much more you have to learn."

After gunnery, students faced the graduation exercise from basic training, CQ. Shore training for CQ consisted of flying around and around the landing pattern at the airfield logging seven or eight landings on each flight. On each landing, pilots worked hard to maintain the yellow light, the meatball, exactly in the center of the mirror beside the runway. They worked to keep the airplane lined up exactly on the center of the landing area and to keep the airplane speed precisely at the required number. A landing signal officer, LSO, stood at the end of the runway and graded every landing the students flew. Deviations high or low, fast or slow, left or right from ideal were recorded and debriefed after each flight. "Close enough for government work" had no place around a carrier. The LSOs seemed to measure those deviations from perfection in Angstrom units. As far as the landing grades went, words like "nice," "good," and "outstanding" were never used. A very good landing was graded as OK, which implied the standard for performance was perfection. Satisfactory performance was high praise. Earth-bound mortals weren't expected to comprehend such a measurement scale.

And there were no excuses. Sun in a pilot's eyes, crosswinds, tailwinds, bumpy air—the worst thing a student could do was to whine about one of those minor inconveniences. Once a carrier pilot rolled out behind an aircraft carrier, his life boiled down to the management of three commodities: meatball centered, on lineup, and on speed.

It was Friday, October 11, and Jon was scheduled to CQ aboard USS *Lexington* on the seventeenth. Then he and his family would move to Kingsville, Texas, for advanced training.

He finished early that Friday and arrived at their rental home on Santa Rosa Island by 1100. Donning his shorts and tennis shoes, he ran on the beach. When he returned, he went to the sliding screen door in the rear of the house that opened into a great room.

"I'm back, Teresa," he hollered.

"Babies' room," she yelled back.

It was something they did ever since they moved from Meridian. It mixed "Honey, I'm home" with "I really need to know you are okay."

After lunch, Jon sat on the beach on a folding chair with his feet in the water. Another thing they started since leaving Mississippi was taking fifteen minutes each, sitting on the beach alone. Jon had been bothered by dreams: shoe boxes of dynamite blowing up in the babies' room, Teresa riddled with machine gun bullets on their lawn, the North Vietnamese sailor's hate, an evil white pickup truck. Teresa knew about the dreams; no one else did.

After the shoot-out in their front yard, Jon's XO suggested he see a psychiatrist.

"You ordering me to see a shrink, XO?" Jon asked.

The XO shook his head.

Jon shook his head too.

"Stubborn. Stubborn Magnet-ass. Worst thing. Get the hell out of here, Zachery."

Teresa had talked with a Navy chaplain priest at Pensacola. He came up with the idea of personal reflection time.

"Reflection, meditation, quiet time." Jon shook his head.

"You don't want to do any of those things because you think they sound sissy," Teresa said. "Consider it take-that–stump time, except without the stump."

"Huh," Jon said. Teresa bloomed a funky smile. He shook his head. "I smell Rose Herbert in how you put that."

Teresa made a lip-zipping motion.

He saluted and figured she knew it was for Rose also. The first time he sat on the beach, he took the double-bit ax and leaned it against his chair.

He didn't bring the ax anymore, but he sat on the beach every day and never tired of the view. To the left, the low bridge connected the island to the mainland. In front of him, two miles across Santa Rosa Sound, a handful of white two-story buildings interrupted the long stretch of green trees and cloudless blue sky.

That day, gulls coasted above the water's edge, eyed Jon, found nothing to eat or squawk about, and sailed by soundlessly. He caught an aromatic hint of something green and slimy exposed by a receding tide.

Since he began taking fifteen minutes with his feet in the white sand or in the water, he slept well. If he dreamed, he didn't remember.

77

Sam Germaine drove a Plymouth from his used car lot north to meet Jimmie at a Flying A truck stop. Sam parked and did as Jimmie instructed. He went inside, used the restroom, bought a Coca-Cola, and climbed back in his car. He looked for Jimmie. To his right, ten semis sat side by side, neatly parked. Nobody stirred around those. The two diesel pumps for the trucks looked lonesome. Half of the gas pumps for the cars were occupied by pickups and station wagons. The men pumping the gas were all older than Jimmie. Women, none worth a real look, hung on to the arms of toddlers intent on escape and hollered, "Be careful," to older kids bursting with pent-up energy as the bodies surged toward restrooms and the restaurant. No Jimmie. Sam took a sip of his soda.

"Sam."

Sam started coughing, and he reached for his handkerchief to mop the soda off the front of himself.

"Goddamn, Jimmie. You scared the hell outa me."

"You wanted to talk."

Sam couldn't see Jimmie in the rearview. "Yeah, Jimmie. I need to know what's going on. Is the Klan folded with Ike and John Calhoun in jail?"

"Not folded. I need to know something too, Sam. You gonna hold up, or you gonna be a problem?"

Sam's Adam's apple bobbed. "Whyn't you sit up?"

"You gonna hold up, Sam?"

"Yeah, yeah, I—I ain't goin' nowhere. I got a business."

"Okay. Saw Ike's lawyer couple of days back. Ike says this is a minor setback. We are starting to come back. Chevy Henley was taken care of last night. John Calhoun should be released tomorrow. Without Chevy, they got nothing on John Calhoun, Sue Ellen being his wife. If we can find where the feds have her stashed, they won't have anything on Ike."

"You do Chevy?"

There was no answer from the backseat. Sam wondered if Jimmie the ghost had slithered away and he hadn't noticed. He started to turn.

"Don't."

"Okay, okay."

"No more stupid questions. What did you want to see me about?"

"Harry Peeper called. He says the Klan owes him twenty-five thou."

"Harry, huh? Wondered what became a him. Cyril Henley disappeared, and we lost track a Harry. He say if John Calhoun's boy Rafe was with him?"

"He didn't say."

"Where you meeting?"

"Desires Diner. Eleven p.m. We gonna give him money?"

"We gonna find out about Rafe is what we're going to do."

* * *

Harry trimmed his thick black hair to stubble. The makeup Cyril had bought for Rafe made him look pale, but it covered effectively. Besides, when he walked into the dingy, dim diner, nobody would pay much attention to his face. Rafe shaved his legs and wore panty hose and a dress. Harry wore slacks. The flats Rafe wore were a bit tight, but they worked.

It was two days after he had shot and disposed of Rafe in Tennessee, and he was meeting Sam in a Jackson diner at 11:00 p.m. Sam really sounded nervous when Harry called, and he did not want to meet. Harry insisted. Harry wanted money to fund his relocation out west. Harry figured Sam and the Klan owed him. Sam reluctantly agreed to the meet and the money.

Harry trusted him as far as he could throw the fat slob. With his bad left shoulder he probably couldn't even lift him.

He watched Sam park his white Cadillac by the diner two minutes late and enter under the "Desires" sign. Harry watched for a minute, and then he parked next to Sam's car and went inside.

Harry stood just inside the doorway. Sam occupied the same booth he had that night when he and Amanda Sue had met him there, halfway down the length of the former railroad dining car. None of the other booths that he could see held a customer. The wall hid the first booth, and he couldn't see if it was occupied or not. Harry took a breath, let it out, flicked open his switchblade, held it along his leg, and stepped forward.

Harry knew someone was going to be in that first booth. *Maybe that rough-looking guy from before.* He wasn't expecting to see Jimmie. Jimmie wasn't expecting to see a well-dressed, well-endowed, six-foot-tall blonde smile at him. Harry saw the surprise on his face.

He saw Jimmie frown, and in that instant, Harry knew they were going to do him just like he'd done Cyril. He flicked his wrist, the knife stuck in Jimmie's throat, and he heard Jimmie's gun drop to the floor.

Harry pulled out his forty-five and pointed it at Sam. Sam raised his hands in front of his face.

"I'll get you money, Harry."

"You don't have it with you?"

"See, Harry—"

Harry shot him, spun, and fired a round into Jimmie's forehead. His knife was on the bench seat next to Jimmie. Harry wiped it off on Jimmie's T-shirt sleeve, which was about the only place not covered with blood.

Sam was slouched back in his seat. A waitress opened a spring-loaded door from the kitchen. Harry pointed the gun at her. She ducked back and the doors closed.

Harry looked at his reflection in the diner window. A scarf knotted under his chin held the blonde wig in place. A light raincoat open in front framed the Ds poking out. She didn't have a bad-looking face for an Amazon.

Harry glanced back at Sam. *Thought you could handle me like that marshmallow Cyril, did you? Sam, I am one mean son of a bitch.*

78

Teresa answered the rap on the carport door, let Greg in, and hugged him.

"Thanks so much for flying in from Beeville, Greg."

"Sure. I hitched a ride with a guy who needed to log some nighttime. And I'm always glad for an excuse to see you guys. Where're the kids?"

"Sally Billings has them. Her husband Slick is grounded for an ear infection, and they live on the other side of the island. Sally likes to have the children for a couple of hours once a week."

"Before I knocked," Greg said, "I peeked around the corner and saw him sitting out there by the water. Jon doesn't know I'm here?"

"I didn't tell him. I wanted to be able to talk to you," Teresa said.

"You're worried because ever since that night in Meridian, he's too serious?"

"He's so protective, which I probably encourage. He never cracks any of his lame jokes. I'm worried, and I don't know how to help him out of whatever he's in. Maybe that experience changed us. Maybe things will never be like they were again."

They walked to the sliding patio door and looked out at Jon. A brisk breeze whitecapped the surface of Santa Rosa Sound. The sky was clear and pure blue except for a few contrails. "Baby angels finger painting," Jon had told Jennifer, just the day before when the cold front pushed through and she asked about the contrails.

Teresa glanced up at Greg and back at Jon. "He was having dreams, mostly about bad things happening to the babies or me, and he couldn't protect us. A chaplain on the base suggested we do some reflective, quiet time. The quiet times helped with the dreams. But before, he was, I don't know, happy with himself, I think. Now he's not happy. He's not having the bad dreams, but he's not happy."

Greg slipped off his shoes and socks and headed for the carport door.

"What are you doing, Greg?"

He put his finger up to his lips, slipped out, and quietly closed the door behind him. Teresa inched the sliding door open, and Greg walked around the edge of the house. He signaled *shh* again. It was funny, watching the big gorilla tiptoe up behind Jon. *He might get away with it,* she thought as the wind whistled around the house.

When Greg was about ten feet from Jon, Jon jumped up and turned. A smile bloomed across his face. "Tutu!" Teresa heard joy in his voice.

Greg charged across the distance between them, grabbed a handful of sweatshirt over Jon's chest, grabbed Jon's crotch, and hoisted Jon above his head. Teresa froze, terrified, just like the night of the dog poop and the night the white pickup came the first time.

With Jon over his head, Greg ran out into the water until he stumbled, fell forward, and they both went under.

Teresa pushed open the door and ran out screaming, "Greg, stop it."

Greg stood up and faced Teresa. He raised his arms over his head, a huge grin on his face. Teresa stopped halfway from the house to the water. Where was Jon? He hadn't come up.

Suddenly, Greg pitched forward. Jon had tackled him, and Greg went under and came back up, coughing violently.

Greg sat and tried to catch his breath. Jon stood back from him and grinned like an idiot. Teresa had gone from concern over what Greg was doing to Jon to disgust over their boyish behavior.

"I'd help you up, Tutu, if I could trust you," Jon said.

Teresa put her hands on her hips. "You two juveniles get out of the water. You'll catch your death of a cold."

Greg stood up and faced Teresa. "Let's throw Teresa in."

"No," Jon bellowed and drove his shoulder into the back of the big man's knees and toppled him forward onto the sand and half out of the water.

"Stop it, you two," Teresa shouted.

She ran to them to pull them apart. Greg rolled over. His big paw caught Teresa on the buttocks, flung her across him, and she fell facedown in the water. Jon sprang up, grabbed Teresa around the waist, and pulled her upright, and then he turned to face Greg.

"I surrender," Greg said, holding up his hands.

When Jon turned to face her, Teresa spit water in his face.

Teresa laughed, standing in the water. Greg laughed, lying in the sand. Jon shook his head and smiled. Then he laughed too.

*   *   *

"I'm going to miss living on the beach," Teresa said.

She held Edgar Jon. He and all of them were bundled against the chilly breeze. Jennifer enjoyed being carried along the beach by her father. Behind them, the sun slipped below the rim of the earth.

"Sure glad Greg talked me into renting the place."

"You said even off-season rates were too expensive. He said you were a cheap screw. Live large for once in your life." Teresa squeezed his arm. "I love you, Jon Zachery, on the beach on Santa Rosa Island, even if you are a cheap screw."

They stopped and Teresa kissed him. Jennifer didn't object, but Edgar Jon did.

Teresa said, "Alright," as Edgar Jon pushed them apart, and they started walking again. "Jennifer, what's your daddy's name?"

Jennifer pulled Jon's lips apart. "Toofless Roof," she said.

"I hope the Navy doesn't make me pay for another set of fals—teeth."

"Even if they do, I think it was worth it, even if Greg did scare the liver out of me. How do you feel, Jon?" Teresa glanced at him.

"I feel good. I think my heart was heavy, and I didn't know it was until the weight got taken away. Wrestling with the big ape, I don't know, it worked a lot quicker than a take-that stump would have. Wish he could have stayed over the weekend."

Teresa looked behind them. The sun was below the horizon. She tugged Jon's arm, and they turned around and started back toward their house.

"Can you tell me what was bothering you?"

"I don't know. I'll try." Jon kicked a bit of broken shell with the toe of his tennis shoe. "I thought I had the world sorted. The US isn't perfect, but it's the best the human race has come up with. What happened in Meridian, it was like the country attacked, not me, but you and the babies. The protestors, I pretty much had them characterized as 90 percent wrong. Now, I don't know."

"Fifty-fifty?" Teresa asked.

"Fifty-one percent wrong," Jon said. "But if we can't go to Meridian, Mississippi, and sit with a colored girl in a Catholic church without having someone attack us, then it is high time there was some protest. Still, I can't go fifty-fifty with them. Anyway, there are no real answers.

"I worried some about things in the Bible. In one of the epistles—James, I think—there is the business about faith not being enough, that there has to be good works too. In at least one of the gospels, Jesus is hungry and goes to pick some figs from a tree and finds the tree barren. And Zot strikes it like in the *BC* cartoon. And Jesus says the poor are always going to be around. There is a time for every purpose under heaven—I don't know, that just didn't seem quite adequate. See, it was just a jumbled mess."

"Having a teeth-knocking-out fight with Greg solved it though?"

"Sort of. I was so worried about losing you, I forgot something my first CO in VT-7 told me. 'She is a tough lady,' he said. I guess you had to get in the middle of Tutu and me for me to remember that."

When they were back at their house, Jon said, "I've got new mysteries for our rosary." He knelt on the sand, pulled her down beside him, and said the "Glory be the Father." Then he said, "In Meridian you created *The Terrorful Mysteries* for the rosary. We need *Thanks-be-to-God-for-the-beach-house-on-Santa-Rosa-Island* mysteries also."

*　　*　　*

Teresa got up from the sofa and turned off the TV at 2205. The bodies of three college students had been discovered buried in a recently reforested area west of Meridian. One of them was Clarissa.

"I thought it would be good to find out what's going on in the world." Teresa shook her head. "Now I don't know."

"Clarissa would want her body found and shipped back home. It's good they found her, and it's good we know."

"Yes, you're right. Still, it sort of feels like she was killed all over again."

Jon took her hand and kissed it.

"I'm glad Greg called when he got back to Beeville tonight," Teresa said.

"Sure," Jon said. "He wanted to know if he should patent his therapeutic mud-wrestling technique. It would have been nice to spend another day with him."

"I'm just glad you didn't hurt each other. When I saw him pick you up, I didn't know what to think."

"He is one strong dude," Jon said.

"He is one strong friend," Teresa said.

Teresa used the bath off the master bedroom, Jon the guest bath. When she was finished, she crawled into bed next to him and they said a decade of the rosary. They had three intentions: Clarissa and her family, Greg, and Jon's lost teeth.

They put their rosaries up and kissed good night.

"One minute," Teresa said.

She got up and padded down the short hall to the babies' room. The babies were both sleeping peacefully. When she came back to the bedroom, Jon had his hands under his head, and he was smiling beatifically at the ceiling.

"Last one in's a rotten egg." She threw her nightgown at him and headed for the sliding door.

"The water's too cold," Jon said from behind her.

"Rotten egg," she said.

It was close, but Jon was the rotten egg.

79

When Harry showed up, Jolene didn't want to let him in.

"You should have called," Jolene said.

"I could have," Harry said. "Let me in."

"I heard you was dead."

"Almost was."

"I'm not taking in a broke outlaw."

He pulled a roll out of his pocket. "I'll give you half, and I'll pay for groceries. Let me in."

She was interested in the money but continued to stand behind the screen door and stare at him.

He knew she'd let him in. She did and held out her hand.

"Inside."

She got out of Harry's way as he entered the kitchen and sat at the round table. Nothing had changed since he had bought the DeSoto from her.

"You got coffee?" He started peeling bills and making two stacks.

Jolene slid a mug across the red-and-white–checkered oilcloth tablecloth, and he pushed a pile of green to her.

She counted it. "A thousand." Her little smile formed tiny wrinkles at the corners of her mouth and eyes. Her dark eyes twinkled.

"How you making out, Jolene?"

That killed the smile. "I been selling stuff, like the car, you know?"

He asked her about her husband. Earl had hit a guard and wound up in the prison infirmary with extra time to serve. She didn't have much left to sell, except the place. A fellow did make an offer. He liked the pens Earl built to hold his fighting dogs. He would have liked to have the dogs too, but Jolene sold those off first. They were a pain to feed and take care of.

He watched her get a mug of coffee, put milk in it, sit back down, sip, and stare at the coffee. *She was looking at her future*, he thought, *and it didn't look good*. He pointed at her pile of bills.

"More where that came from."

"Where?"

"Who's got a lot of money?"

She looked at him hard. "Bank? You gonna rob a bank? What the hell do you know about robbin' banks?"

Harry took a newspaper article out of his shirt pocket, unfolded it, and handed it to her.

The headline was: CLARK GABLE AND MARILYN MONROE HIT THIRD BANK.

"You?"

Harry didn't answer. "I know some about banks. You interested in helping? I'll split it with you, after expenses."

"I'll listen."

"No. First you tell me you're in, and then I'll tell you how we'll do it."

"Where?"

"You in?"

Jolene got up and looked out the window over the sink. The empty dog pens seemed to be falling apart before her eyes.

"In," she said to the window. To Harry she asked, "Where?"

"Right here. Biloxi."

"You crazy? I live here. I'm not helping you do a bank here."

"Jolene, hear me out. I got it planned. Marilyn'll pull the job. Then we do another one in Pensacola, Florida. That'll get us a stake to move out west."

"Where out west?"

"Don't know for sure yet, maybe all the way to California."

Jolene leaned her buttocks on the cabinet under the sink, folded her arms beneath her bosom, and scowled. "You want more coffee?"

Harry held up his mug.

"You still got your husband's guns?"

"Yeah, but a guy is coming to look at them tomorrow. I told him I'd sell them to him if he wants 'em."

"Still got a Thompson?"

She nodded.

"Call the guy. Tell him someone broke into your place and stole the guns."

She didn't want to do that.

"Call him. Pissing off a local isn't going to be a problem when we blow Mississippi in a couple of days. Call him."

"I'll call him. Then what?"

"I'm going to take a shower, if that's okay. I could use some help scrubbing my back. My left side is still messed up some."

Jolene didn't move. "How much you figure we'll get from a bank here?"

"Hard to say. Sometimes you get lucky and hit twenty-five thousand. When you're not lucky, maybe only five. See, even bad luck isn't that bad."

Jolene turned and rapped on the wooden windowsill, and she held up her hand with the fingers crossed. Then she went with Harry to scrub his back.

Harry didn't mention that he had other plans for the Thompson. He'd settled with Sam and Jimmie. When he thought about that little bastard Navy guy who shot him, it set termites gnawing at the inside of his belly. He needed another chance to show that guy a machine gun.

That would make a clean break with Mississippi before heading out west.

80

On Monday morning, Jon and most of his group of twelve completed their carrier qualification check flight. Two of the twelve were set back into the next group to see if they could master the art of flying the ball after another full round of shore training. On the port side of the carrier landing area, a lens displays a yellow light, the ball, and a row of green to a pilot. The pilot's job is to keep the yellow light exactly lined up with the green. If the yellow light is high relative to the green, the pilot will miss all the wires and bolter and have to try to do better the next time. If the ball is below the green, the plane is getting dangerously close to flying into the steel cliff at the back end of the boat, in which case the LSO would likely hit the wave-off lights.

On Wednesday the ten students who got an up on their check flights were scheduled to fly out to the USS *Lexington*. On the *Lex*, they'd get a shot at qualifying to land aboard an aircraft carrier.

A tropical storm named Gladys meandered randomly northwest of the western tip of Cuba and posed a potential problem. A complex set of weather systems boiled along the coast of the Gulf of Mexico and complicated predictions of Gladys's behavior. The most likely scenario:

strengthen and make landfall at Pensacola. On Tuesday, plans for Jon's group to CQ were put on hold. Jon was told to go home but to stay close to his phone.

He left the squadron at 1100. Forty-five minutes later, he drove across the bridge out to Santa Rosa Island. He thought about how quickly the time had passed in Pensacola. Sometimes a student got lucky in the training command and zipped through the program. Other times, things dragged.

Jon had asked one of his instructors about the training pipeline slowing down. Refly thought it would do just that.

"Think about it," the instructor said. "We're trying to convince the North Vietnamese to negotiate a settlement with us. If it looks like we're quitting and slowing things down, all they have to do is wait us out, which is probably what they're doing anyway. But at this point, just keep plugging."

Whatever was happening at national and international levels, it was good to be moving smartly through flight training. If the hurricane didn't develop, or didn't hit Pensacola, he could finish CQ in a day or two. He was, in part, disappointed to see the time in the beach house near an end. He wondered if he and Teresa would ever again live in a place so special, and Jennifer and Edgar Jon deserved a period of normalcy after those nights of terror-interrupted sleep.

Jon had talked with Tutu about how the Pensacola flight instructors seemed to treat the students better than those in Meridian had, more like regular people. "Sure, they're treating us better," Tutu said. "Primary and basic is more about weeding out the ones who shouldn't be flying than it is teaching someone how to be a Navy pilot. There will still be weeding out as we go through advanced, but not as much as in the first two phases of training. Once you leave Meridian, you're expected to complete advanced."

"Yeah, and in Meridian, they expected us to DOR, right?" Jon asked.

"Your buddy Refly looked at it that way," Tutu said.

Santa Rosa Island was special, he decided, however, good things didn't last forever. But, after two months, it felt as if he and Teresa had finally put Meridian behind them. He was ready to move to advanced training.

When Jon entered the house, he found Teresa and the children at the table. Jennifer bit off a corner of a peanut butter sandwich as Teresa steered a spoonful of baby cereal into Edgar Jon's mouth. Jon kissed Teresa and Jennifer. He patted the baby on top of his blond head, a reasonably clean area.

"I'm going to wash up, then fix a sandwich. After that I think we should pack suitcases. Just to be ready in case we have to leave the island because of the hurricane," Jon said.

Teresa nodded.

"Are you okay, Teresa?" He wasn't the most perceptive of husbands, but something was wrong. A pile of used Kleenex lay in the center of the table. "Did you catch a cold when we went swimming?"

"I'm okay. Go wash up."

When he got back to the kitchen, the baby's diaper contents assaulted Jon's nose and he grimaced. Teresa was staring at a corner of the table. Edgar Jon waved his little arms. Invariably, he protested the end of the baby food even when his diaper desperately needed changing. Jon got the baby's face cleaned up and started lifting him out of his infant seat.

"I'll change him," Teresa said. "Eat lunch."

"Something happened to my appetite," Jon said, wrinkled his nose again, and headed for the children's room.

Before he got the baby's ensemble totally reassembled, the phone rang.

"It's for you, Jon," Teresa called from the kitchen. "It's the squadron duty officer. He says it's urgent."

Teresa took over with the baby.

"'Tenant Zachery," he said to the phone.

"Took you a while, man. Christ! I got lots of calls to make. You gotta get in here. You have to brief for a flight out to the *Lex* in an hour."

"The *Lex* is out? I thought we were indefinitely delayed."

"Don't argue, Zachery, and don't ask any more questions. Just get your butt in here. They just came up with this new plan, and the *Lex* is pulling out right now. You brief in one hour."

Suddenly, driving rain from the south pelted the windows on that side of the house. *What about Teresa? What about the hurricane? What about our babies? Wait!* he wanted to say to somebody. He looked at his watch: 1217. An hour.

Then he was doing it. Feet moved him to the bedroom. Hands stuffed uniforms and skivvies into a hanging bag. Teresa came into the bedroom with the baby on her shoulder.

"The *Lexington* is pulling out. It's going to move to the western end of the Gulf of Mexico. They want us students aboard. We might even get qualified tomorrow."

As soon as he said the last sentence, he knew he'd blown it. He should have said something about leaving her to handle the storm by herself. The resignation of a martyr showed in her eyes. It would have been better to see accusation there. He checked his watch.

At forty-six minutes to brief time, they were on the bridge to the mainland. The water on both sides was choppy and angry-looking. Gust-driven sheets of rain overwhelmed the windshield wipers every few minutes. There wasn't much traffic, but the car in front of them moved slowly on the two-lane bridge.

Seven miles an hour.

Jon glanced at Teresa. She still hadn't said anything. The kids were quiet. Jennifer watched the storm out her window. Edgar Jon nodded. Riding in cars always knocked him out in a hurry. The little guy was in danger of whiplash. Teresa usually held his head.

Once on the mainland, the rain quit abruptly. It was still overcast, but the ceiling looked high. So the rain was just a cell, not a large system, and not associated with the tropical storm. It was still way south.

Teresa stared out the windshield. She had to be mad at being abandoned. *God knows I would be,* Jon thought. I'd want to hit somebody. He was mad at himself though. He was abandoning her, with a hurricane coming and two little ones to care for.

Hell no, I won't go. That's what I should have told them, he thought.

"Jon." Teresa looked at him. "I was sick this morning."

She turned back to the front. He forced himself to also, so he wouldn't drive onto the sidewalk.

They got to the hangar, but he couldn't remember a detail of how he drove there.

Say something, he told himself after he put the car in park, but there wasn't a thing to say that wasn't ugly, rotten, stupid, or shameful. He was all of those things, and he felt worse than he ever had. When he'd been seasick, death always seemed like a cure. If death wanted to come when he was seasick, he didn't think he'd fight it. But then outside the hangar in Pensacola, death didn't seem like it could cure what he had at all.

"Just go," she said.

He started walking toward the door in the side of the building. *Keep going, keep going, keep going,* he told his feet. Before going in, he paused, thought about looking back, but took a breath and stepped inside. The heavy metal door clanged shut behind him.

In the ready room, the duty officer told him that the preflight brief for the flight out to the *Lex* had been pushed back an hour.

*   *   *

Teresa heard the heavy personnel door to the hangar bang shut. It was like waking up in Meridian. Her heart beat fast. Ever since she'd finished slicing bananas onto her Rice Chex cereal and rushed to the sink to throw up before she'd even taken a bite, she'd been sleepwalking.

She'd had morning sickness with Jennifer, and after trying for two years to get pregnant, it was such a joyful thing, as soon as the stomach-clenching spasms passed, to vomit into the kitchen sink. Pregnant!

This time it wasn't joyful.

She moved around the car and got in on the driver's side. Edgar Jon was asleep. With him, she had not had morning sickness.

As long as she was nursing Edgar Jon, she hadn't expected to get pregnant. It wasn't a foolproof thing. Still, she had expected it to keep her—what, safe? With Edgar Jon just seven months old, she was pregnant again, without the spike of joy. That bothered her.

And Jon. She had wanted to tell him that morning, but CQ was the most dangerous phase of training. She decided to wait until after he qualified on the carrier. But then, all morning her pregnancy weighed her down. She needed to tell him and wrestled with herself to keep the news to herself. While Jon packed and then drove them across the bridge to the mainland, she had wrestled.

As much as the white pickup had hung over their lives in Meridian, that issue, sex and birth control, hung over them too. Teresa had not wanted to go to the priest in Meridian. The church was clear about that issue. And the bishops had reinforced the church position on birth control every few years.

Jon told her once that he would rather die than have to be with her and not be able to touch her. Rhythm was just another form of Russian roulette. He said that he couldn't help the feelings he had, and when he got horny—it seemed like a dirty word, but "twitterpated" from the *Bambi* movie was just as bad in the other direction—he felt resentful if he couldn't touch her. But he was afraid for her. He didn't want to disobey the church, even though using some kind of birth control seemed like less of a sin to him than endangering her life through his lust.

Another pregnancy right away would endanger her life. That was what her doctor had told them right after her second emergency C-section. But after leaving Meridian and finding the beach house, she'd wanted Jon too. Not the way he wanted her. Men were all hot and impatient and sweaty. She wanted him in a warm, slow, clean way.

"Mommy cwying," Jennifer matter-of-factly observed from the backseat.

"When the going gets tough," Rose said, "first, blow your nose. Second, get tough. Third, get going." Rose would know how to deal with hurricanes. For that matter, hurricanes might even be afraid of Rose and steer clear.

81

THE *LEX* HAD PULLED OUT while Jon drove to the base. The weather was too rough to let a student try to land on a carrier for the first time. Four instructor pilots flew the planes, with Jon and three other students in the backseats. The other six students walked aboard the carrier before it left port.

Peering down from altitude through the clear sky, Jon thought that it didn't look bad. The *Lex* sailed sedately. Surface winds were forecasted to be forty knots, with gusts as high as fifty around thunderstorms. He could see plenty of whitecaps, but the carrier seemed too big, too majestic, to be bothered by a little weather.

However, when the flight descended to eight hundred feet and flew up the starboard side of the ship, the *Lex* no longer appeared to be sailing sedately. The back end of the carrier rose and fell as it rode through substantial waves. A very strong surface wind ripped the tops off the rolling waves. The carrier's bow rose on a wave crest and dropped into the following trough, and as it did, the landing area gyrated through crazy slopes up and down. Ashore, runways just sat there. Ashore, keeping the ball in the center was enough of a challenge without the runway moving.

No amount of practice ashore could prepare a man to land on that!

Jon's pilot Rick flew the number-three position, on the right wing of the lead, in the four-plane formation. At the bow, lead signaled the number-two plane on his left wing to break. Two rolled smartly to the left. In seventeen seconds the lead would execute the break turn. Jon started counting, *One potato, two potato,* to count the interval, but he became fixated on watching Two.

Two never rolled out of his left bank but dropped the gear and flaps still in the turn. The lead plane broke, and seventeen seconds later, Rick executed a snappy roll that smacked Jon's helmet against the canopy.

Over the radio there was an insistent "Wave off, wave off, wave off!"

Rick read the landing checklist and then asked, "You set back there?"

"Yes, sir," Jon squeaked.

It seemed to Jon that his pilot had turned awfully early. During the preflight brief, they had talked about having to turn early because of the high natural winds. Still, it had looked insanely early. Rick turned the interior communications system to hot mic. Jon heard him breathing hard and fast.

The plane rolled, wings level behind the boat. Jon thought that they couldn't possibly land with the back end of the boat at an unnatural down orientation, but his IP kept flying toward what seemed like a guaranteed crash. Then the back of the carrier abruptly rose. Jon looked past Rick's head at the blunt steel cliff they seemed certain to fly into.

Rick, in a voice that might have been asking his wife what was for dinner, reported to the landing signal officer that he saw the ball in the lens. But as soon as he was finished speaking on the radio, his rapid, ragged breathing filled Jon's ears again.

"Okay, deck's up. You're looking good. Keep it coming. Power! Power!" came over the radio from the landing signal officer, the LSO.

The deck dropped to a near-normal orientation, and they jolted onto the deck but missed the wires. It felt for a second as if they were skittering across a sheet of ice.

"Bolter, bolter!" came over the radio.

Then the nose came up, and the rudder shaker came on for just an instant. That meant Rick had been a little over-exuberant pulling back on the stick. The rudder pedal shaking meant you were getting close to a stall. *Even an infallible IP can goon something up a bit in a dicey situation,* Jon thought.

Rick clicked off hot mic and unsnapped his oxygen mask. Jon heard him screaming. There was an impressive string of profanity, which ended with a self-imprecation "… shit together."

He snapped his oxygen mask back on and flicked on hot mic again.

"So, you want to do the next one, Zachery?" he asked in his what's-for-dinner voice.

"Um, there's no one back here, sir."

Rick started laughing at the same time as he turned to the downwind. He was laughing so hard Jon began to fear he would fly them into the water.

When they caught the wire, Jon was stunned by the violence of it. He was thrown against his shoulder straps. His helmet-weighed-down head felt like it might snap off his shoulders. The engines screamed at full power. Then the IP throttled back to idle, and the ensuing quiet was loud. When the plane rolled backward, Jon had a moment of panic at the unnatural sensation, but Rick added some power, and they rolled forward and out of the landing area.

Jon was relieved that the landing was over. But then the winds coming over the flight deck buffeted the plane. It didn't feel secure. It felt as if those winds could pick up the puny trainer airplane and blow it over the side, as helpless as a bit of dandelion fuzz in a gale.

The taxi director brought the plane right up to the starboard edge of the deck. They seemed way too close to the edge and in danger of dropping into the huge waves and angry seas fifty feet below. Jon thought about his destroyer and what it would be like in those seas. He'd probably be puking into a bucket if he was on the smaller ship. On the USS *Manfred,* there were dangers to watch for, but nothing like what he'd just experienced on the *Lex.* Not only the landing but even taxiing to a parking spot seemed like skating right up to the ragged edge of a fatal disaster.

You volunteered for this, Zachery, he reminded himself.

82

Jon climbed down the side of the airplane. He felt a sense of relief when his feet touched the flight deck, but it didn't last long. The gale whistling around the plane and tugging at his legs seemed almost too powerful to resist. He wondered how the flight deck crew could work in those conditions.

The green-shirted maintenance men and the yellow-shirted traffic directors walked, leaning way into the wind. Maintaining footing was a huge challenge, never mind trying to complete a task.

Rick put his mouth close to Jon's helmet and shouted, "Come on. Let's get out of the way of the next airplane. Be damn careful though. You fall down and you'll leave a lot of skin on the nonskid."

The flight deck was covered with nonskid, essentially a mixture of paint and sand. It dried like coarse sandpaper. When it was dry and there were no aircraft on the flight deck, the nonskid worked well. Rain, sea spray, spilled hydraulic fluid, oil, and fuel turned the deck treacherously slippery. Even though it got slippery when it got wet, it was a lot better than painted steel would have been.

Jon shouted back, "I'll get the bags out of the nose."

"Let the plane captain get them. He'll bring them to the ready room. Follow me."

Jon followed Rick, taking baby steps, and they made it to the tall structure rising above the starboard side, called the island, without incident.

The IP dogged the hatch behind them, took off his helmet, and said, "With a little bit of luck, after a tour with a fleet squadron, you could get a job as flight deck officer on a carrier. Spend sixteen hours a day out there." Rick grinned. "We always like to give students something to look forward to." He turned and started down the ladder.

Teresa. The hurricane. He hadn't even thought of her since they started the briefing back at the base. *Teresa, I am so very sorry.* But *sorry* was so very inadequate.

As he thought about Teresa, he failed to start down the ladder behind his IP. He had to wait on six sailors ascending to go out onto the flight deck. After the last one dogged the door to the flight deck, Jon started down. The press of bodies on the ladders and in the passageways was so much greater than on the destroyers on which he had served.

Duty on destroyers, with crews of three hundred, did not prepare him to understand the size of an aircraft carrier, with a crew measured in the thousands. By the time he got to the third deck, he had no idea which direction was forward and which aft. Fortunately, compartments were numbered, so even though he started forward when he intended going aft, he quickly figured it out. The compartment numbers were getting smaller. Going aft they got bigger.

The ready room too was large, at least for a destroyer sailor. It seemed as big as the mess decks on the *Manfred.* Several of the students who had walked aboard were sitting and watching the TV in the upper corner of the right side of the room. The TV showed the landing area with a T-2 on final approach. The deck rose and made landing impossible. The plane waved off.

"Whoa!" came from six student throats. They were having a good time, watching from the ready room.

The SDO was Ensign Billings. He was medically grounded and lived on Santa Rosa Island too. He was called Slick. Word was that when he'd been in the swimming pool for the one-mile survival-swim test, he'd left an oil slick behind him from the bear grease he used to hold his thick black hair in place.

Slick sat behind a battered gray metal desk that looked like it had been there since World War II.

"Slick," Jon said, "any news on the hurricane?"

Without looking away from the TV, he pointed to his right, to a Plexiglas board on which the side numbers of the planes coming from the beach were listed. A piece of thermal printer paper was Scotch taped to the bottom of the board. The outlines of Florida and Cuba were drawn onto the paper. The symbol for the storm was north and west of the western tip of Cuba, at about the latitude of the southern point of the Florida peninsula.

In small print, the latitude and longitude of the center were printed. The course of the center was north-northwest; the speed was three knots.

"Any other word on this?" Jon asked the SDO.

The SDO didn't turn away from the TV. On the screen, a T-2 had just rolled, wings level, behind the *Lex*. He held up his hand. The ready room was filled with quiet and the anticipation of a held breath. On the TV, the deck cycled down and then up. Then it momentarily settled, and the T-2 smacked onto the deck and caught a wire.

"Okay, one wire!" someone shouted, followed by a general roar of approval.

There were four wires across the landing area. The target was the number three. Generally, a one wire got you a very poor landing grade, but in conditions like those raging outside that day, any one you caught was worth a good grade.

The SDO turned to Jon and said, "Weather guessers say Gladys's most likely scenario's still landfall at P'cola. And they expect it to be a cat-one hurricane by morning."

"You know where meteorology is?" Jon asked.

"Yeah," he said. "We're not supposed to bug them though. The OINC said any student that bugs meteorology will get squashed like one." He shrugged and turned back to the TV.

"So, who's the OINC?" Jon asked.

The SDO replied, still focused on the TV, "MO." The MO was the maintenance officer.

There was a "Jesus Christ!" from one voice and a general shout and laughter, almost like at a ball game, when a home team player hit a grand slam.

"What was it?" a voice asked after the roar petered out.

A voice answered, "A hanging bag blew out into the landing area and caught on the two wire. The LSO waved off the plane in the groove. A flight deck guy ran out, grabbed the bag, threw it up, the wind caught it and took it over the end of the flight deck. Somebody's skivvies just got tossed into the wake of the ship."

Jon wasn't really paying attention to the TV. He had his eyes locked on the MO at the rear of the ready room.

"Bolter, bolter, bolter," the voices roared together.

The MO was behind the counter at the back of the ready room, where one checked the maintenance records of the plane one was going to fly. A skinny sailor, probably thirty-something, wearing a green long-sleeved turtleneck, stood beside the MO.

"Goddamn it all to hell, Hall," the MO said. "Every damn airplane needs a hard landing inspection. You'd think one of these instructors could make a landing without breaking his plane!"

"MO," Jon said.

He was several inches taller than Jon, bald on top of his round head with gray stubble sidewalls above small ears. Under his chin, a pouch sagged like a pelican with a mouthful of seawater and fish. He had a large MO stenciled in black on his green flight deck jersey. "What?" he asked.

Jon's eyes dropped to his belly, which pooched out just under the MO. He looked like he was in his third trimester.

"The hell you want?"

"Sir, is anyone back at the squadron worrying about our families? Any way to find out what's happening with evacuations? My wife is on Santa Rosa."

"So, what're you really saying? Your wife, she doesn't have enough sense to get her ass off the island? And you want the Navy to take care of her?"

It was warm in the ready room. There was a drop of sweat hanging from the MO's chin pouch. He and Petty Officer Hall had their sleeves pushed up.

Jon had sweat on his forehead and upper lip. His armpits were soggy. He glared at the MO, clenched his fists, and just managed to keep his lips pressed tightly together. He charged out of the ready room.

83

Teresa felt worse than when she was newly pregnant with Jennifer. Her head hurt. She was hungry, but everything she considered eating made her want to throw up again. A baked potato—she thought she could keep that down maybe.

Jennifer was happy with her dinner, and Edgar Jon was enthusiastic about his cereal.

The evening news broadcast started with a weather report and a long discussion about jet streams, high- and low-pressure areas, and a cold front.

What about the hurricane? she wanted to shout to the boob tube. She was trying hard not to frighten the children.

She kept seeing that hangar door close, kept hearing it clang, kept feeling utterly abandoned, kept feeling fear tingle like an electric charge inside her aching head.

Where she got the presence of mind to stop by the commissary to stock up on groceries, she didn't know. Since then, it was hard to think about what to do. Her mind dwelt on Jon leaving her. The Navy authorities probably didn't even know she existed or that she was out on Santa Rosa. They were occupied with saving their precious airplanes.

Santa Rosa was just a bunch of beach houses stuck in the sand. It wasn't clear if there was any kind of municipal organization on the island or not. Even if there was, she was an off-season renter, not like a real citizen. It was like being in Meridian, except that instead of being threatened by Neanderthal bigots, here it was violent weather.

Finally, the weatherman got to the storm. Gladys hadn't moved very far during the day, but it was expected to speed up in the next twenty-four hours. It was still expected to make landfall at Pensacola.

Landfall, she wanted to scream again. Is that the best name you can dream up for a hurricane smashing into the coast and obliterating off-season beach houses?

Then the migraine started. In one moment it felt as if her brain was being sliced with a razor blade, and the next moment if felt more like a jagged-toothed rusty saw ripping through her skull. With her eyes closed she saw the white lights. She needed a migraine pill, but the thought of any kind of medicine in her stomach made her run for the bathroom.

There was nothing in her stomach, but still she retched up frothy brown bilious foam. The retching sucked the strength out of her. She was totally exhausted.

The wind and rain lashing the house were associated with the other weather pattern, not the hurricane, according to the evening news. Still, the threatening sound intensified her feeling of being helpless and alone. Claws of panic tried to rip apart the gossamer veneer of control she struggled to maintain. She had to maintain control. The babies needed that from her as much as they needed air to breathe. They needed her to hang on to control.

Call Sally. Sally Billings. She and Slick had a house on Santa Rosa too. She picked up the phone. Dead.

She wanted to pack and leave, but the migraine affected her eyes. Her vision blurred. She got the children in their beds, and then she fell into her own. *Rest first,* she decided. *Then pack and leave.*

When sand started striking the bedroom window, she jerked awake and rushed to the bathroom.

It was 10:15. She'd slept two hours. From the great room, looking out the patio door to Santa Rosa Sound, it was pitch-black. In front, the streetlamp cast an eerie pattern of dancing ghost light as the wind thrashed the light pole.

With her last bit of strength and energy, Teresa grabbed her rosary, a pillow, the exercise mat she had given to Jon for Christmas in 1966 so that he wouldn't rub his behind raw when he did his sit-ups, and the Mickey Mouse sleeping bag her mother had given to Jennifer. In the babies' room, she placed the sleeping bag on top of the exercise mat on the hard terrazzo floor. As soon as her head hit the pillow, her misery, the storm outside, and her two babies sleeping peacefully in the room with her disappeared.

84

John Calhoun called a phone number Ike had given him for a guy named Harlan and set up a meeting.

"Meet you at 8:00 p.m.," Harlan said. "Supper crowd's gone. Drinkin' crowd's settlin' in."

John Calhoun walked into Satterlys, a combination bar, restaurant, grocery store, and gas station north of Hattiesburg near Easterbucky, and stood just inside the door. The dim light rubbed the rough edges off the ugly of Satterlys. He knew what he'd see in better light: paint and varnish wearing years like a ten-year-old coon dog. His nose caught hints of beer, fried catfish, and hush puppies, fighting for recognition amidst the cigarette smoke. Two women and two men sat at one of four round tables. Smoke rose from the four like fog over a river on a chilly morning. A waitress placed a pitcher of beer on their table. The other three tables were empty. Five men sat on barstools. The second stool from the right was empty. A man sporting a long black ponytail sat on the stool at the right end of the bar.

John Calhoun scooted up onto the empty stool and placed his feet on the six-inch high plywood footrest.

The door to Satterlys opened, and four men filed in. Even in the blurry mirror, John Calhoun could see they looked city-clean.

"Probably got two more outside," Ponytail said.

"I made three cars followin'," John Calhoun said.

"Nothin' to worry on."

"What happened to Sam Germaine and Jimmie? I heard they went under."

"Word is a tall blonde woman done 'em. Switchblade and a forty-five. Can't feature Jimmie being ambushed like that."

"Switchblade? My daughter's son, Cyril, said that Harry Peeper was real good with a switchblade. Rafe was with him. But Cyril's disappeared, and so has Harry, and my boy too. We need to find Harry."

"Ike's lawyer said we was to get on with finding your wife. We get her, they got nothing on Ike."

"I want to know where my boy is."

"No. Ike never said nothing about your boy. We supposed to get your wife."

"Second," John Calhoun said. "We get her second. First, I find Rafe, and that means finding Harry."

"Nope, Ike said Sue Ellen."

"You go find her then. I'm going to find my boy."

John Calhoun started to stand up, and Ponytail put a hand on his arm.

"Hungry?"

"I could eat." John Calhoun glanced at the thick black beard. "Harlan."

Harlan's face hair split, and a big white-toothed grin flashed at John Calhoun.

"Barkeep," Harlan said. "Pitcher a beer and two catfish dinners to a table, if ya please."

"What about those?" John Calhoun hooked a thumb at the four City-cleans.

Harlan grinned again. "Tunnel. We eat, we drink our beer, and they's liable to be a fight. Those city boys might get caught up in it. Then we take to the tunnel."

Harlan spun on his stool and led the way to a table.

85

The muted yellowish light felt solemn. He heard scrapes, bumps, and thumps, indistinct announcements over the ship's 1MC (the ship's general announcing system), and whistles (signals from sailors moving planes). The sounds were outside though. Inside the tiny ship's chapel, Jon sat immersed in silence, as if the noises he heard tried to get in but were denied entrance. At another time it would have bothered him that noise and silence coexisted.

Gray metal folding chairs, three rows of six with a center aisle, provided seating. Jon sat on the aisle seat in the back row, alone in the box of a compartment. Thoughts tried to enter his head, but like the outside sounds, they were denied entrance.

The door next to Jon opened and a lieutenant chaplain entered. He was five ten and slender and had light-brown hair.

"Are you Lieutenant Junior Grade Zachery?"

Jon stood and nodded.

"Your squadron is looking for you. We were about to do a man-overboard muster. I knew there was no 1MC speaker close to the chapel, so I thought I'd check before calling away the muster. You need to get to your ready room, and I need to call the bridge and tell them you once were lost but now are found."

Jon grimaced. The chaplain laughed and said, "If you're not going to be polite and laugh at my joke, I'll just do it myself."

The chaplain led Jon to Ready Room 3, which had been assigned to the training squadron. Ready 3 was a deck down and three knee-knockers aft of the chapel.

Carriers—warships, in general—were constructed such that sections of the ship could be sealed to isolate fire, flooding, and fumes. Watertight doors set into bulkheads afforded sailors access to all the necessary spaces, but the sills of the doors were located a foot or so above the deck. Sailors routinely banged shins on the sills, but the sills were called knee-knockers, not shin-knockers. Distance and directions fore and aft on the ship were routinely measured by knee-knockers. A helpful sailor explained, with more detail than he'd wanted, when Jon asked for directions to the chapel.

The MO gave Jon a major chewing-out for causing the squadron and the entire ship such a pain in the ass. Jon absorbed the tirade and apologized to the MO.

"Expect this kind of screwup from a brand-new never-been-to-sea-before ensign," the MO said. "Go see the duty officer. He's got more good news for you."

Jon approached Slick, who sat behind the duty officer desk at the far end of the ready room from the MO's station.

"Your hanging bag blew over the side," Slick said. "Tough."

Jon felt a hand on his arm. It was the chaplain.

"You're running quite a string of bad luck," the chaplain said. "You had anything to eat?"

Jon followed the chaplain forward to a crew's mess where hamburgers were served all night. The chaplain, Father Marshall, extracted basic information from him as they ate: status in the flight-training program, marital status, children, address, and length of time in the Navy.

Jon didn't really want to talk to Father Marshall, but he answered the man's questions.

"You're really making me work," Father Marshall said.

Jon shrugged.

"Something pretty heavy is bothering you. That's clear. I might be able to help if you tell me what it is."

The priest probed. Jon fended him off, but the man didn't seem like he was going to quit. Jon was trying to think of a way to end the interrogation, when a sailor approached and offered to take the tray and dirty dishes to the scullery. Father Marshall thanked the skinny, pimply, towheaded kid. Jon watched him walk away.

"I don't want to keep you up all night, Father," Jon said.

"Then help us both get to bed. Tell me what's bothering you."

Jon looked at his hands on the Formica-topped table. He'd gotten Teresa pregnant and threatened her life. He never thought he'd put the Navy ahead of Teresa on a priority list, but that was just what he had done. He'd considered protecting Teresa as his number-one priority, but he'd left her to cope with a hurricane and two children. One day sitting on the beach, he thought about Abraham putting Isaac on an altar to sacrifice him to God. He decided that day he'd never be able to do that with his children and not Teresa either. He wouldn't sacrifice her for God, but he did for the Navy. Jon shook his head. He couldn't say any of that.

He took a deep breath, let it out, and met the priest's eyes. "I'm worried about my wife. We live on Santa Rosa Island. I want someone to check and make sure she got away."

Father Marshall had been leaning on his elbows on the table. "That's the tip of the iceberg, I expect. I can do something about it though. I'm attached to the admiral's staff in P'cola. I'll send the staff duty officer a priority message. He'll check on your wife. I should get an answer in the morning. How about if I meet you in Ready 3 at 0915? According to the forecast, the hurricane should be off Tampa in the morning, so we can see about that then too."

Jon gave Father Marshall his address and phone number. They shook hands and left the mess decks, Jon to his room and the priest to send the message.

His room was half a dozen knee-knockers aft of Ready 3. In the nearby head, he washed his socks in a basin with hand soap from a dispenser. After washing his hair with hand soap, he scrounged bits of soap from shower stalls, showered with the fingernail-sized slivers, and toweled off with his T-shirt. Not much maybe, but it constituted luxury in his circumstance.

The next morning he awoke at 0700. His T-shirt was dry, a little stiff, as if starched. The socks were damp, but that couldn't be helped. An industrial-strength dose of athlete's foot loomed before end of day. No toothbrush or paste. No deodorant. He checked his wallet. Twenty-six dollars. Enough to buy skivvies, socks, deodorant, essentials, if the ship's store carried those items.

He started pulling his flight suit on and stopped with one leg in. It hit him. The things he'd confessed to himself the night before would change things forever between him and Teresa. Those were the kinds of things that were immune to forgiveness. For the rest of their lives, they would never be in love again. They would discharge their duties to Jennifer, Edgar Jon—and to the new little person.

Jon's shoulders slumped, and he sighed. Then he stood up straight, stuck his chin out, and finished getting dressed. He noticed the ship's motion and heard the creaking and groaning of the hull as the waves pushed, pulled, and twisted at the steel structure. Going forward and entering the ready room, he found a sign taped to the duty officer's desk. "Flt Ops Cnx WX." Flight operations were cancelled because of continued bad weather.

He ate in the "dirty shirt," an eatery for aviators and officers who worked on the flight deck. Uniforms were required, flight suits specifically forbidden, in the formal ship's wardroom.

After breakfast, he went to the hangar bay.

The bay was crammed with airplanes and maintenance equipment. Planes were parked with noses nestled up into wing roots of other planes. Boxy yellow hydraulic power units were nestled into available nooks between aircraft. Tie-down chains secured the planes and equipment and added a kind of knee-knocker maze to the challenge of walking across the bay. Aft on the port side, he found a T-2 with the canopy open and a sailor sitting in the front cockpit, reading a paperback book.

Jon rapped on the side of the fuselage. "I'd like to climb up and sit in the aft cockpit for a bit. Okay with you?'

"You want the front seat, sir?" the sailor asked.

"That's okay. I'm going to imagine flying the ball. I can imagine being in the front too."

Jon told the plane hello and climbed up into the backseat. He went over the start-engine checklist. He imagined flying practice CQ landings back at the field at Pensacola. He recalled the flight out to the *Lex* the day before. He recalled both passes his IP had flown, the bolter and the landing. He recalled the taxi to the parking spot.

After an hour, Jon climbed out of the cockpit and thanked the sailor.

"You think we're going to fly today, sir?' the sailor asked.

"Feels pretty rough out yet. Maybe it'll calm down as the day wears on. Maybe the ship will steam out of the bad weather."

"A lot of maybes, huh, sir?"

"A lot of maybes."

Jon was about to turn away from the plane, but he stopped and put his hand on the fuselage. It occurred to him that every time things started going well, some kind of disaster was sure to follow. Every time something bad had happened before though, he and Teresa had managed to make things right again. This time he'd done something for which she'd never forgive him.

Flying is all that's left.

Jon entered Ready Room 3 at 0900. The maintenance officer was behind the counter just inside the door. He stared at Jon.

"Good morning, sir," Jon said and looked him in the eye for a moment.

Slick was behind the duty officer desk. "Hey, Zachery. I called the ship's supply officer. He got the ship's store opened early. I bought you a toothbrush, deodorant, that kinda stuff."

"Thanks, Slick. How much do I owe you?"

"Nothin'. Coupla us chipped in."

A student called Doglips, whose lips were tinted bluish, piped up from the second row of ready room chairs. "Yeah, man. We watched the tape of the flight deck sailor tossing your bag over the side twenty times last night. Better'n any movie aboard."

A sailor handed Slick a piece of paper.

"It's from meteorology," Slick said. "Gladys hooked a right at Tampa. Tampa and Orlando caught hell, but it won't be going to P'cola. Goddamn!"

"I wonder if they evacuated Santa Rosa Island before she changed direction," Jon said.

"I don't know," Slick said. "At worst it was a pain in the ass for the women. But everyone is safe. That's all that matters."

The chaplain walked in and took Jon's arm. "Got an answer to my message. You know Commander Pabst?"

"Yes, Father. He was my first CO at Meridian."

"He's on the admiral's staff now. He answered the message. He checked on Teresa, and she is fine. He said I should tell the Magnet-ass to get carrier qualified."

However, none of the students got carrier qualified. The ship moved west for two days, but the line of foul weather stayed with them. Then after having spent a week aboard, and with the *Lex* in the western part of the Gulf of Mexico, the students were flown off to Corpus Christi and then on back to Pensacola. They would be rescheduled for CQ.

86

Harry had been lying on the floor in the backseat of the stolen car as Jolene drove them six blocks away from the bank. He peeked over the backrest as she parked right behind his own car on a residential street. Harry got out and put the two duffel bags—one with the money, the other with the two blonde wigs and the other disguise material—into the trunk. The Thompson, wrapped in the long lightweight raincoat, went on the backseat. He got behind the wheel, and Jolene took the passenger seat.

Harry grinned at Jolene as she shook her thick black hair she'd had stuffed up under the wig. Her mouth twitched as if it didn't know whether its face was going to smile or cry.

"Told you. Piece of cake," Harry said.

He checked the side mirror and pulled out onto the street.

He screwed the rearview around to check his face for residual makeup. Looked okay, he decided.

"You did good, Jolene." She glanced at him. "I think we got a good haul too. Next one'll be easier. Got to expect the first one to knot your skivvies a bit."

Harry looked at her. He wished she'd say something. She didn't. He stopped pushing, drove back to her place in silence, and followed her into the house. She put the coffeepot on, and he started segregating bills. Then he counted his stacks. "Seventeen thousand four hundred sixty-four dollars," he said.

Jolene still didn't say anything, and he could tell she was doing some heavy thinking.

"You worried about doing the bank in Pensacola?" Harry asked her.

"No. I'm worried we're not going to Florida to do a bank. I heard you call information and get the address of that Zachery guy. He's the one that shot you."

"I owe him one. Then we'll scout out a bank to do."

"Bull," she said. "You kill a Navy guy and we'll have ta split. We won't be able to scout or do no bank."

Harry glared at her. She glared back.

Damn, Harry thought, *just when she got useful.* He started reaching for his forty-five, but she'd had her hands behind her, and she brought her thirty-eight out and cocked it.

"I'd shoot you right now, Harry. Only, draggin' your worthless ass out and burying it would be a pain in mine." Then she smiled.

"That's the gun I gave you for the bank. It wouldn't be right to shoot me with that."

She smiled bigger.

"I been thinking. Seventeen thou'll do me for a while. You don't need it. If I keep it all, no reason for you to come back to get even with me. I done plenty for you. That right?"

Harry seethed.

"Need an answer, Harry."

"Even if I did come back looking for you, you wouldn't be here, would you? You're going to California."

"That's why I'm not shooting you. You'll never come to California. Now, take your forty-five out and put it on the table. Careful. Pull your shirt back so I can see if your finger gets close to the trigger."

Harry laid the gun next to the stacks of bills.

"Leave the Thompson too. I left the shotguns in the trunk of your car. But I took the shells. So get up slow and easy like. Then walk out to your car and drive away."

"Can I take a cup of coffee for the road?"

"No harm in that."

"Pour you one?"

"I'll get my own."

The coffeepot was on the stove. A block with six knives sticking out of it perched on the countertop next to the stove. Jolene moved a couple of steps closer. *Ten feet,* Harry thought.

"I'm not going to go for one of your knives," Harry said, rose, got a white mug from the cabinet above the knives, filled it, and turned so his right side was away from her. Raising the cup to sip with his left hand, he said, "Gonna miss your coffee."

He flicked his wrist, and his knife embedded in Jolene's belly. Her gun went off. The bullet *thwipped* past his ear. He dropped the mug, ran to her, and grabbed the gun as she was trying to cock the hammer with her right hand while her left held her belly. He pushed her to the floor. She landed on her back, her brown eyes locked on him, bright with hate. He shot her in the forehead, which turned her head sideways.

After pulling the knife and wiping it on her pants, he folded the blade and stuck it in his watch pocket.

Too bad, he thought. *Traveling west with a woman would have been better than being alone.* He thought briefly of Amanda Sue, longer of the Navy guy, Zachery. Once he got him, it would be like getting clean. *Too bad, Jolene,* he thought again.

She is—was a fine woman. Some would have called her big boned, which was true. But she had a lot of woman hanging from those bones.

Tsk.

In the bedroom, he stuffed his clothes into a seabag. Back in the kitchen, he put the money back into the duffel, along with the thirty-eight, looked around, considered setting the place afire, thought better of it, slung the seabag strap, carried the duffel with his left hand, the machine gun with his right, pushed open the screen door, and stopped.

John Calhoun stood under the pole light, holding a double-barrel leveled at his belly.

"Where's my boy? Where's Rafe?"

John Calhoun was too far for the knife.

"I wanna know where Rafe is. Now you answer me or I'll blow one a your legs off at the knee. Where's my boy?"

As soon as John Calhoun started lowering the gun, Harry dropped the duffel and the machine gun and dove behind the wall to his left as he pulled his forty-five. The shotgun went off. Harry's lower leg burned. He fired a full clip blind around the wall. Harry shucked the strap of the seabag, ejected the empty clip, inserted another, and jacked a round into the chamber.

Harry peeked around the wall. John Calhoun lay on his back, as if he was watching the bugs circling under the dish-shaped shield over the pole lamp. Harry stood up, intending to make sure John Calhoun was dead. His right shin hurt.

Suddenly, something smacked him hard in the back. His head filled with white light. He landed on his face and tasted dirt in his mouth. Then he went away.

He came back when he felt a hand on his shoulder. He was rolled over onto his right side. He looked up at a tall skinny guy. His long black hair was pulled back into a ponytail.

"Who—" Harry coughed. "Who're you?"

The man reached down, felt around Harry's waist for weapons, and stood up again.

Harry flopped onto his back with his feet toward the house. He was vaguely aware of the man walking away from him and entering the house. Then Harry went away again for a while. He didn't know how long he'd been gone.

Harry felt for his knife and smiled. It was there. He flicked open the blade and raised his arm above his head. His vision was blurry. He couldn't breathe right. He felt like he would go away again. He gritted his teeth. After Ponytail came back out of the house, after he got Ponytail for shooting him in the back, then he'd go away.

But not until.

87

THE PLANE SHUT DOWN ITS engines at Naval Air Station Pensacola five minutes before midnight. Jon was exhausted. He'd abandoned Teresa to qualify as a carrier pilot and spent a week aboard the *Lex* but had accomplished nothing. He'd worn his flight suit for seven days and feared he was like a skunk, unable to smell his own stink. He'd scrubbed his underwear in the sink every night, but his skin sensed vermin living in the boxers and tee. He'd experienced a bumpy ride from the carrier to NAS Corpus Christi, had no time to call Teresa, and then boarded a Navy transport plane for an even rougher four hours bucking a hefty headwind and persistent turbulence with sudden drops off a cliff, slams to a stop, and abrupt rises. The approach into P'cola had been bumpy too. The reunion with Teresa would be even bumpier. He could still see that look on her face when he told her he had to get to the base, that he was leaving her, with her pregnancy and her children, to deal with Hurricane Gladys.

The turbulence they'd flown through that night was nothing like the turbulence he'd feel in his soul when she hit him with the cold, silent treatment, which he deserved.

Jon was the second-to-last student to climb down the wheeled passenger stairs. A hundred yards across the ramp, a single shielded bulb over the door into base operations melted a feeble hole in the dark. His fellow passengers trudged in a row toward the light. Outside his head, it was quiet. Inside, he still heard the drone of the engines. Jon stepped to the side of the stairs. Slick was behind him.

Jon waited as Slick joined the line of zombies. He had the strap of a hanging bag over a shoulder, a barf bag in each hand, and he trailed a whiff of puke in the clean night air. In the plane, it had been a lot worse.

Jon had nothing in his hands. He had a toothbrush and toothpaste in a pocket in the left leg of his flight suit. All the rest of his survival toiletries were left in a trash can on the *Lex*.

Three of the six students had gotten airsick. With the vomit smell and all the bouncing around, Jon thought he would get sick too. On his destroyer, he'd suffered from seasickness. But his stomach held on to the cheeseburger he had for dinner on the *Lex* before flying off.

Go figure, he thought and joined the line.

Halfway across the ramp he heard, "Zachery, hey, Zachery."

Jon saw Commander Pabst standing under the light.

The commander walked down the steps to meet Jon. "There's something you need to know."

"Teresa!"

Commander Pabst waited for the door to close behind Slick. "The day you left, Jon, Teresa got sick with a bad case of the flu," he said. "She's okay now, but she had gotten severely dehydrated."

"She's pregnant. The baby?"

"Baby's okay, and so is Teresa. They kept her in the hospital for two nights mainly to pump her full of fluids and get her strength back."

"The kids?"

"We took care of them," Commander Pabst said. "They stuck me on the admiral's staff until the Bureau of Personnel works up new orders. I was the staff duty officer when we got the chaplain's message to check on Teresa. I tried to call, but the phones were inop, so I drove out. When I got there, she was trying to get Edgar Jon into his car seat. She was at the end of her rope but knew she needed to get to a doctor."

"Why didn't anybody tell me?" Jon practically shouted.

"She didn't want us to. She was absolutely insistent. 'Do not call him,' she said."

Jon looked at the darkened two-engine transport plane. He couldn't look at the commander.

"Why didn't she want me to know?"

"She knew how you would take it. At that point, telling you would have just screwed up everything for no good purpose. She wanted you to get carrier qualified."

"But we didn't. I left Teresa on the island and we didn't get a thing done."

Commander Pabst laughed. "That's what I said to Teresa this evening. She said, 'You had a chance. You had to try.'" Commander Pabst clapped Jon on the shoulder. "Some kind of woman you got there. She found the letter you started writing to her."

Jon had been so sure Teresa would hate him for abandoning her. He forgot about the letter. He had planned to finish it and leave it with her the day he had been scheduled to go to the *Lex*.

"She asked me to have you read this," Commander Pabst said.

Jon held the envelope up to the light.

"She used the good stuff," he said with a shaky voice.

Teresa's aunt, Sister Agnes, had been in Rome for several years. She always sent Teresa a Christmas present. Two Christmases past, the gift had been stationery. Teresa was stingy with it. Even Rose only got one letter on the good stuff.

Jon stood up and got closer to the light over the door.

Dearest Jon,

The last three nights before you left, you didn't make love to me, and I know you laid there awake. I should have asked what was bothering you. I thought you'd tell me when you were ready. In your letter, you said that after you made love to me, you felt like afterwards, it was like tying me up and placing me, like Isaac, on

Abraham's altar; then just waiting to see if the angel of the Lord will come and save me from being pregnant.

I believe that it was part of God's plan for you and me to be together. I don't want us to be apart together. I think that's how you described it in Meridian. For right now we are having a baby. I am not tied up on an altar waiting to "have my gizzard sliced out."

A lump tried to clog his throat. He looked out at the dark airfield, the blue taxiway lights, the green threshold lights at the end of the runway, and the stars above it all.

While I was in the hospital, I talked to a wonderful OB doctor. Dr. Erling told me that we need to be careful with my health, but that there is no reason for us to be afraid, and that there is no reason for us to feel like this is a death sentence. He talked to me straight, not like I was a person with half a brain. I am happy to be pregnant. I will confess, until I talked with Dr. Erling, I wasn't. But I believe we will be okay, all five of us. I trust in the God who planned for us to be together that we will be okay.

Without that trust in God, each and every day, when you went to fly your airplanes, I would see you climb up on that altar to sacrifice yourself. Every day I would wait for the angel of the Lord to give you a thumbs-up or a thumbs-down. We both have things we *have* to do. We have to do those things, and then we *have* to trust Him.

Commander Pabst and Evelyn have been so wonderful. They took care of Jennifer and Edgar Jon while I was in the hospital, and they insisted I stay with them until you got back. We will never be able to thank them enough.

I am so glad you are home. You, Jon Zachery, are a fine hunk of man. When you get here, I will show you, or maybe we'll wait until we get back to our house on Santa Rosa.

With all my heart and soul,
Teresa

Jon sat on the second concrete step from the bottom. His body tried to let loose a sob, and he muscled a hard lump of it back down his throat. A trickle of a tear leaked out of each eye.

"Teresa is waiting in the car in front of base ops," the commander said. "Interested in seeing her?"

88

At 1000 on a clear, bright end-of-October day, Jon Zachery rolled his T-2B wings level behind the *Lex*. For an instant, time seemed to stop. Through the windshield, he beheld the blunt fifty-foot steel cliff at the back of the ship, the ship riding smoothly through the fifteen knots of steady breeze and whitecapped wavelets, and the cloudless blue sky above, but only for an instant. He blinked and found things happening incredibly fast. During practice landings ashore, seconds ticked at a normal rate. Behind the carrier, a demented celestial timekeeper seemed to push the second hand around the clock at five times normal ticking and tocking.

His initial pass at the *Lex* was tailhook up for a touch-and-go. After he got airborne and turned downwind, he lowered the hook, and he was set for his first carrier landing. He rolled out for his second pass. Again seconds ripped by. He anticipated the sudden stop, being thrown forward against his shoulder straps. That did not happen. He boltered. He knew what he did wrong. After a pilot rolled out behind the ship, he had to worry about three things: meatball, lineup, and airspeed. When he got close to landing, he did not worry about lineup or speed. At that point, those two parameters had to be good or the LSO would have hit the wave-off lights.

In close, the pilot scanned ball, ball, ball. He had let the ball get away from his scan in close and missed all the wires across the landing area. Jon didn't miss the wires again. He needed four landings to qualify. As he rolled out for his fourth landing, time seemed to be going normally. Tick, tock.

Let's not get cocky, Zachery. One more landing to get.

*   *   *

Originally, they had planned to drive north to Missouri through Alabama and avoid Mississippi, but then Jon's promotion came through. He had been promoted to lieutenant (jg) six months ahead of standard time. Lieutenant came a year earlier than had been the norm. Vietnam was still driving things hard. Once again, Refly had been proven wrong.

After the promotion, Jon told Teresa he wanted to visit Junior McCauley's grave and leave one of his sets of lieutenant collar devices at the grave.

"We'll drive into town, visit the grave, and leave. We'll be out of Mississippi before the sun goes down. That okay with you, Teresa?" he'd asked.

"We owe Junior a lot, the lives of our babies. We should visit him," Teresa replied. "Do you think we can just drive through without getting into trouble, Magnet-heiny?"

"No problem. Maybe we can even visit your square peg made from a round bole."

He said it in an attempt to be funny and had no intention of spending any extra minutes in Meridian.

At 0900 on November 7, studly, carrier-qualified Lieutenant Jon Zachery regarded the road ahead of him through aviator sunglasses.

Jennifer was in the backseat with her head bent over a coloring book. Edgar Jon was zonked in his infant seat. Teresa napped against the passenger-side door.

Jon backed off the gas at the "Speed Limit 35" sign. Teresa sat up, stretched, and moaned but was reluctant to push aside the luxurious sun-warm blanket of sleep.

"Meridian?" she asked.

Jon nodded.

"I was dreaming about Clarissa. It was just like that Sunday, except that instead of trying to avoid her pew, everybody was trying to get into it. I wanted to sit with her, but the usher kept pushing me back so a Meridian person could get a seat."

"It'll be a while before something like that happens," Jon said. "I was wondering if there are ten decent people here."

"Like Sodom and Gomorrah—I am sure there are more than ten decent people."

"Junior McCauley was one, and he's dead."

"Even Mr. Binford was nice to us when we left."

He thought about saying it: "So we're back up to one."

It was quiet for a moment.

"Clarissa," she said.

"Clarissa," he said.

Jon looked at Teresa and reached in front of the baby's seat to take her hand. Clarissa's body had been released. There was to be a funeral Mass and burial on Friday. Teresa had gotten in touch with Clarissa's mother through Clarissa's college roommate. They were going to attend the funeral before going to Missouri for two weeks of leave. Then Jon had to report to advanced training in Kingsville, Texas.

Jon thought about Harry Peeper. He thought about that night and Harry loading a fresh magazine into his machine gun. *Harry must still be out there,* he thought. As far as he knew, Harry had never been apprehended.

They'd probably never come back to Meridian. If the VT-7 XO knew they were even driving through, he'd have a cow. But they owed Junior a last visit. The XO would never find out.

"I want to drive by the house," Teresa said.

"I thought you didn't want to see it."

"I do now."

Jon looked for something to answer her with but came up empty.

"Clarissa Johnson and Junior McCauley made a difference. If we visit Junior's grave and scurry out of town—"

"I thought we agreed on how to do this. We didn't want the kids to be scared again."

"We did agree. Now, being here, it's different."

Jon turned onto Fortieth Street. "Feels like we've been gone for years."

He pulled into the driveway and stopped.

There were new bricks around the front door. It was subtle, but if you knew what to look for, you could tell. There was a Binford Real Estate sign in the front yard, where Junior's body had fallen.

"Thanks, Junior," Jon said as he reached over and took Teresa's hand.

"Thanks, God, for Junior. And thanks, God," Teresa said and squeezed Jon's hand, "for the other man who was here that night."

Edgar Jon stretched and wrinkled up his face. Jon rubbed his hand over the fine baby hair.

"He's wondering why the car stopped," Jon said, "when everybody should know he sleeps better when it's moving."

Jon looked up at the streetlight on top of the pole on the corner. The dinner plate–sized shield over the light had bullet holes.

"Visit Junior?" Jon asked Teresa.

She nodded and said, "Then we get a motel and RON. I'm going to call Melody. I'm going to tell her I appreciated the opportunity to get to know her just a little, and that I hope she's doing well. I'm going to invite her to have breakfast with us in the morning."

"Um, Teresa, I think we're pushing it with seeing the house. If the XO or Captain Morgan knew—"

Teresa said, "We'll be okay, Jon. Trust in the Lord." Teresa laughed at the look on his face. "Oh, I know what you're thinking, Jon Zachery. You're thinking I trust in Him, I praise Him, but I'm still ready to pass ammo, like that Navy chaplain at Pearl Harbor."

"Do you think she'll come?" Jon asked. "Melody, I mean."

"I think it's more important that I ask than whether or not she comes."

Jon backed out onto Fortieth Street.

"I can just imagine what the XO would say about this Meridian sleepover idea of yours, Teresa Ann Velmer Zachery." Jon shook his head. "And with a Magnet-heiny husband, no less."